THE IMPORTANCE OF BEING DANGEROUS

THE IMPORTANCE OF BEING

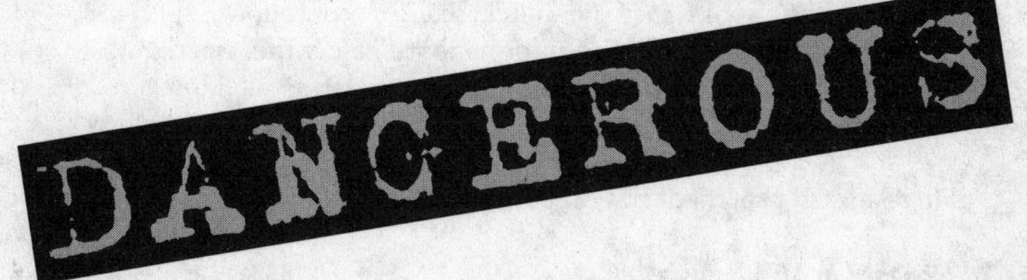

David Dante Troutt

An Imprint of HarperCollins*Publishers*

This book is a work of fiction. The characters, incidents, and dialogue are drawn from the author's imagination and are not to be construed as real. Any resemblance to actual events or persons, living or dead, is entirely coincidental.

A hardcover edition of this book was published in 2007 by Amistad, an imprint of HarperCollins Publishers.

First Amistad paperback edition published 2008.

Designed by Mia Risberg

The Library of Congress has cataloged the hardcover edition as follows:

Troutt, David Dante.
The importance of being dangerous / David Dante Troutt. — 1st ed.
p. cm.
ISBN: 978-0-06-078929-9
ISBN-10: 0-06-078929-8
1. African Americans—Fiction. 2. Revenge—Fiction. I. Title.
PS3570.R643I48 2007
813'.54—dc22

2006050417

ISBN 978-0-06-078930-5 (pbk.)

08 09 10 11 12 DG/RRD 10 9 8 7 6 5 4 3 2 1

For Naima and Shawn

THE IMPORTANCE OF BEING DANGEROUS

| 1 |

BEFORE SHE WAS A BODACIOUS QUEEN of the game, and two years before her fortieth birthday surprise, there were often days when Sidarra wished she had the skills to bargain at least one parent back from death for a visit. She had lost them both at Eastertime, and she could feel the second anniversary approaching. Maybe years later the ability to communicate by postcard or prayer would do. But in 1996, the wound still fresh, she needed a little time with their faces, to laugh into their eyes, or cry into their arms.

Sidarra got off the subway in Harlem, still distracted by what had just happened that day at work in Brooklyn. Once again, life proved to be pretty cheap at her job, the New York City Board of Miseducation, as she called it. Sidarra climbed the steps up to the street sure in her thoughts that her boss, Clayborne Reed, was finally going to pull the trigger on her section. Given her long rejection of his advances and her own advancing years, she figured he would at least retire her. For three months straight, he and most of the male management had been fixated on age, specifically the twenty-four-year-old white phenom named Desiree Kronitz. Clearly she made his dick too hard with her tight polyester skirts and red-lipstick-dripping talk of "downsizing" and "administrative waste," which was all Clay needed to hear anyway. He was already getting pressure from his boss, the city schools chancellor. This Long Island chick with the blond dye job, midnight pumps, and aggressive push-up bras had opened his nose wide enough to make him want to fire everybody who hadn't finished St. John's University with a bachelor's degree in public management. Sidarra had no proof of course, but she was sure from the looks of the man that he regularly fantasized being together with Desiree's little tight ass. Over time, signs here and there told her that the obsession was directing his judgment: people like her were being demoted. Pressure was building in his pants and from his boss. Soon, while Miss Chick moaned in mock delight, Sidarra would be standing in the unemployment line, waiting for some idiot to say "Next!"

She didn't even see Tyrell following her down the first street. Nineteen, lean, long, and just stupid enough, Tyrell was always trying to be the trouble not seen. He was smart enough to make himself invisible, had she ever thought to look back at him. He side-winded into corners and phone booths like a snake, following the flex of her calves after the click of each heel on the sidewalk. His loping, uneven strides began to quicken and doubled the pace of hers as he gradually caught up. Sidarra kept thinking about what would happen to her if Miss Chick won the undeclared competition between them. She and Raquel were alone. Sidarra couldn't let anything happen to her daughter. She couldn't lose the apartment they shared on the third floor of a brownstone. Tyrell's longer strides loped faster, homing in on Sidarra's brown leather purse as it swung in slow motion from her slightly slumped shoulder. Just before she turned onto her block on 136th Street, Tyrell was right up on her, close enough to grab her ass.

Suddenly a spider sense ten thousand years old sprang up in her chest, and Sidarra whirled around two steps before reaching her stoop. "Don't do it," she whispered.

Tyrell stepped real close in front of her. "What?" he said, three inches from her face. She could feel his breath heavy on her cheek and she knew his body was already aroused by something. She also knew what his darting eyes knew: that there was no one out on 136th Street right then. Five fifty-two in the evening, yet no one. She smelled the bad mix of cigarettes, a blunt, malt liquor, and bad gums with each quickening breath.

"I need to talk to you about something, Miss Sid." He looked all the way around. She felt his long, thin arm make contact with her body. He tried to distract her. "Where's your pretty little girl?"

"Upstairs waiting for me, Tyrell."

He leaned on her just slightly, urging her up the brownstone stoop. "Then I'll walk you upstairs—"

"With her daddy, who's about to beat my ass for coming late," she said, trying to hide any fear. While he thought about that, Sidarra got a step's worth of separation, but couldn't get her key out without opening her purse to him. She lifted her eyes over his shoulder, pretending to say hello to someone passing on the street. That got her another step away from him. When Tyrell looked back to see, she slipped her hand into her purse, got the key out and a folded-up five-dollar bill. When Tyrell turned back to her, she knew he wasn't going to wait anymore.

"Look here, Tyrell. I'm glad I saw you today, because I've been meaning to give you this carfare." Sidarra looked deep into his eyes and mustered all of her twenty extra years on earth to tell him, "Don't think I forgot about getting you that job down at 110 Livingston. I can't remember the man's name I want you to see down there, but here's some money. I'll get you the name next time I see you. You're a *good* man, Tyrell. Don't think I don't know that. I've known you a long time. I'll do what I can. Now, this ends right here, 'cause I got a baby to take care of, okay?"

Tyrell stopped, took the money quickly in his fingers, paused long enough to stare at her breasts, and turned back down the stairs. "A'ight," he said. "Thanks."

And that was all there was to it this time. As Sidarra stepped safely into the vestibule, she let out a long breath. Her hand trembled furiously as she turned the key inside the second door. The mailman had slipped two pieces of mail for her onto the floor under the crack. Her mailbox was broken again. She stooped to the dusty tiled floor and picked up the letters, but before she could read the address another man appeared in her face.

"Wha—" she gasped in the near-darkness.

"Just who I was looking for," said the male voice. The man stepped out of the darkness at the foot of the stairwell.

It was her landlord. "Oh. You, uh, startled me, Mr. Simms."

Mr. Simms was a tall older man with glasses and a strong frame who left Harlem years ago and had not smiled since. "How are you, Sidarra?" He didn't wait for an answer. "I'm on my way out. I came into the city today to see you, 'cause your rent is late and I'm not having it this month."

"I know, Mr. Simms. I tried to leave you a message on your answering machine."

"Uh-huh."

She smiled with whatever loveliness Tyrell hadn't scared out of her. "Raquel had a problem with her teeth last week. Her father said he would cover it, and when he didn't, well, I had to—"

Mr. Simms searched her face for truth. "Look, we can't keep playing this game. You know I like you, Sid. I'm sorry about Raquel. You've been good, quiet tenants since before she was born. But I can't do this with you. Harlem is changing. You're a smart woman. You know and I know both that I could get twice what you're paying for them four rooms."

She didn't want him to go on much longer, because he might work himself into evicting her if he thought enough about it. "I tell you what, Mr. Simms. I'll write you a check right now for half and get you the rest by, well, Tuesday, given the Easter mails, okay?"

When she finished writing the check, she waited at the bottom step for him to disappear down the street. Before starting the walk upstairs, Sidarra craned her neck to look up the narrow rectangular gap between the handrails to make sure no other surprises were making their way down to her. She could hear loud music playing as she passed the apartment on the second floor. Once she made it to the landing on her own floor, she found the courage to check who the mail was from. The first letter was from the cable company; her service was being disconnected and it would cost an additional $75 to restore. The second was from the IRS. She owed another $250 from an error in last year's taxes. This year's were due in about two weeks.

"Mommy!"

"I'm home, baby." Sidarra dropped her purse on the hardwood floor along with her keys and the bad news, and grabbed up her daughter. Just moments ago she couldn't be sure she would hold this eight-year-old body again. Sidarra stroked her fingers across Raquel's plaited hair and kissed again and again at the soft brown skin of her cheek. "Why was the door unlocked?" she asked Raquel.

"I made you a picture at school. Want to see it?"

"Of course I do. Where is Mrs. Thomas? Why was the door unlocked?" She looked around the foyer, expecting Mrs. Thomas finally to appear. "Mrs. Thomas?" she called out. She heard nothing in return.

Sidarra wanted to think only about leftover Kentucky Fried Chicken and getting out of her dress. A bath after dinner would be nice, too. But she looked around the house with no lights on and only the weak evening sun trying its last to make it to the hallway through the kitchen windows. No one in the kitchen. She walked to the doorway of the large front room and saw Mrs. Thomas, all eighty years of her, fast asleep in a chair while *Jeopardy!* played on the TV.

"Mrs. Thomas! Mrs. Thomas, I'm home."

The old woman shook herself out of a snore, grabbed at her skirt above the knees, and lifted her groggy head. "Mm-hmm. You're back. That's good. How are you, Sidarra?"

Sidarra stood in the doorway for a few seconds, too pissed off for words, Raquel's long, skinny frame still hanging from her hip. What could she say that she wouldn't regret? She had lied to Mr. Simms, just as she'd lied to Tyrell. There was no father for Raquel at the end of the day. There was just Mrs. Thomas, who lived on the first floor, and she looked after Raquel in exchange for favors.

"Why is it so warm in the house?" she asked no one in particular. Raquel slid down her mother's body and looked up like she hadn't noticed.

"I think the oven was on."

"The oven doesn't work, Raquel. You know that. It's got to be fixed. Who turned the oven on?"

Raquel put a guilty finger to her lips and twisted her body back and forth. "Want to see the picture I made you?"

"In a minute, baby. Mrs. Thomas?" Mrs. Thomas had fallen back to sleep. "How long has Mrs. Thomas been asleep, Raquel?"

"Since the news came on." That was over an hour ago.

"Mrs. Thomas, let me walk you back downstairs, please. Thank you again for watching Raquel."

Down they went in slow motion, two steep flights of creaky old stairs that slanted to one side. At any moment it seemed the old woman would give out for good, and Sidarra was glad she hadn't said anything in anger.

Once she had seen Mrs. Thomas safely into her musty apartment, Sidarra and Raquel went back upstairs and turned on lights. "How was your day, Mommy?"

"Pretty damned awful, sweetie. How was yours?"

"Good. I had a good day. We had a spelling test, and I only got one word wrong."

"That's wonderful. Mommy's very proud of you." Sidarra took off her heels and walked into the drab, light green kitchen in her pantyhose. On her way to the stove, she nearly slipped on something greasy and had to catch herself on the back of a metal chair. When she caught her balance, she looked down in disgust to see what almost killed her. "What is that?"

"Chicken," Raquel mumbled.

"Chicken? What chicken? Why is there chicken on the kitchen floor, Raquel?"

"Galore."

"Galore?" Sidarra almost bit her top lip in half. "Raquel, you'd better stop playing with me this second. Now, what the hell has Galore got to do with this chicken? Whose chicken is this, anyway? This better be Mrs. Thomas's chicken."

Raquel fidgeted badly under her mother's angry glare. "Mommy, she was hungry. She kept crying all over the place. I asked Mrs. Thomas what I could do, but she couldn't hear me."

A gray cat considerably fatter than the one Sidarra remembered seeing that morning sauntered slowly under the kitchen chairs. Sidarra named her Pussy Galore because she was a big James Bond fan. Having an inactive cat with an action-packed name was as close as Sidarra would likely come to an action movie life. "Raquel, don't tell me that's why this oven is on."

"The chicken was cold, Mommy. But I kept it in the tinfoil just like you do."

"And you fed it to the cat?"

"Yes, ma'am."

"Raquel! Dammit! First of all, you must *never* go near the stove. You know better than that. It's *broken*. That's probably why Mrs. Thomas wouldn't wake up. It's probably leaking gas! You both could have gotten poisoned to death, or burned up in a fire. What were you thinking?" Raquel stared at the scuff marks, holes, and deep cracks in the old linoleum floor. "And second of all, that chicken was your dinner. That's all we have tonight. Mommy doesn't even have any money. I just spent my last five dollars . . ."

"We could look in the pockets of your coats."

"Stay out of my goddamned pockets, Raquel! Jesus Christ."

Sidarra suddenly felt too heavy to stand and collapsed in a chair. She put her head in her hands and stared into the tabletop for five solid minutes. Raquel timidly moved beside her and stroked her mother's arm with her hand. "Sorry, Mom."

"Okay, baby. Now you know."

It wasn't really okay that evening. Sidarra went into her bedroom and got undressed in front of the mirror on the wooden dresser. She locked in a stare-down contest with herself for a while, but lost when the sight of a hole in her new bra distracted her. When she tried pulling out a drawer, it wouldn't budge. When she tugged angrily at it, the little round handles finally broke off in her hands. If her father were alive, he would have fixed that. The stove would work, too. She could call her brothers for long-distance advice, but even that would mean a favor. Favors from them meant drama she didn't need. While Raquel drew pictures on a pad across the bed, Sidarra put her hair up in a scarf. She was hungry. She was out of red wine. Somehow she was broke again, but she wouldn't have gone back out into that street to buy some anyway. If her mother were alive, she wouldn't need wine. She would be fed on a day like this. Of course, this day *was* the two-year anniversary, she suddenly realized, the day before Good Friday, when her parents were killed together on a curb. Since then, she'd become acutely aware of her disappointments, wearing cheap drawers with holes in them, surrounded by cheap furniture with bad handles, the stuff she'd bought on layaway at one of the Arab stores on 125th Street. And she had their furniture, most of it stowed away in the junkiest room of a junky apartment. The apartment was so addicted to its junkiness, no amount of love or time or good taste could get it in shape for more than a minute.

Instead of her parents taking care of her when she really needed it, she had Michael, who called while she and Raquel were watching non-cable TV. You could say Michael was her boyfriend. He called a lot like a boyfriend. He wore too much aftershave like a boyfriend. He chewed his food loudly, kept his money in a fat wad of singles, and laughed at his own dim-witted jokes like a boyfriend. But Michael was slow-moving and over fifty, with extra weight he couldn't carry well, like an old friend, not a boyfriend. Over the telephone, he talked too slowly about his day in the token booth where he worked downtown. She could only hear so much about a day selling tokens to New Yorkers from behind a bulletproof glass.

But when she interrupted to tell him about how she felt pretty sure that she was either going to be fired or demoted in a reshuffling at the Board of Miseducation, he relaunched a favorite rescue mission that backfired in her ears.

"You need to give that stuff up, Sidarra. You need to quit grieving so hard and trying so hard all the time and let a man run the show for you and Rock." That's what he called Raquel, his Rock. "Why you don't let me take care of things I know better about, huh? Get you out of that dump, once and for all. The Bronx is not so bad, baby. Beats the hell outta Harlem."

His words ran across the screen of her mind like the subtitles on the television while the mute button was on. Michael didn't get it. She had just turned thirty-eight, and he talked about her like she was old enough to retire down South. He had never known what it was like to want a job because of the work you might achieve. Nobody *wants* to become a token vendor, you just end up there. And Michael's often telling her to get over her parents passing so soon after her loss helped nothing. He was just tired of hearing about things he didn't understand. But she told him she loved him anyway and got off the phone as quickly as she could. "How 'bout some peanut butter and jelly sandwiches?" she asked Raquel, who was barely awake at nine o'clock.

Raquel nodded. They stumbled together to the kitchen in their night clothes and turned on the light.

"Mommy!" Raquel screamed.

There, crawling gingerly out of a hole smack in the middle of the kitchen floor, were two of the meanest, fattest water bugs that ever lived. The light didn't scare them, and they both turned their flying antennae toward mother and daughter as if to say, What? You wanna piece of me?

Few things scared Sidarra like water bugs. Cockroaches were bad enough, and the old brownstone had enough of them for sure. But water bugs were fearless creatures of wretched filth and pugnacious attitudes who made Sidarra feel poor. She would love to have had the courage and the shoes thick enough to crush them back to where they came from, but she did not. That's one reason she had a cat. Galore sat not more than three feet away, resting on a kitchen chair looking down calmly at the intruders.

"Do something!" Sidarra screamed at the cat. But the cat was too fat. She was still full of warm Kentucky Fried Chicken, and she wasn't leaving that chair for a plate of mice, let alone these things that were known to fight back.

So they turned off the kitchen light and went to bed hungry that night. Afraid of the giant roaches, they slept together in Sidarra's bed with the light and the TV on. Raquel had no problem sleeping curled up against her mother's smell. But not Sidarra, exhausted as she was. Instead, she sat up and read from some papers she'd put on the nightstand, things she had been meaning to get to but had been putting off. She put a lot of things off, especially if they involved money, but this caught her eye. Now, it couldn't wait any longer. It was an advertisement along with a couple of pages of explanation, something a friend down the block had given her. Not a pyramid scheme, not some expensive seminar to get ripped off at. In fact, the more she read, the less it intimidated her. It was just a no-obligation invitation to come to a meeting and learn about a local investment club that was getting started. Stocks. Portfolio investing. Estate planning. For people like her who knew nothing and had little but a job. While Sidarra still had hers, she decided she was going to have to join this investment club and get serious about herself again. Just the thought of that, or the hope, put her soundly to sleep without tears for the first time in a long time on the night before Good Friday.

| 2 |

THE LAST TIME Sidarra had been in church, her parents' caskets lay like bookends before her in a final display of horror and absurdity. Sidarra had never gone to church regularly and swore that day that she'd never be back. Yet she gave in that second Easter Sunday and went because it seemed time that Raquel learn to think of things beyond the world of her days and to know that some things were just right and some just wrong. For herself, Sidarra didn't expect church to be more than two hours of pain and bad memory, from which she intended to distract herself with thoughts about the first meeting of the Central Harlem investment club.

Reverend Anderson was up to the task that day, talking about how the people mourned when Christ died and wandered around the rock in grim despair. Try as she could, Sidarra couldn't really ignore what she heard. She saw herself there all of a sudden, transported, missing the greatest love of all. The choir swayed as they sang softly behind the Reverend's great, booming voice. He would say this about the feeling of being lost, then that. Between each sentence, the choir would moan melodically on the rise. It grew louder and louder, and everybody in the church, even Raquel, knew Jesus was coming back, that the story ended with love.

Praise music soon reached a crescendo, sending chills through Sidarra's body. As it tapered down to a hum again, the invitational began. Reverend Anderson's warm, deep voice surrounded her as he asked if anyone wanted to join the church today, if anyone wanted to be saved. Sidarra watched as one, then another person rose a little sheepishly from the pews and made their way down the aisle into the Reverend's outstretched arms. "And He loves you," the minister boomed. The choir soared with him. "And He loves you." The choir grew more powerful each time he spoke. "And you and you and you, He loves you." The voices seemed to lift out of the church. The Reverend looked right at Sidarra. "Listen, sister, you are loved."

Aunt Chickie, her mother's sister, reached over Raquel's lap and held Sidarra's hand in hers.

"Why are you crying, Mommy?" Raquel asked.

Sidarra couldn't answer. This was one more thing about her pain, its stubborn silence. She just looked quickly at her daughter, then into her aunt's face, the one so much like her mother's, and almost imperceptibly shook her head. No, Sidarra didn't believe he was right about God.

THE CENTRAL HARLEM INVESTMENT CLUB meeting was held on a low floor of the Theresa Hotel in the kind of broke-down old room that made it real clear exactly who was probably not going to make a lot of money on stocks. A man named Charles Harrison seemed to be in charge of greeting the dozen or so folks who showed up there that Tuesday evening. He stood near the window of the shabby conference room that belonged to a number of organizations on the floor; apparently not one of them had the responsibility of cleaning it, watering a plant every once in a while, or making sure the seat cushions weren't falling halfway off the chairs. Sidarra got there on time at six o'clock, brought a pad and a No. 2 pencil as she always had back in school, and sat in one of the chairs closest to the door. The people already there looked like her, probably about her age, shopped for the same reasonable clothes at H&M's and Lerner's, and had no idea how to keep a buck, but plenty of reason to try. There was Brenda, her neighbor from down the block who worked for the post office. A man named Dennis whose asthma was bad enough that he kept using his inhaler. Several prim women who might have been West Indian sitting in the front row. A sort of goofy-looking guy wearing a bright orange warm-up suit with matching Pumas and a salt-and-pepper goatee. Sidarra didn't catch his name when he introduced himself to the group. The others streamed in while Charles Harrison was explaining how an investment club worked and drew a few chicken-scratch diagrams on an erasable marker board he'd propped on a chair.

"It's pretty straightforward what we're supposed to be doing," Harrison explained. "You're going to have to work for your money so your money can start working for you. That means a lot of research into how stocks work and what sectors you're comfortable with, et cetera, et cetera, et cetera."

"Be more specific," said a woman who looked Korean, like she was getting impatient. "You keep saying 'et cetera, et cetera.' "

Harrison let her have it. He was already in two other clubs, he told her, so this wasn't really about him. He looked over her face for another moment and directed himself to everybody else. "Look, you all said so when you introduced yourselves, you got people to support. You don't know how to save. You struggle all the time, can barely get up the courage to balance your checkbook—if you even know *how* to balance a checkbook. You play Lotto. You probably waste more money on Lotto or the numbers than you would ever lose if you just did some basic research into what's out there. You could specialize in doing dumb shit with money—excuse me—but you know it's true. You've got your name on a lot of dumb financial decisions you'd like to take back, but you can't afford to. You were pretty sure it'd be different by now, but it's not. Nobody in here's a kid. You know what's going on out there lately, how people in the nineties are making a damn killing on the market, et cetera, et cetera, et cetera. But still you wouldn't touch the *Wall Street Journal* if it had naked pictures of your favorite whoever on every other page. Plus"—Harrison looked straight at a short Puerto Rican man who was hanging on every word—"you're aware that people are starting to make money all around you in Harlem, people are moving in and moving other people out, people who own property are bumping out people who don't in this, this Harlem Renaissance."

"C'mon, brother," sighed a tall bronze man with hazel eyes who had come in late but looked like he already knew everything Harrison had to say. "Please don't use that term like that," he added quietly.

Harrison stopped and looked across the room at the guy. "What's your name, brother?" he asked, down with the challenge.

"My name's Griff."

Hearing the man's name interrupted every channel in Sidarra's head.

"What do you do, Mr. Griff?"

"I'm an attorney. I work in criminal defense."

"All right then. What's wrong with that term?"

Griff was cool all right, as a matter of principle. But he didn't want to shake Harrison completely out of his groove. Griff wore a dark brown suit and black leather boots, a manila yellow shirt with no tie, and two gold rings on his incredibly long fingers. "I don't mean any disrespect, Mr. Harrison—"

"Charles."

"Charles. But I don't have to tell you that the real Harlem Renaissance in the 1930s was one of the most important times for the development of black arts, letters, business, and intellect. This today ain't that. Nobody here is worried about being priced out of Harlem by black people. We're all just trying to keep this thing from running over all of us, that's all I'm saying. Excuse me for interrupting, brother."

Harrison looked across at Griff like he'd reunited with an old war buddy. "Not a problem. Show you're right, my man." And he went on to explain how the people who joined the group would have to commit to each other, not in terms of financial trust, but to being part of a reliable research team. Everybody would have to be patient, no matter how much money anybody chose to invest. "And you have to realize that, like everything else in life, asset investment is a game of angles."

Sidarra suddenly found herself thinking wildly about other kinds of angles. This man Griff might be reason enough to stay with this particular venture. To her, he was the kind of crazy fine man you have long stopped waiting for—kind of. Not only did she notice that his teeth were perfect and white, and that he had the sculpted cheeks of the African warrior chiefs you used to see on those beer commercial posters in the '70s, but he spoke in the low and righteous tones of a brother who had a genuine clue about how things worked. If *he* was down with the Central Harlem investment club with his law degree and concern for the ancestors, well, she was probably down too.

As Harrison took more and more specific questions from the interested folks trying to get ahead in the financial world, Sidarra stole looks at Griff. He fit a fantasy she'd been keeping to herself for years. It was nothing less than the dream of a passionate marriage to a guy who was at least her equal. Griff had been to school. So had she, though maybe not for as long. She had a master's degree in education from City College. She could remember herself back when she still felt like one of the most beautiful women in the room and before a long, painful accumulation of very unwise near-misses. She had specifically imagined meeting this man when her body and mind were a little readier: before Raquel, when her parents were there to say "There you go, darling." Griff resembled the man whose mind contained the unpredictable kindness of radical affection. They would help each other. They would listen endlessly without interrupting or boring each other. For this man, she could rise up with all her energy, and they would pursue each other's growth and pleasure. This was the dream back in the day when everything was going to be all right. This was the bell before a lot of false alarms that fooled her into standing out in the cold nearly buck naked, her best lingerie making her curves look foolish in the streetlight, while some trifling guy, already dressed and looking around for his next piece of booty, would take off into the night, et cetera, et cetera. No, this guy Griff was her guy.

"How ya doin'? I'd like to introduce myself," Griff said, walking up to Sidarra after the meeting was over. "I'm Griff."

"Hello. My name is Sidarra."

"Sidarra." His eyes brightened, and he wasn't too cool to take a flirtatious breath. "That's a beautiful name. I appreciated the questions you asked."

"Well, we're all trying to be clear about things, I guess. I thought your little history lesson was right on point."

He looked away for a momentary blush. "I was just breaking ice, you know." It occurred to both of them that their bodies were swaying slightly, like kids at a school social deciding if they had the courage to join the dance. "That's a lot of stuff we've got to digest," he said. "The small-cap funds. The, uh, tax-free shelters. CDs that don't play music. This is kind of a first for me."

"Tell me about it."

"Are you walking somewhere?"

Of course she was. She was getting ready to walk half a mile home to where Michael would be waiting to tell her what a silly idea this was. "Sure. I'm heading uptown."

Griff wanted to take a photograph of that smile, the exact one that followed her last word. He had not seen one so fresh in a long time. It made him feel familiar, not that he'd known Sidarra before, but like he had somehow met a kindred spirit in the middle of something that usually confused him: making money.

That's mostly what they talked about as they walked up Lenox Avenue, how each of them had felt a little ashamed hearing news all the time about people taking advantage of the stock market, all the IPOs and Internet millionaires.

"But you're a lawyer," she said at one point. "I wouldn't expect to find a lawyer at a meeting like this."

He smiled brightly and looked down at the sidewalk. "Not all lawyers make a lot of money. I'm a criminal defense lawyer. I try to keep black men out of prison. I probably don't have to tell you that black men facing time don't have much to pay a lawyer."

"No, you don't," she said. And next thing you know, they were having a cup of coffee, talking about black men they knew from their work. Sidarra grew passionate about what happens to poor kids in the New York City public schools, and how she felt like she had done practically nothing to help them in all her years in the system. Griff found that fascinating, so fascinating that he kept asking questions about her work, about exactly what she did all day.

"Oh, I really don't do much," she answered half seriously. "Perhaps you've seen me before. I'm one of those people who was gonna make a difference. I taught junior high for a while. When I felt myself burning out, I went back for an administrator's degree, which landed me a once-in-a-lifetime position matching 'disadvantaged teens' "—she made quotation marks with two fingers on each hand—"with shamelessly advantaged corporations. It was a special program." She paused to see if she'd bored him yet, but Griff seemed to want her to go on. "My kids would spend a few hours a week in midtown corporate offices. They would learn in detail just how little they offered this world and just how much white folks really have. If an executive didn't have quite everything—like a cup of coffee or a fresh pencil—my kids would go get it." She stopped and looked off somewhere as if she were still undecided about that part of the story. "I'm not really a liaison anymore—just somebody with a foot in the door, working at the Board but paid by the program. Hanging on. I answer phones a lot. I know change comes slowly, but this is not the best time at work for me right now." Graciously, she smiled. "So, Griff," she asked, playfully exaggerating the single syllable of his name, "have you seen things improve for black boys down at the courthouse all the years you've been there?"

"No. I can't say that I have." His voice could be so deep. "I'm like you. Just trying to limit the thug multiples they face."

Sidarra smiled quizzically at his choice of words. "I'm sorry. Thug multiples?"

"Oh, that's what defense lawyers worry about. You have a client, he's been charged with some stupid thing—it's small, it was an error of youthful judgment or something. But because of who he is, how people see him, and how he thinks about solving a problem, it's probably gonna get worse. One bad decision is gonna multiply until he fits the profile of a thug. Other people's misdemeanors are his felonies. Everybody makes mistakes. But black boys get the multiplier quick—"

"In the public schools," she interrupted.

"In criminal justice," he finished.

"Well, there you go," she declared with a very certain smile. "That's just what I'm talkin' about, my friend."

That's what Griff might be for now, her friend. And that's where they left it at about eight-fifteen on a street corner two blocks from her apartment. The goodbye had the look of all business. They shook hands, smiling. But they shook lightly at first, as you might a stranger, and that wasn't good enough. So they rocked on their heels for a few more awkward moments, reminding each other of when the next meeting was and what they were supposed to do in preparation for it. With all the rocking and coming up with last-minute things to say, they forgot to exchange phone numbers. They didn't even know each other's full names. By the time they went in for a final handshake, they each did it with both hands, holding more firmly this time, letting each other know how truly good it was to make this acquaintance.

Her hands were long, delicate, and lovely in his. His hands were strong, large, and honest in hers. And as Sidarra walked alone down the street with Griff's eyes still on her, she could still feel the distinctive bump of his wedding ring.

SIDARRA HEARD THE GIGGLES from outside the front door, and the smell of McDonald's French fries was all over the hallway. Michael and Raquel were inside yukking it up as usual.

"Well, if it isn't the two partners in crime," Sidarra said, staring at the sight they made. They were draped all over the couch, with enough ketchup-stained napkins, several cups of strawberry soda, a few half-eaten cheeseburgers, and more fries on the floor than a small army of water bugs could eat in a week.

"Hello, Ivana Trump," Michael laughed from behind his big glasses and bushy mustache.

"Hi, Mommy!"

"What you guys been doin'?"

"Watching videos, baby. Come on in, we saved you some food."

Sidarra had to laugh. She gave each of them a kiss. Nobody got up. She just joined them on the other side of Raquel and let them finish the scene. On the TV screen the blurry bootleg showed Eddie Murphy and Dave Chappelle joking about each other's mother, and Sidarra slid down into the cushions to giggle. It didn't take long for the fast food to take full effect on Michael and Raquel. By nine o'clock, Raquel was curled up asleep and Michael's mouth was an open hole of snores.

Sidarra watched the screen go blank blue and squeezed out from under her sleeping daughter's legs to turn it off. She stood in the room, a wave of fresh energy washing through her, and decided now would be a good time to clear some work space in the storage room. The investment club research was something she'd have to do at home, at a desk, which she never bothered to set up. Her father had left her his desk, but it was gathering dust in the small back room. Worried about water bugs, she summoned Galore and made her go into the room with her. Things were everywhere stacked in cardboard boxes and covered in a patina of dust. A drooping shoe tree with all manner of shoes sulked beside a wall. Leaning against a corner was a long, thin case made out of stretched leather that held her famous uncle's billiards cue. Yet the walls looked orderly. Pictures of her parents hung in frames. There was even one or two of Sidarra sitting safely in the middle of her three brothers. Her mother's mirrors hung on sturdy hooks here and there. Looking at the images all around her, Sidarra saw pictures of who she'd been and who she'd become.

By one o'clock in the morning, she had surprised herself by completely clearing the old brown desk and dusting down its sides. All the papers from the investment club were stacked in their own cubbyholes. Her pens were on one side, a hole puncher and stapler on the other. Sidarra tried out the seat and sighed. Fatigue finally started to kick in. The excitement of the day was almost over, except that she had met a tall, handsome married man. Her body came alive at the thought of Griff. They'd had the first serious conversation she'd had about those things in many years.

A box in the corner suddenly called to her. Inside was a chaotic mixture of odds and ends—a radio, some old scarves, her mother's best shoes, and a few pieces of jewelry her grandmother wore. She plugged in the radio and was surprised when it worked. The channel was still set to her father's old jazz, as if you might hear old jazz on the radio now. But there it was, full of sweet horns and a gentle rhythm. Sidarra pulled out a lavender hat with a wide brim that was partly folded under other things. She put it on and found a silk scarf to match. Next she found a long strand of faux pearls and placed it over the hat and around her neck. She tried on three pairs of good shoes before finding the ones that lifted her with a little magic. And there she was in the mirror, fifteen years younger, beautiful and ready to sing like she used to. In her house as a child, everyone knew what Sidarra would become: a singer, a lounge singer, with a rich, mysterious voice like Nancy Wilson, Diana Ross, or Lena Horne. She would wear long, glittering dresses that hugged her strong figure like a mermaid's scales. She would cast shadows on adoring men who stood no chance of having her, but she would give them all her heart through her songs. And that night in the mirror, all alone with the past, she thought she glimpsed hope.

| 3 |

SIDARRA WAS ONE of those people who believed that almost everyone gets up in the morning and tries to do the right thing that day. She figured that if you believed differently about people, you'd go crazy waiting on evil—especially living in New York City. Lately, only the Board of Miseducation made Sidarra question her belief in the goodness of folk, and at the Board of Miseducation building in downtown Brooklyn, there was one person in particular who seemed to set evil in motion: Desiree Kronitz.

Desiree's problem might have been that she was a young white woman with a black woman's first name. Apparently she felt she had a lot of compensating to do for that at work in Clayborne Reed's Special Programs division, where all the other women were black or Latina, but most of the men were white. Desiree had to rise quickly, speaking up constantly in staff meetings, adding her own agenda items, or being the first to report on the progress of a project. She thought nothing of interrupting coworkers fifteen or twenty years older than herself. Only men seemed to like her—a trait Sidarra shared—but the origin of their affection for Desiree was ambivalent: they dreaded the sound of her voice but looked forward to the sight of her butt. She was as well known for the inappropriate comment as she was for the thong line visible atop the back of her waist. Either way, men didn't mind being around her. Particularly Clayborne Reed, the head of the unit, whose managerial responsibilities included standing behind Desiree when she happened to bend over and pick something up two or three times a day.

But what made Desiree more than a pain in the ass was the fact that she was an Eagleton type. Jack Eagleton was the not-so-new schools chancellor appointed to cut bureaucratic waste and improve standardized test scores. Eagleton came in with a plan to run the schools like a corporation and make them "profitable" again. He immediately directed his new programmers to create a simple computer designation for unproductive but belligerent staff—"Control-86 Transfer Command"—which with a few keystrokes would remove them from the books at central administration without the usual termination hearing required by the collective bargaining agreement. For the employee, it meant job oblivion, practically without a trace, and months of costly searching to retrieve lost files of your employment history in the event you wanted back pay, benefits, or reinstatement. For Eagleton, it was legal subterfuge, a secret high-tech hammer held over the heads of longtime Board employees who dared to resist his changes. Under this schools chancellor, schoolchildren were now referred to as "educable units," teachers became "learning associates," a curriculum was really a "paradigm," and success meant "investment returns." Eagleton was known around the office simply as "that bastard." Desiree was the new breed of hatchet man, the kind who speaks wistfully about "makeovers" and "reorganizations."

The first thing reorganization meant was no more offices for certain staff, like Sidarra, just cubicles. Desiree made a beeline for Sidarra's cubicle one morning in late May. When she got to the half wall, she planted her silk-bloused elbows on the edge and peered down as if she were looking into a cage. That morning, Sidarra was stuck answering random calls to the central office when a frantic assistant principal called to report an emergency at a Bronx school. Desiree, gesturing wildly, interrupted the phone call.

"Good news, sweetie!" She giggled like they were close friends.

Sidarra looked at her in disbelief, shook her head, and returned to the phone. "I'm gonna have to call you back," she said into the mouthpiece. "That's very disturbing. We'll get you a school safety investigator by tomorrow. Make sure to keep somebody with the families. Try not to worry. Kids are tough." Sidarra hung up the call and looked up at Desiree. "What?"

"What was that about?"

"District 11. Two children had seizures during the morning test session and no one was prepared to help them. They're still testing out there, but a few of the kids went to the hospital in ambulances."

"That's not school safety, Sidarra! You oughta know that," she said in that thick Long Island accent that always makes you want to chew a piece of gum. "That's Communicable Disease Suppression and, oh my God, Legal. Those parents could sue us."

"Thanks for your input, Desiree. What's the good news?"

"The chancellor issued an early draft of his reorganization report to some of us. Guess what?" Her face brightened as if she sincerely meant it. "You're not getting the early retirement ax after all!"

"What? How did you—?" Sidarra looked around and tried to

blink some sense into a moment that had caught her totally off guard. "What's happening to our division?"

Desiree gleefully ticked off the names of a few coworkers, men and women who had been at the Board for decades. *They* were getting a "package." One or two would be transferred. A new person, a specialist, was being hired from Chicago. "And you'll be reporting to *me*! Isn't that wonderful?"

"But, Desiree, I'm senior to you."

"Apparently not anymore. But don't get stank with me until you talk with Reed, because it was his recommendation, sister-girl." She thought that talk was funny in a black way. "C'mon, Sidarra. Don't be upset. This will be good for the management flow. You and I will have to get along eventually."

And she was gone. Everything in Sidarra's head went numb. She stared blankly across her desk, past the mounds of files, the computer she rarely used, to a picture of Raquel as a toddler smiling sweetly. How could this be? she thought. What would this mean? Then the old, Whatever happened to our union? Sidarra nearly blacked out from the shock. Slowly she rose from the seat, but she was too distracted to avoid the sides. As she stood up, her thigh caught on the jagged edge of the old swivel chair and the metal tore her pantyhose, her dress, and drew a thin line of blood. Sidarra balled up her fists. "Cheesy fucking dress!"

Ripped clothes and all, she marched away from the cubicle and straight to Clayborne Reed's office. He was on the phone when she walked in and closed the door behind her.

He put the phone down. "Do we have an appointment?" he asked, grinning sheepishly.

"I think so," she said. "Desiree just gave me some 'good news.' Is she on crack or something?"

He shook his large round head and chuckled to himself. "No, Sidarra. I'm afraid not. You know your dress is ripped."

"I'll survive."

"Why don't you have a seat. You were going to find out Friday anyway." Sidarra sat down and Reed began to explain that there was nothing he could do about the latest changes the new chancellor wanted. They'd brought in management consultants from Wisconsin, conducted efficiency studies, and reviewed each member of the division's staff. "You're lucky you still have a job. Most of us are lucky to be around. Desiree is even going to train you to enter the Control-86 Transfer Command. Can't fall through a trapdoor if you know one's there."

That wasn't good enough for her. "But why was no one *here* consulted? Lots of us have good ideas. I have a whole folder of proposals I've wanted to make to improve things. Don't I deserve that after ten years here? And how, Clayborne, how in the world . . ." Her voice trailed off as she tried to collect herself.

"Seniority will only get you so far in this man's world," he said. "Desiree's skills are fresh. She knows the database systems they use. She's familiar with the whole test regimen we'll be implementing. This is not a knock on you, Sidarra."

"Did you go to bat for me, Clay? Did you at least fight for me?"

He wouldn't look at her. He just pressed his fingers together and redistributed his girth in the chair. "I did what I could," he nearly whispered, still not meeting her eyes. "The demotion in title could have been worse. The pay cut coulda been *a lot* worse."

"The what?!" she screamed.

It was no use. Before long she was out the door and on the way back to her cubicle, leaving a fresh bloodstain on his chair.

THE CITY'S PUBLIC SCHOOL STUDENTS seemed to be in a perpetual state of test taking. The chancellor had doubled the number of standardized tests given to city schoolchildren each semester during the spring testing dates, but school staff were struggling to handle the logistics. Four girls in the eighth grade at P.S. 76 in the

Morrisania section of the Bronx found themselves four students too many for the classroom's legal maximum. D'Amaya, Kimara, LeJazz, and Jennifer were friends skilled in coordinating class disruptions. Because of overcrowding, the only sensible place to move them was to a large maintenance closet where some chairs and a round table were squeezed in. A proctor could monitor them through a window in the door. Everything worked well enough during the first part of the day of testing, but late in the afternoon an old dumbwaiter shaft that connected to the room through a vent began emitting a weak gassy smell. The girls complained about having to take a test in such a nasty place that stank so bad, but both the supervising teacher and the custodian detected nothing more than the astringent aroma of floor cleaners. The girls went home for the day. But the next morning, the emissions from the little vent became visible as a thin film in the air, which made the girls dizzy and nauseous. When two of them complained again, the young proctor thought they were trying to get out of finishing the test. Then the gas really started to fill the tiny room. When one child lost consciousness, the proctor finally decided to open the door and call for emergency help. Because the school was on testing lockdown, the commotion didn't set off the normal relay, and it was several minutes before the four girls were actually removed from the closet and sent to the hospital, violently coughing and vomiting in loud, raw spasms that horrified the students who had to hear them pass. The story ran on all the local TV news channels that evening. The girls had not suffered from "communicable disease," as Desiree had thought. It was the toxic union of too much gas, asbestos residue, and asthma.

MICHAEL WAS GOOD about one thing. He agreed to relieve Mrs. Thomas of babysitting duty whenever Sidarra was at her weekly investment club meeting, and he was always on time with videos and cheeseburgers for Raquel. Michael was right about another thing: that Sidarra might lack the patient temperament of a successful stock market investor. A couple of weeks into her first attempts to invest some of the savings her parents had left for Raquel's college fund, Sidarra began to wonder if she was a stupid fool, or just a damn fool. Mr. Harrison advised her to wait a bit longer before she actually bought any stock. He thought she might want to keep evaluating the best portfolio for her. But he also said that she seemed like a very quick study. That last part was all she heard. Sidarra felt a little too desperate to be patient.

After that particularly bad day at work, she arrived early and waited alone for the investment club meeting to start in the dank, poorly lit conference room in the Theresa Hotel. She had an acute need for power. It wasn't just the surprise demotion by the chancellor that made her feel vulnerable. It was what happened to the four little girls in the Bronx, too. She realized that, in a way, it could have been she who was forced to take that test in a dangerous little room, in which case, had she survived, she would be forever disabled and her life would assume the involuntary mission of undoing the Board of Miseducation's carelessness. Or, more likely, it could have been her own daughter trapped in that room, in which case Sidarra would suddenly have had to take on the lifelong quest of the pitiful parents you see on the evening news, looking small and sweet and pathetic in their tired search for justice, accountability, and, failing all that, a little peace. The unexpected chain of events starting from the Bronx school accident had suddenly set fear off inside her—the phone call from the frantic school administrator that she happened to answer, the Board's self-protective response by Desiree, the slow-breaking news about the girls' condition in the hospital, the sight of their anguished parents on television, the insipid prevalence of danger to girls. It all struck home for Sidarra. She could see herself under the bright reflection of a helicopter spotlight, scanning for storm victims amid twisted wreckage and instead finding her, huddled and shaking. Sidarra didn't want to be caught out there. So once Charles Harrison began the meeting, she asked as many questions as came to mind; she answered questions she wasn't responsible for researching. And when the goofy-looking guy who wore the colorful warm-up suits tried to redirect the day's topic into tech stocks, she checked him politely, but firmly.

"But I know a little something about this," the man said. "I'm a computer tech. I mean, I do programming."

"Please don't misunderstand me," Sidarra told him, creasing her prominent eyebrows. "I'm not saying you don't have valuable information to share. I'm just reminding you that you don't have the floor right now."

She raised all the lesser eyebrows in the room with that one. But she was right, and the club members who were left—about eight people down from the original thirteen—went back to reading charts on manufacturing.

After class ended Sidarra tried to get the goofy-looking tech guy's attention by gently tapping his shoulder. "Excuse me. I've forgotten your name. Excuse me." He wouldn't turn around. He had his hands in a satchel. "Excuse me." When he still wouldn't acknowledge her, she decided he might hear her better if she stood in front of him. "Look, I've forgotten your name—"

"Yakoob," he said without looking up.

"Right. Yakoob, I just want you to know that I didn't mean anything when I cut your questions short."

He looked up at her from his chair. "Then you shouldn't have done it. You're a rude person. I don't know why they'd let such a rude person up in here."

She stood back. "You serious? I really offended you?"

"Hell yeah, lady. What's your problem? I don't need somebody stepping on the microphone like that. Shit. I'll talk when I wanna keep talking."

"You're funny," she smiled.

"You're not," he smiled back, and stood up. Then they both started laughing. "I'm just bullshitting with you. It's all good."

They got to talking. Like most women with a pulse, Sidarra was well versed in men's attentions. Not that a man was necessarily attracted or was ready to make a move. But men can't help signaling whether there is any room for sexual interest or not. It had nothing to do with being married. It had to do with being a man, and it had to do with being the particular woman she was. No matter how jacked-up she might have looked that day, and in spite of whatever the heck happened to the good taste and style she used to flaunt a million heartaches ago, she knew what she looked like naked. And that almost always had an effect on men. But not Yakoob. As they talked, Yakoob never gave a hint of that kind of interest. She felt safe in his presence.

"Hey, I'm getting ready to break out of here and go shoot some rack, so unless you wanna get down, it was nice meeting you. I'll see you next week, Sidarra."

"Pool?"

"Stick, darling. Yeah. Pool."

"I play pool. I mean, I like to." She had to scratch her head at the novelty of the idea. She thought about Michael and Raquel stuffing themselves with movies and French fries back home. "I should ask my friend. Have you met Griff?"

Griff stepped up as if he'd been waiting in the shadows for his cue. The short walk uptown and cup of coffee had started to become a nice little habit between them after the weekly meetings. That's when they realized that all three of them were tall people. Sidarra was almost five foot eight. Yakoob was a shade under six foot two. Griff was six foot four, and as he stepped up to eye Yakoob and shake his hand, he sort of presented his superior height with a little extra meaning. "Let's go," he said.

"I know a place downtown," Yakoob said.

Sidarra called home to Michael on her cell phone to say she'd be running late, and off they went.

They drove in Yakoob's old Chevy to a billiard parlor upstairs on Amsterdam in the Seventies. As the two men talked and laughed in the front seat, she sat back and watched the city out the window like a girl playing hooky. All of a sudden, life, after one of Sidarra's worst days at work, had served up this scene: her in a car with two brothers from an investment club heading the wrong way from her man and her daughter, about to shoot some rack.

But that was as far as her mind would wander. She didn't even really want to talk. She wanted to get the kind of clarity that comes with a stick in your hand and pure angles before you. The pool hall was warm, low-lit, and long.

"What'll you have, hon?" Griff asked her.

Oh, probably just a glass of the house red, Sidarra was about to say. Then it occurred to her to be exotic without knowing exactly how. "Can you recommend something exquisite?"

Griff's eyebrows lifted. "Exquisite? Hmm." He squeezed his fingers to his chin and stared at her as if he were taking a drink measurement. "My mother—I mean my second mom—was a sophisticated lady and very sweet. I remember she used to drink an old-fashioned martini named a sidecar. This is the kind of place that just might know how to make it. Want to try one on me?"

Did she ever. Exquisite—a word she never used—was just right.

By the second sidecar, she was feeling smoother. She had a quiet storm musical thing going in her temples as she played the games. Later, when she saw Griff's figure striding back across the wide-open room to their table, she was feeling good enough to do something she would never have done if you'd asked her to the day before: she dropped her eyes all over his hips until he was standing right in front of her. "For you," he said, holding the third sidecar.

"Delicious," she declared. "Whose break?"

"Yours, Sidarra," said Yakoob, Tanqueray in hand. "Um, got a question before you do."

"Mm-hmm."

"Just how much goddamned pool do you play, sister?"

She looked up from the green felt of the table to see them both waiting heavy for the answer. "Oh, well, almost never. Anymore. But I used to play a lot, you know. Back in the day." That made them chuckle into their drinks. "I had an uncle who played quite a bit, and he taught me how to line things up correctly and all. It's fun. I forgot about pool."

The strange fact was, they *all* could play. You put your average three strangers together to play pool, especially three people off the street without their own personal cue sticks or gloves, and each game is going to be a long game. They're going to miss a lot, laugh, and generally talk about the world they live in. Not these three. These three could play. By the third game, balls were pocketed with regularity. Sometimes it looked as if somebody might not even get a chance to shoot. Sure, they talked. They talked about trying to keep faith in the stock market. They talked about who had a family at home (all, so to speak) and who could stay out all night (none of them). But apart from the conversation, each seemed to choose shots with a high degree of difficulty. When they made them, they stopped pumping their fists pretty soon and just went on shooting.

For Sidarra, pool felt like a sudden return to her heyday, when she was fourteen, almost beautiful, and she got to play for hours under her mysterious uncle Cicero's watchful eye, the balls gleaming on the bright green table like jewels for the taking. Always in the background was his deep and complicated jazz music, like the birdfighting of crazed horns amid a soft rain of cymbals. "Gwon, girl!" Uncle Cicero would grunt as she'd dream up some uncanny angle. "Good idea." Then *pop!* She'd drill it. "Smart girl," he'd mumble as the ball slow-rolled down the tunnel. "Don't take a bow. Just think ahead."

To Uncle Cicero, pool was the perfect game. On a proper table and a level earth, it is the only game decided completely by the skill of the player, he would say. The physics merely are what they are, and each player controls force and spin, angle and outcome with no one and nothing else to blame. For centuries, the games humbled kings and focused the minds of monks before prayer. Men could learn a lot about themselves around a pool table, he'd say, and so could she.

Except that, by ten o'clock, those sidecars were starting to work on Sidarra, and Yakoob was a little drunk too. Griff alone was Hennessy, and Griff was cool.

"My man here is a law-yuh, and homegirl is an administrator," Yakoob said.

"Was," Sidarra mumbled. They heard that even over the bad rock music and looked over at her. "I don't wanna get into that tonight," she said.

Yakoob went on, banking in a shot. "You and your lady got kids, Griff?"

Griff kept his face in his drink. "Nuh," he coughed.

"All them years and no kids." Yakoob took another shot.

Sidarra wasn't too drunk to take note of that answer. Griff was caught wondering if he had actually told them how long he'd been married. Maybe that was the Hennessy. "What about you?" he asked Yakoob.

"Daddy? Me?" Yakoob sighed. "Can't say so yet, I'm afraid." He giggled nervously. "Five years in the pen with my old lady and still no luck trying to bring me home a son." The statement seemed to make Yakoob miss. He sat back down on a stool and, instead of finishing a thought he left hanging, let out a loud, unconvincing yawn. "But you're blessed with a little girl, huh, Sidarra?" He watched her nod as Griff stood up to take a turn at the table. "Lucky she wasn't caught up in that fire in the Bronx. Can you believe that shit?"

The mere mention of the four little girls sobered her instantly. "It wasn't a fire, Koob," Sidarra explained. "It was a small explosion in a furnace, all the way in the basement of that school. It was the fumes that got the girls. Toxic fumes."

"And they all had asthma." Griff spat from a crouch before shooting at a ball. *Pop!* He let go and the balls scattered loudly. Griff had seen the evening news.

Yakoob looked incredulous. "Well, if there weren't no flames, no smoke, no fire, why didn't they just get the girls out?"

Sidarra shook her head. "I don't know. They were in a little room—a janitor's closet, taking a test, Yakoob. The proctor assigned to them was just an aide, an untrained young person just there to watch. She probably panicked. She was probably afraid if she stopped them from taking the test, all hell would break loose in the district office. By the time she finally came back to the room with someone who could make the decision, the fumes had overcome one of the girls."

"What the fuck's the matter with them people?" Yakoob asked in disgust.

"They work for the New York City Board of Miseducation," she answered matter-of-factly.

"But you work for the Board, too, don't you?" Yakoob followed, smiling at her. Sidarra didn't enjoy the tease. "Sorry," he said. "At least that's gonna be four little rich girls when Al Sharpton gets through with the school."

Sidarra pulled up and stared bitterly into Yakoob's face. "No, baby. No, not four." Yakoob looked back at her quizzically. "You didn't hear? Two of those little girls died. The toxins set off an asthma attack. They died of asthma attacks. Another was clinging to life when I left work today." Yakoob wasn't a funnyman at all anymore. He seemed to take the news personally, scanning the dark floor of the pool hall. "So only two may live to see any money," she said somberly.

Griff had been angrily shooting balls in the background. "No they won't," he said flatly, and took another loud shot across the long table. "From what I understand, it looks like the company that fucked up the air ducts is an independent contractor. They'll get sued, but the city will be immune." *Bip!* Griff shot a ball into the corner pocket. "The company will have limited liability, and its insurer will drag out the suit until the girls' families take a low-ball settlement just to pay off their attorneys." *Bang!* He took another angry shot without looking up. "That's how it works. Two, three years from now, those poor girls won't see shit. You gotta have money to sue companies."

Yakoob sat mildly stupefied on his stool. Sidarra held her knees and sighed. She didn't know about the legal obstacles facing the girls' families. And she had no idea how this back-page story from her daily work had made it into the mood of her clandestine pool game with two men. She certainly didn't expect to be sharing her outrage about it with them. Now, only sarcasm came to mind. "And if I know the Board of Miseducation, the company that's responsible for the accident will probably get the contract to fix it."

"Ain't that a bitch," Yakoob said into his gin.

"This is the real reason you need money," Griff said, resting his cue on the table and walking over to where they were sitting. As his presence drew closer, Sidarra looked up his long leg and smiled naturally. "Protection against fools. Avoidance of a humiliating death, you know?" Finally he noticed Sidarra's eyes glowing slightly beside him. "And maybe some well-deserved good times, am I right?"

Their glasses touched.

The game changed. It went quiet for several turns. No looks. No handclaps for good shots. No helpful groans when somebody missed a tough one. Just playing.

"So you're a computer whiz, huh, Koob?" Sidarra asked.

Yakoob smiled. His friends called him Koob. "To pay the bills, baby, but not really. Don't laugh, y'all, but I'm a comedian. I guess you could say that I'm about as much a comedian right now as you're an administrator, Sid."

She liked that. Her friends used to call her Sid.

| 4 |

TUESDAY NIGHT WAS GETTING TO BE THE STRANGEST NIGHT of the week. The investment club met then, and that meant Sidarra would come home late to find her daughter groggy or already asleep. It meant Michael would be staying over, and it meant she would have enjoyed a night having coffee with Griff or playing pool with him and Yakoob. A few weeks had passed since her demotion at work. The first paycheck with the pay cut had come, and Sidarra found herself a little deeper in debt. Because he had bought her gold hoop earrings as a consolation present and was helping her by staying with her child, the debt was piling up to Michael in particular. Especially for sex.

"Why don't you put that paper down, girl," Michael said from the bedroom doorway. Sidarra was sitting up in bed reading the stock pages of the *Wall Street Journal*. "I suppose those numbers might move if you don't watch them, but I doubt it. Hey, I know a happy little number that's about ready to move up and down for you."

She appreciated the joke and that he didn't laugh at it for a change, but she was not feeling sex at the moment. He was. Michael wore an old-style satin boxer's robe he'd caught on sale at Macy's. He found his own body irresistible in it. He stepped toward the bed and did a little shake-and-bake punching dance, then tugged at the sash until the robe opened. "The champ wants to know if you're ready to go a few rounds."

The champ wasn't quite ready himself, but it wouldn't take much. She glanced up at Michael's heavy paunch, the tiny knots of black curls on his chest, and the tight hydrant of a penis, still flaccid but alert to sirens in the distance. Sidarra smiled politely, folded the paper to the side, and stood up. In real life there's no such thing as being beyond another's hopes, even if the mismatch is obvious to all. Whatever Sidarra had, Michael wanted badly. He often acknowledged the physical mismatch between them with a trembling heart and premature ejaculations. Yet no one else had presented himself to her with any lasting kindness or flattered her sincerely. She didn't like to admit it to herself, but she knew her body was his secret solace, the dream that had eluded him for fifty years. Every time they had sex he was as grateful to her for giving it to him as he was the first. Sidarra wanted to feel like that too one day.

She put a hand on his chest and gently pulled the satin collar closer to her on the bed. He let out the first low moan once he was sure this was no tease. When he lay back, she let her own housecoat fall open, revealing her full round breasts in a white lace bra, the hourglass curvature of her tummy, and the delicate white lace panties that seemed barely able to stretch across her wide brown hips. Still wearing glasses, his eyes thrilled with hunger. Wagging tall above his formidable stomach, his little champ grew heavy, then hard. Sidarra was not the kind of lover who liked to hold his penis in her hand. She had never held it in her mouth. But because she felt she owed him tonight, she pulled off her lingerie slowly, kept her eyes on him, and slid down the bed. When her mouth was just an inch or so above his dick, she hummed to it, opened her lips, and let a thin line of saliva cool down the bulging head. His legs shook around her shoulders, and over the horizon of his belly she could see his eyes roll back in his head. Wet with spit, his penis rocked between her breasts. She held each with her hands and rolled him into a stupor.

"Lord Jesus, you been so good to me!" he called out.

And it didn't take long to be too much for him. Sidarra, who couldn't remember the last time a man's sperm had met any part of her face, lay on top of her spent boyfriend as cool semen dripped from her chin.

"Oooh! Thank you, baby," he sighed, still breathing hard.

"That's what you're supposed to say when it's all over, papa. It ain't over." She got up from the bed and wrapped her housecoat around her shoulders. "I'll be right back."

This could be another effect of the sidecar martinis, she thought as she wiped semen from her face in the bathroom mirror. She took a hard look at her body. She leaned over the sink to see her hips and pubic bush below. She studied and craned, pushing the porcelain corner of the sink between her legs to see her sides. The cool thick edge touched the lip of her vagina just lightly enough to send a ripple up her spine. She leaned again, held the sides of the sink in both hands, and let the weight of the feeling last another second. Masturbation didn't surprise her. What surprised her was feeling so horny for Michael. That just didn't happen very often. When she went back into the bedroom, ready to take him inside her, she found only a large body deeply asleep to a chorus of snores. Before she could get mad, Sidarra was back at the bathroom sink. She locked the door and thought of Griff. That's something she never would have done before. Now, it was something she could not wait to do again.

BY THE END OF THE SUMMER, the newspapers kept reporting record stock market gains for just about everybody except Sidarra. It wasn't for lack of trying. Sidarra would stay up late at night, studying charts on the computer and comparing stocks. The language of investment was slowly beginning to make sense, but it was a challenge. Many of the reports Charles Harrison recommended turned out to be a bit dated or erroneous; magazines she found on her own proved more helpful, but still intimidating. For all her hours of work, she hadn't lost any money. But her $7,500 investment was now worth all of about $7,610, and it was time for Raquel to get new school clothes. They chose one of the hottest days in August to walk to the shops on 125th Street. And because she heard they would be getting shoes, Aunt Chickie asked if she could come along, too.

Chickie was Sidarra's mother's only living sister and was seventy-four years old. She had been called Chickie since the early days when she was the pride of the Dean girls. They all had moxie, a little extra style, and above average minds, but Chickie was the only one who looked the part of a starlet. She lived the part, too, as a young woman married to a Harlem showman who took her to Paris to live for a while in the fifties. Aunt Chickie's visits were always an event when Sidarra was growing up. She spoke French in between English sentences, wore perfume nobody had ever smelled before, and brought clothes you couldn't find in the United States. Her husband Melvin, the entertainer, was a chocolate-colored man with chocolate-filled suit pockets. The sight of them together started Sidarra's pubescent dream of being a lounge singer. They seemed to live the best way a person could: with cash, with the world's respect, and without barriers. And they were kiss-on-the-street in love the way she never saw with her own parents. But that's where it all ended. One night on the Champs-Elysées, Melvin had a stroke and collapsed at the side of a white female acquaintance. He was dead before the ambulance reached the hospital. After that, Chickie came right home to America, poor and brokenhearted. Now, she was an arthritic woman with diabetes, surviving alone on Social Security in a two-room senior apartment on Edgecombe Avenue. Like a long-forgotten tattoo, the only thing left of her former glory was her name.

"Why are we going in *here*?" Raquel asked as Sidarra led them into a Payless ShoeSource.

"Thank God it's air-conditioned, that's all I know," said Aunt Chickie.

"We're pretending, that's why," Sidarra told Raquel.

"Pretending what?"

"We're pretending that we're poor and this is the best Mommy can do this year. Try it. It'll be fun."

"Oh, I'm real good at this game," Aunt Chickie said, slowly making her way over to the first place to sit down.

Raquel wasn't sure she liked it, and walked down the long, dark aisles of shoes in her size wearing a distinctly funky face. Sidarra's plan was to wear her out by looking upstairs and down at every possible pair of shoes she might like, making her try them all on, then bringing the five or six finalists over to try on again in front of Aunt Chickie.

"How 'bout these? I like these okay," said Raquel. She was pointing to an open-toed pair of patent-leather heels.

"They're a little hoochie-mama, don't you think, Raquel?" Sidarra asked, holding the shoe up to the light. "I mean, this is a little more heel than I think you'll be needing for a few years, sugar. And how you gonna wear that one in the snow?"

Raquel was undeterred. "I guess I could wear some other shoes when it snows. Or we could just get some boots to wear over them, couldn't we?"

She sounded so reasonable that Sidarra was being pushed into an absolute "No" when she had hoped to avoid that. Being in Payless was bad enough. "Oh, Raquel. We can't get these as a matter of conscience. Yeah, I've read about this manufacturer. Scobi. Yes. I recognize the name. I own a few shares of their competitors. Did you know that the thing about Scobi's is they use forced child labor? That means that kids your age make these shoes in Taiwan. They're not allowed to go to school or play outside. All day long, separated from their parents, they put 'em at a long table and make them make shoes."

Raquel listened with great interest as long as she believed her mother, and Sidarra maintained a look of grave concern on her face. "Really?"

"Isn't that terrible?"

"Yeah."

"So let's not support that kind of stuff. Why don't you put 'em back on the shelf?"

Raquel didn't hesitate. She practically threw the shoes down in disgust and wiped her hand on her shirt. For the next hour or so, Raquel was distracted, her brows furrowed, wondering to herself how an eight-year-old could make a shoe like that.

Finally they got back to Aunt Chickie with four pairs of contenders to choose from. Aunt Chickie was sitting right where they'd left her, holding a Payless bag and talking with an elderly gentleman standing above her with a silver-handled cane in his hand.

"Pardon me," Sidarra said to them. "I thought you needed shoes, Aunt Chickie?"

"I'm fine, honey. Thank you."

The man smiled broadly, revealing two gold teeth. He bowed his head, winked at Aunt Chickie, and turned for the door. "I'll see you then," he baritoned on his way out.

"Who was that?" Raquel asked.

"He had a lovely smile, didn't he?" Aunt Chickie answered, watching the man walk gingerly into the sun.

Sidarra looked down at her aunt. Still so beautiful, she thought. Body broken but the spirit unbeatable. That's how I was gonna be. "Well, here are Raquel's choices."

After spreading them out to lots of exaggerated oohs and aahs from Aunt Chickie, Raquel made her selection. Two pairs costing just $12.99 plus tax. Sensible blue with the silver buckle and brown suede Timberland knockoffs for styling. Raquel actually looked happy as she walked up to the register with her mom. Sidarra pulled out her last good credit card and handed it to the teenage cashier. They waited. And waited.

"Ma'am, your card's been declined," said the expressionless teenager with all the quiet discretion of a boom box.

"I'm sorry?" Sidarra asked. "The card is fine. It must be your system."

"Run it again!" Raquel demanded.

Her daughter's tone caught Sidarra by surprise. She didn't even know Raquel knew what that meant. "Raquel. Don't use that tone with her."

"Run it again!" Aunt Chickie called out from her seat by the door.

The teenager ran the card again. And again. Chastised by an eight-year-old and an old woman, she must have figured it was better to wear out an arm than to argue. But the card was declined every time. Sidarra had exceeded her limit. Maxed out on just fourteen bucks. So she asked the young woman to hold the shoes for her and told her she would come back after she went to an ATM. Sidarra hoped that was true, for her sake and her daughter's, and they walked back out into the stifling August heat.

"Ghetto shopping, baby," Aunt Chickie said. "That's what happens. Broke-ass machines. That's all."

Sidarra and her only aunt did not always get along well, but given her brothers' unwillingness to help her out, she was left the duty to look out for her. Their mutual reluctance and Aunt Chickie's diabetes episodes were the reasons Mrs. Thomas had been pressed into babysitting service most days after school. But there were times like this when Sidarra wouldn't want anyone but Aunt Chickie with her.

"Did Mommy embarrass you a bit in there?" she asked Raquel.

"Nah."

"Well, that's just how it goes sometimes. I'm not sure whose mistake it was—probably mine. But the important thing is I'm working on it, so don't worry."

They needed to walk as far away from that embarrassment as they could. Sidarra took them each by the hand and marched them back and forth, a half block this way, a half block the other, totally indecisive. But Aunt Chickie could barely walk, and the sun was beating her up bad. In front of the Apollo Theater they crossed 125th Street between the cars. They made it to Lenox and crossed the wide avenue. Once they reached the other side, Raquel was annoying them with questions about how kids could make patent-leather shoes, and Aunt Chickie was breathing hard.

"I gotta stop," she gasped, her eyes almost closing and one hand on her chest. "I, uh, need to get into some cool, Sid."

Sidarra finally stopped. She and Raquel looked over at the old woman and nearly panicked. "Okay. You right. Let's just ease over next to the building there and get some shade. I'll think of something."

She thought about the Theresa Hotel, which was just back across the street. Maybe they could sit down in the investment club conference room and pull themselves together. Maybe there would be air-conditioning in there. But all of a sudden Aunt Chickie spoke up.

"Would you look at that," she said, her eyes fixed inside the huge pane of storefront glass beside them, and her finger rising to point.

"Wow. That's a beautiful dress, Mommy," said Raquel, her mouth open.

It *was* a beautiful dress. A knockout dress. The kind of dress four hundred and fifty women believe they must own and only three can wear. It was a strapless gold lamé evening gown, with a low-cut V revealing maximum cleavage and short slits at the top of the calves. You had to have the calves and the cleavage to wear it. Then you needed to have a statue's neck and only the most sculpted African shoulders. Even if you had all that, plus height enough to show how it all worked, you had to have the figure of a most bodacious mermaid to make it look like skin.

"It's gotta cost a fortune," said Sidarra.

"Let's go see," Aunt Chickie decided, and they went in.

The store was one of a thousand identical cheap clothing stores on strips like this all over the country. New York City had at least half of them. They stretched cheap evening gowns and party clothes from hooks on the walls and ceilings. Neon-colored two-piece outfits hung everywhere on hangers from above. If it wasn't tacky in some way or another, the Arabs or Asians or Colombians or Russian Jews who owned the place refused to stock it. Somehow you rarely saw anyone ever wearing such clothes. Yet in spite of all the hundreds of thousands of clown outfits hanging on racks throughout the huge place, there was this gold lamé wonder in the window.

The store was crispy cool and totally empty except for two eager brown salesmen. "Young man, I'd like to sit down near the dressing room. My niece would like to see that dress in a size eight," Aunt Chickie ordered.

"Well, maybe a ten, too," Sidarra added.

The salesman led the three of them through tight pinball rings of circular clothing racks to the middle of the store. Aunt Chickie had ambled her way to a bench when the man came back holding two dresses and gesturing toward the changing room door. Raquel wanted to come in with her mother. They crowded into the small cubby together while Sidarra undressed. She was relieved when the size ten was too big. Raquel sat cross-legged on the floor. As soon as Sidarra had managed to get out of the first one, Aunt Chickie was sticking her head between the lime green curtains.

"What's goin' on in here? What's taking so long? Y'all stealin' something?" Sidarra just laughed, standing in her underwear, ready to step into the dress. Aunt Chickie looked her up and down as only an old aunt or a mother could do. "Well, look at you, Sid."

"What?" Sid blushed, bending her knee to pull the dress up.

"Raquel, take a good look at your mother. *That*, my dear, is a body. And you gonna have one too. Apparently for a very long time." Aunt Chickie pulled her face away and disappeared back to her bench. Still in earshot but out of sight, she added: "Don't give that thing away, either. I mean, who knew?"

Sidarra paid her no mind and finished slipping the dress up and around her torso. The size eight was it. That much she could tell in the sliver of a mirror on the wall. And from the look in her daughter's eyes. "Wow, Mom. You look mad fine. Like a queen. Or even a princess."

"Really?"

"No doubt."

Sidarra smiled sweetly and stepped out into the fluorescent light of the big, open room. "Ta-da!"

Aunt Chickie put her hand to her mouth, not for herself but for her sister, who was not alive to see her own child shine so beautifully. "Incredible," is all she could say, her graying eyes slowly going over every inch of the dress fitting perfectly on Sidarra's frame. "It's like they made it for you, Sidarra. My God, that's a pretty sight."

Like Cinderella at the stroke of midnight, the fantasy ended. There was no way in the world she could afford that dress. The longer Sidarra stood there wanting it with them, the deeper her disappointment would be. She had just been unable to afford Raquel's cheap shoes. Letting this go should be easy. This was a luxury. She didn't have any money. Simple as that.

"We gonna make you autograph the others," said the salesman. "I give you a good deal on that today. Serious."

Sidarra shook her head and started back into the dressing room to take it off. "How much?" Aunt Chickie asked.

"Every day, three hundred dollars," the guy said without blinking. "Today, for lovely lady, two hundred and fifty."

Even Raquel joined in the you-gotta-be-joking look he got. Everyone knew these stores ask for twice as much as they ever hope to get. There was a long silence, like a bunch of gangsters waiting to see who'd shoot first.

"I'll give you a hundred and fifty," Sidarra suddenly spat out.

"A hundred and seventy-five," he shot back.

Silence again. "C'mon, Mommy. Nothing you have is nice."

"What? What do you know, little girl? You ain't even got any school shoes."

"Do it, woman," Aunt Chickie said, searching in her purse for a piece of gum. "You'll be old tomorrow."

"Well . . ." Sidarra fidgeted and fumbled, standing there in the dress like a bolt of light. "I can't do it today, but we can do that price. I'm a little short today. I'll give you a small deposit to hold it. You give me a receipt, and, uh, we'll go from there."

"No layaway," the guy said, trying to be firm about it despite the fact that the big store was just as empty now as when they came in.

"It's not layaway," she said, quickly coming up with investment club knowledge. "It's securitization. I give you something as collateral, and you hold it in trust for me on installment."

That seemed to work. Sidarra gave him ten dollars, saving just enough for three hot dogs when they got out of there. She left with a receipt, and they walked out into the setting August sun. Raquel smiled ear to ear all the way home, saying not another word about children making shoes in Taiwan.

A few blocks from home, while Raquel was busy singing, Aunt Chickie had to say something she had been keeping back. "I wished I coulda helped you out back at that store, Sid. I truly do. I wish I coulda bought Raquel's shoes, too. I wasn't sure how to ask you, but I'm in a bit of a fix myself right now. My rent is due, and I had to buy some medication I lost on the bus. They only pay for it once, you know. I see 'em kick old folks out if they get behind more than a month, the lists are so long. But I think I'm okay. I think we gonna make it anyhow."

Raquel kept singing into the thick evening air. Sidarra held both their hands and kept them on a slow, even pace uptown. She knew without a doubt that she might as well have given that ten dollars to Tyrell, because she was never going to see that dress again.

| 5 |

AFTER SIDARRA'S PARENTS DIED, she became the kind of person who sleeps with the TV on. She was never that way before, though she knew many older people, especially women like Aunt Chickie, who regularly fell asleep to the sounds of old movies and commercials and awoke to morning news shows and more commercials. They did it for the white noise, she discovered, because they preferred that to their own thoughts. For her it had been better than reenacting her parents' violent death in her mind. It was better than thinking about the stubborn silence that commenced soon afterward between her and her oldest brother, Alex. That stupid breakup kept sadly repeating itself, an unavoidable fixture of her nighttime mourning, until she discovered how white noise could distract her into sleep. The TV also interrupted the endless replays of demeaning conversations she had at work. When he slept over, it could drown out Michael's long, throaty snoring, which had always managed to remind Sidarra of her loneliness—even in

Michael's presence. And most of the time the TV could even overcome her worries about Raquel. The TV's white noise muffled the sound of a bad song her life kept playing in her head.

Yet a strange thing started to happen to her: the song of Sidarra's life seemed to change just a bit. It still held the halting low notes of Tyrell creeping up on her from behind a corner, and the tired blues chords of every day at work. Her shame inside the Payless kept up its steady reprise, and a soft requiem for the four schoolgirls still lingered. But it had some high notes now. It was her own curiosity about a life with less fear that led Sidarra to a stock market investment club. She discovered friends again when she had forgotten how, a crew with its own stuff to talk about, and she had at least one night a week when, led by her uncle's beautiful pearl-handled cue stick, she could play in the green glow of a pool table and talk tough about business. She felt different and talked different. But usually the best thing to think about in bed was this long, brown, intense man, Griff. He had good voice. He had good tone. And she loved the way he said her name. She could listen to that all night. Which is why Sidarra began to sleep with the TV on but the sound turned off. It would still be several weeks before she would sing her new song aloud. For now she began instead to dream.

"Sidarra," Griff said. "It's your turn, baby."

They were playing in another beat-up place, an underground pool hall on West Twenty-second Street, when the second sidecar martini allowed Sidarra to turn the mischief of a private worry into words, which she was now ready to spit out. "Is anyone interested in making some money? Because I need some money," she asked.

Yakoob smiled. "You're not saying you wanna start some action up in here, are you, baby?"

"Not pool, Koob. Stocks. I hate to admit it, but I really need to see some profit. Soon." She almost began to whisper, as if she'd be embarrassed if someone could hear her over the blaring rock music. "I mean, I might have to sell off some of my positions. Did you ever expect making a little gain would come so slow?"

The ice above the river of moneymaking discontent was now officially broken. Griff and Yakoob each wore looks of pure commiseration. They had all learned a lot in the investment club, but they had made almost nothing yet.

Yakoob pulled himself off the stool and prepared to take a shot. "Well, I'ma tell y'all a little secret. This ain't likely the unit that's gonna bring down the cash, you know what I'm saying? This club is carrying some low-level yokels."

Sidarra and Griff didn't want to hear that. They wanted to keep drinking and playing in the hopes that someone would come up with something reassuring, like a stock tip. But shot after shot Yakoob kept pressing his point.

"I'm not kidding. I know. Y'all keep talking like the *group* could do this, the *group* that, combine shit, whatever: *ain't gonna happen.* That Spanish dude who sits in front, Julio? He ain't got no money. He got more idea than money, y'all, and I promise you he ain't got *no* idea. Nice guy. No clue. Maybe invested eleven hundred dollars at first. Been sold off over six hundred and fifty by now. *Six hundred and fifty dollars!* Think about it." Sid and Griff put down their cue sticks, and Yakoob went on to recite detailed financial information about every single member of the investment club.

"Koob, how the hell do you know all that shit about these people?" Siddara asked with a hand on her hip.

"I know."

Griff squinted and walked up on Koob real calm. "The fuck you know?"

"All I need to know, blood. I know their names."

"Social Security numbers?" Griff asked.

"That's not a problem." Both Sid and Griff had to take a second before saying more. Yakoob continued. "Not to mention that the broke blind is leading the blind broke," he giggled, a little impressed with his own wit. "Harrison's real assets, bless the nigga's heart, look like a paperboy's. He keeps his gains in a piggy bank, and it's a small one. The only thing he owns is a state-subsidized cooperative apartment, but he couldn't sell it at market if he wanted to."

"He's a good group leader," Sidarra said.

"Yeah, but this ain't summer camp, sweetheart," said Yakoob, back on his stool, getting serious. "If it is, it's the Fresh Air Fund for little street niggas like us and we supposed to be glad to see a real tree."

"Okay, you can learn this stuff, but can you manipulate it, too?" Griff asked.

"It can be reached," Koob answered, making a tap-tap-tap gesture with his fingers on an imaginary keyboard. "Most times, a name, maybe an address, will get you through to account numbers, credit lists, available funds statements. Nowadays people are dumb enough to e-mail credit reports all over the place. You don't even need to break into databases."

"PIN numbers?"

"PINs, too. Eventually. It's easier than you think."

"That is some real shit!" Sidarra exclaimed. She was stuck trying to figure out in her head what all that could mean. "So you don't think this club's in any position to make real money soon? That's what you're saying? You just like to play pool with us?"

"Not really. It could," Yakoob answered. "And yeah, I like playin' with y'all."

"Hold up, Koob," Griff said. He had to be clear about something. "This is your chance to tell me you did not do a check on me." His eyes were hidden in the shadow of the pool table lamp, but his meaning was unmistakable.

"Not you, Griff," he answered, and they shook hands in relief. " 'Cause you're a fucking lawyer, and I'm not interested in all that."

"Good, 'cause I know people who'll kill you if that ever happens."

Yakoob kept his eyes down on his cigarette. "I probably know 'em too, but okay."

That was uh-oh for Sidarra. Suddenly she felt like she wasn't wearing any clothes. "You wouldn't," she said, squinting and pointing a finger at Yakoob.

"Well, gorgeous," Yakoob sighed, and smiled at her. "Let me just say I'm sorry about that bullshit at Payless. I coulda helped you with that one if I'd known ahead of time."

"You motherfucker!" she screamed. Now she really felt naked.

"For real. I could," Koob went on. "Emergencies, baby. Just emergencies. Look, before y'alls' looks get too hard on a brother, remember, I'm in the class, too. I'm trying to go legit. I'm trying to learn just how the game is played. But at the end of the day, we gotta do what we do to do what we gotta do."

Griff took a long shot that thundered down the whole table and spanked a ball in the pocket like the crescendo pop of somebody bowling a strike.

"I don't know what you mean by emergencies, Koob, but I was just trying to get my little girl her school shoes," said Sidarra, hiding her curiosity badly.

"I can set you up with a new card, with a new name. Just for emergencies."

"It would be someone else's, though," Griff said.

"Probably so," Yakoob answered, and lined up a shot. "Something to think on."

They continued to play pool. They learned some, but not all, of what a hacker can do. Yakoob knew people who were serving time for getting too crazy. Or just being foolish. And he learned enough about their mistakes to know he was not easily persuaded to use his gifts like that. That is, he could be persuaded to use them, and he at least felt the potential for persuasion amid the three of them. Though he never said it out loud that night, what could change things was knowledge. Knowing how to do certain things with computers didn't always mean knowing *what* to do with them. He might also need a crew.

Sidarra started to act a little high on the secret, missing trick shots all over the table and enjoying forbidden thoughts about what good this new credit card could do for her world. And the company she was in. She enjoyed that more than the heavy sweetness of a sidecar martini. Mischief had not occurred to her since she was about Raquel's age. It hadn't been known to Griff since high school. Once again, Tuesday night had put everything into a different perspective.

| 6 |

GRIFF HAD THE KNOWLEDGE, born of hundreds of hard cases. Working for so much disadvantage had taught him a great deal about advantage. Then along came the story of the four Bronx schoolgirls, which quietly broke his calloused heart. Now he was ready to make a decision—or at least to make a game out of it. A few mornings after playing pool with his new investment crew, Griff's wife Belinda called him a bitch. By the end of that long day, he'd start to build his case to the contrary.

Griff arrived at the ugly gray building on Centre Street, ready to do a defense counsel's losing battle only he knew how to win. His client, Robert Billingsley, was supposed to stand trial that morning, or cop a plea. Mr. Billingsley had decided one day that his four-month-old baby boy should have a yuppie fold-up stroller, the kind made in Germany out of the finest, safest craftsmanship. Mr. Billinsgley was sixteen. The cop stopped him with the aluminum stroller two blocks from the playground in Central Park where he'd taken it; the owner's baby was not in it. The baby was in the playground with his nanny and the other babies and their nannies. Mr. Billingsley was charged with theft, the second felony on his record, and with resisting arrest. The cop told him to "C'mere, bitch," and the term didn't sit well with him. The combination of charges against him meant that, if convicted, he could get either one year, two to four, or, if he was charged as an adult, four to six.

Griff wore a charcoal gray three-button gabardine, a Joseph Abboud tie, and a crisp white shirt. Jeffrey Geiger, the spanking new assistant district attorney in charge of the prosecution—known as A.D.A.'s—wore Syms off the rack. His supervisor sat in the back of the courtroom. While Robert Billingsley's mother and his baby's mother waited two rows over, Mr. Billingsley was being brought up from the Tombs, the basement way station where people waiting at Rikers for their trials go the night before. He had been at Rikers two months already, and he looked like it.

"Good morning," Griff told the A.D.A.

It was clear the young A.D.A. was just trying out his power for the first time. Where Geiger probably came from out on Long Island someplace or Queens or the still all-white sections of Brooklyn, this tall twenty-something man with the square jaw and firm handshake was the business. But to Griff, who had tried his first case when the A.D.A. was running on the freshman track squad in high school, he was another whiteboy in the way. And it wasn't a good morning at all. Everything about it was wrong.

"Good morning, sir," said the A.D.A., surprised to have to look up to meet Griff's eyes. "We got a change of plans."

Griff didn't blink. The friendship was over. "Let's let the judge have a listen." The A.D.A. hesitated and followed Griff over to the judge's bench. "You were saying?"

"Our office has decided not to accept the defendant's plea in the alternative. In fact"—he choked a little on his words—"in fact, we've decided to charge Mr. Billingsley with felony assault on the arresting police officer and to insist that he be tried as an adult."

Griff began talking in measured tones, but his thoughts were already in high gear. He couldn't get mad. There were only so many things he could do. Robert Billingsley was sitting at a table, a court officer behind him, and he looked about as clueless as a high school student (because he was one). Rows behind him was his mother, who looked about as helpless as a new crossing guard facing rush-hour traffic (because she was one). His young girlfriend and infant son looked like specks of brown too small to see (because in that place they were). And Griff knew there was no way Mr. Billingsley was getting the option of a year in prison anymore. Griff was fighting for two to four max. Why? Because that could mean less than three, and less than three years in prison meant that when he got out Mr. Billingsley's infant son might still be small enough to be pushed proudly around by his dad in one of those yuppie strollers.

That would beat the time Griff had with his natural father—or his mother. Griff's heroin-addicted parents lost their parental rights after escaping a tenement fire without him when he was two years old. Because his investment banker wife Belinda thought it would be very black of them to live in a renovated Harlem brownstone, they happened to move down the same street from where his life went up in flames about forty years before. Griff was a smart kid. He bounced from foster homes for two or three years, and sure enough he was eventually adopted by an upper-middle-class black family and moved to a suburb in Westchester. Griff was bookish, serious, and sensitive, unless he was fighting or playing pool in his foster parents' basement—then he was just serious. Because he was tall and athletic, his friendships with the white kids around him were shaky. They expected certain things of him, but never to compete with them in class. Winning there meant being alone, so he spent a lot of time alone. By his second year in college at Brown University, Griff was really alone. His foster parents died of cancer within eight months of each other. They left him a bit of money and a plan. He was going to spend all the money on higher education—he was going to be a lawyer. And as a lawyer, he wasn't going to make any money if that's what it took to keep black families together.

He met Belinda Chambers at Brown. She was a year behind him, but more popular. Belinda was the color of dry sand and had long, straight auburn hair Griff once wrote poems about. She had a tight, bony face, legs like a model's, and wore beautiful clothes that camouflaged her small chest. Belinda was an economics major who, at eighteen, knew she was going to business school. She was going to be wealthier than her parents. And her man was going to "partner" with her—that is, he was going to equal all those things or better them. Tall, angular, smart, and a little radical in an independent thinker sort of way, Griff was the catch to make it all work out right. They looked like an airbrushed ad in *Essence* magazine except for one small particular: Griff could never really please her. In fact, Belinda could never truly stand him.

It wasn't that Griff was a bad guy or a poor fuck. He disappointed a lot of women when he married Belinda after college, and he could leave her silly with orgasm. It was just clear to her that, after he finished Fordham Law School and she graduated from Columbia Business School, he wasn't going to keep up his end of the financial bargain. Forget the cause, defense lawyers like him didn't make any real money. Yeah, she made seven figures at Smith Barney, but the point was equal or better. He was supposed to do that, and he was way off. No matter how long he argued with her for his own value as a husband, a win one day was back to a loss another. Belinda only had to open a catalogue to remind herself of what she was missing. This time was for her, she used to say throughout their twenties and well into their thirties. She'd give him no kids until he could afford the things she deserved.

And she'd be damned if he thought she planned to be a working mother. He knew the terms. Lest he forgot them, as he must have that morning before leaving for court, she was ready to remind him.

"Got it, bitch? Or I'm finally gone," she said.

You can never be too sure why two people stay together in a marriage. Maybe it was sixty-nine, which, in the absence of making babies, they each had a strong taste for. Maybe it was that she was the only person he knew who could beat him at chess three out of four games. Twenty minutes with Belinda and you understood which financial trends mattered and which were pure bullshit designed to fool small investors. Maybe it was because she dressed so damned well and made sure he did too. They looked like movie stars whenever they were forced to go out together. But the truth probably had something to do with the fact that she kept Griff running toward some kind of financial greatness he couldn't quite figure out but which he always wondered whether his parents, all four of them, would have wanted him to achieve before he died, too. He wondered.

Sidarra posed the perfect problem for him. She was a long way from the best clothes and took a fraction of the time on her nails, face, and hair than Belinda did. But she was a mother, with all that a mother knows instinctively about the world. Belinda would come home talking Wall Street smack and griping about the idiots she put up with, but Griff would start hearing Sidarra's voice in his head. He couldn't get out of his mind the feel of the grip of her hands in his that first night. All his married-man cool disguised his schoolboy wonderment for her. One morning he even woke up from a Sidarra wet dream. He hadn't had a wet dream in twenty-five years. When Belinda asked him what the fuck was wrong with him, he blamed it on her. She went straight to the shower. He stayed in the white six-hundred-count sheets and waited for Tuesday.

Back in the courtroom, Griff played the gentleman motherfucker for Robert Billingsley. He made calculated procedural arguments that made the A.D.A. blink too hard. He recited chapter and verse from the boy's file, showing how his record was made worse by unreasonably aggressive young prosecutors scoring points for their careers and quota-happy cops trying to bait a large black kid into some fatal mistake. The boy didn't fall for it, Griff explained. The only thing Robert Billingsley resisted was humiliation. When the cop called him a bitch, he had the right *not* to remain silent. After that, Griff was able to get his client, shackled and terrified in an orange DOCS jumpsuit, to stand before the judge and politely answer the judge's questions about his priors. The kid was clear. The kid was sincere.

"This is a good kid, your honor," Griff told the judge after Robert finished. Then he pointed out the boy's mother. He asked his girlfriend to stand up with the baby. "We don't really know if he stole the stroller that day, but we can't blame him for wanting one, can we?" Then he pulled out the final stop. "He reminds me of myself," Griff told the judge. "He's a young man trying to impress. He could've been you long ago," he told the old white man in the robe. "Or him," Griff added, pointing a finger directly at the A.D.A.

The judge appreciated good lawyers, especially among the overworked court-appointed attorneys who hardly knew their clients. Yet he could not allow himself to be swayed by emotion. "Counsel to the bench again," he demanded. Griff and the A.D.A. stepped up. The judge looked over his glasses at the young white prosecutor. "Mr. Geiger, after hearing what's been said today, do you still stand by your original position regarding Mr. Billingsley?"

Jeffrey Geiger refused to meet Griff's eyes. He was not much older than Mr. Billingsley, so it seemed, and he looked like he would have been much happier drunk under a beach umbrella during spring break. "We do, your honor. Nothing has changed. This is the defendant's second and third felony offense."

"What is the point?" Griff asked with calm exasperation.

"I don't need to explain myself to *you,*" Geiger said, finding the courage to repeat the words he'd been taught weeks ago in an A.D.A. training workshop. "I need to make a conviction."

"That's not a reason," Griff went on. "That's got nothing to do with this young man, his life, or his infant son's life. There has *got* to be some point to it. Why are you trying to do this?"

The A.D.A. looked irritated. Finally he turned to Griff and said, "Because I can."

Forgetting the judge, Griff asked, "Well, who the hell are you, young man?"

The A.D.A. was ready now and looked Griff in the eye. "I'm the state, sir. And you're not."

That's how Griff's decision got started. The judge decided that, given the circumstances, Robert Billingsley should be considered an adult and convicted, but would be sentenced to a minimum of two years and a maximum of four. Maybe not for Mr. Billingsley's infant son, but that was what Griff would call a victory in his line of work.

That night at home, he lay spent on the living room sofa and hoped for sleep, occasionally interrupted by Belinda's heated telephone conversation with a colleague from work. Her voice could still echo with monetary ferocity even at midnight. As usual, somebody on one side of a deal was fucking up again, a guy named Brett Goldman she kept calling "Dick" with a vengeance. Some company, "Solutions," was too heavy to carry such a lightweight executive. The "bitch" was in over his head, she fumed, losing paperwork, not answering his phone, letting investment companies she'd never heard of into the "angel round" of financing before satisfying due diligence requirements. She was storming around the sleepy Griff, back and forth between rooms, cussing and fulminating about details he wished would say good night, when he noticed the glossy papers and thick prospectus on the coffee table in front of him. Griff never paid attention to this clutter before, but tonight the Solutions, Inc. logo caught his eye. He began to read part of a deal memo lying on the couch beside him. Suddenly he realized this stuff was not Greek, that he could make sense of it. It didn't sound all that different from the deals a few of his "better" clients went to jail for. While Belinda recounted her frustrations to her friend, Griff learned about the Solutions, Inc. conglomerate and the many public businesses it owned chunks of. Not an angel on the list. Prison construction companies. Public school consulting contracts. Welfare reform "intermediaries." Defense contractors. Third World "conflict assistance" management consultants. All the kinds of activities people like him usually slept through. But he was awake now.

And that is when Griff made his decision: that till now he had had too much respect for a game that could never respect him, or Robert Billingsley, or four little schoolgirls trying to take a test designed to show their ignorance. For years he had wrapped himself in earnestness and legal rectitude while being seen as nothing more than some sandtrap on the government's favorite golf course and a mere bitch at home. Now, maybe he could play a little. A sumptuous sister and a round-the-way sidekick had shown Griff how to play again. They too could play people like pawns. They too could invent their own rules as they went along. And, in honor of the people who had brought Griff to these conclusions at last, he named the game Whiteboy.

On the Tuesday next, Cicero Dean's Investment Club was about to be born.

| 7 |

"SO FIRST WE'RE PLAYING POOR," Raquel started as they stood in line at a checkout. "Now we're playing rich, Mommy?"

"Not rich," she answered. "Comfortable."

It turns out there are many different kinds of emergencies. There are the emergencies that come by phone, like the one Sidarra got about three years before when her parents were killed on a city street by a driver who had jumped the curb while trying to avoid a cab that had cut him off. Then there are some that different people would define differently depending on how they're affected by them, like money problems. For instance, a landlord's money problem is a very different money problem from a tenant's, yet both tend to call them emergencies and both do what they have to do to get through them. Sidarra had been living in a black-and-white world, one in which an emergency wasn't an emergency unless a siren was involved. But ever since the day she decided she had to join the Central Harlem investment club, she started living in the gray. Her emergencies were not subject to the approval of anyone else, and she wasn't waiting for sirens anymore. That's why she decided to take Yakoob up on his offer of a fake credit card.

But nothing would let her go back to that Payless ShoeSource on 125th Street—or any other Payless. Raquel got her shoes all right. Sidarra discovered that, just as she had thought, the shoes they had picked out there were not real leather anyway. How could they be for six bucks? So Sidarra took her daughter down to Herald Square, where they finally did some *real* shoe shopping, the leather kind. One pair had buckles, but not the kind that change color after a couple of rains. And they had good arch support, so the saleswoman said, which justified the price—fifty-five dollars a pair. They bought three different color pairs. And some real Timberlands, and several pairs of socks. Then they went over to Macy's, where they bought Raquel some tights, a few dresses, and new underwear for both of them—Sidarra bought lingerie, nothing too exotic, but sexier replacements than she had allowed herself in years. By the time they were done, Raquel would be the best-dressed girl in her class.

Even at eight and a half years old, Raquel let very few things get past her. This could be a worry for Sidarra. Like other school administrators, Sidarra knew which schools—even which teachers—a person expecting to send their kid to a good college would want to attend. There weren't that many of them, and most of those were nowhere near where they lived in Harlem. In fact, Raquel's school was not known for stimulating young minds at all. But it was safe. At that point, safety was about the only thing Sidarra felt she could assure her child, and P.S. 27 did that well enough. Raquel might not learn to write full sentences anytime soon, but she'd more than likely live long enough to try.

So Sidarra protected Raquel from news of a little new money in their lives. When she could, she'd shop alone after work and bring the clothes home for Raquel to try on.

"What is 'comfortable,' Mommy?" Raquel asked. They were still on the checkout line, and Sidarra waited until they were outside the store before she answered that one.

"Well, comfortable means just enough and maybe a little more."

"What's a little more than just enough?"

"It could be something a little extra, just in case. It could be something special, like a treat. That's about it."

And for several months, that's all it was. The $3,000 credit limit on her alias charge card bought the comfort of a new wool pantsuit gracing her skin as she slipped into it. Comfortable meant not being afraid to get help and attention at Bergdorf's or Bloomingdale's. And good shoes, not great shoes, not fabulous, but good shoes, more than one pair. And boots for the winter, with strong high heels that lifted her a little taller over her female colleagues and put male colleagues closer to eye level so that no one talked down to her. For many months, that's what comfortable meant to Sidarra. Comfortable also meant something she could never thank Yakoob enough for: cash advances.

One Tuesday out of Griff's earshot she mentioned to Yakoob that she was afraid to shop at the same place twice.

"That's probably a good idea," he said.

"I have a brother, Kenny," she explained. "Kenny took chances. He's the only one of us who does. Well, Kenny has spent most of his adult life in prison. He's a thief. *Was* a petty thief," she added nervously. Yakoob just nodded in understanding. "I'm not a thief," she giggled. "But I'm not trying to get busted."

"That's never gonna happen, Sid."

"Right."

"But you could use a little cash on occasion is what you're saying."

"Right."

So Yakoob got her a personal identification number for the card, which enabled her to take a cash advance at ATMs—though never the same one twice. Cash advances meant another kind of comfort. It brought Aunt Chickie closer when she needed to be because Sidarra would call up a car service and send for her. It was only ten dollars here and ten dollars there, but it was cash she could never spare so easily before. She and Raquel would have to go get her, or wait for Michael to come down from the Bronx and drive them. It wasn't even a mile away. The cash advances closed that distance in a hurry.

With a little more courage, a cash advance could do more wonder than that. The Board of Miseducation had great health benefits for its regular administrators, but Sidarra was irregular; the small staff of Special Programs received the cost-cutting minimum. Sidarra's health plan got her and Raquel regular checkups at a clinic within walking distance from their home, and the wait was never more than two hours. But there was no dental coverage. By the time Sidarra got through taking care of Raquel's teeth, her own were left to the team of Dr. Crest, Dr. Colgate, and Trident the hygienist. None of them could fill a cavity or replace a broken filling. Sidarra had two of one and three of the other, which for years she would quietly nurse with Tylenol, finger massages, and true grit. All until cash advances went to work on her smile.

Just enough and maybe a little more, that's what comfort felt like. The paint on the walls of her brownstone apartment still cracked and chipped to the floor under the winter's steam heat. It faded ugly with the sunlight of spring. The gold lamé dress still hung on deposit at the store on 125th Street, but dollar by dollar, the deposit inched upward. Sidarra took care of some things and left others for later. She kept Raquel's questions to a manageable minimum. She even found a way to take some of that cash advance into a bank and put a little bit of Raquel's college fund back into a money market account.

"The rate will change eventually, but right now it's almost two percent," said the little man with the blue suit and the uneven shave.

"Is it safe?" Sidarra asked.

"What do you mean?" he asked.

"Can I lose it?"

"No, no," he smiled, surrounded by the strong marble walls of the bank behind him. "There's no way you can lose any of this. And you can make deposits as you go, ma'am."

She could have done without the "ma'am" part. Her thirty-ninth birthday was approaching soon enough. Her teeth no longer hurt. Her stockings had no rips or tears hiding under her pantsuit. She did not need to be called "ma'am" yet. But she was glad this modest contribution to Raquel's future was safe from the ups and downs of the stock market.

"Okay then," she said.

It wasn't until she was back at her desk that day that Sidarra started to feel like a player again—maybe not a lounge diva, but nevertheless a player. She had taken care of a certain amount of business. She was in the game even if she didn't completely understand it yet. When she sat with the bank officer and opened the money market account, she knew most of what he was going to say before he said it. That had never happened before. The investment club had done something for her. And when a report crossed her desk about test scores and dropout rates at New York City high schools, Sidarra did not tremble as she used to or take a moment in the bathroom stall to curse in private. She just read the numbers with the cool of a poker player—or a pool shark. She checked the statements against data in the appendix. Discrepancies she might have missed before stood out now like they were written in red magic marker.

GRIFF AND YAKOOB SAT IN KOOB'S CAR parked on a side street and waited for Sidarra to come out of the meeting. Griff was too pissed off about the trial of Robert Billingsley to attend, and Yakoob was steadily losing interest in Charles Harrison's pep talks. Months of playing and scheming together had forged a cynical bond between them that Sidarra—who still had some faith in the Central Harlem investment club—could not join yet. Griff actually listened to Yakoob's discovery of an online betting operation that paid out when certain terrible things happened to famous people. Sidarra probably wouldn't hear that. Besides, Griff was brewing his own ideas that he wasn't quite ready to share with the one woman whose voice alone had opened his nose.

"Everybody's listed somewhere," Koob said, drawing on a joint. The smoke whipped in a circle near the cracked window, then was sucked out into the night air.

"That's good to know, but the issue is how they're connected," said Griff. "Two hundred and seventy-five million free-floating motherfuckers does you no good unless you can see who's connected to whom, right?"

"I hear you."

"Here's what I'm talking about." Griff pulled a folded piece of yellow legal paper from his coat pocket and handed it to Yakoob. It contained stock symbols attached to full names of companies attached to various financial indicators and dates, all in his own hand. Griff's demeanor seemed to lock into a different seriousness than ever before. "You wanted knowledge. That's knowledge. You check it out, see what else you can do in twenty-four hours. Roll this piece of paper around some cheeba, smoke it, and bring me back the ashes and the odds."

Yakoob studied the paper, squinting in the streetlight. Griff watched his mouth slowly open as he worked down the page. An "ooh" turned to a full-toothed smile real quick. "What's this?"

"This is a guy's address and a couple of background facts about him I got from a directory. His name's Jeffrey Geiger, but I'm not writing that down," Griff said. "Some things belong to oral history." Yakoob smiled and slapped Griff's hand.

Griff heard her footsteps as she turned the corner and adjusted the rearview mirror so that he could study Sidarra's form as she approached the car.

"She back?" asked Koob.

"Like sweetness," Griff mumbled, fixed his collar, and jumped out of the car to let her in the back door. Like that, his demeanor unlocked into something easier again. "Hey, baby," he said, and wrapped his arms around Sidarra. She peered up out of a hug she didn't really want to leave and smiled into his face.

"Hi," she purred, "sugar." And she kissed him gently on the mouth. He squeezed her a little closer to him, and she could feel him jump beneath his long winter coat.

Yakoob tapped the horn, and the two got into the car.

At the pool hall downtown, it was all business. For this night, they chose an upscale billiard parlor with a crowded top floor and a downstairs that remained empty on Tuesdays. They put their coats on hooks beside a secluded back corner table and removed their cue sticks from their cases. They racked the balls, paid the waitress, and washed back the first tastes of alcohol.

"I'd like to propose a little game," Griff announced.

"If there's money in the motherfucker, the table's all yours, dog," said Koob. " 'Cause this nigga's trying to get paid."

Sidarra nodded approvingly at Griff. He drained his sniff of

Hennessy and chalked his cue before breaking. "All right then. It's called Whiteboy. It's my turn to persuade. If I don't lie, I don't die. If I'm alive, you all come with me."

With that introduction, Griff tore up the break. The three of them watched as the balls went spinning in every direction. Four balls dropped and the others spread out magnificently. Before he began to pick them off, Griff described a group of black folks from a book he'd once read. In it, they form a secret society of seven assassins who avenge the lynchings of black people depending on whichever day of the week the victim died.

"Oh yeah," Koob said. "That's by that dude Toni Morrison."

"She's not a dude, my brother," Sidarra gently corrected. "I know the book."

Whiteboy was a billiards game of selective reprisal and secretly just desserts. Griff invented it over the course of the day that began with his wife calling him a bitch and ending with the young D.A. trying to unload the weight of New York State on Robert Billingsley. The shooter had to reach "persuasion." You nominated somebody who had excelled in the business of humiliating black people. That was it. You named the target on the break and you tried to run the table without letting another player get a single shot in. When that happened, plans would be made and the victim would soon find himself very short of cash. Yet winning wasn't just about skill at pool; Whiteboy was also a game of talk. For each ball you sank, you had to state a reason, something from the victim's résumé that made him deserving of his fate. If you missed and another player disagreed with your nominee or one of your reasons, they could "intolerate" by sinking enough balls to keep you out of the game. But if you made your eleven straight, that was a "joint," or persuasion, and nobody could change it. The victim would get hit at some unspecified time in the future, and the crew would take the spoils.

The problem was, before anybody could nominate Whiteboy's

first victim, they had to find suitable investments in which to grow the booty. Griff first had to persuade his friends about where their new money was going—and why.

"Okay, so here we go," Griff continued. His expression started to lock up again. "I owe you a reason and at least one ball in a pocket every time I step to the slate." Sidarra and Yakoob grinned at each other and waited for Griff to start. He had eleven balls to go. "The first is, there's a new bonus structure in the D.A.'s office downtown. They give Christmas money to the ones who can put the most brothers in jail by New Year's." *Bang!* Griff shot with authority. Two balls went into opposite corner pockets. "Second, there's a Southern company, Great Walls, it's public, that does new prison construction. They had profits last year of seven billion dollars, but most people never heard of 'em. They specialize in high-tech solitary confinement units. Lockdown—that's where the money is. Twenty-three-hour days inside, no inmate contact, workouts in a cage, electronic monitors watching you all the time. Drives sane brothers mad, makes mad brothers kill themselves, but it cuts manpower needs by about sixty percent." *Spank!* Griff let go and dropped another ball in the side. "Thirdly, they have two wardens on their board of directors, I found out, one from the largest penitentiary in Georgia, the other from Texas. Each of their prisons has already broken ground on a combined total of twelve hundred new solitary units." *Bop!* He aced again.

"Here's the really sick shit. The governors of both states once sat on Great Walls' board. Each state legislature appropriated the money for the construction projects as a discretionary item in recent crime bills. Really can't be reviewed or challenged in court." *Spop!* Another ball dropped in the far corner. "Just so happens, with heavy lobbying from political action committees from these same two states, Congress just passed a federal statute changing the designation of certain felonies—particularly those connected in any way to crack cocaine—to fall in line with tough mandatory sentences." *Pop!* Two balls dropped cold. The cue ball spun on the edge of a pocket, but would not fall.

Griff waited until the ball stopped spinning before he continued. He had now given five reasons and dropped at least as many balls. "The states are gonna use that federal law as a model. By next year, half of them will have the equivalent penalties under their own laws." *Bang!* Other than the cue ball, there were just two colored balls left on the table. He'd shot so efficiently he had to pause to align his reasons with the few remaining targets. "But check this out: The statute also comes with a special designation for certain kinds of prisoners. If they exhibit one of like three behavioral signs or commit any prison infractions, they're now eligible for solitary." Griff looked up to make sure they followed him on the point. "Solitary used to be considered cruel and unusual, reserved for the baddest of the bad. But with Congress making it ordinary well, now an inmate could get it for pissing on the toilet seat." *Spop!* One ball left. "If they *had* toilet seats in prison."

"Wait. Wait. How can they do that nonsense, Griff?" Sidarra interrupted.

"Because they can." He lined up the final shot. "And wanna hear the kicker, my love? Three members of the board of this Southern company I've been talking about are president, CFO, and CEO of another company, a shadow conglomerate. What did you say was the name of that educational consulting firm that's got the contract to overhaul New York City's public school curricula?"

"Solutions, Inc.," she said.

"There you go." *Boom!* Down went the last colored ball. "I, uh, I rest my motherfuckin' case."

The table was still except for the Whiteboy spinning in the middle.

Yakoob sat back in his chair with an expressionless gaze in the manner of a person who had just gotten hip to something that might have increasing importance to him if he allowed himself to grasp it. He knew the room had just expanded, if not his world. He couldn't wait to get at Griff's list of companies and names.

"Seven billion dollars?" Sidarra asked.

"Blood money, baby," Griff said, leaning his palms on the felt. "So I've nominated Great Walls as a target investment, and," he added, sizing up their approving looks, "I think I got persuasion."

"Wait a minute, Griff," Sidarra interrupted, spreading her fingers in the air. "If this is so good, why don't we just sell off our current stocks and use our money to buy Great Walls stock? There's nothing sneaky about that."

"Because none of us really has any money, baby," Griff answered matter-of-factly.

"You got that right," Yakoob muttered.

"And even if we did, I'm not about to use my own hard-earned money to buy into this evil, unethical machine. Why should I when I can use some other evil bastard's money to buy up this evil on my behalf?" He was dead certain.

Sidarra and Yakoob were still thinking. "Not our own money, huh?" Sidarra repeated.

"No, baby. Not ours," Griff confirmed, his eyes intense. "Triangle trade. From bad money to blood money to us. Next we gotta play for the names of bad folks to bankroll us. Okay?"

Sidarra pulled a ball from a pocket and tossed it around in lone angles around the felt rails. She remembered something Yakoob had said a while back about the alias credit card: that nothing was free, that what they got they got from somebody else. She thought about Desiree Kronitz at work. She remembered the day she peeked into the chancellor's office and saw Desiree in a tight pink outfit surrounded by laughing white men in suspenders. She even thought about her boss, Clayborne Reed. Then she remembered her brother Kenny.

"Nothing can be traced back to us?" she asked nervously. Griff and Koob seemed to watch her nervousness extra carefully, which only made her more nervous. "I mean, you're talking about running around cyberspace—or whatever you call it—with somebody else's wallet. Don't they call that identity theft? Don't people go to jail for that?"

Koob spoke up softly. "I don't think so, but that's Griff's department. Look, anything can be traced unless it's done right. You have to keep the amounts small. You gotta take off your boots and tiptoe, you see what I'm sayin'? The people who get caught are the dudes who get too greedy, sleepy, and I'm not trying to do that."

"Trying is not quite what she's talking about, brother," Griff said. "People do go to jail for this. Shit, it's stealing—even if it's justified. So before anything happens, before a dime flips our way, we're gonna have to see what you do, how you do it, and how nobody knows who takes from the pot, Koob." Griff held him in his gaze. "Now, Sidarra asked you the ultimate question: Can *you* do it right?"

For once, as he looked down at the floor, no joke could be found on Yakoob's face. Which was suddenly very important to Sidarra. Griff's conviction was palpable and seductive, but she wasn't sure at this moment if some of it wasn't what a lawyer learns to do with words. Yakoob was different. What you saw you got, except for his hidden gift—to work the mystery of computers. She had to believe in that on faith, and that he would do it right even if she couldn't understand it. For Koob it was a step beyond anything he'd ever imagined doing. He had never been the key to anything before. Their gazes rained down on him like the judgment of parents, but they weren't his parents. They were his friends.

He composed himself and looked back up at them with a firmness. "Yeah, I can do it. I can do it right. It'll be tricky, but with a little help, some knowledge, I'm on it."

Both Sidarra and Griff exhaled in relief. "All right," Griff said calmly, and turned toward Sidarra.

She realized her hands were trembling a little as they clutched the pool cue. Sidarra knew she needed money in the worst way. She couldn't go on limping along forever without collapsing. She could feel the many aches this plan might heal, but wasn't sure about the anger. It seemed that, like Griff, this required getting in touch with a certain kind of anger. She admired his anger, she was intoxicated by his words, but she was also done taking her cues from other people. Maybe she had to want this business with her own anger. Sidarra's pains had to come together with other people's pains—poor people, helpless people, black people—and theirs with hers. Personal revenge alone wouldn't justify it. Or maybe she should just go along to sustain the crush. No, at this point in her life, wanting Griff wasn't enough to take this risk. No, maybe not anger, and definitely not infatuation, but something else, bigger than both, would have to justify the very adult decision to play this game: protection. Sidarra decided she was finally going to protect herself. That felt instantly right.

The long nails on her fingers stopped trembling, and she looked up hopefully at both men. "Okay," she said.

"There you go," Griff declared, then reached for a new rack.

They named themselves after Sidarra's famous uncle Cicero, the first black pool champion. Over the next several games of Whiteboy, they played for names, the nominees whose bank accounts and credit cards became "joints" for Koob's modest withdrawals. For the first (and last) time, Koob wrote them down on the yellow slip of paper Griff had given him and took them home. Cicero Dean's Investment Club was officially in business.

| 8 |

IT TOOK YAKOOB MUCH LESS than the twenty-four hours Griff gave him to check through the list, test some security walls, and devise a strategy for getting cash access. Alone late at night, his wife Marilyn asleep in the next room, Yakoob enjoyed a cannabis-induced meditation before the computer screen. What was once a lock picker's hobby to break code was now becoming a mission of personal redemption. He got so good he surprised himself. The firewalls never talked down to him, never called him stupid or questioned how much schooling he had. They would merely stand fast against his keystrokes until he could go through them, becoming one brick, then another, until he was his own hole and the barrier was broken. Staring, staring at the glowing symbols, Yakoob patiently typed permutations until eventually, one night or another, he'd find himself inside a program, where he could have his way with multiple identities and the federally insured fund amounts representing other people's luck.

If withdrawing their cash was painstaking, the stock payoffs took even more time. That was the idea, for the club members to let time pass slowly, to let a gain arise imperceptibly, as if it never happened and wouldn't be missed. That's why nobody's life became a lavish affair. To the world, each of them tried to stay pretty much the way they had been before, despite the roles they were playing and the way it made them feel inside.

One day back in mid-October, Jeffrey Geiger, the young assistant district attorney, went to the ATM near the courthouse where he always went after work, put in his card, entered his PIN, and discovered that he had –$76.21 in his checking account and $96 in savings. His square jaw dropped in its sockets, and within minutes he was on his cell phone to his father. Before he could get out a full sentence, his father was cussing loudly into the phone.

"What the fuck happened to my money market, son? I gave you access because I was sure you would—" and the cell phone went dead. His phone bill check had bounced.

Jeffrey pushed all the buttons he could, but the phone company was two steps ahead of him. "Out of Service" flashed for about ten seconds on the little screen before the thing shut down.

That was how the grand strategy began. Six months, some lawyer fees, and several hundred hours of telephone and letter-writing grief later, "joints" like Jeffrey Geiger and his no-nonsense father would probably get their bank to insure the fraud. But by then Cicero's Investment Club had used the cash to start an offshore shell corporation based in the Caribbean with accounts in Swiss banks. Yakoob named Griff president under the initials "G.H.C." only, himself the chief executive officer with just "Y.B.J.," and, with her permission, made Sidarra the chief financial officer with the alias he'd used for her fake credit card, "D.G." They had each made short lists of people they knew had profited from humiliating black folks; they subjected the nominees to grueling games of Whiteboy; and the losers soon learned that they were on the hook for small nuisance losses of about $2,500 apiece—they took $5,000 from Geiger. The shell corporation accumulated a quick infusion of about $50,000. They would buy stock in the meanest, richest companies they could find, like Great Walls. That stock kept rising. By the final quarter reports of 1996, not even a full year since they had all met at the Central Harlem investment club, Yakoob, Griff, and Sidarra had, on paper, twelve times their original stock investments.

FOR SIDARRA'S PART, the money was a balm to her many still-open wounds, but it was not what completely accounted for a distinct sexiness she often began to feel. Having money made her open to new things. Making money with Griff made her especially open to him. The magical way Yakoob could turn a game of Whiteboy into cash on paper made her life begin to seem a little unreal, like she had been simply walking on the wrong side of the street all the time. Somehow, with her grief perhaps lifting a bit, she crossed over. It didn't seem to take much more than that.

One night, she and Griff decided that it was time to see Yakoob perform onstage at an underground club in Harlem.

"But why, sweetheart?" Michael pleaded with her before she left. "Why can't I come out with you tonight to see this guy you know? I love comedy. You know that, Sidarra."

"It's people from work, darling," she explained. "It's not something I want to do. It's something I *have* to do. Please, baby. I promise I'll be back early."

Michael had no idea. He'd heard of Griff only when he wasn't listening. He let Raquel distract him. Whenever she was around, he had a tendency to focus on the child. When Sidarra mentioned her investments, he had the attention span of a pigeon. So that night she left him for her new mischief. And somewhere in her heart, a song.

Sidarra met Griff at their coffee shop wearing caressable silk and rayon just in case the comedy club was dark. He wore a black trench and black suit with royal blue shirt and smiled without speaking when he saw her, then grabbed her firmly into his chest. However much he held back, she was getting to know the intensity of his feelings. It would break through immediately when they met alone, then he would have to do something awkward to regain his composure. After all, he was out on the streets of his own neighborhood with a woman not his wife. This time he followed up the hug with an oddly generous exchange with a panhandler.

"Griff, why would you give a crackhead five whole dollars?" she asked as they walked away.

"Because he's being priced out of Harlem," Griff quickly replied with a laugh. "I don't know. Because I can. Maybe I shouldn't have. Next time, he just gets a buck." This was how he burned off his jones for her. "I promise."

Because Sidarra was crossing streets and living mischief, she slipped her arm into his and they continued walking the several blocks toward the comedy club.

"Tell me. Were you always gonna be a lawyer?"

"Pretty much."

"That sounds like a lack of imagination," she said.

"It was. I thought about being a state assemblyman, but I would have to run for office. You have to get people to like you if you're gonna run for office, and I don't really like people that much. A more creative person—like you—probably could have made more with that dilemma, but I'll be all right."

People were looking at them, and he was flirting badly. By now Griff had realized that he enjoyed people looking at them together; his being excited to be beside this woman deserved attention. He enjoyed flirting, too. The last time it felt so good he was too young to cherish it. Yet Griff was a stranger to this side of the street, and he occasionally looked nervously to the other side.

Blood-money stock investing with stolen identities sat surprisingly well with him. Griff had concluded that the proper balance of his life might actually require some low-level criminality. The only thing that scared him was his wife.

"What did *you* do to be creative?" he asked Sidarra.

She stopped to think. "I sang my heart out in long, floppy hats." They laughed together. "Usually in front of the mirror." They kept walking and turned down a side street. "I used to believe I was channeling God. Nothing made me feel better."

He stopped and looked into her eyes. "Would you sing for me, Sidarra?" Griff asked sheepishly. "What would you sing if you sang to me?"

Everybody needs life to happen to them, and nobody knows when it will. That's why Sidarra let her shoulders go. She took a step backward with Griff's hands in hers and giggled. His eyes looked so expectant alone under a streetlamp. The air turned warmer all of a sudden. The solid faces of brownstones on both sides of the block turned the winds away.

"Donny Hathaway or Temptations version?" she asked.

Griff looked baffled by the question. "Um, Donny. Whatever it is, give me Donny Hathaway's version, sugar."

Sidarra cleared her throat and right there on the quiet side street she began to sing Donny Hathaway's version of "A Song for You." She looked down as if she were waiting for her voice. *"I've been so many places in my life and time . . ."* she began. Her voice had the clear quality of pearls flying. The song swelled in her chest. Sidarra closed her eyes and pushed the notes even beyond her register. Griff's eyes glassed over in disbelief. He knew only to keep holding her hands. Sidarra paused for the chorus, took a deep breath, and came up from down under: *"I love you in a place where there's no space or time. I love you for my life. You're a friend of mine."*

The song ended. The night suddenly blew cooler. Griff opened his coat to swallow her up.

"Thank you, Sidarra," he said, holding her a little more freely. "That was you, precious. That was precious." He pulled back and looked into her face. "You know?" he started to say. Instead, Griff leaned forward to kiss her. She closed her eyes and waited for the touch of his lips on hers, but they landed on her cheek. It was the right feel—warm, moist, assertive—but the wrong place.

AT A COMEDY CLUB tucked in an underground bar, Griff and Sidarra sat together in the darkness, smiling expectantly and holding hands to a song still in their heads. Yakoob was going on about an eight-year-old son he didn't have.

Kids are a trip. Nowadays they're just full of opinions and whatnot. Like, now my son wants to be a criminal when he grows up. Ever since we saw a cop riding horseback down the street in New York City. Blew his mind. He says, "Hey, Dad, why the fuck they got cops on horse? Doesn't that ruin the element of surprise?"

Funny or not, something about Yakoob's set made Sidarra go out the next day and buy that gold lamé dress once and for all.

| 9 |

BY THE END OF THE YEAR, the Board of Miseducation released its preliminary autumn standardized test scores. In the districts that always did well, the scores improved. In the poorest ones, they stayed the same or declined. But an inside joke was emerging for those who looked hard enough to see it: enrollment was dropping in many of the districts where failing kids struggled. Somehow the dropout rates remained the same but the kids were disappearing. Sidarra knew this had never happened before, yet no one in her unit was talking about it. The newspapers missed it too. Instead, they reported small miracles occurring at one school or another under the chancellor's new plan. But the praise was lies to Sidarra. She came home to the truth. She saw her daughter's homework. Even the teachers didn't deny what was up. At Raquel's school, learning had gone to pot.

However, the biggest challenge for Sidarra at work was not standing out. For someone struggling with a pay cut and demoted to boring tasks well beneath her abilities, she sure looked good. Her nails were always done. Her perm was always fly. Her clothes had become Desiree Kronitz's envy. It takes a fair amount of energy to camouflage success. Before she got to work, she'd have to take off certain jewelry and put it in her purse. Sometimes she would cut the labels off her blouses so no one standing behind her could sneak a peak at her shopping habits. On Tuesdays especially, Sidarra would leave for work perfectly made up. A block from her office, she'd go into the same restaurant bathroom and wipe some of it off. She'd return at five-fifteen to put her face back on. The waiters there adored her.

"Something is different about you," Desiree said one morning, confronting Sidarra in the hallway. She looked Sidarra up and down and wagged her finger too close to Sidarra's face. "I'm not sure what it is, but I'm gonna find out."

You keep wagging that finger like that and you're gonna find something else out about me, Sidarra wanted to say. Instead, all she said was: "I'm sorry, Desiree. Did you say something?"

"Don't play dumb with me, sistergirl. What's going on with you?"

About this time everybody needed to just back up and take a puff. Sidarra decided to walk on. "I'm in love. That's all." And she returned to her cubicle.

ON THEIR WAY DOWNTOWN to play pool, Yakoob told Sidarra and Griff that he had to make a stop. "To get that good shit," he smiled. "Just a quick hookup with my boy."

"I don't have a lot of time tonight," Sidarra said.

"We're not even getting out the car."

This time they were heading to a hall on the East Side, a small place for gamblers and serious players who minded their business. If you were too good in some places, you could draw a crowd.

Here they could care less. Time taught these things. Time also rearranged the seating in Yakoob's old Chevy Cavalier. Sidarra and Griff preferred to sit in the back on the cracked vinyl upholstery.

Koob's pager went off on his hip. "This is the cat you get your cheeba from?" Griff asked him while they speeded down Second Avenue.

"Yeah. Raul's no joke. He's kind of a kid. Don't be mad if he doesn't smile at you. His dope is strictly two hits and you're good."

"Wow, it's been a long time," Sidarra said. She was still deciding whether she'd get high. "Last time I smoked pot I remember you had to smoke a whole joint."

Yakoob knew Raul from around the way. Raul always had a hookup for the kind of whiteboy weed that's particularly hard for many brothers to find. It seemed odd that as the millennium approached, white guys continued to enjoy such an advantage in weed quality, but so it was. Raul, however, was the ambassador of high-octane at a reasonable price. On East Eighty-eighth Street, Koob turned the corner and pulled over to wait for Raul to come out of a building. He double-parked and they sat. The wait grew long. Finally they saw a short, squat Puerto Rican-looking guy in a Kangol and black baggies leave the vestibule real quick and hurry toward the Chevy, checking both ways over his shoulder. He looked fresh out of jail, with frizzy cornrows slept on about two weeks too long.

"Uh, damn, Koob," said Sidarra. "This your boy? He looks a little hard."

"And dangerous too," said Griff.

"He is," Koob said as Raul made it to the passenger door. "But we're gonna drop him off in a minute."

No they weren't. Raul had a little trouble with the handle, and they could see his wide-bottom jaw getting very serious under his long-haired, half-slice mustache. Sidarra didn't say anything, but she thought he looked like a muskrat. Raul got in, didn't smile or say hello, just said, "Drive this thing, brother. On the quick, I ain't playin'."

Even in the dark, Yakoob could see that Raul had blood on his AND I's. Suddenly he too got real serious and took off down the street.

"What's up? What's going on?" Griff asked, like he had radar.

"Who dat?" Raul asked Koob.

"Tha's my boy. It's cool. He a defense lawyer and she a teacher."

"*Was* a teacher," Sidarra mumbled.

They drove to the FDR Drive real quiet. Koob didn't know which way to go all of a sudden. "Which way, motherfucker?" Koob asked.

"Up. Go up!" Raul said.

"Hey, excuse me," Sidarra finally said. "What's going on?"

Nobody said anything. Raul was breathing kind of hard, and Koob, who you'd think would speak up for the two in back, was mum. They got to the Willis Avenue exit, and the old engine chugged and strained to get up the ramp. They listened to the wheeze of the tires roll onto the grates as they headed over the bridge to the Bronx. That's when Koob finally asked what happened back on that block.

"I smoked him," Raul declared with the flat tone of someone finishing a cigarette.

"You mean you *got* some smoke?" Sidarra asked.

"You what?" Koob asked again.

"I 'on't know, man. I had to. Motherfucker just tried to get big on me for the last time, you know wha'm sayin'?"

Nobody did. What happened was, this white guy named Blane sold high-quality pot to white folks. Blane even delivered. But not to people like Raul. It was once the other way around. Raul used to hook Blane up, used to connect him to dealers Raul knew in Washington Heights who could get cheap dope from Jersey. After a while, Blane found a high-end source and got too large to need Raul anymore. Raul became a regular old customer who got no breaks, no discount, nothing even for his own stash. For a long time Raul thought all that was kind of fucked up, but what could he do? Raul was a criminal. And he smoked *a lot* of weed, almost all the time. So what could he say? Well, that night, Blane got too bold with him. Blane tried to punk him, short him on the weight, but Raul figured it out and asked him what the fuck he was trying to do. Blane had no answer. He was just doing it 'cause he could. Raul was not the kind to play that smug shit, and he didn't get played. So when Blane told him to just get the fuck out of his house if he wasn't happy, Raul made himself happy, pulled out a .45, and shot Blane dead in his face. Then he took about a pound of weed and walked out.

"Hold up," Sidarra said in that voice to keep a scared thug calm. "Nobody dies over marijuana, now c'mon."

"This had nothin' to do with cheeba," Raul said. "He disrespected me."

They were all quiet again for a minute while Yakoob drove the car up the Deegan to no particular place. Sidarra was the only one who did any talking. Raul seemed to listen to her; she made him explain. Yakoob was straight scared. He and Raul had grown up in the same neighborhood, but he was older than the kid and he wasn't like that. Griff had one hand to his forehead and the other in Sidarra's. As he stared out the window at Yankee Stadium, he knew right away this was all about as fucked up as it could get. The only thing he didn't know was whether this vitamin-shaped roughneck Raul was finished shooting. They needed to get Raul out of the car so they could figure something out.

That happened naturally because homicide had worked up Raul's appetite. He directed Yakoob up into some uncivilized piece of the Bronx where he liked to go for Chinese takeout. Bloody shoes and all, Raul got out and left them at the curb.

"Hey, y'all. I'm sorry," Koob tried to tell them. "I didn't know. I just had no idea."

"Well, let's just go, Koob," Sidarra said. "Just drive the fuck away, now! Let's go!"

"Can't do that, Sid. He's smarter than he looks. He'll come back after me. He might even come back after *you*."

"Well, we have a choice," Griff said. "As it stands, we're in this. It's pretty unavoidable. D.A.'s gonna try to charge us as accessories even if we turn right the fuck around now and give him to them."

"What? For some dumb little nigga with a grudge?" Koob asked him. "No way, man. How's that gonna happen? What about you? You got friends down there. That's your world. How they gonna charge *you*? And if they can't charge you, how they gonna charge me and Sid?"

Good thing there was a line in the Chinese restaurant. Everybody on it looked like they were on lunch break from a murder. "He shot a *drug dealer*," Sidarra said. "C'mon, Griff. Aren't drug dealers expendable down at Centre Street?"

"Not white ones who live on the Upper East Side and sell pot to other white folks. Get ready to see his family on the news already represented by a lawyer. Get ready to see it made into a break-in. He's not even gonna look like a drug dealer when the *New York Post* gets into this. *Those* are his friends. For all we know, the D.A. on this one could be a customer. They're damn sure not *my* friends. Once they know who I am, who Sid is, they're gonna blow this thing up. They might try to use us to charge your boy with capital murder."

"What's gonna happen to us, you think?" Yakoob asked like he was eight years old.

Griff stopped thinking fast for a second and sighed out the window. "We testify in exchange for a deal. I doubt we could serve any kind of time for this. But my career and Sidarra's career, well them shits mighta just ended tonight."

Sidarra grew cold. She had her long fingernails up around her temples and she was staring down into her lap, thoroughly and completely pissed off. Her heart raced in her chest, and when she looked up again she could see her own shadowy face in the rear-view mirror. Raquel. Aunt Chickie. Even Michael. Sidarra suddenly became very cool and to the point. "Look, this is very ugly. Koob, I don't know your stupid little friend, but I work too hard to go down in any shape or manner for this thug or the silly sonofabitch he just shot. Now, Griff, what if I just don't cooperate? Before this little muskrat motherfucker comes back in here with his shrimp-fried-rice afterglow and really makes me mad, just what other choice do you think we have?"

Griff clasped his hands together and stared at the back of Koob's seat. Raul had made it up to the front of the thug line and was handing some dollar bills to the guy behind the counter. Griff looked up at both of them, his face dark. "Cover him. Try to make this shit straight-up go away. Put his ass someplace on the down low for a few months, I don't know, lose him somewhere in Philly. If they ever catch him, we're his highly credible alibi."

"Yup, but he gotta pay something for this," Koob said, stiffening up in the seat. "For real. You can't just roll a human and slide like that, can you?"

They all seemed to exhale at once. They imitated each other's nervousness, running their hands through their hair and shifting in their seats. "All right," Sidarra declared. "I'm clear. For now, he's in the club."

By the time the little rock with creases for eyes and not even a bag for the carton of Hunan chicken he was wolfing was back in the car with them, Cicero's Investment Club was telling Raul how he was gonna work for them from now on. And, yes, you *can* roll another human and slide back into the daylight if you're a thug with no other shit to do and you've got three adults directing traffic. If he would aspire to henchmanship, Raul could be useful; and they would make it so until the debt was paid.

The funny thing is that the same weed Blane died for was so good that, after smoking a single joint of it back up at the Cloisters, they were already thinking of a list. On that particular high, they began to devise a purpose and new financing angles. They didn't exactly say it all yet, but some version of it was in all three of their heads at some point that night. They found a place to put Raul till they could get him to Philly. Then the three of them found a safe place to have drinks and talked. While they schemed, Yakoob announced a major discovery: Solutions, Inc., the educational consultants, was taking steps to go public as early as the summer. Griff discovered a side of himself that took no prisoners. Koob found out he might prefer to be rich than funny. Sidarra felt what it was like to be the accidental queen of a small kingdom. And Raul, sitting up on somebody else's couch watching TV, discovered the importance of being dangerous.

| 10 |

"RAUL'S BACK," Yakoob announced as Sidarra stepped into the truck. Two subwoofers and a blistering rap made it hard for her to hear. "You'll see him tonight. How do y'all want to handle it?"

"You know what?" she said. "I don't even think I want to see his ass. I'm just really not in the mood. Is he trained yet? Can you just ask him to obey or something?"

"It's all good, baby," Koob replied.

"We got a new place we're going to, sugar," Griff said, trying to ease her mind. "Enough of that downtown bullshit. You could use a castle."

I could use an unmarried Griff, she wanted to say. Sidarra was on her period this particular Tuesday, and it would be three or four more days before she was due for good humor. "Whose car is this?" she asked irritably.

"It's my new ride, baby," Koob proudly answered. The truck was a shiny black Cadillac Escalade, tricked out to the max with

Corinthian leather seats that swiveled a half dozen ways, a navigational system, two DVD players, a 50-CD changer, a drink cooler between the second and third row of seats and Sprewell rims. "Since neither of y'all even own a vehicle, I'm 'bout to be the only nigga making car jokes from now on. Dig?"

Sidarra made the same sucking sound with her lips she once made daily in high school to show how unimpressed she was. "This is no way to lay low, Koob. This car beats the hell out of that jalopy you had, but it's too ostentatious."

"What the fuck does that mean?" he wanted to know as they drove up St. Nicholas. "You tryin' to say I got my head in the sand?"

"Nah, dog. She means you're showing too hard," Griff explained.

"And could you turn the damned music down just a few decibels, please?" she said.

He lowered the volume on the stereo. "Damn, Sid. Are things that bad?"

She didn't answer.

"We're doing pretty well, actually," said Griff. "And we're in a position to start some shit."

"Well, I would certainly appreciate that," she said. "I'm not feeling so good, okay?" Tonight, Koob and Griff sat up front together while Sidarra sat in the back and ached. "I don't want to know details, Koob, but I was wondering," she asked. "Raul's been lost in Philly for almost four months?"

"Mark my words, girl, Philly is the biggest motherfuckin' place on earth as long as you a nigga. I can't speak for the others. You might could find them. But I kid you not: a well-stashed nigga with a fresh haircut is as good as gone forever in Philadelphia."

The brand-new tires eased like Isaac Hayes onto Edgecombe and rolled further uptown. As the quiet street inclined, all of Harlem spread out below them. A few blocks later, Sidarra's view from the window was interrupted by the brick wall of a narrow alley between two buildings. Koob one-handed the squeeze into the private little lot in back, and within minutes Sidarra found herself and her company standing inside the doorway at Q's club, the Full Count.

Q, a tall, dark brother built just bigger than a bull yet quicker on turns, stepped his bald head into the low light of the doorway and hugged Griff, then Koob. Q and Griff had become poker acquaintances in the Full Count's back room, but if Griff had ever run for office, Q would have managed his campaign. He was a loyal ex-cop, a careful businessman, and looked like he could still play linebacker at a Division I school. "My brothers," he said like he was ordering his favorite drink, "your boy's already in the back. Oh, you gotta be kidding," he said, pausing to look at Sidarra. "Who made this creature?"

"I'm not your 'this,' " she said, walking past him. "And I'm still in progress."

"This work of ancestral beauty, darling. That's all I meant. Females couldn't *buy* disrespect inside these walls. I'm Q. Welcome home, baby." He shook her hand like a giant gentleman. "What you drinking?"

"Sidecar, Mr. Q."

"Like you never tasted. You got a coatroom in the back. Griff'll show you."

The Full Count was underground, an old-school whiskey bar without the knife fights. It still smelled like 1973, though, and the carpeted areas were low shag. Back in the day, it was one of several preferred after-hours homes for Harlem's political power brokers; with new power brokers came new haunts. Now, it was a neighborhood bar, a well-kept hole in the earth with no windows. Except for red bulbs and blue on the ceiling, the low neon lights burned up into the faces spread across the oval-shaped bar. Marvin Gaye spoke for everybody from several speakers embedded in the walls. The pimp or two in the house was the low-lying and discreet kind. He was probably sitting near a postman, a bookkeeper, or an older middle manager. It was two-to-one men to women, but half the men were fifty-plus; most of the women were quicker than that. As the three of them walked through it all to a maroon curtain in back, Sidarra had to wonder why they had never been here before.

"Check this out," Griff said, standing before the curtain. He pulled it back and Sidarra stepped through to what had been a nasty poker den until a few weeks ago. Now, it was a true VIP lounge; fully equipped with its own sound system, several dark blue velvet couches built into the walls, three small tables surrounded by comfortable stools, a bathroom and changing area, and smack under the long light fixture in the center, a $12,000 Brunswick eight-footer with brick-colored felt. "This is *my* ride," he beamed at Koob. "I should say ours now. I named her Amistad." Their eyes studied the pool table, then roamed the room with kiddie delight. The place made you want to take off all your clothes and just play. "We needed a new office, and the rent's not so bad."

But seeing Raul sitting on one of those couches at the far side of the room momentarily put the play on pause. His compact, bulging body was somehow cut into a very dapper gray suit with faint brown pinstripes. His Guccis shined. Just as Koob said, Raul's cornrows were gone, replaced by a short Dominican curl with a nice fade above his ears and the most impeccably sculpted facial lines a barber ever cut. Raul sat tight, reticent and extremely glad to see them. He was ready, as he told them, for business. "Help yourself to some candy," he said in his flat murmur of a voice, and pointed to a huge cache of Nestlé Crunch, Snickers, and M&M's candies with which he had decorated the tables before they'd arrived.

"Would you please excuse us for a bit, my man?" Griff asked him.

Raul nodded respectfully and disappeared into the darkness of the room beyond the curtains. The pleasure was all his. Out in the Full Count's main room, Raul could finally exhale. Once he settled onto a bar stool alone, it struck him that he'd never felt like this before. His whole body swelled up, and he could not hold back a constant grin. Raul had never been in anybody's VIP lounge. And though he'd been asked to leave, being in their company, even briefly, made Raul more visible than he could ever remember being.

Inside the curtains, Griff had new business on his mind. Something big and dramatic to match the new setting. His eyes focused elsewhere as if he were preparing to make an opening argument. "Not a lot is liquid right now, but we're seeing some filthy gains, my people," Griff reported. "The stakes are about to climb, and I think the game needs more justification. That's just my view. The target person or company has to be a major player in the black people humiliation business. That much hasn't changed and I think you should still have to nominate a target like before, but I think you should have to kill at least thirteen balls straight to reach 'persuasion,' not eleven. If you have a problem with somebody's nominee, wait your turn. If you get a turn, you gotta drop at least four balls—not just two anymore—to 'intolerate.' Okay? It should be harder all the way around. Comments, questions, suggestions?"

There were none. So such were the new rules of Whiteboy. As if on cue, Yakoob fired up a monster spliff, the Ohio Players grooved from the stereo, and the game was on.

"Nominate, Griff. It's on you, dog," Yakoob told him.

Now for the argument: "I've been thinking about something Sid said to me on the way to Koob's comedy act," Griff started, toothpick in his mouth. He walked over to her with his stick in his hands. "She said that life may be too short to ever sacrifice your voice."

"I said that?"

"Something like that. I don't remember it exactly, but it was very powerful. It got me thinking about getting some real power and a booming fucking voice."

"I'm hip," Koob nodded.

Griff was excited to find a taker and stepped toward Yakoob. "Did you know that Solutions, Inc. is a Fortune 500 company already?" From their expressions it was clear they did not. "Well, I think we have to get in on this Solutions, Inc. IPO. We gotta own a big piece of that slave ship right now, on the cheap, just before it goes public. So I nominate the whole fuckin' company."

He stood before the break, settled his eyes on the fat rack, and lowered his body down into the kitchen like a crane. Griff had the best break of them all, but he usually scratched. Scratch on a break, you just sweeten life for the next up. *Pop!* The stick punched whitey, and Griff's whole body snapped out of its sockets like a bad bone. The thirteen, four, eight, and eleven balls all dropped on the break in that order, and Griff didn't scratch. Sidarra was still skeptical. Now he had to declare his point.

"One point two million kids in the New York City public schools, about half black. That alone makes those bastards eligible." Griff's eyes never left the Amistad. The balls spread virgin across the table, loose change looking for a pocket. He was ready to run them all down. Griff had too-good power yet bang-bang aim, and he preferred the real long balls on a line. He could hit 'em so hard they got dizzy for holes. *Bam!* Four in the corner, sets up the six opposite side. Griff's body did a James Brown spin.

"This is only their sixth year in business," he declared next. "They already remastered a dozen school districts in cities across the country—thanks to Sid's boss, Eagleton, the star director on their board. Six, cross corner, whitey splits the nurse, ten in the side." He stroked, jerked English underneath, and the cue ball dropped the six, spun back between two balls touching, and sent the ten right where he said he would. By rule, Griff needed only one more ball for persuasion.

Yakoob had been deep in thought, studying the balls arrayed before them like a poker hand. "This one ain't gonna be easy, brother, gettin' hold of private company stock," he said. "Shit," Koob laughed, "it'd be quicker to place a bet online, kill the fucking schools chancellor, and collect."

Griff looked over at him and grinned. "I thought you were a badass."

"Nah. *Raul's* the badass. I'm just good," Yakoob answered.

The air was too thick with testosterone, and it was time for Sidarra to cut through the nonsense. "Hold up," she snapped impatiently. "There's no way for us to buy Solution shares before the IPO, Griff. And the price will be too high afterward. You know that. You're either in already or you're invited to buy in at the offer price. But we're strangers. Koob can't just hack our offshore funds into a purchase. C'mon."

Yakoob immediately deflated, but she was right. Until then they had managed to gain as Solutions gained by following its portfolio and buying stock in the companies it owned stock in. If they could have bought Solutions stock before, they would have done it outright. Sidarra seemed to intolerate without having to take a single shot.

"No, baby, but he doesn't have to. We can do it all together."

"How so?" she said, sliding back on her stool and folding her arms across her chest.

Griff let his cue rest against a velvet wall, walked closer to them, and leaned back on the Amistad. "This is the angel round of financing for Solutions."

"The angel round?" she repeated skeptically.

"Yeah, the last one before the IPO. This is when preferred venture capital and affiliated investors get invited to pump them up before they go public. I even know one of the vice presidents who handles the deals there."

"You *know* him?" she asked incredulously.

"I don't know him personally, but I know who he is. Apparently a real dick named Goldman. My wife's investment house is one of the banks doing the offering."

The mention of his wife, even if not by name, broke an unwritten rule in her head, and Sidarra's skepticism got a jolt of bitterness. "It sounds convoluted, too many steps," she said. The look on his face as she spoke indicated for the first time that maybe Griff had a problem with people disagreeing with him. So she pushed it. "I don't think it's worth doing. I think we probably leave it alone."

But Griff was not angry. He leaned his fingers on the table and searched for words. All the dance of body English was done for now, and he reached for another type of persuasion. "You're right that it's not easy. And it's probably risky. We would have to be angels. This is how they do it. This is how the ones who know each other make each other richer and more powerful. So we'd have to become one of them—or come off to Goldman like one of them."

"How do you do that, homes?" Koob asked, not sure whose side of the argument he wanted.

"We have to create an entity that sounds like one of their affiliated investors, their angels. That entity buys in as if it should have been in all along."

"How're they not gonna know we're not who they don't know?" Koob asked, twisting up his lips. "We don't even know who they know, and that shit's probably locked up in company files. I can't just go online and learn that."

Griff took a deep breath, stood up, and held his cue with both hands in front of his chest. "Well, we're gonna need to get some inside knowledge about that somehow, because Belinda's taken all that stuff back to her office. And then we're gonna have to get a little lucky. One of us is gonna have to catch Goldman at his desk when he's in the right mood to fuck up. From what I hear, he's either flustered or half drunk by late afternoon. If we sound like money he knows, the phone call should be quick. Then I'll follow up with the paperwork and we wait for the day to come."

Sidarra's doubts relaxed just slightly. "How much are you thinking about buying?"

Griff smiled. "As much as we can. At least two hundred thousand dollars. We'll stand out at less than that."

"Nah, sweetie," she said. "That's most of what's there."

"It's a risk, no doubt," he quickly responded. "Bu, it's not our money anyway. And the payoff will be enough to turn all of us white, even Koob."

"Yeah?" Koob said, ignoring the joke. "How much?"

This time Sidarra answered. "I would think it's on the order of eight, maybe ten times the purchase value, depending on when and if we sold."

"Then finish the game," Koob declared.

"Don't blink now," Griff said. His best shot coming up was a high-line diagonal, two in the downtown corner, with a slight kill so he could smoke the company joint with the five off the cushion.

"The percentage of black male children under fourteen diagnosed with special ed needs, learning disabilities, or pharmacologically treated conditions is, like . . ." *Bam!* Whitey came rushing, crushed the two across the table, dropping it with a thwack. Griff jumped out, straightened up, and spun. He especially liked to spin.

"Sixty-four," Sidarra said suddenly, smiling now with butt-naked approval. "Sixty-four percent."

"Okay then," Griff exhaled gently.

There was a pause. "You sure you wanna do some Securities

Exchange Commission federal-style shit?" Koob asked a little nervously.

"Practically every single one of my clients in a holding pen today came through Chancellor Eagleton's watch," Griff declared. "That's one dangerous motherfucker." There'd be no more intolerance this time. The game was done. They all looked at each other for a minute. A song ended. A brief moment of silence ensued. "Koob, you better let your boy back in here."

Koob went to fetch Raul from the bar. Sidarra smiled all the way over to where Griff was standing to say: "You pretty damned pleased with your fine self, huh?"

His grin took on a little mischief. "Yup." He couldn't hold back the giggle. "What'd the man say a while back? Let no one fuck asunder."

"How's Raul gonna work on this?"

Griff turned away from her. "We'll see. Koob's always got ideas about how to use him. The guy can find things we don't want to be around. Maybe he finds some executive's briefcase in a cab. Surveillance. You know."

"That's all?"

"I don't see why not."

"Okay then. Please be right." She leaned up on tiptoes and kissed the side of his lips. "And thank you, sugar."

Yakoob came back through the curtain with Raul behind him. They sat down on one of the velvet couches to finish a drink.

It was now time not to let all Griff's body jive and gyrations go to waste. Sidarra promptly challenged him and him alone to a round of straight pool. And though his body was just as magnificent doing its theatrics after every shot, Sidarra just as promptly beat him three games in a row. Because she appreciated how to play the balls gently and the value of a slow roll.

| 11 |

MONEY CAN BUY HAPPINESS, but it can't aim at hurts. Money's joys distract from old pains, but cannot cure them. Happiness, or money, just seems to work that way, which may be why drug addicts wake up from nights of euphoria only to hate their lives all over again. Sidarra did not hate her life. At times now it even seemed to hold a little promise. Like Raquel. Like a roomful of men, not her brothers, who worked for her survival and a little more. What she hated in a deep, unspoken place was not being able to share any of that promise with her mother or her father. A little bit of grief always lingered behind every accomplishment that went unshared with them. She also hated that she was nearing forty and had not found the love who would share the limelight she once imagined singing under. She hated not really knowing for sure if she was desirable to a special man. Sometimes she hated her brothers for not protecting her from bad men. She hated that, other than herself, her daughter had only Mrs. Thomas to rely on, sometimes Aunt Chickie, and some occasional fast-food laughter with Michael, a good but inadequate older man. She hated the bad decisions that seemed so right at the time. Money couldn't answer those "whys" or buy out the regrets.

The Full Count was nice, almost perfect, except that Sidarra always thought she saw men like Raquel's father sitting at the bar there. It had the look of the places men run to. Her mother's mirror in the storage room brought these unkind thoughts alive one afternoon. Sidarra had taken a personal day from work and planned to catch up on paying bills that had accrued to her real name, not her alias. That didn't last long before dresses in boxes and hats on hooks distracted her. She put on her favorite Anita Baker album and joined every note. Anita Baker's band would fit a place like Q's well, she thought. But it didn't take long for all those "sweet surrender"-type lyrics to bring back Sidarra's regrets. Like the image of Raymond, Raquel's father. Ray was not a postman or a pimp. He was a camcorder man she'd met one day at a hot dog stand outside of City College where she was a senior. He was a sophomore, he said. The conversation should have ended there, since Raymond was not in fact anybody's sophomore. He was just a hungry guy with thick black curls, the right lines, and a frankfurter jones. Sidarra was already twenty-nine. He was like fourteen, or so he later seemed. She had missed out on a straight run of college; she got interrupted by career misguidance, course credits that didn't add up to anything, debt that did, and the substitute teaching jobs she had to take in order to stop asking her parents for money. Her brothers had cost them enough. Along came Ray.

Ooh. He has green eyes, she thought, almost aroused already. Green eyes. Long, pretty lashes.

"It's better without the bun," Raymond told her. She knew it was a stupid line, but he didn't seem to mean it that way. There was no furtive look, no ridiculous tongue action. He was either very young or kind of mysterious. "I mean, you split it open, you mix mustard *and* ketchup in the slit, and the juices sort of come alive in your mouth. Why am I telling you this?" he asked.

Because he really *was* stupid. Raymond was what Aunt Chickie later declared "a stupid fool." Yet there had been so few of them in Sidarra's life until that point. Everyone needs at least one completely stupid fool. They make life fun and interesting. They talk about what little they know as if it's the only thing in the world, which conveys a kind of sincerity, and sincerity can be sexy if it's attached to green eyes and long lashes. Sidarra already knew that she was boring. Men might whistle at her ass on the street, but it was certifiable fact by the time she was about twenty-seven: she was nobody's lounge singer. She was dull. A substitute teacher. Someone who loved children. Someone who suffered from poor advice. So this time, when Raymond asked her if she wanted to actually share a naked hot dog and see if he was right, she ignored all good sense and said yes.

They were in bed together three hours later. The size of his dick alone told her she was right to act on impulse. He wouldn't stop slapping her with it. He waved it all over her body like a metal detector wand. He wanted her to hold it, cup its pulse, squeeze it, slide Vaseline on it, and put it inside her the way she liked it. And he said these things sincerely, things that had been said in other ways before but were clearly lies. These were not so clear. It would take months before she admitted what lies they were. Instead, she just wanted to feel good. Raymond could grope her for hours. He was the first man to hold her vagina in his mouth. He sucked her nipples like a wild infant. It didn't matter if he was a boy. She was a girl in more ways than she cared to confess. In her room on lower Morningside Avenue, she played catch-up on fun with him. She had never thought through her pussy before. She had never had orgasm with a man. She had never masturbated after lovemaking. Clearly she was in love. In love at that age meant admitting the part about masturbating; it even meant allowing him to see her do it. Which led to the whole thing getting out of control, his filming her with a camcorder he produced somehow, and Sidarra drinking too much cheap wine from a box a few times so he could record more sex. If you could string together onto one film all the hours Sidarra backslid with Raymond, it would not seem like a lot for one life. Yet the tape would always contain those precious few moments when one afternoon Raquel was conceived.

The aborted engagement, like the end of a fond dream, remained a burning moment in Sidarra's life. Like the videotapes Raymond disappeared with soon after he learned she was pregnant. His attentions were not love after all. He was only twenty-one, it turned out. Had maybe one job. Might have been bisexual, she heard from a friend of his she bumped into on Christopher Street. Whatever Raymond was, he was wrong and he was gone. And after Sidarra went on to finish her final graduate credits with Raquel showing under her shirt, her parents helped her see the truth of it all: she had been a stupid fool (but would not stay that way) and she would be a mother (forever).

The cat was staring up at her now, sensing something was not right. Sidarra turned off Anita Baker, folded up the dress she was wearing, and went shopping. Her alias credit card had not yet visited Saks Fifth Avenue.

IT'S NOT EVERY DAY you find yourself inviting a twenty-two-year-old murderer over to your house to sit on your couch and look at your stuff, but money can bring that too. Raul had never been to Yakoob's apartment before and sat, quiet as dull pain, in his pinstriped suit, suppressing his awkwardness. Yakoob had a lot of things—several computers on a wraparound desk, stacks of manuals, hundreds of music CDs, clean rugs, nice plants, some artwork, soft, deep furniture—and everything was neat. He watched a little nervously as Raul's tiny eyes scanned what would be nice to rob. It was good that Marilyn was at work, that she knew nothing of this part of investing, because out of all of it she would hate this guy the most.

"How's your moms?" Koob asked. Raul just nodded. Koob poured a little gin into two glasses sitting on the coffee table between them. He raised his and said, "To your pops, man." Raul smiled, reached over, and touched his glass.

Koob sat with his hands on his knees and tried to figure out how to have this meeting. "Okay then, nigga, as you know, you owe." Raul nodded again. "I mean, that Philadelphia shit for four months was cheap, but not free. There's some heavy stuff in the works, and you gotta do your part for us." Again Raul just nodded. "You gonna have to leave that thug shit behind, 'cause this ain't that kind of game, son."

Raul reached into his coat pocket and pulled out a fat, cigar-sized blunt. "Yo, can I smoke in here?"

"Yeah, yeah. Do your thing. Now," Koob continued, "there's things you gotta know and things you don't ever need to know. We need you to get some information." Raul's eyes perked up in the middle of a long toke, followed by three very abrupt gasps, which Koob waited for. "You ever been inside an office building in midtown?"

Raul exhaled in a mad cloud and began coughing loudly. "No," he blurted.

"How 'bout a corporation? You know what a corporation is?"

Raul shook his head and looked at the joint. "Nah."

"Think you could tell the difference between a desktop and a laptop?"

Raul casually wheeled around in his seat and gestured toward Yakoob's desk of computers. His eyes opened as wide as they could. "You know, basically," he said, and held another large toke in his chest.

Damn, Koob said to himself, shaking his head a little. "You ever been in jail before, nigga?"

"Hell yeah, nigga."

"What for, nigga?"

"Nigga, it's done, a'ight?"

So Yakoob had to school him right then and there, sometimes about things he was still learning himself. While Dr. Dre rapped mad rhymes in the background, Koob pulled out a subway map and showed him where certain offices were. He got on the computer to show Raul the names of companies located in those midtown offices and what their names would look like when he got in there. He explained about corporations, global conglomerates, geopolitical monopolies, and revolving credit—anything he could think of to convey the seriousness of the situation. Raul was duly impressed. He was not quick, but he liked learning his creditors' terms.

After a few hours they took a break and chilled to more music. Raul piped up almost sweetly. "Yo, Sidarra's fine."

Yakoob heard him getting too comfortable and tried to squash it by speaking to him in Spanish. "Don't worry about that. Don't try to get close to that. Just handle your business. Forget Sidarra. Forget Griff."

"He's trouble," Raul answered flatly in Spanish, but it wasn't clear what he meant—good trouble like respectably dangerous or bad trouble like a potential victim.

Yakoob looked hard at Raul. This might be tougher than he expected. He spoke in English again. "No, homeboy. Griff is the reason you're not in fucking prison today. You owe that brother the most." Koob reached for a pack of cigarettes and lit one up in silence. "The trouble is the company I was telling you about before. The trouble is the head of the New York City school system, Jack Eagleton—*that* motherfucker is the only trouble you need to concern yourself about. That's the guy trying to make sure every little blood in school today comes out dumber than me and twice as dumb as you, dig?"

Raul nodded slowly, fooled by the math. He stared at the carpet, thought briefly, and pulled a Nestlé Crunch bar from another pocket. "So let me just smoke him," Raul said in Spanish.

"This ain't *Scarface*, yo!" Koob nearly screamed in English. "This shit is high-tech!"

Raul looked up at him almost plaintively, confused and unconvinced. "So what the fuck y'all want me to do then, Koob? Shit, I want to be down too."

Koob smiled. "We want you to study on what I've been tellin' you and shit. We want you to get up in the company offices, act like a stupid motherfuckin' janitor who can't speak English, whatever you gotta do, however you got to play it, and steal me a laptop out of a vice president's office and then get it *back* in there the next day."

"What if what you need isn't on his laptop? What if it's on another laptop?" Raul asked to Yakoob's utter surprise.

"Don't overthink it, my brother. Don't be all *Mission Impossible* and shit." Yakoob then reached into his pocket and pulled out a small folded piece of paper. "Here's the name and the address of the company. Solutions, Inc. Here's the guy's name. Brett Goldman. Can you do that for me?" Raul paused and nodded again; his tight lips barely cracked a smile. "Solid. 'Cause that's what we need. For you to be the epoxy on this thing."

"What the fuck is epoxy?"

"Glue, nigga. We need you to be like glue, 'cause glue rolls slow before it gets hard."

IF SAKS FIFTH AVENUE EVER GOES OUT OF BUSINESS, it will be because women have given up the dream of happiness. It was a place that in all Sidarra's years in New York City she revered too much to enter. She used to slow down in front of its window displays. She might even get an idea for something she would seek in a cheaper version someplace else. But she understood it as a place for the happiness of others she would never be. Which was okay. As long as the dream remained open for business, flaunting its high-brow perfection between St. Patrick's Cathedral and Rockefeller Center, Saks would exist as the standard below which every other store labored, as the way happiness ought to look when all doubt is removed, and as a place she just might enter confidently one day. That day had come.

Sidarra's thirty-nine years resembled confidence as she walked through the doors in her newest spring dress, but she wasn't feeling it. Inside the bustling lobby, all the beauty and jewelry counters looked cut from the same gem. They sparkled with pinch-me clarity. The suave shoppers in motion buzzed like it was Grand Central Station. She could smell good taste in the perfumed air. Everywhere she looked, it was a great place to be a white woman with a gold card.

Sidarra's alias probably was white, but not all the privileges extended to Sidarra, who started feeling very black in a hurry. The kind of jewelry on view in the cases was entrancing. It was nice to spend time with the genuine version of the handbags she saw copied by the street vendors in Harlem. She couldn't wait for the makeup counter. But none of that prevented Sidarra from the distinct impression that she was being ignored. You try to look past being looked past. You try not to believe it or get hard-faced. Then it keeps happening. The cologne sampler ladies seem to catch some other woman's eye just before they see you. The idle salesclerk keeps remembering something she forgot to do when you approach. It's just a feeling confirmed by the accumulation of small moments. You're invisible—until someone bumps into you without speaking.

"Hey, colored girl," a male voice whispered gently.

"What?" she said out loud. And before she could turn around, she thought: Who would call me a colored girl?

A colored man. "How are you doing today, sweetie? Stop looking like such a colored girl and come over here."

Sidarra was relieved to see a short, dark, round-faced man in his late forties waving to her from behind a beauty counter. His salty hair was cropped very close to his head, his skin and grooming unblemished, but his glasses and white coat reminded her a little of a scientist or her oldest brother Alex. He waved more impatiently at her.

"C'mere, c'mere." She walked over to him, and he took her in with a friendly gaze. "What is this?" he proclaimed. "You're here for a makeover, right?"

She grinned and looked down for a second. "I know we're old friends and all, but are you trying to flatter me?" she asked.

"Not really. I like you. What's your name?"

"Sidarra."

"Sidarra, that's a name you should live up to. You know you have a juicy smile?"

"Thank you."

"My name is Darrius Laughter," he said, looking down at her hands.

Sidarra immediately giggled. His face didn't move. "For real? That's your name? Laughter?"

"Yes. It wasn't always. It used to be Slaughter, but a long time ago my family came together and made a decision about what we planned to be. We planned to be about laughter, not slaughter. You know you've been searching for me a long time, right?"

"All day, if you're the one selling my moisturizer."

"Moisturizer? First of all, it's at least exfoliators for you. Second of all, sit down. We're going to fix this once and for all. This damsel-in-distress number you're working doesn't really suit you. Look at your skin. You have exquisite bones. I *know* I've got a queen at home, but, sister, you could put him to shame if you wanted to. Please want to."

Sidarra sat on the stool with her hands clasped, about to say something when a tall red-haired European woman interrupted. "Darrius, I need you to show me where we've put the Celestier cleanser."

Darrius swung his hips around instantly. "I'm not over here talking to myself, Ruina. This gorgeous creature happens to be my customer." He turned back around to Sidarra. "I'm sure you can find it yourself." Darrius waited about five seconds for Ruina to go back to where she'd come from. "These bitches in here will try your last nerve, I'm telling you. They think every line starts with blue eyes. Whatever. Over here they wait."

Sidarra relaxed into the seat. "I'm open to suggestions. I'd like to see what you got."

"Oh, we got. I'm gonna swab a little of this product—it's a cleanser—over your face first, okay? Then we'll look at some ideas I have. It'll be fun."

It was. He came around the counter so he could stand in front of her. Darrius's touch was professional and gentle. She realized she was being adored by experienced hands and closed her eyes. When he was finished, he pointed to several bottles he had set out on the counter and started to explain what each one could do for her. Then he looked into her face suddenly and stopped what he was doing.

"My God."

"What?"

"It's so obvious I almost missed it. Let me pull your hair back." He reached up, and she didn't object. "Wait a minute." He took quick little steps around the counter and came right back with a hairbrush he'd retrieved from a drawer. "Just let me do this." Nobody in Saks Fifth Avenue's lobby was getting their hair done but the colored girl. Everyone else was invisible. "I thought so," he said, studying his work. "And I was right as usual."

"What?" she said, peering past him into the lighted mirror on the counter.

"Sidarra. Do me and the world a favor. Try never to wear your hair in your face again. Look at you. This is a stunning discovery. And you haven't even spent a dime. Leave now and you'd still be up a million bucks."

"Thank you," she blushed, trying to see in the mirror what Darrius was so sure about. "Let's make it two million, okay?"

"Let's." And they did, all afternoon. Hours passed as she and Darrius talked and laughed and made her beautiful. The counter was crowded with lipsticks and glosses, skin products for mornings and bedtime care, blush, eyeliners, and mascaras in combinations she'd never thought to try. She felt the giddiness of luck at a craps table. Every time she threw the dice, Darrius came back with something that made her look even better. He told her about his family in Virginia. They critiqued certain actresses. She told him about Raquel. They ignored the circling snobs.

When it was over and time for her to go home, Sidarra asked, "So what am I gonna do now?"

"Well, you're going to go on being this vision I call 'you.' You're going to come back with your little girl at least once a month. Here's my card. Home number's on the back in case you're not lying about coming to one of my parties. And today you're going to buy the lipstick and the exfoliator."

She was confused. "But what about all the other stuff, Darrius?"

"Well"—he looked around—"that stuff's expensive."

Sidarra watched him ring up the two items on the register.

Sixty-two dollars and seventeen cents. Then he reached under the counter for a bag, placed the two items in it, and proceeded to pour in about five or six samples each of everything else on the counter—even the things she said she didn't want. He smiled as the bag filled up with a year's supply of the best beauty products she'd ever seen.

"You never know," he smirked.

Sidarra paid cash. Darrius kissed her on both cheeks. She would be back soon.

"You're a good man," was all she could say at the end.

Darrius looked kindly into her face. "Listen, sweetheart, just because you're stopping traffic doesn't mean the light's green, okay? Be careful out there. And, Sidarra."

"Yes?"

"By the next time I see you, get the sad out of your eyes."

"I'll try."

IT WAS NEVER GOOD TO SEE MR. SIMMS, her landlord, but when she got home there he was on the stoop. It had been more than a year since he cornered her over late rent, and things had changed. Still, after being broke so long, she could do without any encounters. He stopped her before she could utter a greeting.

"Sidarra, I'm sorry to tell you, but your neighbor's gone on."

She tried to read his expressionless face. "What? What are you talking about, Mr. Simms? Who left?"

"Mrs. Thomas. You couldn't smell it out in the hall? She died a few days ago."

"Oh Lord, no! C'mon, Lord. You're kidding."

"I'm afraid not," he said. Sidarra started past him, as if she had to see for herself. "You don't want to go in there. It's not pretty. They already took her out anyway. It's just some folks from her church cleaning up and boxing stuff. Place is a right fucking mess.

That's what happens when you get that old. Cockroaches running the joint. I don't believe she could see them."

Sidarra put her Saks bags down and sat on the stoop. "She was my friend," she mumbled into her knees as a big tear welled up in one eye. "She used to take care of my daughter. This is gonna be hard for Raquel when she gets home."

Mr. Simms was not one to commiserate. He had something else on his mind. "I should tell you something else, though the time's probably not right."

"What's that?"

"I'm getting out of this business pretty soon. I've been thinking about it for a while, and with all this new money coming into Harlem . . . I mean, look up and down the block. Well, maybe not this one, but the next one," he pointed. "That one over there. All over. You see those huge Dumpsters parked on the street? That's money. That's someone who just bought one of these old buildings and they're gutting it. It's a whole new day in Harlem. I couldn't buy in here today."

"You're selling the building?"

"That's what I decided. You might as well know now. Gives you a head start on finding someplace else, unless you want to fight it. I hear you'll lose, but if you get a decent lawyer who can drag things out a bit, the new owner might give you something to get you out faster. With the rent laws as they are, all I can do is ask you nicely."

The day had quickly become too interesting for her. For every up there seemed two downs.

"What do you want for it?"

"I don't know yet. There'll be an appraisal or two. I'll let you know if you like."

She suddenly felt exhausted. She wanted to get her kid and her cat and curl up in bed. "Please do that. Please don't make any moves without letting us know."

His eyes brightened strangely. "*You* thinking about buying this place?"

Sidarra regained her wits. "No, probably not me, but my boyfriend might."

"I always knew you'd be all right, Sidarra," he said, tipped his hat, and walked back down the stoop. "I'll let you know."

| 12 |

JACK EAGLETON, THE FIFTY-TWO-YEAR-OLD CHANCELLOR of the New York City public schools, also happened to live in a brownstone. However, his was located in tony Brooklyn Heights. It was the official residence of the officeholder, paid for long ago by the citizens. If it had ever gone on the market, it would have fetched at least five or six times what Mr. Simms's beat-up old Harlem building was worth. The precise reasons for the discrepancy can never be known for certain, but the truth had something to do with the leafy quiet of Eagleton's block, the affluence of his neighbors, and the complete lack of property crimes in Brooklyn Heights. The four-story single-family brownstone also happened to face the lovely pedestrian promenade, which meant it enjoyed wide-open views of the Manhattan skyline, the Statue of Liberty, and the Brooklyn Bridge from half the rooms in the house.

Raul knew all of that—the differences between Harlem and Brooklyn Heights, the absence of people from the promenade after dark, and Jack Eagleton's exact address. Raul was in possession of other relevant facts and accessories. In contrast to the impulsive roughneck he was before his visit to Philadelphia, the pinstriped Raul was steadily trying to change. He was determined to be the Cicero Club's epoxy. His .45 long gone, he'd traded up to a Glock pistol. Unlike Blane, Raul took his debts seriously.

Eagleton, on the other hand, was an established man of few debts. His three-quarter-million-dollar-a-year salary as a public servant was merely round-town cash. He had liabilities which were more than offset on a balance sheet by his assets. He had a full-time maid, a couple of house workers who came in on Tuesdays and Thursdays, a cook for three hours every evening, a dog walker for his bichon frise twice a day, and, during weekdays, a valet for the town car the city provided. He paid only for his wife's personal expenses. Having spent many years roving between educational administration, as a former university president, and private sector consulting companies, as an executive and director, Eagleton had assets too numerous to name. By the end of the 1997 school year, Eagleton already owned 7 percent of the stock of the multibillion-dollar Solutions, Inc. Come June 6, the company's IPO would easily multiply the value of his shares by a very fat factor. Cash simply landed on Eagleton, as it had on his father and grandfather before him, like rain to a drain with nowhere else to flow.

Once the IPO occurred, a storm of cash would land on the Cicero Investment Club too. Raul cleaned Brett Goldman's laptop out of his office. Sidarra reached him by phone before he even knew it was lost. During the telephone conversation that occurred at the end of a long day, Goldman thought he recognized the company name she gave him and set in motion the Solutions stock sale to them. Raul got the laptop back on the man's desk and Griff just as easily secured the flow of paperwork. They were in.

But you don't get to be a good lawyer without wondering

"what if" a lot, and Griff began to wonder what if this Goldman wasn't always so dumb. What if somebody figured out that one of the angels in the angel round had the wrong color wings? What would they do if an investigation of their shell corporation's IPO gains somehow led to any one of them? Griff decided they would need protection. The best protection would be personal information about the misdeeds of the gods. With the threat of embarrassing disclosures of secret transactions there would never be an investigation. They needed to get inside Eagleton's home and borrow a little documentation of his personal deals. So they needed more from Raul.

And Raul wanted more, too. It was true that he had never been inside a townhouse before, but he had never been inside a skyscraper before, either. And when he did that, he found out he could take not only Goldman's laptop but three others without being known. He'd never done any shit like this before or known people who got shit like this done. What he'd already accomplished could be made into a video game. It *was Mission Impossible*. He *could* think it through. He knew exactly what to do. Raul was ready to handle Eagleton.

But Yakoob could be vague. Beyond the basic facts of date, place, and face, the only instructions he gave Raul was to do this one like a pool game. "With every shot you take, you line up the next two options or you play a safety. There can never be an angle that surprises you. Relax. Think of Sidarra's game: the soft touch always beats the bang. You got a lot of bang in you. Just get the man's shit."

Being in the thick of whatever he was in was more than a thrill for Raul. It was the education he never had. He went to school on Eagleton. He figured he'd be caught if he tried to get into the Board of Ed building, but a townhouse was a little different. He learned that Eagleton liked Scotch and he knew where Eagleton kept it. He knew when he had it, and he knew that Eagleton's wife drank something else. He observed that whenever Eagleton himself was home, he was never far from his own briefcase or his laptop. Raul learned that schools chancellors and their wives would rather not shop for groceries themselves. They had it delivered from an online supermarket that only operated in Manhattan. Raul knew that he was too wide to fit under a steel fence above the promenade, so he lost twelve pounds. And, most of all, Raul knew Manny, another dealer.

If Raul had been a small-time dealer of good cheeba, Manny was a chemist with a business plan. Manny was an ex-junkie from the same block, and he had been instrumental in Raul's marriage to angel dust several years before. For a junkie, Manny was lucky. Crack didn't work for him; only heroin did. He could sell crack and do heroin at the same time. Some people's bodies have that gift. The longer he stayed in the game, opportunities for other productive chemistry lessons came his way. Fate kept him out of jail and his flesh bullet-free. So he was around for new drugs, designer cocktails, homemade Ecstasy, things he could make as a hobby. For a dealer, he was extremely lucky, gaining notoriety for cutting-edge shit without the usual stickups and shoot-outs. Friends came to Manny for knowledge, pills, and new highs. Raul came to his heavily fortified apartment on East 112th Street in Spanish Harlem for something slow, potent, and obscure.

"The money is good, yo," Manny said one evening in late June. He was cooking on a laboratory stove. He hunched his long, bony frame shirtless over a flame. "Please, Raul. Don't touch shit, okay?"

Raul drew still again and leaned against a wall. "I already told you it'd be a grip. Don't ever doubt that shit, motherfucker. My word is bond. But you gotta show me exactly how or you might have a hard time spending that cash."

Manny understood. "It's all in the amounts. It's basic fucking biology, man. Just be cool. I'll show you."

MICHAEL HAD NOT GIVEN UP despite the doubts he hoped Raquel would pass on to her mother about their relationship. He sensed something not just distant but stronger in Sidarra's personality. She still had most of her same old insecurities, but as a man with a little more time in the world, he figured she was growing up again. She was accepting those things about herself and going on. To keep her from going without him, he bought her clothes she wouldn't wear. He tried to feed her beauty better than she was learning to do herself. He rubbed her back without request. He reminded her of their old rituals, like reading Sunday papers over Sunday brunch. He offered to take them to dinner if ever she'd go. And hardest of all, he never doubted her investment interests anymore. The success was too obvious. But he tripped up over the brownstone thing.

"Six hundred thousand dollars?" he almost screamed the night she told him Mr. Simms's asking price. "Excuse me. Is he fucking crazy?"

"Michael, please lower your damn voice. You'll wake the baby."

Michael began to pace frantically around the kitchen in his high black socks, boxers, and white undershirt. "That's mind-boggling. That's *mind-boggling,* Sid. That's what he really thinks he can get?"

"He showed me comparable sales figures," she said from behind a cup of tea.

"Have white people lost their damn minds? Who the hell would pay that kind of money for this hulk of deferred maintenance in Harlem? *Harlem!* Don't these yuppie bastards know what Harlem is? What, are they knifeproof? Bulletproof?" He pretended to be a yuppie walking down the street. "'Don't mind me, junkie, sir. I'll just step over you on my way up to my million-dollar personal tenement. And don't waste your bullets shooting me in the back, because, funny thing is, those things just don't affect my kind.' Geez. And these are the same people who watch you count out their change in the token line like you must be the dumb-ass who's sure to short them a nickel. I don't get it, Sid. This uptown madness is gonna end in about ten minutes."

"Look, I don't know why it's happening either, but it's been going on for a lot longer than ten minutes, Michael." Sidarra waved off Michael's exaggerations. "You see those nice people on the street who still smile and wear old clothes and stand at the checkout line and pay with pennies at the bottom of their purses? They used to be all over New York. On the bus. At the park. Where do you think they live? They live in rent-stabilized apartments, Michael. Well, guess what? They're not making any more rent-stabilized apartments. All those people have to go. If you want to stay in this place, you better get rich and you better own, Michael, or they're gonna drive you out. That's just how it is now."

"But, Sid, you *know* Harlem. This place ain't no Broadway musical. Motherfuckers actually live and die here. It couldn't be worth that kind of money even if you had it."

"But it's home. Why should you be the only person in this room who appreciates owning the home he loves?"

"Maybe 'cause I do actually love it and you really don't. Maybe 'cause it's the Bronx, baby! Do you know what six hundred thousand dollars would buy you in the Bronx? Any idea? The whole damn borough only costs about two and a half million."

Sidarra had had enough and bit her lip in exasperation. "What are you talking about, man? Do you know what it means to finally own my own home? Can you imagine what it means to have my daughter see me do that for us? I think I can do this. *I* can do this.

Me. A brownstone. Do you know a brownstone is all my daddy ever hoped to get us—a brownstone and a Mercedes-Benz? And he never got either." She paused and looked out the window with her hand on her hip, then back at him. "So just what are you saying, Michael? Because I don't want to keep running around this with you if you can't be supportive at all."

He held a beer can to his thick belly and sighed at her. "I want to be supportive, darling. You know I do." He scratched the back of his head. "I don't know. Maybe it's time. Maybe we could—"

"Could what, Michael?" she baited him to finally say it. For years he couldn't even talk about marriage and she knew he wouldn't now.

"I don't know," he said, falling back against the kitchen countertop. "What do I know? Apparently you're the one got all the dividends coming. I just think you should at least consider the Bronx."

"The Bronx, no thonx," she said calmly, just as her daddy would have said.

RAUL SAT ALONE ON A BENCH at the end of the promenade one perfect night in June. The air was warm and still crisp. For all the clarity of the sky that glowed with the light of a million Manhattan office windows, nobody walked by to disturb him. Raul would probably enjoy few chances ever to take in the peace of that view again. In fact, he would get exactly three, and this was the first.

He squeezed under the fence bars on a Wednesday evening while Eagleton was still out and the house was empty of workers, guests or Mrs. Eagleton. Raul carefully reached the Scotch carafe in the bar and left a few drops of the future in it. Somehow Eagleton would have to be involuntarily separated from his work and induced to forget about it. Raul was back on the bench in time to see houselights come on in the windows. That was the night of the IPO, June 6. The Eagletons got in from celebrating around 11 P.M.

On the second night, Raul crawled under security gates with Nestlé Crunch bars in his stomach. He had thought hard about the skyline across the river, distracting himself with minor visions of honor and expertise. When his moment came again, he slipped back inside the residence and smeared Manny's mix over the fresh steaks that had arrived earlier by truck. Mrs. Eagleton, he knew, was a vegetarian. That was a Friday. The mix worked slowly through the system. It was hardly perceptible until the toxins had accumulated, but once they reached a certain point, the process would be fast. It needed a foothold in the lymph nodes. Multiplication throughout the bloodstream with just two doses. Then a third and final administration to hasten a deep sleep before the body could panic and seek help. That he took care of on the following Wednesday, again with a belly full of chocolate. By that time he'd grown bold. That time, Raul was still sitting in the house when the potion went down. He had found a dark place to wait and listen. He was a witness to Eagleton's last Scotch of the night. One false move or an errant sound and the Glock would have changed the plan instantly.

While Yakoob and his wife were in an Ocho Rios bungalow feverishly enjoying the fruits of his investment acumen while trying to make a baby, Raul was busy taking his words to heart. He remembered that Eagleton was Sidarra's boss and that Yakoob had called him the problem. Maybe he didn't need to wake from this sleep after all. Mrs. Eagleton had left on Thursday for a weekend trip home to see family in Minnesota. There was only the question of timing and Eagleton's peculiar insides. The chancellor had approximately twenty-two hours in which to die. His heart would simply give out. But Raul had to know; it would determine when and how he'd return the laptop and briefcase to the house. His own heart barely beat from his hiding place in the long curtains of the back parlor. The hundred-and-fifty-year-old floorboards described exactly where Eagleton was in the grand front parlor. Raul tried to imagine the movements he heard. Eventually he heard stumbling. Eagleton had fallen against something. Something had fallen to the floor and shattered. Something else sounded like a groan, but he couldn't be sure. Then Raul heard the unmistakable sound of cell phone buttons being pressed.

"Yes, I'm not sure, but I, uh, I'm not feeling myself. I have a bit of numbness—"

With a soft touch, Raul appeared and dropped the phone to the floor for him. He stayed behind Eagleton's torso and wrapped it in his thick arms. An elbow to the windpipe, a firm palm compressed the chest. That's all the help the system needed to close down. From the little speaker on the floor, a dispatcher was asking questions. Beside it, Jack Eagleton could no longer answer.

"SEE, DARLIN', this is what I'm talking about," Michael said from one side of his dining room table. He had made the omelets that morning along with French toast, a bowl of strawberries, fresh-squeezed orange juice, and imported Sumatra coffee out of his new coffeemaker. "Look at these Bronx listings. It's like another world. Back in the days before Manhattan lost its mind."

He and Sidarra had met for brunch at last that Sunday, and they pored over the newspaper she read now (but he quietly hated most), the *New York Times.* Michael handed her the real estate section and she pretended to study the classifieds.

"It's definitely another world," she said. She took a few more bites and smiled as if the food was better than it was. Michael was always very proud of his eggs. They weren't bad once you got past all the salt. He was busy reading the front page. "Michael, I don't think you should count on us moving to the Bronx. My commute to work, Raquel losing her friends, Aunt Chickie being in Harlem and all. Either buying the brownstone is gonna have to work or we're gonna have to find something else close by. That's what I'm thinking now."

He listened quietly, averting his eyes occasionally as she spoke. When she was done, he said okay and resigned himself to the newsprint again. "Oh, damn," he said all of a sudden. "Ain't that some shit. Sidarra, look at this."

"What?"

"Your boss, girl. Your boss is dead."

"Clay?"

"No, your boss boss. The chancellor. Look here. Eagleton. The man died yesterday of a heart attack, they think."

"You had better be joking, Michael." Sidarra grabbed the paper from him and read a few paragraphs of the article. She rushed her hand to her mouth as her eyes absorbed the words. "My God!" she gasped. "How do you like that?" she whispered.

"Fifty-two. What a shame," said Michael. "That's young for a white man. Did you know this guy, work with him?"

Sidarra could barely think beyond her sense of shock and just shrugged. "Not really. I mean, everybody up there is *near* him, you know, but not like contact. I was introduced to him when he came on. He looked through me on a few occasions after that. I didn't know him."

They read together for a couple of minutes, turning to the page the story continued on without saying a word. "Guy was the real deal," Michael said. "Raised in San Francisco. Yale-, Oxford-educated. Very qualified guy. Loss for the kids. You, uh," Michael turned to Sidarra, "you okay?"

She nodded, still fixed on one particular paragraph.

"This gonna be a problem for you?"

Sidarra had been reading the part about Eagleton's wife, her trip to the emergency room, the end, when she realized Michael had been talking to her. "No. No. They come, they go. It can't probably get much worse for me. We'll see. But, uh, his wife, Michael. I'm thinking about the man's wife. She came home yesterday and found him on the floor. Imagine that. Her man. Just like that, gone."

| 13 |

THE MAN IN THE SECOND-FLOOR APARTMENT wanted eight, but was willing to take five thousand dollars and three months to move out. The boiler was not in bad condition, but the electrical system was underpowered, and many wires had been gnawed into by basement rats. All the plumbing was the original copper. The huge mantel in the parlor apartment where Mrs. Thomas had lived was mahogany under several coats of white, then green, then a fading peach layer of paint. The reconfiguration of each floor into one unit would not be as hard to do, given the convenient position of support beams. And the whole thing leaned east about eight or nine degrees. Sidarra learned all this about the brownstone before she bought it from Mr. Simms, who is still slapping himself. When he purchased the place for $45,000 in 1978, he never expected to sell it one day for $525,000. It was easy to come down off his price. Sidarra paid cash. Mr. Simms danced back to the Bronx. She liquidated most of her Cicero Club gains from the offshore shell company to do it, hundreds of shares in sixteen carefully researched companies. The sell-off made Sidarra the crew's junior shareholder. Yet it came right back. Within weeks of the public offering, they had made nine times their investment in Solutions, Inc.

And there would be more money soon.

"How do you know?" she asked Griff.

"I thought *you* would know," he said over coffee. They sat beside each other in the booth and dropped into hushed tones. "The plan was to get in on the IPO, sure. But we were only gonna hold a few weeks or so, then dump most of it. Koob placed a bet online about a Solutions director." She looked quizzically at him. "You can do that," Griff added, turning to meet her eyes only briefly. "Koob told you."

"Koob never told me that."

"He did. You weren't listening. Or you were high already. This is why I think we need a rule against smoking cheeba until after persuasion." He chuckled and tried to hide his face in a sip of coffee, but Sidarra just waited, a little impatiently, for Griff to come back to the point. "This web site has some nefarious shit you can wager on. It's an online international mayhem casino. You can bet on certain untimely events."

"Who the hell knows about shit like that?" she asked incredulously.

"Belinda. My wife," he said. Sidarra rolled her eyes. "Koob says it's set up by Russians. The risk is ridiculous, Sid, but the payouts are absurd. They list the directors of every Fortune 500 company, heads of state, national monuments, climactic events, terrorism, plane crashes. If anything happens, you can hit. When Eagleton died suddenly, we hit."

"When did you place the bet? How could you have known he would have a massive heart attack?"

"We didn't know," Griff answered, his expression unchanged. "We placed it a while ago, after we decided to get in on the IPO. We placed it on all the top executives of Fortune 500 companies we had a piece of, a thousand dollars in the event any one of a list of directors over the age of fifty died in a month that began with the letter J. Eagleton died in June and paid ten to one. Baby, there was a lot of money at stake with the angel round. We needed insurance."

She squeezed his hand in disbelief, looked away, and choked back a smile to keep it from growing too wide. For just a moment something in Griff's eyes looked false, different; like the news, it threw her off-balance. "I wish I'd known. It's definitely a nice surprise." She paused and shook her head. "But let's get something straight, Griff: I don't ever want to be treated like lady luck by you guys. My brothers used to do that and their luck ran out pretty fast. I want to know about everything before it happens. I want to decide everything before it happens." She looked deeply into Griff's hazel eyes and held his gaze. The old sincerity had returned; he seemed to get it. "Now, I've been thinking about moving into trusts more. I might do that. What do you think?" she asked.

"I've had a similar thought lately, but there's other things too for me."

"And I think from now on we should start coming into Q's through the back door only," she added. "I don't want all those eyes on me every time we walk in there. It's like the Apollo sometimes."

"That's cool," he said. "Hey, by the way, you know Raul's got a crush on you?"

Sidarra turned into Griff's face and got real close. "You should probably worry less about who else has a crush on me and work on your own."

I do, Griff wanted to say. Every day.

MICHAEL WASTED AN ENTIRE DAY off for Sidarra driving her around stores on Fordham Road in the Bronx. His low-cost taste in home materials was exposing his roots, and the whole outing made her impatient. If she'd stuck with him, there'd be wallpaper everywhere. By the time Sidarra refused to stand any closer than the doorway of tile shops, Michael was getting resentful. He barely understood how her money had come so fast, but the change in attitude, the loss of interest in him, started to smell like betrayal. He knew she didn't wear the clothes he bought her, even though he'd outspent himself. Her kind explanations about why her closet was full of dresses with the tags still on them didn't help. Sometimes speaking nicely is a way of telling somebody you're better than they are, or that they don't belong in your league anymore. The truer that felt, the angrier Michael got.

That didn't matter as much to her as the whirlwind construction crew already at work on her new home. Q knew somebody who knew a contractor known for speed, and the race was on. Fortunately, there are stores near the corner of Park Avenue South and Nineteenth Street that sell bathroom fixtures from Italy as well as a full array of marble tiles from the region. Sidarra's new acquaintance Darrius Laughter had his boyfriend fax her a list. She and Raquel went together, free of Michael's constant sticker shocks, and they sat in empty luxury claw-foot bathtubs imagining bubbles. They turned faucets at a rate of ten a minute. They stood under chrome showerheads that looked like sculptures and tried to guess where the water actually came out. They had long dialogues in and out of the presence of salespeople. If somebody got funky with them, Raquel had learned how to lead them right out of the store.

Carpets look the best on newly finished wood floors, and carpets were found in the tall buildings of lower Fifth Avenue. In their elongated windows hung beautifully woven rugs from Persia, Pakistan, and India. This was the template for a thousand forgeries found in Target and Kmart, where Sidarra usually bought area rugs.

Raquel soon took over the day. Her urges moved them along; her imagination colored their tastes. Sidarra followed her daughter through each store with a kind of awe. The older Raquel got, the more she became Sidarra's teammate—even, on days like this, her captain.

"I'm just gonna run a bit, okay, Mommy?"

"Do what you gotta do, Raquel."

Sidarra and the salesmen would stand aside smiling over a $3,000 rug while Raquel, with a look of care and utter determination on her brown face, would do short jogs and quick stops on the fabric.

"She wants to see how the traction works," Sidarra would explain to the person. "I never used to let her run in the house."

"Your daughter is a very serious child, no?" asked the curious salesman.

"I found it, Mommy!" Raquel exclaimed.

"That one, sweetheart?"

"Yup. It should be comfortable. Just enough. This one's right."

Sidarra knew it was her own fault that Raquel wouldn't leave the "comfortable" thing alone. Children have no reason to dismiss the things you say and fewer worries to replace them with. Raquel told all her friends about the shoe-making children of Taiwan. She might never stop wondering about them. Of course, Sidarra had been the same way. That's why she was putting Raquel in a fine Catholic school come the fall. She knew that what had happened to her as a young woman seemed to turn on the moment she stopped focusing on things that interested her. She roamed, then she settled too soon. That was not going to happen to Raquel's mind. That's what comfort started to mean to Sidarra now. That's why spending time buying the details for the house had to be their joint endeavor. It's why she went to such lengths to conceal from coworkers the brochures and catalogues on her desk and spoke in whispers to salesmen on the phone. She couldn't explain it, but she wanted nothing in the way anymore. She wanted clean open space to live in and now she could. As long as her own wits and research turned Cicero's Club blood money into small fortunes, she saw no harm in sending a few bad people to chase after their insurable losses. They'd be paid back eventually. Following some inconvenient bumps in their roads, their way would open again. The only lesson would be the improvement of her life, and one that, for obvious reasons, they would never learn.

THE DUMPSTER IN FRONT OF THE BUILDING had been gone two weeks and the paint dry for one when Aunt Chickie finally agreed to come see the renovation of Sidarra's brownstone. Rain fell hard that late August day. It soaked into the brick along the tops of buildings and darkened the sky by midafternoon.

"So this is what you did, huh?" She spoke under her breath, thoughtfully, and Sidarra didn't answer. "You and that guy. They sure can be useful sometimes."

Inside the door, the vestibule had changed. Sidarra replaced the old mailboxes and hung a chandelier that shined ample light on the fresh white walls. Through the glass door, Aunt Chickie could see a short hallway and rooms opening to the rear of the parlor floor. Sidarra led her aunt into the living room that had once been two and a half smaller rooms. The high ceilings seemed even farther away under the columns of exposed brick, the restored mantel that arched proudly around a grand new mirror and the thin tracks of bright, recessed halogens.

"Mmm, mm, mm," Aunt Chickie said, careful with each curious step. Sidarra watched her eyes for approval. "Your mother," she said, emphasizing the *th* for some reason, "your mother would be very proud of you, Sid."

"I appreciate you saying that, Auntie. Are *you* proud of me?"

This was always the harder part for Aunt Chickie, who never

had children of her own. She nodded reluctantly at Sidarra. "Umm-hmm." Sidarra needed more. She waited like the nine-year-old girl who always hoped for Aunt Chickie to come visit and, eventually, maybe, to compliment her. "Yes, Sidarra," Aunt Chickie added with some vigor. "Yes, yes, girl. I'm *very* proud of you, truly."

Sidarra moved toward her aunt with her hand on her daughter's back, as if to push her four-foot security blanket along with her, and made them all grab in a hug. "Then come live with us. Come on, Aunt Chickie."

"Come on, Aunt Chickie," Raquel echoed.

"This house is too big for just us. Live here where we can be near each other."

"Yeah!"

Aunt Chickie was flattered enough to turn slightly away, as if to take counsel with herself. At that age, the facts of one's immediate life are never far from thought. She was hopelessly poor and spending most of her fixed income on housing at the senior home. She was sick and needed watching. But she was also proud and happy to be nasty when she cared to be. At the old-age home, she had a perfect balance of friends and enemies. And she was watched every so often by nurses. Tough choice.

"You want to put me in the apartment where that old lady died?"

"No! She died over there," Raquel announced, pointing back to the living room.

"Of course not, baby," Sidarra explained. "Come let me show you the apartment downstairs. It's on the street level so you wouldn't have to climb stairs, and it's got a kitchen and access to the back." Sidarra led them carefully down the stairs and walked her through the sitting room in front.

"What's that out there?" Aunt Chickie asked, pointing to the rear.

Raquel and Sidarra smiled at each other. "Come look, Aunt

Chickie." They walked under the low ceilings, across the small kitchen, and through a short pantry hall to a door with a window at the top. "That's the garden. That's *your* garden."

"Garden?"

"Yeah. Mr. Simms didn't even rent out the ground-floor unit. He saved it for himself in case he ever decided he wanted a place in the city again. There's a backyard out there that was full of so much junk and rotting nonsense that you couldn't see it's got two lemon trees. I just found out there's fresh soil underneath."

Aunt Chickie was silent as she stared out the bottom edge of the window. She scanned the yard, but her eyes kept falling on the soil beds. At first she seemed to be trying to guess which way the sun fell. Aunt Chickie was a plant mother, a green thumb trapped in the city. She abruptly changed the subject. "You should throw yourself a party or something, Sid. A housewarmer."

"I'd like that. With Labor Day coming up, I thought maybe a barbecue. I just don't know who to invite." The three of them continued to stare up at the gray sky from the window. "You wanna think about it? Staying here?"

When a face gets old enough, tears fall a different way. Like soldiers who already know the paths they'll march down, it is steady as they go. Sometimes you cannot even tell they've been through except for the wetness they leave in the grooves of the cheeks. After the last one had gone, Aunt Chickie was clear. "No, I'll stay," she said softly. "I'd like to stay."

14

WHEN SIDARRA WAS A LITTLE GIRL, it was always clear to her family when she was having some crisis of conscience. Her skin would break out. Not just her face but her arms and legs would fill with tiny dark blotches that would deepen, fatten, and spread like pox. It never lasted more than a few days, but whenever it occurred, Aunt Chickie used to call it Redbone Guilt. This strange affliction, and the vague fear of going to hell, kept Sidarra from being a child who stole things or lied on people or cheated in school. Aunt Chickie would know, since she had skin light enough to betray her emotions and mischief enough (at one time) to produce guilt. On the other hand, Sidarra's caramel skin shouldn't have been the moral showcase that it was.

For the first time in some thirty years, it was back. The telltale marks of Redbone Guilt had established a beachhead across her forehead, with small clusters on the move inward from her shoulders and her thighs. Now that Aunt Chickie lived in the brownstone with them, Sidarra could only hope the old woman's eyes would fail her, sparing Sidarra the obligation to explain her pimpled flesh. But this time was worse than ever before. This time confused her because Sidarra no longer feared damnation, having decided you had to feel God's love before you could lose it. This time the source of any guilt was unclear—her feelings for a married man? That seemed superstitious; they had only flirted shamelessly for months. Purchasing a dream house with a little of other people's money? Maybe, but they deserved it, it was insured, and they made it grow on their own in any event. Still, that summer the mysterious patches migrated and thickened, preventing her from showing her skin just when she began feeling beautiful again. Even Darrius had no cure. Instead, Sidarra spent a lot of time upstairs in her new room. Which is where she would have gone as a child for the only cure there was.

"LET'S GO IN THE ROOM AND TALK," Sidarra's father used to say. "I don't want your mother contradicting me."

That was his usual line, the signal, but Sidarra knew the room was really chosen because it was the one place away from his boys. He had three of them. They couldn't help what they were, but their presence could annoy the hell out of him at times. When Roxbury Parish finally got a girl, he made sure to get her her own room so that she would always have a boundary line of retreat from the suffering caused by the boys' loud voices and flying limbs. His daughter gave him the opportunity to speak freely about serious issues, like growing up, and that was a pleasure he would not deny either of them for the sake of his sons' jealousy.

The room was down the long hallway from her parents' bedroom and the one her brothers shared next to it. Sidarra's room had been the apartment's second bathroom. Just before she was born, her father ignored every imaginable protest and ripped out the fixtures, painted the walls peach, and installed things he was sure a girl would like. He even made her brothers help in the work, demanding that they learn how to respect a female other than their mother. The room was small—but not to Sidarra, who for most of her childhood thought it was a palace compared to the lion's den her brothers piled up in. She was allowed to hang some of the best family photographs on her walls right next to the one of Dr. Martin Luther King and the life-size poster of Michael Jackson. There was also a large antique mirror her father bought for her at a junk shop on 125th Street. In the corner she had two soft chairs covered in blankets, one for her and one for him. Her father would crouch down and assume his seat, always surrounded in her memory by the glare of the white bathroom tiles that still climbed halfway up the walls. His knees would fork outward, and while they conversed he would raise his elbows and put both hands behind his head. At his feet, she would hear the occasional crackle of ice cubes melting in a glass of bourbon. For a man who was named like a small town in Louisiana, Roxbury Parish seemed more at home with his daughter in that room than anyplace in the world.

"You should always be able to see yourself clearly," she remembered him telling her often, and he would inspect the old mirror for streaks. Taking a rag, he would dampen one end with a little soap and use the other to wipe it dry. "The secret to cleaning mirrors, Sid—are you listening?"

"Yes, Daddy."

"The secret to cleaning mirrors that nobody seems to know is that you gotta keep wiping, wiping, wiping well after you think you should be done wiping. The mirror will let you know when you're finished. The cleaner the mirror, the clearer the soul."

Even as a little girl, Sidarra understood mirrors as her dad's metaphor for the mind. Roxbury Parish simply wanted his daughter to have a mind more capable than his own. Poorly educated, he was smart enough, but his specific aspirations for Sidarra were limited by his horizon. If she had wanted to become a great singer, for instance, that was probably okay with him. Yet she knew he always hoped for something more, something that would develop her mind, like a manager, a manager of something. The best word he could ever find to describe his hope for her was "queen." "Be some kind of queen," he'd urge. But there didn't seem to be any queen openings, so Sidarra became a schoolteacher instead. It wasn't the most original choice, but it was the best she could figure out, and just beyond his raising, it pleased him. He'd come from no place worth mentioning, the son of a preacher whose indiscretions taught Roxbury to distrust God, raised by relatives Sidarra never knew, and he made up his rules as he went along. The story he told of his life before her always began with him wandering for several years, then to New York City in the fifties, and finding work in the subways as a sanitation man. He was one of the men who rode the flatbed maintenance cars that roared very slowly into the stations after midnight, stopping briefly so that they could jump out, empty trash canisters, sweep and spray the platforms down with water, and jump back before entering the tunnels again. It was a job like his journey: stop in a place only long enough to find what's rotten there. Yet once he married, Roxbury couldn't leave.

Sidarra's mother, on the other hand, was a Dean. She belonged to a clan, brought her daughter to church where they sang in the choir, and preferred to have her talks with Sidarra outside the home, like walking through Central Park. Zester Dean loved the idea of Sidarra becoming a singer in a lounge as her sister Chickie had done in Paris.

"Why not?" she would say. "Shoot for the stars, girl. Shoot *at* 'em!"

That sort of encouragement led eventually to the shared coveting of a special hat by Sidarra, her mother, and Aunt Chickie, who happened to be its owner. It was mostly purple, floppy and felt, with a fuchsia bow, garish enough for the burlesque stage with the hippie soul of a seventies album cover, and perfect for a nine-year-old's view of womanhood. Zester had managed to borrow it from her sister after several months of trying. She paid for the privilege by enduring an onslaught of biting Chickie snipes about her lack of the requisite sexiness, charm, and cheekbones to wear such a hat outside. Shortly after the loan, Chickie traveled to Spain with her performing husband. When she returned two months later, it was as though she'd packed a tracking device. She wanted the hat back. She'd even made note of it in the letter telling of their arrival in New York. But Zester couldn't find the hat. The hat was gone. And with the announcement of her Aunt Chickie's return, Sidarra promptly turned into a leopard. Her smooth skin became awash in tight red, then wide brown pimples. Yet she remained mute on the hat's whereabouts, and her silence was catching: Zester and Chickie didn't speak to each other for a full year over the saga of the missing hat.

"Why'd you take the hat, child?"

Sidarra raised her big eyes up at her father, stared for a while, then smiled. "I like the hat, Daddy. For a long time, I liked it every day, in private. I sang in it. I danced in front of the mirror when everybody was asleep. I even hoped that Aunt Chickie would never come back. Then, after a while, I forgot about it."

"Even though you looked so great in the thing?"

"Yessir. I did."

"Hmm."

"What I didn't forget was the bad stuff she said to Mama about not looking good enough to wear it."

"So you thought it would be a good idea to keep it from Chickie altogether? Even when you saw the sadness it caused your mother when they fought and stopped talking. You still thought you'd teach your aunt a lesson?"

Sidarra thought about it for a while. She knew she could come up with any answer at all. Knowing what her father would want her to say and saying the opposite had no predictable repercussions in that room. She could tell it like she saw it.

"Yeah. I think so, Daddy."

Roxbury Parish was quiet. He put his hands on his knees and cast his gaze around the room a few times. At some point he picked up his bourbon, took a sip, and as he scanned around again, he caught his daughter's expectant expression. He raised his glass to her in a customary toast, sipped, and continued his slow scan of the room. "You finished? You ready to come clean and let 'em know what happened?" She looked out the window, then back at him. "If you're done, I think you should tell 'em." She stared at his glass of bourbon and waited for the ice to crack, then nodded. "You wearin' your trouble, you know?" Sidarra looked up at him and nodded again. "And don't plan to go no place for a while, 'cause you're grounded, y'understand?" She nodded and actually smiled a little, realizing she was already serving the sentence. He too smiled slightly. " 'Course I'll be here if you need me."

In all the years of conversation in that room, Sidarra knew that her father spoke there as he spoke nowhere else. However, this time was the same, only more so. "And you should always have a room for yourself, like this one, baby queen," he added for no apparent reason.

Her Redbone Guilt cleared up overnight.

Years later she learned that on that day her father had been fired from his job of nineteen years. It was the beginning of his end. He hid the firing from her and her brothers for a long time, speaking in whispers about it to her mother, leaving and returning home at the same time each day, for years finding only part-time work at best. At his age, he could never find as good a job. Eventually it all merged into an unexplained poverty, with each child who could helping out.

Sidarra was slow to become the queen of her father's wishes, and she failed to keep her mirrors clean. Instead of grinding toward her teaching certificate, she went to school in fits and starts and worked as a substitute teacher. She had finally finished college with a baby and a certificate when she got her own classroom. There she saw the horror of her dreams. For all of her own doubts and delays, she came face-to-face with pure failure. Sidarra saw the trying-hard faces of lovely doomed spirits soon to be quit upon. Not every child, but too many children. Especially the boys, like Tyrell from her block, whom she first met as a bucktoothed, gangly thirteen-year-old whose sweet eagerness took steady leave of his personality with every day he was shunted to a program for slow learners, sent away to a counselor for disciplinary misdeeds, or ignored. There was nothing for them, she realized, nothing intended. Sidarra tried for five years to be the difference in their lives, just as she was doing alone in her East Harlem apartment with Raquel. She thought she'd gotten a lucky break when a well-known philanthropist—a "white knight," as they were called then—decided to donate his millions into a special schools program. He wanted fresh, bright, and untainted professionals to administer his plan to expose junior high school students to internships at corporations. Sidarra had already enrolled in school administration classes when she was hired on and moved into an office at the Board of Miseducation in downtown Brooklyn. And there but for the grace of God, she left the classroom and its neglected faces for good. Yet because it looked to her father like a promotion and because he had wanted so little and gotten much less, Sidarra never shared her unhappiness with him.

Her parents were happy before they died. Her father had discovered a problem with his blood. It was killing his bones. The flow to the joints had ceased and the edges were rapidly collapsing. Soon he would not walk or sit comfortably in a chair or make love without great pain. In short order the doctors said he would need his hips, his knees, and possibly his shoulders replaced. There was no money for all that. So her parents decided to get in all the strolling they could before his health prevented even that. Arm in arm, they walked the city, visiting parts and places they had only vague memories of from years before. One such day, they stood on a midtown street corner together, waiting for the light to change, when along came a terrifying screech, the quick blue smoke of a car's tires, and the errant twist of a steering wheel. Careening over the curb to avoid a swerving yellow cab, the car hurtled straight into their bodies and decided everything once and for all.

After that, trouble seemed to become always for the Parish children, especially Sidarra's big brother Alex. The cabdriver, lucky for him, was soon deported, and her other brothers, mad at an unjust world, wandered aimlessly for a long time. Sidarra needed help with her parents' effects, but the men couldn't find the strength. Alex argued a lot with her; he refused to be her backup. Alex tried hard, but he couldn't move. He too had been crushed. Then one day Alex did move. He moved out to the desert with his young family, to New Mexico, where he became a plumber. And years of silence between Alex and his beloved little sister commenced.

A LITTLE MORE THAN THREE YEARS LATER, Sidarra found herself defiantly examining her naked body in the mirrors of her converted room, wondering just why the smooth bronze skin she was now all too willing to share with Griff chose now to turn into the hide of a poisonous butterfly. The rash was more venomous on an adult body. It had tracked clear across her breasts, tattooing one nipple with laughable discoloration, and freckled the slight paunch of her tummy. Never in childhood would it dare approach her genitals, but now the spotted march was on with a vengeance upon rounded hips she'd come to love again, down her strong inner thighs, and even populated among her outer pubic hairs. In disbelief, Sidarra stood there itching.

The transformation of the storage room into a sanctuary for self-examination was painstaking. The plaster was blasted clean of a hundred years of neglect. One wall had been replaced with hand-carved teak, insets for pictures of her parents were cut, special frames were ordered, and beneath it Sidarra had put in a Yoruba mask and shrine for the ancestors. The other walls were red. The windows that never existed behind old blinds and boxes were replaced by one huge pane that looked down on the garden. The boxes, loose hats, and shoe trees were in an attic space now. Sidarra had replaced them with a bank of deep couches covered in plush cream-and-mocha-satin-covered down pillows. To the left as you entered was an electronic piano on a stand. Beside the instrument was a cabinet with an encased sound system. At least eight speakers of different sizes were cut into the walls and ceiling. And everywhere were mirrors.

Before she began speaking to her father in the room, Sidarra felt she had to cover her body in a robe. He would know why the pox had come. "It could be the Whiteboy money—I mean, the money we play for and invest," she began aloud. "But I don't think that's what broke my skin out this time Daddy. Making that money is very abstract. You don't even experience it until you can turn it into a house. And I'm pretty clear about the sources. They're scum. I'm not saying it's right. I'm just saying I don't think I regret it enough to go Redbone over it. Maybe the bet they won when Eagleton died. That wasn't cool at all. His wife is grieving while I'm furnishing a brownstone with her loss. Maybe that's had an effect on me. You never know what it is. It's unconscious anyway. That's what you always said.

"No, I think it probably has something to do with this guy I'm starting to love. You know, it occurred to me the other day, and it's funny: no matter how much I think of him, no matter how long I'm at it, there's no 'but' about Griff, Daddy. I mean, everybody gets a reservation. You got reservations about family all the time. You have reservations about even your best friend. Things they've said you never forgave 'em for, things they do, something you wish they'd change. The longer you know somebody, the farther they are from perfection. Look at Michael. He came on a lifeboat of reservations, and he's been docked there ever since. But not Griff. I've known this guy for over a year and I *like* him, like being around him and what he says and how he says it and how the man looks when he says it, and I got no particular place I'd rather be than with him. I harbor not a single reservation. Not one." Sidarra dropped her hands to her sides. "Except the fact that he's married.

"I'm not even sure if this is my problem, Daddy, or his. I can feel it coming off of him all the time, and I'm forced to deal with that. I don't even know how Griff feels about his wife, or how much he hides from her—or from me. I just sense sometimes that it's the only thing that could blow his cool, and I am heavily invested in this man's cool. Crazy, huh?

"That's probably why I've grounded myself up here in this room so much, where I can do no trouble but grow a few more scales or horns. Of course, if you could talk back, I'm pretty sure none of this would have happened. I wouldn't be out at night with Uncle Cicero's pool cue, I wouldn't be playing the stock market with bad white folks' money, I wouldn't be goo-goo for a married fella, and my skin would be lovely and clear. So I suspect all this is the trouble without you, Daddy."

| 15 |

SIDARRA'S FATHER WAS RIGHT about the unconscious cause of her skin condition. The itching got so bad that she went to a dermatologist, who diagnosed it as a nasty case of pityriasis rosea. Such a beautiful name for a problem conscience, much better than the clever labels she and Raquel made up in front of mirrors. Mocha Revolt. Streaking Tiger, Spotted Frog. Neither Noir. Red Arrests Rust. Raquel was also the only person other than the doctor who saw the whole quiet storm of color as it progressed from cute red pimples to burning brown swathes to flaking, itchy blobs. She helped administer the anti-itch creams as well as the historically offensive "de-pigmentator" called Fair & White. Yet none of the new information about the disease solved the mystery of just what Sidarra felt so guilty about—furnishing her new home with ill-gotten gains, marrying a married man in her thoughts, or something else.

By the time she held her Labor Day housewarming party, the

brownstone was ready for company even if her skin was not. Aunt Chickie stood on her feet all Saturday afternoon in the kitchen making collards, macaroni and cheese, and potato salad. They'd bought steaks, ribs, chicken, and fish for the new grill in back. Michael was scheduled to be the master cook, but he decided he wasn't coming. He and Sidarra had loud words the night before. A little too much vodka and Michael let her have it about all that was on his mind, including how her bad skin was a punishment for ignoring him. So Sidarra let him go. That way they would both be spared the head-to-head comparison with Griff.

But pityriasis rosea complicated her own inevitable meeting with Griff's wife, which increased her nervousness and in turn made her itch. Sidarra tried to conceal her troubled hide with tight white pants and a billowy white cotton blouse. The top had a Queen Elizabeth collar, which covered her neck at the expense of looking a bit silly; it was that or a scarf. She was also nervous about inviting enough people. Her old friends would become jealous and wonder too much about the price of everything, and in any event, she would look uncharacteristically showy. That excluded them. The creepy Raul was nobody's housewarming guest (though he managed to keep himself close). That left only the crew and some odd choices. Yakoob brought his wife Marilyn, a short, pear-shaped Puerto Rican woman with big thighs and a high-pitched giggle. Q showed up with an unknown girlfriend, Jeanette, who looked so young that maybe he picked her up at a bus stop on the way to school. Darrius Laughter brought his partner, Justin, a white man. Both were dapper in light suits and white shirts. To fill things up, Sidarra invited the contractor, Joseph, and his wife Evelyn, as well as the painter, Harry, and his wife Pearl. Of course Griff appeared at the top of the stoop with his wife, Belinda Chambers.

The cat, Pussy Galore, took one look at Belinda from the top of the stairs and decided it was time to leave.

Belinda had clearly intended to be the vision of note among whatever human females attended Sidarra's affair, and from the git-go Sidarra had to acknowledge that she was. Just the sight of them deflated her a little. Griff arrived wearing a spectrum of browns, like the parlor walls—an auburn button down shirt with a wide collar, a honeycomb linen four-button summer suit and pony brown clogs. Belinda followed him in like the sun shining on earth. She was lighter-skinned than Sidarra had imagined, a well-tanned butterscotch complexion, and even taller in high heels. Her thick reddish hair flowed just below her shoulders, framing her long, angular face, green eyes, and weak mouth. For an investment banker she boldly wore tight suede slacks in marigold yellow, her long, thin legs striding confidently inside. Belinda was small-chested beneath a cranberry-colored vest, but her arms were elegantly muscular, her neck like an antelope, and her exposed belly noticeably firm. The woman worked out. The woman never said no to herself.

Which included not wasting time where she didn't care to be. Belinda had no interest in spending their holiday here, but gave in at the last minute. Griff asked her to make the best of it; out of curiosity, she said she would. But the more she heard of this Sidarra woman, the more her anticipation grew caustic. Belinda took no prisoners and that included party hosts. Her first sight of Sidarra released a slow drip of competitive juice down her spine until it tasted like salt or blood down the back of her throat. Their introduction was all eyes and no blinking. The girlie handshake they approached with was quickly tossed for a real grasp. Then they took turns measuring each other's details. Once everybody was seated around the living room, Belinda took advantage of Sidarra's momentary shyness, put a choke hold around whatever initial unease her own insides brewed, and did what she was famous for at work: she ran the room.

"So tell us, Q," she began from her privileged position on the love seat beside her husband, "what do you do?"

The big dark man in the royal blue shirt smiled to everyone. "Would you believe I'm a cop?"

"Not if you're a friend of Griff's," she came back.

"*Ex*-cop," Griff added.

"Retired actually. I run a bar."

Belinda clasped her hands together, leaned up in the couch, and nodded approvingly. "And you?" she asked, looking at Q's girl.

"Oh, I'm Jeanette," she said with a round-the-way meekness you knew wouldn't last and a thick Harlem accent that would. "What do I do? Cosmetology."

"Cosmetology!" Belinda repeated in case everyone hadn't heard. "That's great."

"Jeanette, we have to talk, girl," Darrius piped up from a leather stool beside Justin. He sipped his martini through a plastic stirrer.

"Darrius," Belinda said, turning to him next, "what do you do?"

The natural flow was to settle into Belinda's third-grade circle and wait your turn, but no one had told Darrius that. "Oh, you don't know?"

"No," she said, looking deliberately cute, and waited for him to tell.

"I'm Sidarra's stylist, only *I* pay *her*!" His strong voice carried around the large room, and everybody laughed. "Isn't that right, my queen?" he added, calling over to where Sidarra leaned against a doorway at the circle's edge. She laughed and waved him off.

"Okay, so we got Hugo Boss in the house. How about you over there?" Belinda pointed to Justin. "Are you Calvin Klein?"

"If you'd like me to be, darling, but just for today," Justin said, and broke up the room. Justin was a striking young white man, clean-shaven like a model, but delicately built, a brunette tussle of well-coiffed bedhead with blond highlights up top. When he opened his mouth, no *s* went unspoken. "I'm Justin," he waved to the group. "And I'm a funkaholic."

"All right," Belinda went on, applauding playfully.

"You gonna keep running this thing, Oprah?" Griff turned and said to her.

She ignored him. "How about you, sweetie?" Belinda asked Yakoob's wife. "What's your name again?"

"Marilyn," she said with a tart Nuyorican accent that rolled the *r* in "Mari" and licked the *leen* in "lyn." Marilyn was the color of butter in the pan, with straight, nearly black hair pulled tight in a ponytail and a pudgy, beautiful face. Kind as pie, said her full cheeks when she smiled. Her thin brown eyes gleamed with good nature, and her pretty teeth never stayed hidden for long. "I work in the pharmacy, in the Duane Reade," she told them, sitting up, rubbing her husband's thigh for brief social support.

"Which one, baby?" Koob joked in a soft voice, looking into her ear.

"Quiet, bu," she waved toward him.

"Nah, baby, tell 'em which one."

She sucked her lips and elbowed him. "You know the one downtown on Duane and Reade streets?" Everyone sort of pretended to be right there. "That's the one. That's the *original* one."

"That's how that shit got *named* Duane Reade, y'all," he added.

"And, Koob, you're a comedian, right?" Belinda asked when the giggles subsided.

"If I am, somebody in here owes me fifty cent for that last one."

"I get half of it!" Marilyn added. The group laughed nervously. "So what do *you* do, Belinda?" Marilyn asked.

"Yes," Darrius said, "what *do* you do all day?"

"Well," she pulled up to the edge of her seat again, "I'm an investment banker."

Long silence from those who knew what that was. "Oh yeah?" Marilyn said with a little excitement. "At what bank—like Citibank? That's my bank."

Belinda tried to be gentle. "No. Not that kind of bank. I'm with Smith Barney."

What else could anyone say? They'd all seen the TV commercial with the fat white Englishman smoking a pipe in a library somewhere and bragging about what he had and how he'd *earned* it. Marilyn, her hand on Koob's knee, just nodded and smiled. Game over, people started to stand up.

The pairing off began at once, mostly so folks could peek around the house, at least the parlor floor. Q immediately asked about the grill. When Sidarra hesitated about who was cooking, Q stepped up. Darrius and Justin strolled over to Jeanette, and Jeanette and Justin wound up outside in the yard beside Q for the next hour. Raquel spent some time slapping Koob five, until she decided to show him and Marilyn how well she could run and stop short on the new Persian rug. Aunt Chickie was polite with the construction people for a while, then left them on the bench and went back to the kitchen. Belinda stepped in and out of conversations but mostly circled her husband.

"I want the tour, Sidarra. Frankly, I think it's overdue," Darrius said.

"Okay, Darrius," Sidarra answered, but nervousness shot through her again, and the skin behind her left ear began to itch a little. With other people in her home, she could really see the extravagance and reached instinctively for the presence of Griff and Yakoob. "You got it. But hang on just a bit and let me get some other folks, too."

Sidarra collected Yakoob, Marilyn, Griff, and Belinda and they were soon heading up to the third floor.

"It looks like I need to join this investment club y'all got," Darrius said. "My God."

Silence on the stairs. "Let's go up to the top floor first," Sidarra said. "That used to be my apartment. Now our bedrooms are on the third floor." They reached the top and Sidarra stood aside as they walked into the open space. "This is our family room," Sidarra declared with muted pride.

Several old walls with chipped and fading paint could no longer contain loneliness or grief or the smell of fast food up there, and Sidarra tore them down. The natural light they used to trap scattered freely over the shiny floors and nestled in the Oriental rugs. Most of the remaining walls were now blues, aquamarines, and periwinkles like sky. Artificial light fell on a few framed pictures, a painting of a reclining brown woman stretched across the longest wall, two large philodendron trees arched from ceramic planters, and sparse but comfortable furniture invited calm. The group broke up and started walking around individually, peering at things, inspecting politely, asking questions, oohing on occasion.

Belinda eyed Sidarra from behind. She watched the physical closeness shift ever so slightly between Sidarra and Griff. She watched Griff for signs of anything at all. Bad rash or not, this was a beautiful woman, Belinda thought, with the thick, curvaceous musculature black men coveted most and a warm complexion. This house explained a lot about Tuesday nights, more than Griff ever told. Nothing he ever described in the past mattered now. Sidarra and her husband were clearly "good" friends. They could be hiding a deep privacy, for all she could tell. The question was, how good was this friend?

Yakoob stood in front of a raised platform on one side of the room. Sidarra had built it to replace her office, and her father's desk sat in the middle below pictures of him and her mother. A computer table stood beside it.

"Well, damn, Sid! Ain't you gonna even plug your PC in?" Koob laughed. "Look at this. Poor little gigabytes. Dust all over the keys and shit. Somebody musta told you this was modern art. Hate to tell ya: it ain't."

"It's just a badass job," Griff told Sidarra when they were almost alone in a corner of the loft-like space. The apparent privacy allowed his familiar tone to return, and she allowed herself to blush. "I'm very happy for you. This is what you worked for, Sid, what you deserve."

But someone had been eavesdropping. "Amen," Darrius declared near a window overlooking the street. "Magnificent! You done it, girl!"

"What's in here?" Belinda asked. Sidarra had not intended to allow anyone to see her little room, let alone Belinda. Belinda seemed to notice the mild panic her question caused and planted herself more firmly in front of the door. "May I see it? Is it private?"

Griff's radar went off and he came to Sidarra's aid. "C'mon, baby. This is a housewarming, not an engineering report. That's Sidarra's private space."

"She can tell me if it is."

Sidarra collected herself. "No. Sure, you all can see it. Lemme get the key out of the desk." She walked past Yakoob to one of the compartments in her father's desk. The others gathered expectantly near the door to the mystery room. "I just don't want Raquel in there when I'm not home," she explained. Then Sidarra fiddled with the lock, all eyes on her, and opened the door to the former storage room.

The room's decor was smart-ass proof, so nobody said anything at first. Sidarra walked in, but no one dared follow her into the sanctuary right away. Except Belinda, who slipped inside without hesitation. "What do you do in here?" she asked flatly.

"C'mon, Belinda," Griff said.

"Griff, please," she said, waving a hand in his direction.

"I sing. Relax. Pray. Belly-dance sometimes. Just unwind."

"Oh, you belly-dance?"

"Sometimes."

"You're built for it," Belinda was quick to say, gesturing toward Sidarra's much wider hips and softer tummy. "Kind of Victorian shape. I bet you're good."

"This is a goddamned casbah, child," Darrius said.

"Can we borrow it sometime?" Koob asked.

"You so stupid," Marilyn laughed. "It's very peaceful, Sidarra. I like it."

Belinda strolled up to the shrine to Sidarra's parents, a stranger at the altar of her tears, and Sidarra's stomach tensed up. Belinda quietly studied and scrutinized the wall, the pictures of Sidarra's family and the Yoruba sculptures.

"I'm sorry, Sidarra, but I'm a little curious," she said. "Why would you have a fertility totem?"

Sidarra was near the limit of her hostessness and good nature. "What are you talking about?"

"This is Yoruba, isn't it? From Nigeria."

"Yeah."

"Right. I have a great interest in these kinds of pieces, and this one's beautiful. The condition is remarkable. It's just that it's a fertility piece. See?" Belinda pointed to two symmetrical carvings on the sides that vaguely showed a coital embrace between male and female forms. "And, of course, these are breasts," she added, pointing again.

"Of course," said Darrius, barely concealing his sarcasm. "You're good."

"Not good really," Belinda shot back. "I just know what I'm talking about. I love this stuff. I studied this stuff for a few years. There's nothing wrong with a little fertility at our age, Sidarra. I just wondered why."

"Because I like it. I find it very powerful. I mean, prayerful,"

Sidarra said, unable to hide her embarrassment about her possible confusion. She'd put a lot of hope and money into that shrine. It was like the guy who boasts the Chinese character tattoo all the way down his arm, only to learn from a Chinese friend that it didn't mean "Never say die" after all. It meant "Soup, five yen a cup."

"Well, all I'm saying is you might want to watch who you dance with in here unless you want Raquel to have a little brother," Belinda added with pleasure.

Yakoob and Marilyn were still wrapped together in the doorway and looked privately into each other's eyes. They said nothing out loud, but the idea of dedicating a space to fertility prayers was nothing to laugh about. It was like stumbling together on a hope they had been a very long time without.

"Who's hungry? I know I am," Darrius said.

He headed out of the room for the stairs. Before Marilyn and Yakoob followed, Marilyn turned to Sidarra and said, "That's the most beautiful room I've ever seen. Congratulations, girl. I don't even know how you did it." Her eyes searched Sidarra's face more plaintively, then she smiled. "Do you think the fertility thing from Nigeria probably works?" Sidarra didn't have the words to fill the long, awkward pause, which only made Marilyn ask if maybe Sidarra didn't need the sculpture and might sell it or give it away to friends interested in its powers.

"I'll think about it, sweetie," Sidarra told her. "Or maybe you and I can go find you one together."

That suddenly left Griff, Belinda, and Sidarra together, a troika of pure tension. Before leaving the floor, Belinda had to suggest a good place for Sidarra to put in a gym for herself, particularly an ab machine, maybe a treadmill. Sidarra shook it off. They started down the stairs toward the third floor while the others continued on to the kitchen. At the landing, there were two oak doors. One led to Raquel's bedroom, which Sidarra proudly showed them.

The other led to Sidarra's master suite. When they got there, she opened the door and let Griff inside. When Belinda started to follow, Sidarra filled the space with her body and stopped. She stood in the doorway and leaned her arm against the jamb, keeping the Yoruba expert in the hall.

"You're pretty knowledgeable," she turned and told Belinda, who needed a second to realize she'd been banned. "If this were stock advice, I'd probably owe you the place by now, huh?"

Belinda only smiled and waited awkwardly in the hallway, unsure whether to go back downstairs.

While Sidarra held her at bay, Griff stood inside the long room and scanned the luxurious comforts. His eyes widened in awe at the beechwood California king on stilts with its sheer cotton canopy drooping like a sail. A stone fireplace sat within a few feet of it. The walls were sponged in terra-cotta, and the several rugs lying around like clouds were lamb's wool. A long wall of bookcases full of books covered the side next to the door, and at one end, beyond two wicker chaises, was an open bath with marble Jacuzzi, bidet, and a regiment of candles in every size holder.

Sure that Belinda couldn't see him, Griff kept making faces of wild approval toward Sidarra, pointing to things. The moment was a little surreal for her, too. She had Griff exactly where she had imagined him a thousand times since beginning her renovations—beside her bed, undressing in her dressing area, entering her bath—and here he was with his wife just outside. Griff regained his composure and returned to the doorway. "Dope floor tiles, Sid," he said calmly, and winked at her.

Sidarra was first down the stairs. Belinda held Griff back for a moment of marital confidence. When she was sure Sidarra was a good five or six steps below them, she turned to her husband and whispered through a laugh, "Have you seen a single fucking book in the whole house?"

"I'm sorry," Sidarra called up the stairs at her. "What did you just say?"

Belinda had trouble with her own cool then, but got it back in time. "Oh, pardon my French. I asked my husband if he'd ever seen such a fucking renovation. We've been through it, and you obviously had much better luck than we did. Contractors will kill you."

"Okay then," Sidarra said, turned, and walked off the stairwell.

Q was not playing about the food. Gone from the ribs, the steak, the chicken, and fish was the bonanza of salt Michael favored. Sidarra missed him by now, but she was glad to see a backyard of satisfied friends, their heads spinning with Tanqueray, their mouths full of good food and laughter. Marilyn liked old-school music, and she took over the stereo. Darrius and Justin wanted Raquel to show them all the latest fourth-grade dances in repetitive detail, and she was happy to take them to school. Jeanette could groove too. Soon, only Belinda, Aunt Chickie, and the construction crew sat playing bid whist while the Gap Band, Isley Brothers, and Peabo Bryson got jiggy with it. The sun passed beyond the rooftops, and the yard soon turned to shade. Twenty minutes after firing up a blunt outside, Yakoob was half asleep in his wife's familiar lap. Sidarra had answered all the house questions and could be her own self again with braids down. After a while, folks found their way back inside the living room. Belinda cornered Sidarra and Raquel about schools, wanting to know why an educator like herself had taken so long to put her daughter in private school. Griff called her off with a distraction. Darrius and Justin stole her seat, and eventually the voices got loud again. Over it all, the doorbell rang.

Sidarra jumped up and excused herself. Raquel, sure that Michael had finally arrived, ran after her mother and disappeared into the vestibule. It wasn't Michael. It had been many months of careful, even calculated avoidance, but there in the well-lit doorway, behind the glass, was Tyrell.

"Party still goin' on?" Tyrell asked through decorative bars on the glass door.

"Tyrell," Sidarra said. Then she felt Raquel at her side. "Go on back inside, honey." She watched her frightened daughter move back to the living room doorway but stay within sight of her mom. "Tyrell, you can't come here, you know that. You can't come to my home like this, man. C'mon."

His expression lingered between hope and mischief. He was dirty again. His breath smelled awful. He was wearing too many clothes for such a hot night, and there was no telling what he hid under his layers. "Just let me in for a minute. I just wanna talk to you."

Though Sidarra had had to admit Tyrell's dangerousness to herself as he got older, this amount of boldness—coming to her door when she probably had guests—could be special trouble. He was probably high, too. Sidarra searched his eyes. She wanted to show good faith and to appear cool, so she opened the door as wide as the chain would go. "Can you hear me now? You gotta go."

From a little ways down the block, Raul squinted his eyes and watched intently as a conversation started to unfold.

"Miss Sidarra, Miss Sidarra," Tyrell repeated. "You s'posed to talk to me, right? Right?"

He wouldn't budge. Gin had foiled her wits somewhat, but she wouldn't do anything stupid. She didn't have to. The shadow that suddenly rose up behind her was Q's.

"Excuse me, baby," said Q, muscling his frame in front of her. All she could see was a great wall of back. She stepped aside further and watched his bicep tighten as his hand reached back to pat a service revolver tucked into his waistband. "Whatchoo want, blood?" he asked sharply with a menacing flatness.

Tyrell looked up into Q's eyes. Q was gonna make this quick. "No need, dog. This really ain't your business, man. Me and my teachah got something to work out."

"Your teacher? Uh-uh." Q raised his huge arm up to lean it against the doorframe, which made Tyrell step backward and also put one hand a lot closer to grabbing anything the intruder pulled out. "Check this out, youngblood. It don't happen tonight. It don't happen here. You wit' me?" His baritone never wavered. Tyrell hadn't faced such a clear choice in years. Q turned slightly to Sidarra, but his eyes never left the junkie. "I got this, baby. Go on back inside." She backed away. Q's eyes turned mean. "Now, look at me, motherfucker, because I will take your life if I have to. Quick. Am I clear?"

"Yeah, dog. We cool."

"Nah, we ain't cool. We just clear. Now back your stank ass off the stoop."

Tyrell was gone with a quickness. Not far behind him were most of Sidarra's guests—with a description from Q and a light warning to watch their backs on the way to the subway. Koob and Marilyn were first to go, with Marilyn hugging Sidarra extra hard and promising she'd take her up on her offer soon. They were followed immediately by Belinda, who had reached the limits of her graciousness, and Griff, whose still-anxious eyes appeared to be busy trying to put the whole experience in a distant place. Q already had. He just had a good time, kissed Sidarra on the cheek, and headed out with Jeanette on one arm and a bag of leftover desserts in the other.

Darrius and Justin were in no hurry to leave. It was only nine o'clock, and they needed more coffee before they were set to go to another friend's party that night. So they helped Sidarra and Aunt Chickie clean up and wanted to talk about the other guests. They started with the contractors and saved the best for last.

"I'm sorry about Miss Clairol," Darrius said from the couch.

"By the way," Justin began, "Belinda was wrong about your sculpture. I hope you don't mind, but Darrius took me up to see it. I work with collectors all the time. Your shrine is beautiful, but it's not a fertility piece. It's often used to commune with dead ancestors. There's a great history to those pieces. I have a book about them if you want to borrow it." Sidarra could not hide her relief.

"See?" Darrius beamed. "See what happens when you bring along your own whiteboy?"

"What'd you think of Griff?" she had to ask.

The two men looked at each other from over the coffee table. "Well, first of all," Darrius said carefully, "the man does brown like the Lord himself. And he's fine enough to clone. Little serious, but you'd be too if you came home to *that* every day." Sidarra enjoyed a guilty smile that her Aunt Chickie looked disapprovingly at. Darrius seemed to check with Justin before he went on. "And secondly, the man's nose is wide open for you, sweetie. I'd hate to be his insides. He's gonna sleep all day tomorrow, all the work he did today—unless she kills him first. 'Cause she may not be the most likable legs in suede, but she's no dummy, that's for sure."

Sidarra didn't need to hear anymore. Raquel was dozing off to sleep on her lap, and she herself was nearing the time when she just wanted to be alone with a glass of wine in her room and think back on the day. Darrius and Justin left her kisses and a few final words of skin care encouragement. Then off they went into the night.

"Why are you looking at me like that?" Sidarra said to her aunt as she was about to lift Raquel into her arms and put her to bed.

"Because your friend is right."

"About what?"

"Not all of it, but some of it, it seems to me. That Belinda is a horrible girl. She's mean, kind of calculating. She's one of those siddity girls who gets humbled late." (Aunt Chickie could have been talking about herself, Sidarra thought.) "You can hear how she's uncomfortable with what we used to call the 'vernacular.' I can't even tell where she's from, her accent going back and forth, back and forth. Anyway, I'll just say this. I don't think she and that Griff are in love either. But I don't believe it's the host's role to publicize a fact like that. And in your own way you did. Now, I'm going downstairs to bed. It was a nice time today. Nice people. Good night, baby."

Raquel's sleeping body weighed a ton on the stairs up to her room. Sidarra struggled with her while she rewound her aunt's words. As she undressed her daughter, it seemed to her that both Darrius and Aunt Chickie had her confused for somebody that gave a shit what Belinda thought. Griff's interest in her or lack of interest in his wife was the province of the man, and she bore no responsibility. All she did was open up her home. It was time for wine and dreams.

16

IT MUST HAVE BEEN MUCH LATER that night when Sidarra and Griff entered the Full Count through the alley door. For some reason it was very important that they work on a difficult shot adjustment on the cue ball called the Cicero Spin. When you tag the cue just right—almost a quick flick-and-retreat of the tip upon the upper left quadrant of the ball's surface—whitey goes crazy. The spin makes it do an impossible arc just like a candy cane—and twice as sweet. But Griff was having trouble doing it consistently. So was Sidarra, and she had had enough of the embarrassment. Nobody else was there. Even the club was deserted.

The pityriasis rosea was gone. Her skin had healed completely.

Tall drinks were already sitting on one of the small tables, her sidecar and his Hennessy. She turned on the lights while Griff put on Marvin Gaye's "Come Live with Me Angel."

"I love that!" she almost screamed. It was just what she wanted to hear.

He stepped into the light of the table still wearing his browns to the nines, but began eagerly to take off his jacket. Sidarra leaned her body on a corner of the table and watched him shed the coat. Without the mad pox and cloudbursts of mocha distorting her smooth caramel flesh, Sidarra now wore a white netted jumpsuit that squeezed her curves like a wine sack. The lights close above her gave the caramel diamonds of her protruding skin an added shine. Griff's eyes followed.

"I never told you how much more delicious you look with your hair back like that," he said, twisting the mother-of-pearl handle of his pool cue in his hands. All his cool returned, backed by deliberate intention. "This is where I wanna be, Sid."

"Me too. We're gonna have to put in a coffeemaker, though."

The Cicero Spin. That was the object of the game, and it was hard to spin it like that. There was just one cue ball, so they each took turns close beside each other, shooting. Over and over again until it became natural. It's not so much a kiss as the gentlest twist between your fingers, she said. Loving fingers. But the shot is absorbed into the body as soon as it's released, he said. Isn't that a kiss? Their bodies would arch down again over the table together and wait for the angle. No, baby, it's a rub, the gentlest rub, not a kiss.

This went on like that, it seemed, all night. Hours must have passed. The same music always returned, but the room got hotter, and neither of them had ever asked Q how to work the thermostat. So Griff took off his shirt and laid it on the nearest velvet couch. His feet were also bare. She watched him, getting the best look she never had before.

Griff looked across the width of the table at her. "You know I'm sorry about this afternoon."

"I know, man," she purred.

Griff did brown a lot better with his clothes off. His body was finally there to prove it. The angles were as magnificent, the symmetry of the muscles just as she had many times imagined them arranged. But not the tightness of the skin, or the pure invitation of its shine, or how it rippled in the right places. That was better than the wish.

"How come you're not supposed to be home now?" she asked.

Griff looked like he'd been waiting to be asked. "Because she's never in my dreams anymore. We're never together there. So I figured I could." His eyes were so sure. Sidarra blushed warmly at his words. "And I learned a lot today," he went on, easy yet determined to explain something.

"So did I."

"Not just what you're thinking, baby. Your sanctuary upstairs—the whole house, really—but the sanctuary with the red walls is the right thing to do. I see you free there, which is why we had no business going in." Sidarra sauntered halfway around the table to him. "And that's a little piece of how I start to feel so free here."

Her breasts were nearly already out of the netting. "In this room?"

"Not particularly," he shrugged. "With you, Sidarra. Just being with you."

There was no music. A song had ended. She lay her cue stick down along the rail. Griff rested his against the side of the table. She strolled over and stood in front of his tall frame. In the moment before Stevie Wonder's voice dripped into the soft intro to "As," Sidarra raised her arms out from her sides and slowly leaned her pubic bone against the swollen tip of his pants.

"Touch," she cooed from the top of her breath. And the song began.

Griff's long arms swallowed her. His full lips bounced gently against hers. He kissed her cheekbones and tongued the crease of her mouth. He kissed her neck at the vocal cords, and Sidarra began to sing the lyrics. His hands untied the white strings of her jumpsuit and rolled it down, down her curves. That soft mouth followed the luscious unfolding of her skin, down, down between her breasts. She sang at the top of her lungs. He lapped at the bottom of her breasts. Lower down, his pants were descending. Lower, he knelt down on the carpet, pressed his thick elbows against the slope of her pelvic bones, held her breasts in his hands. Taste, taste, he repeated lovingly into her skin, tasting her hard dark nipples, taste, he kept saying, and Sidarra sang. But when Griff kissed a triangle all the way around her vagina, the song paused in her mouth. She could not control her tongue. She lost control.

He lifted the whole guitar of her open body into his arms, pressed his thick, waving penis up against her nascent wetness, and kissed deep inside the walls of her mouth.

This is a kiss, he said to the body he pulled to him.

This is a kiss, he said to the shoulder he honored.

This is a kiss, he gave to her belly button.

But there's something more, he confessed to Sidarra, laying her naked back gently upon the auburn felt of the tabletop. The song came in and out of her moans. She fingered through his hair as his head dazzled her lips and his sure touch slid inside of her.

This is a kiss, he told the sweet clitoris. But this is the rub, said his fingertips.

To me, baby, she called out. Oh, to me, baby! she could only say. The words to the song escaped her busy senses. The rest of the sentence eluded her consciousness. Her whole body rocked more and more severely under his serious touch, pushing her, moving her more urgently with each stroke of his full tongue and every soft rub of his pinched fingertips inside. Her feet flexed back and forth in spasms. Her toes arched in desperation. Her orgasms screamed with the choir, rising and swirling with the song's momentum. Griff was saying something he'd only been thinking every day before, and she heard him, she heard his whole body say: I'm reaching for the heart of your love.

And when he pulled up his body and suspended the descending armor of his abdominal muscles over her, when his breath shook at the welcome reality of her wet pussy awaiting him, Sidarra twisted her ass around and slid him between her in rhythms. He complied with the frenzy, rocking up and down with her, ravishing the skin on her back, her hips, her ass, and her thighs with wild hands while they smiled. They laughed loud and savored. They dripped sweat and teased madly. Until they twisted back around and their eyes found each other again.

I love you, Sidarra.

She remembers his hazel eyes then, how honest they were, how complete their hold on hers and the tender surrender they let free. She held his face and stared into his feeling as Griff's thickness spread her gently around with each stroke. The sweet pendulum rocked steady like that for luscious days until she abruptly rolled his whole wet body over on the table and straddled the great Y of his pelvis:

I love you, Griff. I *love* you, baby. I love.

The fact that he couldn't stop kissing her. The way his passion pumped enormous up through her. The way his hands washed every inch of her ass. The liberated joy across his face. When he arched upward to suck her breasts again. That she could have fucked him all night and tomorrow forever. That the fine rage of her last orgasm rushed against the explosion of his head in time for her eyes to see the blur of it all before rolling back into her own head to sleep. To sleep. Spent, embraced, completed. Right atop the Amistad, they slept until morning in the cool puddle of their abandon. Griff never left her body.

SHE WOULD REMEMBER EACH FEELING. She would remember every sound. But when Sidarra woke up, the best thing still hers was the fact that she would not have to go to work that day. It was Labor Day. The night was a dream. She woke in her bed alone, her troubled flesh on fire, and got up to take her skin medication.

MOST OF THAT DAY and just a few blocks away, Tyrell lay bleeding under some metal stairs with his face caved in on one side. Q was helpful, but Raul was more thorough. He had followed Tyrell up the block, sorry he hadn't moved on him when he saw him go up Sidarra's stoop looking sideways. Harlem streets can offer up a variety of loose weapons—a carburator on the curb, a broken telephone somebody left on the street, a tin garbage can top, or bricks near a Dumpster. When Raul prepared his choice, he searched ahead of Tyrell for a suitably discreet place to have him. The encounter was brief with very few words. Raul asked him if he believed in reincarnation. Tyrell pulled a .22. Raul asked if he'd rather be shot with his own gun or find some other way to be somebody new. Tyrell laughed too hard at that one. The one round he got off missed Raul badly. Moments later, his legs were broken in several places below the knees and three ribs were cracked. When Raul was finished there and Tyrell understood the nature of the punishment, Raul dragged him to the stairway and busted him in the face with the brick. Tyrell wasn't supposed to go back to Sidarra's again.

AND LATER THAT NIGHT, at a small bar downtown, Yakoob was once again nearly bombing onstage. He was telling one of the stories about his make-believe fatherhood, and as often was the case, the tiny audience didn't know whether to laugh or cry. It wasn't that they knew Koob's observations about being a dad were fictitious; most believed there really was a boy who did the things

Koob described and said the things Koob said he did. To most it wasn't that he was a wannabe dad. It was more that he was a wannabe comic without faith in his own stories. And since his memory loss as a result of pot smoking meant he could remember a few names but never entire jokes, Koob tried telling stories to make people laugh. Like so many, Monday wasn't a good night for it.

17

THE FIDELITY INVESTMENTS BRANCH OFFICE on lower Broadway was smack in the heart of the financial district, two blocks from Wall Street, three blocks from the World Trade Center towers. Yakoob's job as a computer technician was located in an innocuous old building a few blocks from the Ferry Building at the very tip of Manhattan. Every day after he worked, rain, snow, or shine, he would walk several blocks up Broadway, past the Fidelity office, and on to City Hall Park, a few blocks south of Duane and Reade streets. There by the fountain he would meet Marilyn, and they would ride the subway home together.

That Tuesday was important for a couple of reasons. People seem to mark the Tuesday after Labor Day for some of their most serious pursuits. It is the day summer ends and seriousness begins for adults everywhere. For Marilyn it was particularly important, and Yakoob knew it. That Tuesday, Marilyn had an appointment on Madison Avenue to see a fertility specialist, a doctor with an international reputation who wouldn't accept insurance payments of any kind. A year ago, Koob could never have paid for his wife to see such a person. Only a year ago (and for most of their time before that), Koob and Marilyn's romantic friendship was challenged loudly, sometimes dangerously, by money problems he knew he alone had to solve. He was doing that now. Marilyn had waited four months just to get the rare 6 P.M. appointment because, she was told, most of Dr. Vershak's patients were either still in the Hamptons or just getting back to the city from there. Marilyn was already thirty-nine, and four months felt like eternity for a woman wanting to get pregnant. Koob even paid the consultation fee in advance. He had put aside a liquid account just to pay for everything involved in conception. For all the fights between them over the years, there was no debate about one thing: this was their final chance to have a child of their own.

That Tuesday was also important because Yakoob had made a decision about his money. The whole idea had been to get some and be smart about it. But it was also to *be* smart, to *show* smart like Griff did. Koob had never in life done that. The Cicero Club proved he could be clever, but it was all down low, and a lot of the knowledge about trades and companies came either from Griff or Sid. Yakoob decided to step into the daylight and be a man with his money. Sidarra had sold off most of her stock to buy the brownstone, and Griff was buying property, too. It was high time Yakoob invested some money the way regular investors did. He wanted to finally walk his own walk and talk his own talk where the big dogs ran. And he would buy Marilyn some security. Preferably in her own name.

He arranged to get off work at three-thirty that day. This would give him time to walk up to the office, meet with a broker, discuss his plans, look at some options, and be done there in about an hour. That might be cutting it a bit close, he admitted to Marilyn, but he'd still have time to meet her by five easy. At rush hour the express train on the Lexington line would get them to the Upper East Side in more than enough time for their appointment. His hair in fresh cornrows, Yakoob wore a light blue suit left over from the wedding of one of his boys ten years ago. It still fit except for the waistline, but it was better than the casual clothes techs usually wore in their back-office cubicles. In his breast pocket, Koob occasionally passed his fingertips over the edges of a thick envelope that contained fifty $500 money orders he'd gotten from six different check-cashing stores—checking to make sure it was there.

Fidelity Investments was located in the reconfigured lobby of an old bank building. You climbed a short flight of gray stone stairs before you crossed between two enormous pillars and through two glass doors. The place did a quick number on his heart. The ceilings were so high his eyes kept glancing up at them. He wasn't sure at first where to go among the different modular oak desks. A pretty blond receptionist stopped him before he could wander deeper into the place and asked him to fill out a form for new investors. When he was finished he should go back and wait in the seating area by the front window. Somebody would be with him momentarily, she told him with a smile. She was all of twenty-five years old. In his head, he named her Heidi.

"Yes, ma'am," he said, pulled out a pen, and took a seat.

Try as he could, the chandeliers made the words harder to read in a way only being from the projects explained. There were already two other people waiting to be seen by an account associate or broker or whatever the receptionist had called the people who advised you and opened your accounts. The customers were both white, a man and a woman, middle-aged, briefcases at the ready, and they looked a mean combination of busy and bored. If he could help it, Yakoob never wrote a single thing down in longhand. His penmanship revealed too much about going to JFK

High School and his early flight from words. So he turned his body to one side to make sure these two folks weren't watching him fill out the form.

Marilyn was going to be amazed, and that kept him going. That was her job in his life. Only Marilyn understood how Koob explained the difference between his programming ability and poor longhand. He'd achieved a small, often secret brilliance with the one. With the other he was quite obviously another ignorant nigger.

An Asian man in a navy blue suit walked in like a regular, met no one's eyes, and took a seat on Koob's far side. Yakoob's nod meant nothing to the guy, so they both averted their gazes.

As he filled out all the personal background information and asset questions, Koob couldn't help reviewing the reasons he had no business in that room. He'd never gone to college. The GED exam was a struggle. He probably smoked too much weed. Now, folks were looking at him in that suit like he was the ringleader of a circus or a member of the Platters. Just in time, Koob's cell phone rang.

"Where are you, baby? Are you on your way?" Marilyn asked a little frantically.

"Everything is fine," he said so that the whole seating area could hear him. Cell phones did a good turn for black men. They came along and made a lot of men's idle moments look important and gave them something else to do with their hands. Koob stepped away to a corner. "I just gave them the form they make you sign. Don't worry. I'll be on time. There's hardly anybody here."

"Koob, you better be here. This is not the day to fuck around, man. I need you with me. I'm not trying to wait out there and be all anxious."

"It's all good, baby. Count on your boy. You gonna like this. I'll see you in a minute."

That's when he decided to put the account in Marilyn's name no matter what. Two more people walked through the doors, spoke briefly to the receptionist, and sat down in the waiting area. Yakoob even considered putting a little of the money in a high-risk, high-yield account for his unborn child. He sat back down and waited.

"Mr. Elliman? Mr. Cavanaugh can see you now," said the receptionist to the first man waiting. It was 4:14 by Koob's Rolex.

Did the receptionist have his name? Of course she did. He gave her the form. It was probably like the DMV, only better, a place as professional as this. They didn't need to take numbers. They weren't selling ice cream. Koob's knee began to bounce a little. He was next after the woman. He would just state his business. He knew what he wanted. He'd been over the script a hundred times in his head. Four twenty-six. The white woman ahead of him was called on. Two other people entered and made their way to the seating area.

If his mother were still alive, he probably would have called her now. Koob took a deep breath at the thought of her and felt the bulge of checks press against his chest. If his mother were alive, he would want her in the empty chair beside him now. She simply would not have believed his words alone and would have to hear what he was about to say.

At 4:35, the receptionist approached the carpeted seating area. Koob started to move out of his chair, but she went directly to a young white man who had come in after him.

"Todd Dukovny?" asked Heidi. "You may be seen."

Koob looked up at their backs in a question he wasn't about to ask. He was not about to tangle with his image as a six-foot-two-inch dark black man in there. He had a goatee to stroke, so he stroked it. He stroked and strummed, looking out the window at lower Broadway's old-fashioned façades and waited his turn.

Another man, the Asian guy, stood up at 4:42. Koob looked to find the receptionist, but she hadn't called the guy. Mr. Cavanaugh himself was motioning to him from his desk.

"Yes, Mr. Yamaguchi," Heidi intervened. "Go straight back."

Koob figured it was an appointment. It *was* almost 4:45. Asian cats come early, he thought. He went back to waiting. Marilyn's voice grew more shrill in his head. He'd be seen when he was seen, but he wasn't gonna make no scene. He had his most serious business to do. When one of them brokers finally saw what was large about his front pocket, he'd never wait again. New guys must wait, he thought. I still got time. Downtown, in this man's world, motherfuckers make you wait.

He couldn't understand why the receptionist never met his eyes, though. Yet he had no words to say anything about it, so he just politely waited. Uptown he wouldn't have waited so well. He would have said something by now. In fact, Koob would have said a lot of shit by now, or be gone. This was different. This he had to do the way they do it.

Marilyn always complained that when Koob was late—which was almost always—he wasn't thinking of her waiting someplace for him. He wasn't thinking about the danger she might be exposed to or how bad it felt to be sitting somewhere wondering what might be happening wherever he was. But he could see her now. He could often see her; she was wrong about that. He knew that by now she was leaving work. He could imagine her clothes, her hand around her purse, and the strides she made in heels all the way to the fountain at City Hall Park. This made him fidget like a boy. Fidgeting seemed to make him sweat. As soon as he realized his brow was wet, Yakoob noticed that no one else's was. Four forty-nine and another person behind him was called by a broker to enter the desk area. Koob watched in disbelief, trying not to show anything irregular, but pissed just the same. He saw a third broker way in the back rise up from her empty desk, push in her chair, and grab her coat. He caught Mr. Cavanaugh's eye. Cavanaugh was about to be the last one left in the long room of desks. The other remaining broker, an older white woman with white hair, also seemed to be finishing up for the day.

It was just Koob and a white woman left. She was maybe fifty. He caught her looking at him and smiled. She grinned ever so slightly as she turned her eyes toward the window. Five to five and the receptionist promptly came for her.

"Andrea Roisman? Just this way," Heidi directed.

Marilyn would be there by now, nervous, pissed, and preparing all her disappointment in a rage he really didn't want to hear. The waiting area was his alone now. Koob spread his legs in the chair. His fingers pinched the money in his pocket while he sank into the seat-cushion. Now, he just looked stupid. By the time someone came to speak with him now, he'd have to get right up and leave. His time was almost up. But still he waited quietly.

"Sir," said the receptionist, who managed to come up from behind him, "I'm terribly sorry, but we close at five on Tuesdays—I don't know if you read the sign as you came in." Koob looked up into her sparkling face. She looked like one of those "people people" who pretended to ask you something when they were really telling.

"But I been here. I was here before most of those people. You don't remember?"

"That may appear true," she said, not budging, "but your form required only Mr. Cavanaugh to see you since you're a new account, and he's got to finish with a client. If you like, you can take your form with you or leave it with us for your next visit. We're not taking any more clients today."

Yakoob looked down at his watch again. Five oh-one. It was already gonna be a sprint to Marilyn. He tried to think, but this was the last place to think.

"Okay, okay. I better come back. Let me take back my form,

like you said. I'll come back to see him. Maybe I'll call." Koob realized he was trembling slightly and wanted to fly away through the window. "Can you give me something with Mr., uh, Cavanaugh's name and information on it?"

"You mean a business card?"

"Yeah, sure. That would do it. Thank you."

Yakoob tried, but he couldn't run in a suit to meet his wife. He was already sweating pretty badly. He was already late, and he wasn't sure whether he would ever tell anybody anything about what had just happened to him. She stood alone by the fountain in a light red jacket. He could see that Marilyn had been crying.

"How could you, Koob? How the fuck could you?" she spat in a restrained yell.

"I'm sorry, baby." He tried to hug her, but she was unhuggable. "Let's just go. We'll be all right. C'mon."

They hurried toward the train station. "Why didn't you call me? Why didn't you answer your phone?"

Only then he realized that his phone hadn't gone off. He had no answer for her. That was just bad technology or bad luck. She looked at her watch and cursed.

"We're not gonna make it, Koob. They gave me a special evening slot. The doctor goes home. We'll miss my cycle." They hurried down the street. "You know they charge you the full fee even if you miss the appointment."

He didn't know that, but he wasn't planning on missing the appointment. "Baby, don't trip. C'mon. We got like thirty-five minutes." She reminded him they had a five-block walk to the doctor's office once they got off the subway uptown. "Then let's take a cab."

"Are you sure? It's rush hour, Koob. He gotta go straight up through all that midtown traffic."

Koob was running out of ideas and dripping sweat down his tight collar. "It's cool. I'll tell him to take the FDR. We'll just shoot up the highway. And we can call the doctor and tell him we're coming."

That sounded good enough. She clenched his hand and they stood together in the street looking for a taxi. At five o'clock exactly, for reasons understandable only to them, every yellow taxicab driver in New York City changes shifts. That's why there were typically no cabs for a good while after five. Marilyn bounced on her toes impatiently as they scanned the horizon. Finally, at 5:32, they stopped a cab and got in. Marilyn did the explaining. Yakoob told the guy they had to take the FDR. The guy nodded, and they sped off.

Moving swiftly up the FDR, they held each other. Marilyn leaned her head into his upper chest and Yakoob stroked her hair. She wanted to know how it went at Fidelity.

"They bullshit in there," he mumbled. "Ain't doin' that."

"You didn't go with them?" she asked, pulling her head back to look at him. "And we're in a fucking cab late for the most important appointment of my life, but you didn't even do it?"

"Nah, baby. It's not like that. Just chill." He pointed toward the cabdriver beyond the partition. "This ain't how we talk about this. C'mon, sweetie. Later."

A few feet beyond the Thirty-fourth Street exit there was an accident. Somebody cut somebody off near the Thirty-fourth Street on-ramp. It was a mad dash familiar to Westchester commuters who took the highway each day. Get off at Thirty-fourth, race up three or four blocks, and get back on four or five cars ahead of the one you were trailing. But Yakoob didn't know that. He didn't take cabs, he wasn't thinking about Westchester commuters to Wall Street, and when he rode the FDR, it was uptown, and they called it the Harlem River Drive. The taxicab stopped. Marilyn pushed Koob's arm off of her and slid over to the window. Every few minutes, the car lurched a few feet and stopped again. Ahead of them, nothing but red taillights and the faint sound of sirens. If they'd been on a city street, they could at least have gotten out. They could have taken a train. They could have run to Madison Avenue and Eighty-first Street. But there was nowhere to go now. They were trapped in the cab, the length of the wait ticking steadily on the meter.

Marilyn handed him a slip of paper with the doctor's phone number on it. "Call him," she demanded.

Koob took out his phone, punched in the numbers, and waited. Marilyn could hear the phone ring and ring. Koob hung up and tried again. Again they weren't answering.

Marilyn stared out the window at the cobalt waves of the East River, her face stiff but her gaze drifting. A sniffle soon broke the silence. A lone tear rushed down her cheek, but she kept her eyes on that water.

Yakoob sighed hard. "It's on me, baby." He wanted to stomp somebody. He wanted to break open the car door with his elbow. But Koob always reserved any acts of heroism and physical prowess for the abstract safety of a late-night computer screen. "I'll make it up to you, Lyn. I will."

Without looking at him, she reached over, held his hand, and let out a long, angry breath. "We'll get through it, Koob. I guess this just wasn't meant to be."

He squeezed her hand, felt in his breast pocket first for the envelope with the money orders, then for Cavanaugh's card, and without another word looked the other way out the window. Dukovny, Yamaguchi, Roisman, he recited in his head. He might have to go back for the receptionist.

| 18 |

THAT TUESDAY NIGHT, by the time Sidarra arrived, Raul had already decorated the VIP lounge with his customary array of chocolate bars. She'd taken a car and gotten to the Full Count before Griff and Yakoob. Sidarra and Raul had never been alone together. When he saw her come in, he pulled up his low-hanging jeans, made sure the laces on his Tims opened just right, and rubbed his palms across the sides of his head. She wore tight beige pants with a tassel belt that bobbed around, light brown ankle boots, and a low-cut blouse made of red silk. The dull brown splotches across her arms and neck never seemed to register in his sight. Raul offered some quiet compliments on how she looked, but words were no friends of his. He wondered how she was. If she needed anything. He wanted to squeeze her but instead looked for the right place to sit down, someplace dark enough so he could just watch her play. She paused her warm-ups when she noticed him looking around awkwardly and thought about asking him if he played any pool. But before she could speak, she noticed something askew about his pants. It seemed Raul's body was having a very specific kind of blood flow. Not since high school had Sidarra seen such a public display of erection. She decided to let him find his corner and kept on shooting.

"Whaddup, G?" Yakoob asked Raul as he came through the back door, followed quickly by the sound of hands slapping hard. "Hey, Sid. Whassup, girl?" and he hugged her. Koob's tone was different. He sounded on edge and serious. Humor had left his face, like he had just come from a fight, or was headed for one. "Griff here yet? No? Good. Raul, go see if Q got some hip-hop for this motherfucker."

Raul got up and went out the curtains to investigate. It didn't matter. Whatever privileges Q was instructed to permit Raul, messing with the private stereo wasn't one of them. And Griff arrived.

There was more palm-slapping, a man hug, a Sidarra hold, a sweet schoolboy kiss, then business to do about the holiday weekend's untouched resentments. Yakoob and Griff took their cue sticks out of their cases and assembled them in unusual silence. Yakoob hardly met anyone's eyes. Sidarra knocked balls around behind him. Though he pulled a case of CDs out of his leather sack, Griff did not make his customary trip to the stereo yet. He had not shaved since they saw him at the party three days before, and through his grizzled look he seemed distracted and a bit tired. Their bodies weaved around each other as they practiced. Nobody mentioned Sid's party. Raul stepped back into the lounge for a moment and retreated to a corner again to wait until their drinks were dry.

When the table was warm, Griff picked up his CDs. "Well, I brought some nice grooves to play."

"We'll get to it, motherfucker!" Yakoob suddenly snapped at him. "You ain't the ear traffic controller in these parts. This is *my* night. Here, Raul," he said, pulling a home-mixed CD from his large velour pocket. "Tell Q to put this on. I'm not trying to feel 'nice.' We gonna hear some hard shit. Let's play."

And Whiteboy was on. Curtis Mayfield rolled into "Pusher Man" on the speakers. Yakoob shot first. "For starters, I nominate James W. Morrison," he said, chalking his cue after a powerful break. "That's the motherfucker who invented Jheri-Curls. He thought that was some funny shit. Embarrassed half my fucking family for *years.* Well, he gonna pay now." And Koob fired away, naming various family members, celebrities, and random people on the African continent as his reasons. Yakoob ignored specifics. He had entered a zone. Everyone—Sidarra, Griff, even the miscreant Raul—sat back and watched something take angry hold of Yakoob. He shot with authority and righteous exasperation, every ball going to its death with an exclamation point.

"You okay, baby?" Sidarra teased during a break after four straight games.

Yakoob smiled quickly, but neither answered nor looked at her. Instead, he vanquished the fifteenth ball in a row. The table remained his. Next was the Harlem franchise coordination executive for Popeyes Chicken, "the motherfucker who made my wife fat," Koob barked, a guy named Wainright. *Bam!* Balls separated and prostrated themselves for surrender. Nobody had ever been concerned about the health of the table before. It was a $12,000 table after all, made of the best slate, the highest-quality felt and rails, all the materials rare, handcrafted, and professional grade. Yet Koob was beating the shit out of it. And wouldn't quit.

"I'm yo mama, I'm yo daddy, I'm that nigga in the alley . . ." he sang with Curtis.

"May I cut in?" Sidarra asked, finally assuming her turn. Yakoob nodded and fell back into a stool. He looked almost hurt. He was only warming up. The lounge went through an oxygen change with someone else at the table. Sidarra nominated the woman who held the original rights to Barbie dolls because she was sick of Raquel praising blond hair. But after just five balls she missed badly.

"I got it," Yakoob said, sliding off his stool in a hurry.

"It's not your turn," Griff said, slowly hauling his weight off the stool he'd been warming for several games. Griff had been stewing quietly, constipated by an apology he was holding in.

Yakoob stopped and looked over at him with a strange fierceness. "I said I *got* it."

Griff wouldn't step away. "How's that, brother?"

Yakoob stepped back. "Oh. Well, go 'head then." He looked down at his empty glass, as distracted as disappointed. "Damn," he muttered. "I gotta pee."

"We'll wait," Sidarra said quickly as Yakoob rose to leave the room. On cue, Raul followed him out to the bar.

Sidarra locked eyes with Griff and wasted no private time getting in his face. She put her hand on his chest, never leaving his eyes. He blinked first and smiled. "All right, quiet guy," she said. "I was wondering about what happened on Sunday."

He started to put his hands on her arms, then held up. "I'm sorry about that, baby. That wasn't too cool, was it? I apologize for what you had to deal with, but—"

"I didn't actually have to deal with that, Griff," she interrupted. He looked a little confused. "She was a woman in my house. She said what she said, and I could have given her replies she could always remember me by. But I didn't. For you."

"I understand. I hear you, Sid. It's difficult for me, but it was unfair to you. The whole thing was awkward—even for her, though that's not your concern." Sidarra had to love this side of Griff, too. It was much more attractive than his scenes at the housewarming party. It was the real she was often waiting for. "These aren't small things, Sidarra. I felt exposed, you know? I was embarrassed. I've been struggling with it ever since, to tell you the truth."

The man was apologizing for his wife, which was more than she expected. In response, Sidarra got playful, doing a little dance with her body in a circle because, well, she wasn't used to these moments with a man like him, and because love may choreograph awkwardness all of a sudden. "Know how to do a Cicero Spin?" she asked.

"No," he said, staying serious and drawing her back to him. "I'm your biggest fan, Sid, really. I'd kill to keep my front-row seat just to watch you. Few times a day, I just look up and think . . ." He paused for words he couldn't find. "Anyway, I appreciated your generosity Sunday. I really did. You were gracious and"—he took her hands and looked around almost nervously—"delicious."

"I didn't cook. Q cooked."

"I'm not talking about your cooking." He kept glancing over at the curtain, expecting Koob and Raul to part it again. "You don't understand, Sid. I'm not very practiced at this." He searched her eyes. Apparently the apology was only the start. Griff had something he didn't know how to share with her. "I found you in a blind spot, baby. It never occurred to me to look for you before."

They almost kissed. Sidarra stepped into him, but she too could feel the curtains about to open again. "Let me show you my uncle's patented spin."

Yakoob snatched the curtains back and stepped through with his crease-eyed chaperone in tow. His music choices still played defiantly overhead as he sat down with his drink and waited for Griff to nominate. Raul, enjoying special privileges on account of Koob tonight, remained in cahoots with Koob's mood. And Griff, showing none of his confident body language, stepped unassumingly to the head for the break. It was as though Yakoob's play (or Sidarra's face) had drained all the game from him.

"All right," Griff began, stepping to the break and sizing the maroon felt before him, "here's one. That talk show host who raises his ratings by blaming family assistance programs for high taxes. Buford O'Toole." Griff leaned down to shoot. He aimed and fired from a strange angle. While the cue ball raced stupidly around the table, most of the balls remained unmoved in the center. "Okay," Griff said with mild resignation as he moved toward a seat. "Do your thing, O'Toole."

Yakoob was back up at the table, and the hunger in his eyes returned. On cue, classic Rakim rapped overhead against Eric B's shuffling beat, "*Thinking of a master plan/Cuz ain't nuthin but sweat inside my hand . . .*"

"This is a Fidelity Investments joint," Koob declared. "I nominate a dude named Cavanaugh." He proceeded to take out a very certain rage on the break. The shots ricocheted so violently it made the others twitch. Again, the reasons were not detailed. Koob was simply blowing his nominee away in rapid succession, one ball at a time. He would mutter reasons in passing—"by-appointment-only for new accounts, but no fuckin' sign sayin' so." The crew learned only that their friend was humiliated while trying to give an investment house his money. Yet Koob's own good shooting form was feeling good to him. His bad mood could be tempered by a private satisfaction he found in the precision with which each shot was executed. It took him nine shots to drop fifteen balls.

"Todd Dukovny," he declared next.

"Who's that?" Griff asked.

"Fidelity customer," Koob answered without looking up.

For the next twelve or thirteen balls, Sidarra began to wonder if playing mad was a good investment strategy.

"Somebody Yamaguchi," Yakoob said as he stood before yet another break. "I'll get the rest of his name once I'm in." He broke powerfully and lined up to start shooting.

"Who's that?" Griff asked again.

"'Nother customer there. 'Nother motherfucker made me wait."

Griff shook his head slightly. "How many motherfuckers were ahead of you, baby?"

Koob looked up finally. The whites of his eyes held a bitter redness, and his gaze was cold. "These aren't the people that was ahead of me. These are the motherfuckers who made me wait."

Griff and Sidarra sat back and watched Koob dispatch Mr. Yamaguchi. They worried the same thing as the next game went on to Andrea Roisman. It seemed too personal, so personal they didn't quite know what to say about it. Whiteboy had rarely been used to handle very personal scores. When Koob dropped the last ball on his nominee, Ms. Roisman, he looked up.

"I'll have to get the receptionist's name when I go back there."

"Why would you go back there?" Sidarra asked.

"To get her name."

"Maybe Raul should get her name for you," Griff suggested. "Sidarra's right. People remember angry people, and these people pissed you off." Yakoob seemed to think about it. "I mean, from the sound of it," Griff continued, "you're really planning a fucking bank heist."

"Nah," Koob answered, his tone still strangely flat and lifeless, "not really. Cavanaugh's the bank. He's gonna rob his own people, and we're gonna walk off with their shit. The bank's gonna insure it, then these people are gonna fuck him up; he gonna lose his job and Fidelity Bank is gonna start losing customers. At least new ones. I just gotta get in."

Sidarra squinted her eyes, cocked her neck back, and said, "Whoa! That's like biblical-caliber vengeance, baby. Can you do that?"

Yakoob said nothing, but kept shooting at idle balls. "Sid, that's basically what I been doin', right? Robbin' banks. This is just a little better. The banker robs the bank."

The comment slightly lifted Griff's funk. "But you gotta become the banker, right?" he asked. "He's not just gonna start jacking customers out of midlife greed."

"Sho nuff. So I gotta get in," Koob agreed, "the right way."

"Koob, try, baby," Griff said delicately, "try not to let style rule you on this one, okay? I mean, your shit is on fire. You shot a fuckin' masterpiece in here tonight. The man really needs a straight ass-kickin'."

"What are you tryin' to say?" Koob asked, turning to face Griff.

"I think he's asking why you don't just rob the bank the way you've been doing it, Koob?" Sidarra shot. "Why get fancy now? Keep it simple."

"Just 'cause you *can* paint a masterpiece doesn't mean you *should*. That's all I'm saying," Griff added. "There's a certain elegance to stick figures sometimes, ya dig?"

Yakoob chalked his cue excessively. Griff had no real idea how he felt. "A'ight," Koob conceded. "I won't expose myself. I'm gonna try to go in as this bitch motherfuckin' Cavanaugh if I can, but I won't expose myself. I'll figure these ofays out. Don't trip."

The itch that had started to burn down Sidarra's lower back cooled somewhat.

These were more moods than Raul could handle right away, and he looked confused as he stood with a fresh tray of drinks beholding the sudden peace. He sat them down and watched the billiard balls zip back and forth. Then Raul raised his voice above the music.

"Yo, I got a question." All eyes turned on him as if the sofa had suddenly spoken up. "What is it? Y'all hate white folks up in here? Is that what this is about?" It was his eureka moment.

The three looked at each other, all of them wondering who let Raul stay in the room too long. "What kind of question is that?" Sidarra asked him.

"Nah, brother," Griff said without looking up. The song "Purple Haze" came on overhead. "We teach tolerance in here."

But Koob wouldn't have it. He stepped into the darkness and right into Raul's face. "The fuck is the matter with you?" he whispered angrily. "What? Who are *you* now, motherfucker? Ted Koppel?" His eyes squinted sharply and he looked like he was about to slap the assassin. "You supposed to be in Attica, right? You couldn't hate a honky in Attica if you wanted to up there. Now please let me handle my business, and you handle yours, all right?" Jimi Hendrix's music, feedback over lyrics, wailed in the background. "Griff," Yakoob said, turning deadpan to him, "what *is* that shit?"

Matter-of-factly, yet a little unsure he wanted to say it in front of Raul, Griff stated, "It's a rare song about the approach of a male orgasm."

Koob's expression didn't change. "How 'bout you give us a fucking break on the acid trip?"

Griff nodded and headed out of the curtains to change the CD. Sidarra stepped toward the chastened hard-on sitting in the darkness.

"Look, baby," she told him gently but firmly, "nobody's hating in here. We're just borrowing from those who took from us, and that's really about it. You doin' a good job, Raul. Just stay good, my love. And stay quiet, okay? We got you."

Raul straightened up like she had just sung "Happy Birthday" to him. "It's all you, Miss Sidarra," he said with pride.

But Yakoob thought Raul was better off gone and had sent him out the back door by the time Griff returned to the lounge.

"Um," Sidarra began, "*I* have a question." The occasion of Raul's early departure was her cue to raise a concern that had first started to bother her around the time Griff finally told her about Koob's sick bet on Eagleton's death. "How are we paying the roughneck?"

Yakoob and Griff immediately looked at each other. "Salary—" Griff said.

"Small percentage commission," said Yakoob at almost the same time.

"What?" she asked. "Which one?"

"I meant that he always gets something to live on," Griff explained, but it wasn't smooth. "Sometimes we treat him as an expense. Sometimes he just gets a dividend."

"That's some tricky shit," she said, leaning her cue against the wall and turning to face them.

"What I meant was he's got to get something on each take," Koob tried to say, his old demeanor returning. "He gotta get a salary 'cause he's still doin' a lot of everyday shit like little jobs, investigating shit, getting descriptions—"

"Of what?" she asked, hands on her hips.

Koob tried a glance at Griff, but Griff knew better than to look back at him. "You know, places," Koob answered. "Whether a company exists. Whether a guy got what his account statement says he got. You know, motherfuckers say one thing on paper and got a whole 'nother thing for real."

"Uh-huh," she said.

"Sid, if he do a real peep, like he just got through doing for us with the Solutions account thing you wanted, he should get a small cut," Koob said a little more convincingly. "A percentage. Don't you think?"

"You were gonna tell me about that, right?" Sidarra asked, hands still fastened to her her hips. "I mean, just what the hell is that?"

"Be cool, Sid. You just asked how the nigga gets paid," Koob assured her.

"Does he know he'll get a cut?"

Koob again looked at Griff and would not answer until Griff finally looked back at him. There was no hiding the conversations behind her back now.

"Yeah. We told him," Griff answered.

" 'We,' " she declared. " *'We'* told him? I never told him a damn thing."

"That's on me," Griff said. He was abusing his authority with her, and they both knew it. That's the thing about attraction. It sits in the background of conversations that should take place and allows them not to happen. "I was supposed to ask you at your party Sunday, but I, uh, obviously didn't get the chance."

Then the new and improving Sidarra, directed by attraction, did a strange thing with the revelation of being left out: she let it go. Sidarra found *herself* changing the subject and talked on and on about her job at the Board of Miseducation. She updated them on every last part of the new chancellor search, candidates from big-city school districts around the country turning New York down, and how her favorite was the long shot, a black woman named Dr. Grace Blackwell from Gary, Indiana. Sidarra went on about the old chancellor. His widow was in the news. Had they seen it? Just shakes of the head. Attraction seemed to want the evening to end on a pleasant note.

| 19 |

EVEN IF SIDARRA SHOULD HAVE KNOWN BEFOREHAND, there was no mistaking it once Michael received her two gift-wrapped peace offerings: Michael was a person who'd gone giftless for many years. She handed him the boxes and his eyes lit up with pure joy behind his glasses. The skin on his neck inched back suddenly, and he couldn't stop smiling. Michael didn't know he was being bought, yet he was happily sold. In one box was a Cartier watch with the smallest diamond on the tip of each hand. It was hardly the top of their line, but it was more watch than Michael had ever owned. In the other box was a pair of matching cuff links. The set was a closeout package, but Michael could have cared less.

"I think I forgot one of your birthdays along the way," she told him.

Michael stammered in speechlessness and kept staring in disbelief at the gifts. "I don't know what to say, darling. Thank you. Thank you so much."

"You like?"

"I love 'em."

Michael loved them so much that he wore them all the time. For a man who didn't own a shirt with proper cuffs, this was no small feat. He found a way to attach the cuff links to regular shirtsleeves. For a token booth vendor in New York City, he was the lone guy in a system of hundreds who wore cuff links to work. People noticed too, usually women his age and older. They would watch him counting their money and dishing their tokens and occasionally say into the thick bulletproof glass, "Nice cuff links." Unfortunately, he often couldn't hear them. The millennium was near, but New York City had not yet figured out how to make exchanges between subway riders and token booth vendors audible through the partition. The vendors had a microphone they could use when it suited them, but customers would have to yell things. So they did. "Nice cuffs!" Then, all the way down the platform and sometimes over the roar of arriving trains, you could hear Michael's proud voice boom over the loudspeaker: "Thank you, my dear. Thank you very much."

Of course, it wasn't Michael's birthday. It was more like Sidarra's guilt about a relationship that was paralyzed by her infatuation with a married man and Michael's inability to do anything to change that. It was also a calculated setup to get a ride out to the Short Hills Mall in New Jersey, because Michael had a car and no place else to be on a Saturday. They had never gone there before, but Sidarra had heard from enough people that it was Jersey's version of Fifth Avenue. Raquel rode along too. After weeks of constant pestering, Raquel had won out in her quest to have her mother see more of Michael. They all had a date with McDonald's, she said, and other things to go over. Unfortunately, Sidarra and Michael had very little to say to each other. So on the drive across the George Washington Bridge and down the turnpike, they did what people do who are at a loss for words and scenery. They talked about other people and passing cars.

"That man looks like my brother Alex," Sidarra said, pointing into a white sedan. "I heard from Alex the other day," Sidarra said.

"Oh yeah? How's he doin'?"

"Fine. He's very happy about the schools his kids attend. Says they're really good out there. You know his girls are nine, eleven, and fourteen."

"No, I didn't know that. This is the brother in New Mexico?"

"One of them. He and Charles both live there. Charles doesn't have kids. He's not married. Charles and I don't really speak. Alex and I don't talk very often either."

Silence ate up the turnpike again. "That's family for you," Michael finally added. "You don't get to pick 'em."

"True enough." She stared at the lanes of cars ahead of them. "But we had a nice talk. It was good to catch up a bit."

"I bet."

Suddenly Sidarra saw a sleek gold car with a wide chrome grille come up beside them on the passenger side. "What is that, Michael? I think that's the one. What kind of car is that?"

Michael glanced over and immediately laughed. "That's a Mercedes, baby. Want me to get you one?"

Sidarra couldn't take her eyes off it. Raquel pressed her face against the back window to see it better. "Yes, I do. That's the one Alex was telling me about. He said it's a good car."

Michael's face scrunched up a bit. "No question about that. What? You need a car now?"

"I was thinking about it."

"Great!" Raquel squealed from behind them. "Let's get a car, Mommy! That's a great idea."

"Grandpa always wanted a Mercedes, Raquel. That was my daddy's favorite."

"Not this again," Michael sighed. "Where you gonna park a Mercedes where you live? On the street? Ha!"

"Wherever my father would have parked it," she shot back.

"You know how much that car costs? You can't even drive, can you, Sidarra?"

She was barely listening, fascinated as she was by the lines and the slope of the windows. She imagined a debonair Roxbury Parish behind the wheel on his way to the rich people's mall with his wife and daughter and granddaughter beside him. "What are those little things on the headlights?"

Michael begrudgingly craned his neck to the side so he could see out the passenger side. "Tiny windshield wipers, Sidarra." He added a short breath between each word for emphasis, then repeated it. "Windshield wipers. On the goddamned headlights. Wonder what the rest of us will do without a set of those."

Sidarra remained transfixed by the car. "I would want mine in blue," she said.

"Light blue," Raquel chirped.

Michael shook his head, hit the accelerator, and sped away.

SIDARRA AND RAQUEL SHARED A MOTHER-DAUGHTER FACT neither one said aloud: they were not in New York anymore. This place was different. Michael had his own fact to keep quiet: he was getting as lost as could be. Apparently the State of New Jersey wished to keep the exact location of the Short Hills Mall a secret. The signs on the highway—those that existed at all—came up in a bunch and informed him that an exit he needed or a "route" he should take was about ten feet ahead. He missed several. He was always in the wrong lane when the roadway forked or the exit-only lane appeared on the left instead of the right. As Michael cursed the state, its governor, and every other driver on the road, Sidarra and Raquel quietly took in the houses and scenery of another land.

When they finally parked in a lot at the mall, they immediately discovered that the people in this world also celebrated Christmas. But it felt to Sidarra and her daughter like a different Christmas—not their Christmas—they were visiting. The people of Short Hills spared no holiday expense. The mall glimmered with decorations. All the Christmas trees were perfectly trimmed and lit up two shades above a sparkle. The ceilings were bright, the floors shiny and clean, and holiday music played not from speakers but from live quartets of classical musicians sprinkled at various points across the corridors. Raquel had never seen carolers before. There was Fendi, Neiman Marcus, Gucci, and every other store you could want. You felt so good about being there that you wanted to spend every cent of someone else's money.

Sidarra made a mental map of the stores she intended to get to. Some she could do with Raquel and Michael, but for others she'd have to find a way to lose them. For that she'd also need to map their stopping points—an arcade, a Santa line, the food court where the McDonald's was.

"You guys hungry?" she asked. "You're not supposed to shop on an empty stomach, you know?"

"Why not?" Raquel asked.

Sidarra wasn't actually sure. She herself often shopped hungry. "I think it's because hunger makes you stupid and irritable. Suppose you're in a dressing room trying on some clothes you're not sure fit right. How are you gonna be able to make the right decision if you can't think straight and start getting mad at the pair of pants?"

Raquel thought about it for a second. "Is that really true, Mom?"

"For some people it is."

"*I'm* sure as hell hungry," Michael grumbled, still fighting mad about the roads of New Jersey. "And I know straight where we're going—right, Rock?"

"I know too," she smiled.

So Sidarra was able to leave them over McDonald's Happy Meals. She said she just wanted to go back to a window and look at a bag she passed. There was in fact more than one bag. Sidarra's alias bought three, but Sidarra was the one who had to carry them back to McDonald's. And she'd have to come up with an explanatory lie for Michael.

"Can I have this delivered?" she asked the Fendi cashier.

"Of course. Would you like it gift-wrapped as well?"

Pleased with her own quick thinking, Sidarra grinned. "Yeah. Yeah, why don't we do that?" She promptly had the bags sent to her job at the Board of Miseducation. Then she went back to another couple of stores and did the same thing. When she returned to Michael and Sidarra, she was empty-handed; they were fat, full of French fries, and giggling hard. After an hour or so of family shopping, she dropped them again in the kiddie arcade and ran off to pick up a couple of outfits at Chanel. Fourteen quarters of video games later and Sidarra was back with them, not a bag in sight.

The alias could be a strange thing for the old Sidarra, a quiet shopping companion who never said no to the costumes of confidence the new Sidarra wore all the time now. It had become a habit she could now afford to break. If she wanted to come back to the Short Hills Mall, her alias would have to stay home next time. And Sidarra wanted to come back—even if she had to drive herself. She wanted to be the same woman out in the world that she was in the lounge at the Full Count. She also wanted Raquel to see her mother handle her business without having to hide her fear that somebody with a badge might someday tap her on the shoulder. This way of life could not become a way for life, she thought, as they walked toward a Nine West shoe store. It couldn't last forever.

"Hey, Mommy, wanna pretend we're poor?" Raquel said loud enough for half the people in the store to turn around.

"That's not funny," Sidarra snapped in a sharp whisper.

"What?" Raquel wondered loudly. Fortunately, Michael didn't do women's shoes and stayed outside with the latte they hoped would keep him and the fun going longer.

"Lower your voice, Raquel, and stop playing!" Sidarra stared firmly into her daughter's eyes, but Raquel just looked confused. "When I whisper to you, you don't keep talking loudly, okay?" Raquel nodded sheepishly. "Now, we're not playing that game anymore."

Raquel was obviously embarrassed. She glanced around at the strange people from New Jersey looking at her so curiously, and she obediently sat down to make herself disappear. She didn't know what her mother was so mad about. They were in a shoe store. Didn't she remember the game? For her part, Sidarra paid more attention to the scene they made than to Raquel. She smiled one of those you-know-kids smiles to whoever would take it and pretended to take great interest in a pair of burgundy boots. Raquel withdrew. When Sidarra pointed out that they happened to have a small children's shoe section, Raquel politely shook her head and went back to waving her legs under the bench.

"Well, sweetie, how 'bout you help Mommy pick out something?"

Raquel shrugged. This was quiet resistance, a late-blooming insolence Sidarra figured Raquel must have picked up in private school. To things she once got excited about doing, she now showed indifference. It was a tough tactic.

"Hey, Raquel. If these boots were a new car, what color should they be?"

That did it. Eyes widened. Interest returned. And the two embarked on a short search for sensible shoes. When Michael appeared in the doorway, a man-sized presence reeking of coffee, they knew it was time to go.

At the cashier, Sidarra reached in her purse for her alias. Raquel's face was unusually close, and she watched her mother fiddle for her wallet. Her scrutiny threw Sidarra off. Maybe it was the Payless ShoeSource episode coming back to mind, and she wasn't convinced that their poverty was past. Maybe it was the fear of going to jail in New Jersey where her New York friends would never be able to find her again. Whatever it was, Sidarra couldn't bring herself to pay with the alias. There were boxes of shoes on the counter, four for Sidarra and one for Raquel.

"They're all comfortable. How much is enough, baby?" she asked Raquel. "Two is probably just enough," she declared, and told the cashier she would not be needing the other two pairs today. With a little more confidence, Sidarra pulled a few fifty-dollar bills from her wallet and handed them to Raquel. "Handle your business, child."

Raquel beamed and took the bills from her mother's hand. "Okay!"

IT WAS EASIER FOR SIDARRA to buy the Mercedes-Benz her father never owned than it was to explain to her daughter why they weren't playing poor anymore. In fact, Sidarra could do most of the transaction over the phone, and they delivered her sky blue sedan to the brownstone a few days later. It was amazing how few questions got asked with the right size down payment. The municipal credit union was more than happy to finance the rest, and given Sidarra's new and improved credit rating, at a rate even Michael would call ridiculous. Except that Michael didn't get to call it anything. He got left out of the Mercedes loop on account of his demonstrated tendency to interfere with her happiness. It wasn't just the constant attraction to Griff; Michael couldn't keep pace with her. He couldn't follow her money. She kept having to look back over her shoulder for him. Michael was also kept from knowing what Sidarra was fast discovering about having money: every purchase is easier. People who present themselves as having money get breaks, discounts, and a friendlier path than folks who look hard-up. You pay twice for being hard-up. And you wait a lot. Sidarra couldn't have waited for that car if she'd wanted to. It arrived just in time for her to drive herself to work, inconspicuously retrieve her Short Hills "presents" from the mailroom, and drive them home again. Of course she knew how to drive. But as Raquel was too eager to point out, she just drove slowly.

"How'd you do it?" Aunt Chickie asked from her seat in the corner of the living room sofa. "You had got so fat, Sidarra."

Sidarra kept trying on the new clothes. Tonight was the first night they'd ever used the fireplace without the whole house smoking up by accident. It was also a good time to try on her new clothes. At the dining room table down at the other end of the floor, Raquel crouched over her homework and hardly moved. "I was depressed."

"For four, five years?"

Sidarra, wearing only her bra on top and a skirt, turned for a second, shot Aunt Chickie a look, and went back to adjusting a skirt. "There's a time limit? I don't think so. It started before I lost them and got much worse afterward. I'm doin' the best I can. That's all I can do."

"I'm not criticizing. I'm just remembering. Look at you now, girl. That skin allergy you complained about looks almost gone to me."

"Almost. Thanks for noticing."

"Your figure," Aunt Chickie continued, "that's what you call svelte. I didn't wanna say nothing at the time, but, Lord, Sidarra, you were fat." She finally pressed the on button on the remote control she had been holding. The large-screen TV popped on, but it was still too far away for her old eyes to see well. She squinted and sat a little forward on the couch, but it didn't seem to make much difference. "You're taking care of your own self. The only way to go. The *only* one."

"Got that right."

"That one's very nice, Sidarra. Very elegant," she pointed to the blouse. Firelight from the artificial log glowed on their brown skin.

"Yeah, I like it too."

"So you ain't ever gonna marry that Michael fella then?"

Raquel immediately put down her pencil and listened in. When she wasn't sure if she could hear over the TV, she got up and tiptoed closer to the wide doorway. Sidarra caught her in the corner of her eye.

"Baby, you should finish your homework upstairs in your room," Sidarra said. "Aunt Chickie's watching television now, and you need to concentrate."

"I'm just about finished."

"Well, go on up and finish, child," Aunt Chickie added. "We'll be here when you get it all done correctly."

They waited for her to gather her books and papers and head up the stairs.

"That's sort of the question, isn't it? But I'm pretty sure I've known the answer for a while now, Chickie. Michael's a good man. He's kind and he tries to look out for me." She stopped talking, walked quietly to the foot of the stairs in her stocking feet, and looked straight up into her daughter's eyes. "What's the matter? You got a water bug in your room, young lady?"

Busted, Raquel just nodded yes, went to her room and shut the door.

Sidarra pointed upstairs and whispered, "If anything, *she's* the reason Michael's still around. They really get along." Sidarra pulled some fishnet stockings out of a bag, looked at her aunt, and decided to put them back.

"Please do me a favor, Sidarra, and don't waste your precious time on perfection," Aunt Chickie said. "That's why I'm living downstairs and not in some fine suburban house. No offense."

Sidarra looked surprised. "I always thought it was love. I always kind of admired that about you, you know? That you'd fallen in love, been in love, and when you lost that love, you were gonna keep holding out for love."

"Same thing. But it was quite different then. I look at y'all nowadays and I'm afraid it's hard to see how any of you ever fall in love. I'm not so sure you all know what being in love is, so concerned about, what is it, 'making bank'?"

Sidarra finished tying her robe and sat down to face the fire. "Well, I'm in love," she told the flames.

"That's nice," Aunt Chickie smiled softly.

"It's taken me a while to realize it. It's not a perfect situation. But he's as much perfection as I care to know."

Aunt Chickie grew attentive. "Does he love you back?"

"Think so."

"Who is it?"

"The man at the party. Griff."

"I *knew* it!" She mashed her fist on her knee. "Yup. That's a problem. Wish I had some advice."

"That's okay. I'll work it out."

Aunt Chickie's eyes returned to the silent TV screen, but the expression on her face looked irritated. After a long pause, she opened her mouth to speak. "I'm just wondering something, Sidarra." Sidarra stopped what she was doing. "Assuming you could, what makes it okay to take this man from that woman?"

Sidarra thought for a moment and looked up at her aunt. "I deserve him," she said.

"Well, you're not the first," she sighed. "Just be careful, Sidarra, would you? People have a way of thinking the only vows to take serious are their own."

MEANWHILE, IN HIS ROOM surrounded by the crusts of peanut butter and jelly sandwiches, Yakoob confronted Fidelity Investments' firewall for the first time as a customer. It was not just that he truly wanted to go back and get Heidi's real name (Marissa Arpel). It was that, after many days of dedicated attempts, he couldn't hack past the firewall. It surprised him that he couldn't quite put himself in the mind of the bank's programmers. Yakoob had always been able to find the field that revealed the code that opened the database where the good numbers lived. But this couldn't be unveiled without a password. At least not in the time he had.

So several weeks after his successive Whiteboy runs of the Amistad, Koob found himself back at the Fidelity reception desk, his new account application filled out, sitting at George Cavanaugh's desk, angrily biting down on his own jaw. This time he carried just $1,000 in money orders, which he said he wanted to put into a Fidelity money market that he could write checks off of. And he wanted online banking. Koob was no longer afraid or intimidated or ambitious. He never thought of his mother once. Marilyn never knew about the visit. He used their home address but not his real name, and fake IDs. His poor penmanship didn't bother him enough to hide it.

Cavanaugh was not a bastard about their brief meeting. Pleasant enough, he just didn't see Yakoob as completely a man yet, it seemed, but someone in between. Koob could tell this by the low expectations from which his questions came, the busy but charitable tone talking down to him. And as he listened and occasionally answered without the slightest inflection, Koob imagined the man before him crying at his home somewhere, with his wife of a million years distraught beside him, having just gotten the final news that the bank had completed its investigation. After twenty-five years, it was firing him. That he better clear out his mahogany desk immediately and hire a lawyer, because there were probably going to be charges brought. And maybe, just maybe, this man could hang it up—his prospects of ever working for another bank, his pension, and his name—all because one day he looked out at the waiting area and mistook a black man in blue for someone who didn't matter.

20

THE FACT THAT AUNT CHICKIE'S REACTION to Sidarra's confession of love combined careful indifference with a killjoy warning was further proof that she deserved Griff. Sidarra deserved Griff because her own mother would never again react with the excitement and celebration love's arrival demands. And Sidarra would never witness the great meeting she'd always envisioned between her father and the man she'd choose as second best on earth. For the same reason, Sidarra deserved nice clothes, a great brownstone, and a healthy daughter. All of these were not conscious understandings yet. But without her mother and father's love, she discovered, her just desserts in life might never again come unconditionally. She would have to go out and find them, even take them. This too was the continuing work of grief, a kind of soul's work she could get tired of, it occurred to her, as she drove up the Henry Hudson Parkway in her sky blue Mercedes, listening to

Aretha sing for the river beside her and trying to reach the Christmas pageant at Raquel's new school on time. Sidarra deserved two chemical peels to remove the last layer of a three-month descent into disfigurement—and the dermatologist visit early that morning, too. She probably deserved the Mercedes as consolation for pityriasis rosea. She deserved Griff because it was Christmas. But all that would remain inside. There was no one left to tell about her jones. All she could think about were his hands.

ST. AUGUSTINE'S WAS AN OLD RAMBLING STONE building set on a campus that overlooked the Hudson River at the northern tip of Manhattan. By five o'clock, it was bathed in evening sunset. The school was so affluent that Raquel still qualified for a generous financial aid package; its parents were so leisurely that getting to the leafy edge of the island by five o'clock caused no problems at work. When Sidarra reached the parking lot and found a space, her Mercedes joined several others, some Lexus's, Land Rovers, and BMWs that had already arrived. She walked up the gentle, bush-lined path to the main entryway with other parents. The idyllic setting contrasted with the dry faces of serious strangers. With the exception of a few black parents and a few more Latinos, nearly everyone was white. They had name charts of the children hanging on bulletin boards outside the auditorium, and though it's hard to tell a Catholic name, very few people seemed to be Catholic. When the parents were seated and the little show began, most of the biblical references and Catholic twists seemed to sail right over the heads of the audience, including Sidarra's. This was Aunt Chickie's point about "making bank" put another way. Nowadays, you didn't need to be in love or even understand the religion behind the membership as long as being in the membership brought all the other blessings of a good life. In this case, that membership cost about $18,000 a year, depending on the grade.

Attending the religious ritual in a room that looked a lot like a church was just another deposit on your membership dues, not a sign of surrender.

Boys from the brother school across the way joined the girls for the production. Once the show started, the cuteness was suffocating. Raquel only had a part in the chorus, but the other little actors were doing their adorable best to get their lines out, be Jesus, and pretend like they knew how to be somebody from two thousand years ago. There were more chuckles than applause for the third and fourth graders. Sidarra stopped counting the other lone mothers sitting in the rows. All she could see was her daughter's bright shining teeth in her wide-open mouth singing as hard as she could.

"Mommy!" Raquel screamed when she spotted her from the edge of the stage at the end of the show. Sidarra jostled her way among the excited parents to get to her kid.

"You were wonderful!" Sidarra cooed into her ear as she held her up and kissed all over her face. "That was just great. Mommy's very proud of you."

"We didn't make any mistakes at all!" Raquel beamed as they started up the aisle holding hands. "Not one."

"Everybody was great. You all did a great job. Hey!" Sidarra suddenly called out. A little red-haired boy running full blast through the tangle of kids and parents had slammed into Raquel's back on his way to his waiting parents. If Sidarra hadn't been holding her, Raquel would have been knocked to the floor. The boy didn't even turn around. Sidarra looked down to check on Raquel, whose triumphant expression had gone crestfallen as she rubbed her shoulder. "You okay, darling?"

"Yeah. I'll be all right."

Sidarra took her by the hand and they hurriedly made their way through the crowd to the top of the aisle where the little boy was talking excitedly to his parents. Sidarra interrupted.

"Excuse me, but did you see what your child just did to my little girl?" she asked.

The parents looked at her like the intrusion she was, then at each other in momentary disbelief. "I beg your pardon," the father said with a sharp hint of irritation in his voice. "We're talking to our son right now." The mother returned to hear the story her son was recounting.

"He just ran up from behind us and knocked her down!" Sidarra continued.

Silence. The boy looked up at his parents, who were not particularly moved. "It's not my fault. She wouldn't get out of the way."

That response was good enough for his parents. The father shrugged and turned his full attention back to the boy. Raquel began to move behind her mother. "It was crowded. He was excited to see us," said the mother. Her face looked so cold. She finally glanced at Raquel. "She looks okay."

The answer to Belinda's not-so-stupid question about why an educator like Sidarra never put her child in a private school had much to do with her anticipation of moments like these. It was true she had had opportunities to put Raquel in a more challenging place with more dedicated teachers and more stimulating materials. She knew what a wasteland so many public school classrooms were. But her efforts to move Raquel before were hindered by independent school admissions requirements, money, a lack of spots in lesser but closer Catholic schools, and other things she'd never say out loud. Like dealing with wealthy white parents and the sneers on their faces. From a distance, you can imagine a lot worse than what's true. Up close all of a sudden, this was quite true.

"What's your name, boy?" Sidarra snapped down at him. Her tone stunned the child, as if he'd never heard such a sound.

"Wait just a minute—" his mother started.

"I asked you what's your name, kid? Now answer me!"

"Nicholas," he whispered, clutching his mother's leg.

"Nicholas," Sidarra said sternly, "this is my daughter Raquel. If I hear that you *ever* lay a hand on Raquel again, *I* will be back to deal with you so quickly that your parents won't have a chance to cover for your rudeness. Understand?"

Nicholas ducked out of sight behind his mother. His father jumped in. "Who the hell do you think you are to threaten my son?"

Sidarra looked fiercely into his eyes. "The same mother who will deal out some necessary parenting if he touches my daughter again. Now, don't make me ask you *your* name. Come, sweetie, let's go."

She grabbed Raquel by the hand and led her past them to the door. They did not follow as quickly as Sidarra feared they might. She and a visibly embarrassed Raquel walked back down the path through the chilly evening air. Moments later, Sidarra could hear the parents' raised voices as they argued with a school administrator.

"You shouldn't have done that, Mommy," Raquel said in a cowed voice.

"Why the hell not? That rude boy pushed you. You're not to be pushed even if I'm not around."

"But he's rich, Mom. That's Nick Mathews. He was the star of the pageant. And he's really, really rich."

Sidarra could not believe her ears. "So you think if a person's rich, he can have his way, do whatever he wants to do, push whoever he wants to push, even you?"

Raquel was quiet. The expression on her face showed she was dealing with a lot of thought traffic coming from several different directions at once. "I don't know. It depends."

Sidarra stopped them and leaned down into Raquel's face. "Take your finger out of your mouth, sugar. Listen to me. What you just said is ridiculous. There's no such thing as 'depends' when somebody is touching your body, okay? Nobody gets to do that. I don't care how rich they are. Rich doesn't mean you can hurt other people. You don't get to buy your way out of the rules. That's crazy. You just don't."

Raquel seemed only half convinced. The school administrator walked up to them quickly after finishing with the boy's family. Sidarra heard her shoes on the asphalt and looked up expecting to go another round.

"Hi," said a short, chubby woman with a kind smile and a close-cropped nun's hairdo. "I'm Miss Horn, the librarian. I don't believe we've met before." They shook hands pleasantly. "How are ya, Raquel?"

"Fine, Miss Horn," Raquel mumbled with her finger back in her mouth.

"You sang beautifully today." Miss Horn turned to Sidarra. "Her voice is so lovely, she sometimes carries the chorus. We're so glad to have her here." Sidarra was waiting for the other shoe to drop. "I just wanted to meet you in person and to apologize for Nick's roughness. We think it's unacceptable. Sometimes parents have a hard time hearing that, but I wanted to be sure to apologize to you on behalf of the school. Raquel shouldn't be distracted from her fine performance, and we're so glad you could make it up here this evening."

Sidarra wondered exactly where she was. This could not be New York City anymore. "Well, thank you for saying that, Miss Horn. We were just discussing what happened back there . . ." Sidarra didn't know what else to add. The woman kept looking up kindly at her.

After the awkward pause Miss Horn asked Sidarra, "So have you signed up Raquel for the ski trip to Vermont? It's just a few weeks away."

"Oh yeah, Mommy." Raquel's eyes brightened again. "Can I go?"

"*May* I go," Miss Horn corrected. Sidarra had obviously heard nothing about a ski trip. "I wear several hats here at St. Augustine's," Miss Horn giggled. "I'm the librarian, the new diversity coordinator, *and*, this year, I'm responsible for planning the annual ski trip. It's really great fun for the children and very well supervised." She could see unmistakable doubt crossing Sidarra's face. Miss Horn lowered her voice in case other parents could hear her. "In the past, St. Augustine's didn't offer such things. Now, it's part of our efforts to provide the same kinds of experiences that parents pay independent schools to provide. But, to be candid, since we began the trips a few years ago, our students of color—and I'm afraid we're losing more of them to tuition increases each year—well, they just don't tend to come."

"Hmm," Sidarra sighed, pretending to think about it. "Is it covered by tuition?"

"Oh no. I'm afraid not. But it's a terrific bargain at only eleven hundred dollars this year."

"How 'bout it, Mommy? I've never been skiing before," Raquel chirped.

"Well, I'll need to think about it," Sidarra lied, "but it's not likely this year."

"Oh, c'mon, Mommy!"

Sidarra looked down at Raquel's creased eyebrows. "Oh, honey," Sidarra said, "we're gonna need to go home now and take care of what's bothering your eyebrows." She turned back to Miss Horn and smiled. "It was a pleasure meeting you. You all have done a real nice job with the pageant."

Sidarra didn't want to say a word until she and Raquel had safely navigated their way out of the twist of suburban-type roads and back onto the familiar Henry Hudson Parkway.

"Raquel, I want you to listen to me. Don't ever crease up your face at me like that, not in front of other people, not anytime, understand?"

"I want to go on the ski trip," she declared.

"Wait a minute. Are you listening to me?"

"No. Not unless you sign me up for the trip." She crossed her arms over her chest.

"Uncross your arms!" she shouted. Raquel reluctantly complied. "Have you lost your mind talking to me that way? Is your hair red all of a sudden?"

Raquel thought about that one for a minute before answering. "Why not, Mom? Tell me why not. *You* bought a whole building, a car, lots of nice clothes—you buy everything. Why can't I go skiing? It doesn't make any sense. I wanna go. *You* said we were comfortable. Well, then how come we're pretending to be poor just 'cause I want to try out skiing with my friends?"

Sidarra's knuckles turned white on the steering wheel. She hit the power button on the window, waited for it to roll down, and spit outside. Then she waited for the glass to roll back up. "Now, you shut up, Raquel! You just shut your mouth until we get home."

Unfortunately for Raquel, the worst thing about a jones caged too long inside can be the nastiness it might dish out without warning.

GRIFF AND BELINDA LIVED IN A RENOVATED BROWNSTONE on Mount Morris Park, one of the first parts of Harlem to see gentrification. The building had five stories. The top two floors were rented out to tenants, while Griff and Belinda kept the first three for themselves. The parlor floor was immaculate common ground, containing the kitchen, dining room, a small study whose walls were stacked floor to ceiling with bookshelves, and a front room used almost exclusively for company. There was almost never company. In fact, the house suited the marriage well, which might have been one reason Belinda demanded they buy it. Having three floors allowed her de facto run of the third floor and its master bedroom suite. Griff mostly lived and slept on the ground floor.

With Belinda's late hours as an investment banker, they used the parlor floor for little more than spats, quarrels, and arguments. They almost never ate dinner together or breakfast. A maid came in once a week, so they didn't clean up together. Lately that had changed, as Belinda warmed to Griff's willingness and ability to bring home some real money. One night in the living room they found themselves in the awkward position of talking breezily, even laughing, and then, feeling the rare rub of horniness, almost having sex on a leather couch they once purchased for that purpose. But tonight, three simmering issues made them return to fighting form on the parlor floor.

"Look, I didn't go with you because I didn't go, Belinda," Griff said, already weary in his work slacks, socks, and unbuttoned shirt. "There's nothing more to say. Why keep going around and around with it?"

She was quick to respond. "Because if you had, (a) you would have shown some interest in my work, (b) you could have met some smart people who are *at least* your intellectual equals for a change, and (c) you might see why I'm right about letting us set up a DRIP portfolio with that hundred and fifty thousand dollars you've been sitting on. Instead, what did you do? You fucking played *pool* with those fucking people, those same fucking people *I* endured on *our* Labor Day Sunday just to please *you*!"

"Baby, I was tired. I had already tested my mind the day of your office dinner. I won an acquittal on a three-day drug trial. I was tired. That's not disrespect. Those people don't give a shit about criminal lawyers anyway. The people you work with think people who defend poor people barely made it through law school and couldn't get jobs in investment banks."

"That's not true?" She laughed. "I mean, other than you."

"That's not funny coming from the woman who tells me I don't respect *her* work." He tried to soften his gaze on her. Griff didn't want to fight. It was late, past midnight, and she was standing there fully dressed in a black designer suit. Belinda still looked great at that hour. For some reason her makeup was done, but he thought it was time she take off her shoes and have a glass of wine or something. "If I didn't respect your work and your criticisms, why am I now in a position to let a hundred and fifty G's sit till I find the right thing? I'm just not interested in Smith Barney products."

She threw out her hands. "But you would listen to *Yakoooob*?!"

"Yakoob and I have made a lot of money."

"Yakoob is a fucking comedian with a GED, for Christ sakes, Griff! Get real, you idiot!"

Somehow, as usual, he kept his voice low. "What the fuck did you just call me?"

This enraged her. "A fucking idiot!" Belinda kicked a chair so hard her hair flew wild. "Want me to spell it? Would you prefer imbecile, moron?" She watched him steam. "That's what a grown professional man is who ignores his wife's investment bank advice so that he can invest the first real money he's *ever fucking had* based on the pot-induced gee-wizardry of a high school dropout telling nigger jokes with a microphone!" Both hands hugged her hips and her mouth stayed open. "Go ahead and call me 'bitch.' It used to be your favorite word right about now, so you might as well use it."

He was close. But calling her one would be so simple, so pathetically clichéd that it wouldn't sound like anything more than weakness. Besides, until he had started making money, it was she who was calling him a bitch at least once a week. "Go fuck yourself," he said.

"I put *you* to shame."

"You should. You got more practice."

"Fuck you!" She kicked her heels off into the air across the room and started marching toward the kitchen. Halfway there, she stopped and pointed a finger at him. "Stay where you are. I'm not done with you, Griff."

Once Belinda left the room, Griff relaxed again on the couch, pulled the newspaper section he was reading back off the coffee table, and tried to read. He heard glasses and pots occasionally clanging around in the kitchen behind him. A few minutes later, Belinda was back, down to nothing but her lingerie, a delicate periwinkle combination he had never seen, with a silk thong and a mostly sheer bra. She returned with two champagne flutes and a bottle of Veuve Clicquot. She put them down, winked at him, and ran up the stairs. All as if the yelling before was just sport to her. She'd come home, picked a fight, got in a few more shots than she took, and was good to go. Which might have been more titillating when they were much younger, Griff thought as he admired her fleet body whip up the stairs. But he had never signed on to that; he just rather went along with that. It rarely aroused him. It wasn't his style of sport. Belinda was that way all day long with people, putting them in the places they needed to be.

She returned in a silk robe the color of the shallow sea and a warm smile like nothing harsh had happened lately. She strode confidently over to where Griff was lying on the couch. She slowly lowered her bottom onto the cushion near his face so that he could see and smell the thonged pouch between her legs. Then she laughed and began to pour them champagne from the bottle. This was a kind of physical power she had. Belinda was extremely comfortable with her own body. She knew it was beautiful and she adorned it beautifully, down to the lingerie she wore. Lately, as the power balance in the relationship began to shift with Griff's exploits outside the home, he noticed that she was using the occasional show of pulchritude to keep him interested, if not engaged. He suspected she was at it again.

"What's, uh, what's going on, B?" he asked.

She finished pouring. He was not yet aroused—Belinda made him too suspicious for that. But he caught a notion of her arm from underneath and wondered how something so striking could be aligned with someone so stank. She handed him a glass and sipped her own.

"I have the kind of news that will change our lives and our marriage forever. Guess where we're going?"

"I don't know," he said. "They havin' a dinner I can't get out of down at your office?"

"No. Japan."

"Japan?"

"Yup. Probably Tokyo. Maybe Osaka. I'll know Friday for sure."

"Wait a minute, B. I'm not, I mean—"

"What's wrong with the Japanese?"

"Nothing's wrong with the Japanese." He straightened up and she motioned for him to drink up. He puzzled for a moment, took a sip, and set the glass down. "When and for how long?"

"*Six* whole months, maybe seven, if we're lucky. This client is notoriously slow."

Griff's face twisted up like he'd tasted chopped liver. "Six months? Belinda, you gotta be kidding me. Why would you think I could just up and move to Japan for that long?"

Her face saddened. "Because you love me and you don't want me to run off with a wealthy Japanese investor. And because it would be fun as hell. We'd have all kinds of new experiences. We could travel all over the region. See things together we'd never get to see." She pretended to pout. "And because I have no choice, so you need to come with me, sweetheart." She kissed him gently on the forehead. "You're my geisha guy." Then she tried to slide her hand onto his cock.

"Whoa, baby, wait up," he said, scrambling to get up off the couch and face her. "I can't do that. I have a job. I have very important work to do. People count on me. I have clients in jail awaiting trial. What do you think I do all day? How—" He was so incredulous he could barely finish a thought. "How do you think my office would respond to a request like that?"

She crossed her legs, ready to play it his way. "Honestly, Griff? I think they might fire you, 'cause they're probably that stupid. But so what? Listen to me, seriously. You've been fighting the good fight, struggling for the downtrodden felons and drug dealers, for, like fifteen years? How long can you keep doing that at sixty-two thousand dollars a year when kids right out of law school are making a hundred and twenty-five thousand before bonuses? Everybody you came up with is in private practice by now, representing white-collar criminals and making serious bank. That's exactly what you should be doing. Right after you come back from a few months with me in Japan." She was truly pleased with her presentation. "How you like *that*? Baby!" She grabbed him by both cheeks and kissed him wet on the mouth.

When she was through, Griff sat back and just looked at his wife. He saw her as he had never allowed himself to see her before. After fifteen years of marriage, no kids, strong prospects, he never knew how or if the end would come. If it was to be a moment, by then he'd made so many compromises and slept through so many dreams that he wouldn't believe the moment if he saw it. The moment would probably come with death. Griff didn't really see this as the moment. He just knew he wasn't going to Japan. And even if Belinda would not go to sleep that night believing Griff's resistance to following her across the earth, she at least needed to hear why not.

He cleared his throat and his mind. "Belinda, let me confess my greatest failing to you. Somehow I have managed to convince every motherfucking man, woman, and child I have come across in the last couple of decades that I am a man. Except you. You don't know what I do, don't understand it, don't want to know. So tonight you come with all this like it's done, like it's all a matter of what you figured out on your own about *me*. And you, who's supposed to be my partner, the one who really knows me, you mistake me for a punk. Maybe bitch is a better word—you were hot on that one for a minute. Well, darling. I'm really not your bitch. People don't pretend to tell me how my life gets run." Belinda's eyes assumed a fierce defensive gaze, yet she said nothing. He kept waiting to be interrupted, but she wouldn't. So he stood up and took a few steps toward the stairwell down to the ground floor. "So, baby, I'm sorry I can't finish this good champagne with you. I appreciate the thought. But I kind of feel like I've said enough for one night, and it's late. Now that you know a little something about who I really am, I'm gonna hit the pillow. There's a young brother facing twenty-five to life in the morning and they got my name on him."

The celebration was over. And down he went.

| 21 |

FOR THE SUN, the crisp early February wind, and an appointment in the city, Sidarra wore her best. She looked forward to this day once a month when she had a morning round table meeting with the mayor's education staff at City Hall and did not technically need to report to her office in Brooklyn. She could wear what she wanted. That morning after a long shower she dried her newly toned body and suffused her naked skin with Quelques Fleurs fragrance, slipped La Perla lace over her primary attractions, and went to the wardrobe with glee. Her imaginary husband still lay in the white cotton sheets, a hazel-eyed bar of Godiva watching her from beneath the canopy. She put on a blood red Dolce & Gabbana dress that hugged her down past the knee, a pair of Jimmy Choo shoes one shade darker, a fox coat, and shades to minimize the UV and maximize the splendor. Leaning naked against the door, her imaginary husband wrapped her in a full hug, pulled back her bra for a last kiss of her breast, and hoped with his hardness that she would stay a little longer. As she stepped into the bright sun to her car at the curb, Sidarra thought she saw Tyrell approaching from the far end of the block. But when she looked directly, whoever it was had vanished quickly. Her day was her own.

The glamour ended as soon as the long meeting started. As usual, the agenda included a proposed bond offering for new school construction. As usual, yet another good idea was defeated by the end of the meeting. The only good news was that all of the mayor's choices for a permanent schools chancellor to replace Jack Eagleton had finally turned him down—all five of them. Only Dr. Grace Blackwell remained.

But really, Sidarra spent most of the meeting spacing out. She wondered how her daughter could talk like a monster disguised as an angel. She wondered how some people could talk so long at meetings and say nothing. She walked out of the building and back toward the garage where she'd parked and wondered when it was that she stopped having big ideas. There was a time when she did, and being in the palatial confines of City Hall's meeting rooms—even if she was too shy to speak—always made her hungry to retrieve them. There was a time when Sidarra thought she might be a leader, and the reminder made this day different from any she'd had in a long time.

As she pulled out of the driveway in her fabulous German cocoon, she decided there was no way she was going back to her office in Brooklyn. Maybe she should plan for her fortieth birthday. It might be fun to have a joint of some of Yakoob's bodacious smoke right about now. Or go belly-dancing. Sidarra fumbled with the stereo knobs she was still learning to use and pressed PLAY. Anita Baker's "My Funny Valentine" came on like a wish come true. She waited for the light to change at Foley Square and Worth Street, pulled out her cell phone, and started punching in the number for the dance studio in Union Square to find out the afternoon class schedule. She always kept belly-dancing gear in the trunk, just in case. It was two o'clock.

The pedestrians moved along the crosswalk in their typical blur except one, a man still leaning against the light pole. He was tall and wore a long, open cocoa brown wool coat and a dark green suit. Sidarra was momentarily stuck on him, as he was on something in his head. Daydreaming, he had not noticed that the light had changed. He stood alone looking up about halfway into the tall buildings across the street. His expression bore a combination of pain and resolution as well as an ignorance of strangers who might have caught him distracted in his private moment. Alone like that, he was purely beautiful. An innocent strength and a serious wonder came off the fine lines of his long, mature face. Sidarra blinked twice behind the steering wheel and momentarily held her breath. Just as the light changed green for her, she realized. Just when the light turned red for him, he stepped into the street. It was Griff. She honked her horn and he immediately jerked backward.

"Griff!" she called out of her window. He didn't hear her. "Griff!" she shouted ecstatically. "It's me!"

Shaken from his daze, he peered into the windshield and squinted to make out who was calling to him from behind the glare. "Sidarra?"

She leaned her head out of the open window. "Yes! Yes, it's me!" She opened the car door and stood up with one foot still on the floorboard. The row of taxis, town cars, and other hooligans behind her began slapping their horns like monkeys.

His demeanor brightened. His eyes awakened to more than the fact that he had been daydreaming dangerously at a Manhattan crosswalk. They woke to the image of her outside his thoughts. "My God. Hey! It's you. Sidarra. Hey, baby! Hey!"

She motioned urgently for him to get a grip and walk over to her. He eventually complied and stepped into her embrace. The taxi-honking be damned, she was so glad to see him. Griff grabbed her up like an adolescent boy and smooched her fat on the lips.

When it was a few moments past time to let go, she pulled back. "What do you know? My statue man. What are you doing here?"

"I work here," he said. "I'm just coming from court." He pointed up the street to the Criminal Courts Building. "Just got a continuance on a trial that was supposed to . . . What? What are *you* doing here?" His smile was so fresh he couldn't fake it.

"Well," she grinned uncontrollably, "I had a meeting with the mayor's staff like I do once a month." More taxicabs came upon them. Like a law of nature, more honking commenced.

His eyes scanned her face several times before they ventured over her clothes. "You look, baby, you look just marvelous. Can I say that? Damn, it's nice to see you. It really is. Sid, I can't think of another human being who I would rather break my legs than you almost did."

She giggled and pinched his side. "Get in, please. Where are you off to?"

He started for the passenger door. "I didn't know really. That's probably why I was so distracted. I guess I could go back to my office. I haven't eaten. I don't know. I thought I'd be at trial now, but the judge was reassigned at the last minute so we got continued till next week."

"Wanna do something?" she asked, turning to face him beside her.

"With you?" he answered. She nodded a little too happily. "Baby, in the worst way. Whatever you wanna do. I could use some hooky with you. God must be looking out for me today."

Griff sounded relieved, nearly excited except for the weight of preoccupation his eyelids couldn't hide. She watched him pass a heavy glance over his own clasped hands. That's when Sidarra realized she might not just love Griff, she *knew* him. She knew that he did not ordinarily stand dazed at intersections like that and walk out into traffic. She knew he had more inner cool than his worried hands now showed. Whatever was on his mind, whatever made him this way right now, she knew she was the one thing that could make it right.

"Let's eat, baby. Relax," she said firmly. "Whatever happened this morning, let me buy you lunch." She drove west. "The handle on the floor to your right will put the seat back for you." She heard the electric seat recline under his weight and he sighed. Sidarra found the stereo button with no problem this time. "My Funny Valentine" began again.

Several blocks later Griff realized that Sidarra was driving around in circles so that he could rest his mind. "C'mon, turn right here," he said. "Let's go to Odeon."

Located on West Broadway just up from City Hall, Odeon was a fashionable place to be seen eating if you were a reasonably high-level official in municipal government. By the time Sidarra and Griff strode in, the lunch crowd had tapered away and the place had the feel of fresh air returning. The Art Deco detail was good on the eye. The waiters were slowing down. The maître d', who knew Griff, hurried up to greet them.

"How are you, Griff?" the man with the slight accent and full mustache asked.

"How are you, Sergio?" Griff returned.

Sergio looked pleased to see him and turned a warm gaze on Sidarra. "Hello," he bowed toward Sidarra and turned back to Griff. "I have a very nice table for you and your lovely wife, Griff."

Neither of them corrected him because, it struck them privately, there was no better error. And what if they were married? The idea rushed up and hit them on the back of the neck. The world had never seen either of them that way before. It was a damned good idea. So they decided—each in their own head—to pretend to be married, to try out the feeling, until whenever their day together ended.

Once they were seated at a nice half booth on one end of the uncluttered room, their giddy elbows began to bump and they stared hard at each other. Suddenly Griff was brimming with something to say. "How much do you follow astrology?" he asked her (as if it were a sport).

Sidarra laughed and shook her head, trying to decide how much to lie. "I follow it from time to time," she answered (as if it were a debate). She followed it at least twice that much.

"Griff's wife. How nice to meet you," a waiter interrupted, and stepped forward to gently shake Sidarra's hand. "Serge told me you were here," he said in a thick accent, and smiled at Griff. "How are you, my friend?" Griff nodded and warmly took the bald man's hand. "Your husband is the whip, did you know that? This man great lawyer. Bad. Ass. Appetite killer, too. Bad for business. Believe me, I know."

Once again, neither of them disabused the man of his assumption.

Sidarra looked up into the waiter's eyes. "My guy doesn't play," she said.

"Ha ha ha ha ha!" he blurted, and pointed knowingly at Sidarra.

The waiter insisted on a complimentary bottle of red wine, Griff conceded, and the man disappeared. Then Griff eagerly returned to his point. "Well, I don't really follow astrology either, but I have seen a psychic several times over the last few years." He paused, realizing Sidarra probably didn't figure him for that. She didn't. But he could see that she was more interested in what he had to say than in why he saw a psychic. "I first went to her about eight years ago, as a gag, a favor to a friend who swears by her. At first, nothing came of it, but near the end of one session, she gave me an interesting warning. She told me I better be prepared for my Saturn return. 'Cause it was coming up." He raised his eyebrows in fun. "That's supposed to be some spooky shit if you know about Saturn returns. Do you know what a Saturn return is?" he asked.

Sidarra looked away for a second. "Vaguely," she said. "It's some kind of crossroads. A spiritual crossroads? A pure moment?"

"Almost," he smiled, glad that she'd heard of it. His voice grew lighter and full of breath. "As the psychic explained it to me, in every person's chart, Saturn returns to the same exact point in the sky every seven years. I'm not sure how long it stays. But its presence is a very powerful force, especially if we ignore it or make excuses for it. It's supposed to create a time of crisis. We're supposed to surrender to the crisis and make careful choices. It's one of those opportunities to either change course or remain stuck repeating dumb shit in your life." Then, for no obvious reason, Griff reached across the table and gently squeezed Sidarra's hand. "The truly cool thing about this notion, Sid, is that supposedly the return of Saturn coincides with the point every seven years when all the cells in your body have completely regenerated. Every single cell. It's as if you're new."

Sidarra was sitting on the edge of her seat, squeezing her legs together under the table, and with the hand Griff did not touch, twirling red wine around in her large glass every few sentences. "If nothing else, it's some very useful poetry," she finally said. "I like it. You buy it?"

"I do," he answered quickly, with an unfamiliar mischief in his smile. "A year later the psychic was right. Seven years ago I had a Saturn return—my work, my marriage, and I needed some pretty serious medical help." He moved food around his plate and finally filled his fork with salad he wouldn't lift to his mouth. "I don't think I did it right, Sid. I got help for the injury and eventually healed up. But I didn't change a thing about my work. And my marriage, the only thing we did was to buy our brownstone. Some people have a child to save a relationship. We bought a building."

Sidarra smiled into her food and looked lovingly across the table. "Now it's back?"

"Seven years later, baby. *And* I'm forty-two now. I mean six times seven, right? There's no doubt Saturn's back. And there's no doubt I've got an answer this time."

"What makes you so sure?" she asked.

Griff leaned back in his chair, took her in his eyes, and leaned his elbows forward on the table again. "Because this time it followed *me.* I was already changing when it came over me." He sighed with a gentle smile, as if he wasn't sure how much to reveal. Maybe Sidarra was wrong. Maybe she didn't know Griff as well as she thought. First the psychic thing, now shyness. Griff finally continued. He explained how playing pool again was an improvement in his life. His politics had grown stale and apathetic, but Whiteboy had changed that. "My anger's back, but I don't get as mad anymore. That's a good thing, too. You know, you can change by returning to yourself, Sidarra."

"That's true!" she said, emphatically agreeing with him by pointing in the air. "But I'm not sure how to tell you this." She caught the moment when Griff's face registered worry. "I'm pretty sure your psychic got her math wrong."

Now he looked really worried. "She did?"

"I think Saturn returns every forty-nine years, darling, not every seven." Sidarra felt bad breaking it to him. He was so sure.

Griff looked briefly crestfallen and stared down at his plate for a moment. "Wow, hundred bucks a session, she really had me going," he muttered to himself. "How 'bout the cell replacement part? That probably happens every seven years, though, don't you think?" He smiled at her.

"She couldn't be wrong twice." Sidarra smiled back. "Plus you felt it. Either way it's a comeback. You don't have to change into someone else to improve your life. A comeback is change, too."

A natural grin grew across his face. "I like that," he said, fully satisfied. "You on a comeback, sweetheart?"

"More than you know," she admitted. Sidarra started to blush.

At first he had to look away. "All right, I have another question." She waited. "How do you conceal your bounty?" Griff asked. The main course arrived.

She looked around the almost empty room. "What do you mean?" She giggled.

"Like, how do you show up at the Board of Ed in an S450 convertible and your fine vines without causing a civil service scandal?"

"Oh," she laughed, "I thought you meant something else." He'd said "bounty." She heard "beauty."

"Sidarra, I would never ask you to hide your booty."

She giggled some more. "Okay, that stuff? Well, you have to be mysterious. I have a few strategies. Like I park in different places at lots nobody I work with parks at. Sometimes I park in this neighborhood and take the subway one stop over to Brooklyn. I bring a bag of clothes to change into."

"Like a gym bag?"

"Now it's a gym bag, but that's not how it started. I was using a restaurant bathroom regularly for a while till it occurred to me I could just join a gym." She sipped her wine and thought about other strategies to tell. "Sometimes I admire other people's clothes and deliberately call them by the wrong labels. It's gotten to be a pretty exciting game. I feel like Batwoman some days. You have to remember, for years I let a lot of people I work with think I was stupid. It would take a lot to change their minds now." Griff laughed almost out of his seat. "Well, what do *you* do?" she asked, the wine taking over and her smile shining big. "What about your booty? You got pretty things to hide."

He laughed some more. "Not around here. My office is different. I'm a free agent, and the prosecutors all assume we're dirty anyway." He took a bite of his swordfish fillet. "Buying the Full Count. Nobody knows about that but you, Koob, and Q." Griff's face got serious again. "But to be honest, the person I conceal the most from is my wife. For her, it's what's on paper—she'd know in an instant—and by now there's a lot to hide, of course."

Sidarra's guard immediately went up. "How can you say that? I thought she advises you."

"That's what you thought, Sidarra? You thought I was bringing ideas from Belinda?" Griff laughed incredulously. "How 'bout that. Ye of so little faith. No, the only information I learn from Belinda I get from the things she leaves lying around. I never talk to her about investment options for me or the club. And the actual decisions"—he leaned across the table and held her eyes with his gaze—"that's just us, baby. If you've been thinking you had some secret investment-banker backup, think again. We take our own risks. We make our own gains."

It was true that occasionally Sidarra had assuaged an investment doubt with the assumption that Griff was running a lot of ideas through Belinda, who after all was a stock insider, if not an expert. Now, the realization that Griff could be so secretive at home made her uncomfortable.

"I used to be pretty jealous of you, Griff, to tell you the truth. Now, I guess I have to say I'm a bit sorry for you," she said gently. "Your home life's not so good, is it?"

He looked around, or maybe he just looked away. His eyes had some of the distance in them they had when he was being a statue man at the crosswalk. "No. If I were trying to hold on to a bad situation, I'd accept your pity. But, baby, this is the sign of a Saturn return: me. I think I've been preparing myself for a long time, and now, well," he smiled broadly at her, "luck has a way of facilitating things. Belinda's going away, Sid."

Sidarra stopped chewing her food and looked up. "What do you mean? Where's she going?"

"She's going to Japan on business. She can't say when her project will end there. She probably won't be back until the summer at least." His face was resolute, but not sad, as if he was were waiting to take his cue from Sidarra.

"Well, um, how do you feel about it?"

Griff looked at Sidarra and measured his words. "I'm pretty damn cool with it, Sid. I've never been so relieved. I'm not gonna sit here and say that everything happens for a reason, but sometimes they do."

Suddenly her body felt like it had to be someplace else, and she was taking him with her. "Please let me pay," she said, waving down the fanatical waiter.

His face looked game. "Okay, but I had something else I wanted to tell you."

"Let it wait," she advised, hurrying them into their coats. And after paying, they walked out into the crisp chill of the late afternoon street.

They walked the downtown sidewalks arm in arm and slow, a pace so slow they sometimes wobbled. The two glasses of wine each drank helped. Giggles came easy. But their long strides matched, and their hips touched as they bumped paths again and again. When they were ready to resume speaking, Griff had forgotten what he wanted to tell Sidarra. So they asked about each other's favorite secret destination: Paris, France, she said; anywhere in Belize, he said. And Sidarra told him about the charter school she was thinking about starting, leaving the Board of Miseducation to go back to teaching. They laughed at the irony of the chancellor's position being taken over by a strong black woman from outside the men's club of usual suspects. Strange that after waiting a dozen or more years for something like that, Sidarra might leave it as soon as it happened.

Yet it wasn't the talk anymore that mattered, but the temptation of an alley. The icy river, not far off, whispered privacy to them and they walked west. As they passed their reflections in Tribeca plate glass, navigated a patch of cobblestone, onstage beneath streetlamps, the city kept increasing the delight of finding themselves arm in arm at last with no meeting or pool game to go to.

They never made it to the river because a brick wall stopped them cold. "I gotta ask you something I never wanted to stoop to," Griff said. Sidarra nodded. "How have you managed to be as breathtaking and thoughtful and sexy all these years and be without a man who would stand beside you and be done?"

"Be done?" she asked, loving the hell out of Griff's wine-induced syntax.

"Yes," he said into her eyes. "Be done looking anywhere else, finished with himself as a man alone and ready to be a partner with an equal, done with all the bullshit that comes before, when a guy's not sure, and just get on with the honor of trying to be the equal to you. How'd you manage to miss that guy?"

"Well," she laughed, and closed her arm tighter around his and took a step. "First I was stupid for a long time. I kicked a lot of men to the curb on general principle. I was stupid and unnecessarily mean. Then I became sad and fat, then just chubby and sad. After that I went on to being kind of skinny sad, and, as Mr. Harrison used to say, et cetera, et cetera, et cetera." They both laughed and bent a little this way and that, but the alley wall behind her remained unmoved. "There is a man, though," Sidarra finally admitted.

"Yeah?"

"His name is Michael. He's a bit older. He cares about me a

lot. I care about him too. He's a man that should have been a friend, Griff, in a world that offered too little else to me. I mean, we all have needs. I've never been in love with him; he knows that. But we've done the best we could over a couple of years now."

Griff turned and leaned into the old brick of the Tribeca alley. "You've been a little lonely, huh?"

"But not today, baby."

And that's when they knew to lean into each other's soft, ready lips and kiss. He held her head, she palmed his neck, and their coats opened to let each other's warm bodies closer for a great long kiss against the wall. They licked and tasted the delicacy of each other's gums and tongues and teeth. It was the first best kiss of adolescence again, perfected by decades of experience. It was what you couldn't know how to feel then finally happening now. And every time words, suggestions, or declarations came to each of their minds to say, they kept kissing. In time there was no wonder. It was clear what to do next.

Making love didn't need to be like her fantasy to be better than the dream, because it was both of their hopes pent up. It was her red room with the pillows and the shrine, not a pool table in a lounge. It was a weekday afternoon, not a forbidden late night. It was Al Green singing playfully of love, not Marvin Gaye losing their minds. On the drive to Harlem, they held hands and grooved fingers. When they reached her home, they marched up the stairs with singular purpose, giggling, grabbing, and pulling each other upward by the hand. Sidarra was his simple goddess, the actual queen of his senses, and he swarmed her body with his hands, licking and teething her clothes off of her. The foreplay was all stumble, a mixed-up process of getting undressed with can't-wait passion and wet pressure points. As she nibbled his neck, Griff grew so hard, his penis much thicker and more marvelous in her hand than in her dream. Sidarra's curvaceous body rolled over and under him like an insistent tide. He lifted her into his arms and hugged her against his naked body in waves, giggling long kisses into her mouth while looking for the right place to lay her down again. He wandered over her magnificence in search of thresholds to cross. Finally he lowered her gently down onto the sofa and inhaled at the sight of beautiful lingerie she had intended for no one but herself.

"So this is what you look like the other days of the week?"

"I often look like this on Tuesdays, but you never asked to see."

He grinned mischievously. "May I?" he asked, and bent low over her pelvis.

"Do, baby. Do what you feel."

Griff lifted her lower back to him from beneath and electrified her swollen vagina with his mouth. She moaned over the sounds of "You Ought to Be with Me." Griff washed her and soaked her and bedeviled her with slow determination until they were sticky and hysterical, and she reached to pull him inside of her. Their eyes open and locked on each other, the deep meeting of their flesh overcame their breath. They held the gaze from less than an inch away as their lips slid across each other's, as she widened and as he grew. They rolled against the hilt back and forth again and again in long, then tight, then long, then harder strokes, until their flesh was fairly splashing, their mouths wide open for air, legs shaking and rocking to the frenzy of one full-body scream. Sidarra had just come a second time when Griff let go all his might within her. And they were spent.

Sidarra absorbed Griff's loving weight atop her body and listened to new songs play. Her eyes scanned the ceiling and traced the last lines of sunrays seeking the red walls. She held his butt cheeks until they stopped trembling against her. They lay filled up and tired. The truth felt like love, and she didn't dare live to see this truth reduced little by little to rumor someday. Her body decided to never let this man go. Her fingernails gently crisscrossed the muscles on his back, her eyes stuck on heaven. She refused to calculate. She didn't care to reason. Aunt Chickie was plain wrong about love, but still, for Sidarra, to hear Griff say something now would mean the devastating power of simultaneous orgasms was no accident. She couldn't wait to know.

She didn't have to. As if he anticipated her question, Griff pulled his arms up so he could look back into her eyes, grind his torso a touch deeper inside her, and lay a kiss on the moist tip of her noise. "I want you to be clear about something, Sidarra," he declared just above her face. "It's what I meant to tell you when you interrupted me to leave Odeon."

What? her eyes said.

"I love you. I've loved you for a long time. That may not sit right with you. I'm not playing the angles here, though I know there are some. Feel that?"

Griff nudged his penis slightly inside her walls. It was still as hard as if he had never come. "I like that," she said. "What *is* that?"

"My body backing up my words."

"Okay," she purred, and searched for her reflection in his eyes. "Okay, but tell me one more time."

GRIFF STAYED INTO THE EARLY EVENING with Sidarra upstairs on the third floor, walking naked together around the space and lounging to music in each other's arms. Raquel had lacrosse practice—Sidarra's concession to the skiing episode—and Aunt Chickie remained on the ground floor doing whatever she did down there. Sidarra lay back freely on a corner of the sofa and watched Griff wander across the things in the room. He stopped at her work area and took a step up the short platform.

"Koob wasn't kidding," he said, pointing to the computer. "You never use your computer, do you?"

Sidarra closed her legs as if she were a bit embarrassed. "Not often. I mean, I use it to keep track of a few things, you know, basically word processing. But I don't really know how to go online or anything. I'm gonna get around to e-mail one of these days. I really am." Sidarra thought to herself, But I can remember the Control-86 Transfer Command, as if that meant something.

Griff chuckled quietly and continued walking the room. "The view is nice from here," he said, pulling a drape back from the window and looking out.

She savored the long brown wing of his hard body as it became a silhouette in the remaining sunlight. "I'm sure my neighbors think so too."

He stopped, forgetting that he was probably visible from the street. "No, I mean up here you're just above the roofs of the buildings across the street. You can see for miles." His eyes continued to scan. Then they prowled the street, roaming back and forth until something to the left caught his eye. Griff squinted to be sure. Then he pulled back from the window and closed the drapes together. "We have a little problem," he said with a whole new expression on his face.

"What's the matter?"

Griff saw Raul leaning against a gate down the block, completely inattentive to the cold. "I'm hoping it's just a guardian angel," he said. "But we gonna find out." Griff peered through a crack for another moment, thought, He's trouble, to himself, and turned back into the room.

| 22 |

FOR RAUL, being dangerous had not always been such a wonderful thing, but the choice was made for him very early in his life. Yakoob was among the few who could remember that Raul once had a smile, which he wore like a uniform beside his dad back in the time of salsa and Harlem River fishing. Benny's boy was sweet, with an almost pretty face, and a squat, premuscular frame. Not just his father's favorite child, but a beloved sidekick to all those who, like Koob, saw them coming back together, tackle box and rods in hand, from a Sunday sunrise on the pier, or heard Raul's ready six-year-old giggle from behind the bulletproof glass and over the boom box playing EI Gran Combo. Benny went through a lot of jobs but liked to sell tré, nickel, and dime bags of Mexican skunkweed out of a small storefront on Third Avenue. The dark place always smelled of fried food, cheeba, and aged cat piss. Back there behind the partition, eating tinfoil plates of *chichirrón de pollo* with rice and beans next to his daddy, was Raul, usually being admonished to keep his sticky fingers off the merchandise, or hugged. He was one of those boys who, like young dogs, wanted to be hugged often; Benny had been the same way. One day, the music, the hugging, and the smiling ended when Benny stepped out from behind the bulletproof glass to deal with a loud customer and got shot in the face. Raul happened to be the only other person back there, alone to watch his *papi* die. He didn't know what to do.

Neither did his face. Sometimes a look won't take because the look can't set, and what happened to Benny removed from Raul's young face the possibility of any foreseeable smiles. Instead, the pup that loved hugging assumed the cool pose of a very mean dog. Now, in that part of Spanish Harlem at that time, once the boy leaves your face you better look sullen or be looking for a gay way downtown. Boys seldom showed their teeth after age eleven; Koob was excused because he was funny. But Raul took it to the level of a rare few—young guys who had a lot of need, little to say, and felt physical pain many days after other guys did. He *never* showed his teeth, even when he talked. Guys as old as his father, like Koob, knew that that made Raul especially dangerous. And eventually, usually after a spectacular act of heart or evil, guys like him left the block for prison.

There was the time as a twelve-year-old when Raul stood outside the Martinez bodega watching drug dealers play dominoes on one side while a game of chess was under way on the other. Koob was there, drinking malta beside Manny, a sometimes junkie dealing crack in the days when people still called it "base." Manny was winning the dominoes game; across from him was his smack dealer, Hector, who was losing badly to a good customer. Hector hesitated on a move and miscounted.

"Ho, siit [Oh, shit]," Raul said aloud to himself, publicly emphasizing just how bad Hector had fucked up.

"What?" Hector spat, turning around in disbelief to see the kid with dead eyes mocking his game. "Shut the fuck up, little nigga!" he said. "And get the fuck outta here." He pointed for Raul to walk away. The other men laughed in the shade and glanced back at the rickety card table where the game was played. Raul turned and looked over at the chess game for a moment, but he didn't move. "Yo, you hear what I said?" Hector repeated. Everyone knew Hector was always strapped. "I will fuck your little ass up."

From his fold-up chair, Hector stared over at Raul. Raul took a breath and stared back. The man was at least thirty. In those days, everybody spat a lot, especially in the summertime, but for men spitting was always the thing to do. Hector spat almost as an afterthought, or as a prelude to some more emphatic gesture. The gob fell near Raul's imitation Nikes that his moms bought him on Fordham Road in the Bronx. Raul looked down at the spit on the sidewalk, and before it could register with anyone else, he spat back and caught Hector on the shoe. The corner, a cross-generational jury at least eleven men deep, stiffened with shock. Hector broke wild, forgetting it was a kid who spat on him, and pulled a pistol from inside his jacket. He wasn't gonna shoot Raul just like that. He was gonna beat his face and his neck with the handle a few times, make him bleed and cry and eat shit instead of dying. Hector stood up and got in one clear blow, straight across Raul's temple. Raul's switchblade was out of his back pocket before the blood could appear, and suddenly Hector's right shoulder was cut in three places. He was very fortunate that the chess players could hold Raul back; one of them suffered a two-inch gash just for being there. Nobody died that day. But nobody forgot it, least of all Yakoob, who had to love Raul's nerve to avoid it. This was no longer a child. Benny's boy had become a dog.

Raul's grandmother didn't want a dog in the house, and she ran the apartment while his mother was at one of her three jobs. Between Spanish soap operas and Spanish game shows, she had a different idea about what the young man of the house should be doing if he wasn't going to school, like getting a job himself. She never cared for Raul's father, who she thought was an angry loser, and she resented his son for slumping around her apartment like the living monument to his failures. His grandmother only spoke Spanish. When she started with him, he would talk back only in English. That would spark long yelling fights where only he knew what they were both saying. If Raul stuck around till evening when his mother got home, he could hear his grandmother talk bad about him before getting kicked out. Back on the block he'd smolder on street corners.

Cheeba became Raul's best friend, and he ran with it wherever it would take him. Cheeba never looked wrong at him or questioned what he wasn't doing. It spoke Spanish when Raul felt like it, English when he didn't. And when cheeba hooked up with PCP, Raul could fuck and fight all night. Manny called it angel dust or Crazy Eddie. The first time he rolled some into a joint for Raul, it was like light. It clarified just what he wanted to do. It expanded the world Raul knew beyond eight square blocks of Spanish Harlem and sent him on endless subway rides. Pulsing atop a train bench, quivering inside his own skin, Raul could always get there quickly on PCP, wherever "there" was. He would ride until his body stood up and walked out the open doors. He would climb the stairs into the night, winding up in Astoria, Queens, the Lower East Side, East New York, Brooklyn, or Williamsburg, occasionally finding girls who would fuck a crazy guy, often fighting just to see the blur of blows, up for days with a crew of users he'd meet, asleep for days more someplace. Usually near the river, taunted by rats, awakened by another sunrise without his dad.

His grandmother was right: he was gonna have to find a job if he wanted to come home again. Raul only came uptown to get his dust from Manny; back around the way, he might bump into Yakoob and ask him for a couple of dollars. But mostly, working meant empty aluminum cans in the early nineties. The homeless trolled the streets like walking boysenberries, bulging with black garbage bags full of tin. You got a nickel a can, and Raul could collect some cans. You needed fifteen dollars for a Bowery bed, plus the twenty dollars a day for pizza, Puerto Rican fried chicken, orangeade soda, and cheeba unless he was hallucinating. That's a lot of cans. You had to stand around dirty while people finished lunch in midtown. You had to go into the alleys. You had to climb inside of Dumpsters. You had to kick ass just to keep what you had, and since you were kicking ass anyway, you might as well take from a motherfucker who's not trying to make bed money at all, some motherfucker sleeping in a box someplace waiting to get his cans jacked. Which was helped by being dangerous, because the fearful put up less resistance—unless they were drunk. Raul nearly had to kill a big drunk for his cans one night, and that's how he finally went to jail.

At Rikers, Raul got constitutionally clean—he dried out of his PCP addiction—and institutionally mean—he perfected his ability to hurt other men. His chiseled body stayed close to barbells as Raul sought revenge on the power he lost without PCP to guide him. Impressed by his rehab progress and attracted to his efficient violence, some of the guards let Raul smoke straight weed with them. That's how he met Blane, the pot dealer. Blane was a friend of a friend of a Rikers guard who would eventually help Raul find the raging whiteboy weed that had all but replaced the Mexican skunkweed and the dime, nickel, and tré bags it came in.

And that's where Yakoob found him in 1994 or '95, living back home in the projects, thugging on occasion, but mostly selling pretty good cheeba he got from a whiteboy on the Upper East Side. At twenty years old, Raul was master of nothing except the sound of other people's bones breaking. Yet he had a soft spot for the little black boys around the city who sold candy bars to white folks for their ghetto basketball raffles. He had a hope one day for a fine-ass woman to protect just like a queen. And though it seemed doubtful that Raul would ever enjoy another sunrise, he was grateful for an older guy like Koob, who always remembered his pops with a kind word that meant a lot. Oddly enough, shooting a whiteboy in the face on the Upper East Side had been the very catalyst he needed. And by early 1998, over a year back from his Philly makeover, Raul bought all the candy bars he could fill his pockets with, stood sentry over Sidarra much more than she knew, and had sunrise, if not sweetness, in his eyes again.

YAKOOB NEEDED HIM NOW. His Fidelity Investments bank heist had gone well in almost every predicted respect. Once he became a customer and gained a password, the firewalls came down before his tired eyes, and money began to relocate. Through a complex series of steps, Yakoob made the computer identity known as Cavanaugh withdraw $15,000 to $20,000 apiece from the popular identities known as Dukovny, Yamaguchi, and Roisman, and deposit them into Cavanaugh's own IRA. Even Marissa Arpel chipped in a few thousand. Over the space of seven to ten business days, the new money in Cavanaugh's IRA would disappear into the dummy account linked only to a fictitious company located at Koob's address. These became transactions to be proud of. Within just four months, the Cicero Club's stock investments made with the booty were worth three times the initial transfer. This time Sidarra was told.

But what Yakoob neither told Sidarra nor could even share with Griff was that, in his mind, the second half of the plan snagged and had to be finished somehow.

Yamaguchi was the first to notice the hit on his account. He had been a customer of Cavanaugh's for many years; Cavanaugh had attended Yamaguchi's daughter's wedding. Roisman demanded the investigation by the bank; Dukovny called the police. But Yamaguchi was a friend and a techie. He refused to press charges and instead hired his own investigator. Why, he wondered, would Cavanaugh withdraw stolen funds from an IRA days later? He would simply lose a third of his theft to the IRS. Besides, as a techie, Yamaguchi suspected a hacker, even if it was the first at Fidelity, and Cavanaugh was no hacker. Fidelity wasn't so sure, but the evidence was good enough to prevent them from firing Cavanaugh outright.

So Yakoob kept seeing him sitting at his desk whenever he would stop into Fidelity to check. The longer he saw Cavanaugh still in place, the angrier he got. There were days when the feeling got so bad, it seemed Koob might just be able to do what Raul could do—overcome all physical fear and launch his body into another person's. He wanted to take a crowbar to Cavanaugh's knees, smack his ass with a belt, and make him piss on himself. If he could, he would have done these things personally so that Cavanaugh was very clear about who did it and why. But that was not Koob's way. It was Raul's, however. And now that it had shown itself to be a danger he could harness, Yakoob had to admire just what his young friend could do.

| 23 |

EVERY GAME BEGETS ITS WINNERS, and every winner deserves a party to celebrate her prize, but for almost two years the Cicero Club had been quiet about its bounty. Together they had never saluted each other with gusto. Sidarra and Griff had begun to celebrate theirs a little more openly, first to Koob, then, in small but meaningful steps, to the world. Now that Belinda was in Tokyo, Sidarra held his arm when they went places together. They allowed themselves a night at the opera, downtown dinners with a nightcap of Village jazz, and they had strolled the marble halls of late nights at the Metropolitan Museum of Art. But the whole crew had never had a celebration, let alone one in the manner they could now easily afford. Sidarra's fortieth birthday finally provided occasion to get a little loud about their slow roll to mischief.

The milestone, thanks to Griff, came alive with laughter and an unusual game of Whiteboy for one perfect night. Sidarra declared the Full Count a "nigger"-free zone—the word could not be uttered—and wore the gold lamé dress. Yakoob made her open his present first, a silver tiara lined with jewels, mostly rubies, and at least one large emerald in the middle. Raul brought her a giant lavender teddy bear at least four feet high and stuffed with bags of sensimilla and various kinds of chocolate bars. Griff promised her a surprise to come later. And all was good at the Amistad until Clarence Thomas had to get mentioned.

Nobody had ever nominated a black person during a game of Whiteboy before, and both Koob and Griff sat uneasy on their stools, unable to intolerate. Sidarra rolled on, pointing out right-wing decisions the Supreme Court justice had supported. She pocketed three balls in a row off the bad sex jokes Anita Hill recalled Justice Thomas making when he was her boss. Koob and Griff remained stumped. What could they say? They couldn't mount a defense. Plus, it was her birthday. Sidarra was down to her last ball.

" 'High-tech lynching,' " she laughed. "Can you believe the words even left his mouth?" *Spop!* And the last ball made persuasion. "He should be whacked."

Q, who still managed the club Griff now owned, had closed the place down for a private party. The Whiteboy game over, Griff's birthday surprise for her was getting ready in the main room, and Sidarra proudly wore the bejeweled tiara slightly askew atop her slicked-back hair. Yakoob, however, still had something to say about the only black justice on the Supreme Court. But first he had to remind himself he was still in a "nigger"-free zone that night.

"C'mon, Sid," Koob complained, "it's your day, no doubt. There's nothing you don't deserve. But killin' a justice? A super-judge? You can't really be serious about offing the brother."

Sidarra looked up from under the pool table lights. She noticed more than birthday looks in the eyes of the men in her crew. Griff, Koob, now Raul, and even the giant teddy bear with his cheeba and chocolate guts spilling open, they were all stuck on something she couldn't figure out. She lifted her gold-lamé-covered body off the Amistad and rested her Uncle Cicero's cue stick gently against a velvet wall. Then she surveyed their faces again. It was clearly more than the birthday libation and the fine herb. Something wasn't quite right.

"Who said anything about *killing* anybody?" she asked. "I nominated Justice Thomas, who is, at the very least, a stupid fool none of y'all can find a good word for. I got persuasion. He's the next joint, and the motherfucker's accomplished a lot by humiliating black folks, so he *should* be our next joint. Remember, Koob? We do what we do to do what we gotta do." She strode slowly over to the front of the table, leaned back on it, crossed her arms, and took a careful study of each guy. "But who said he's gotta be 'offed'? Maybe a good whack on the head, but not *'offed.'*"

It was as though she had Raul's Glock on them all, the kind of stickup where each intended victim knew better than to even look at the others. So, for a minute, nobody spoke.

"Just a figure of speech, baby," Griff said coolly.

"That's what I thought," she said, stepping closer to his face.

"You right, you right," Koob tried to help out.

"Then what the hell is all the panic about?" she snapped at him. "Y'all act like nominating him or any other black man is, like, um, fratricide. That's not the game," she paused. "Let *him* be a broke nigga for a minute. It might give him some perspective. Right?"

"I thought this was a 'nigga'-free zone tonight?" Yakoob asked.

"It is," Sidarra shot back. "Birthday privilege." She checked them again with a long, sweeping look that accidentally ended with Raul. "So how tough can it be?"

Raul nearly raised his hands. His dick, never within his control in Sidarra's presence, pressed hard against his pants like it had something to confess. "Yes, ma'am," he said.

"It can be done," Griff said calmly, pretending he believed his own words and finally stealing a look at Yakoob as he sipped his Hennessy. "Nothin' but the Secret Service to worry about," he mumbled.

"All right then, fellas," she said, and relaxed a little. "Thanks for picking my birthday to act like I'm proposing some kind of racial mutiny. I mean, damn."

Yakoob tried as always to lighten things up. "Nah, baby. Don't bug out. I'm just playin' with you. It's your joint. Ease up."

The song changed around them. The mood felt sticky. They tried to play on for fun, freestyle. After a few shots, Griff led Sidarra into the dressing room for a private moment while Raul took his first-ever turn on the table.

"Please, sugar, don't let the vibe out there steal your good time. This is your night." Griff squeezed her to his body. The warm feel of his loins against her was now a reminder of private hours before and of a future neither could quite see their way to when they first met that evening in 1996. "There's more to come, baby," he said into her ear. "I told you I have a surprise for you."

Sidarra squeezed his ass to her and stared at his chest for a moment. Then she looked up. There was something more to say. "I had another birthday thought, Griff."

"What's that?"

"I think we should disband the club after this joint. After Thomas. We've made enough money. Raul's more than paid us back. Now, with you and me like this, we don't need, we don't need to keep doing things in the dark. I'm not sure it's right. The more we do, the more we run the risk . . ." She left it there.

They squeezed each other harder. Griff sighed, kissed her temple, and pulled back so he could see her whole face again. "I hadn't really thought about it, but you may be right. With Belinda gone, there's no real need in my life to, you know. So I'll think about it. I hear what you're saying. Then why Thomas?"

"I don't know, I was just reading about him the other day," she admitted. "You talk about humiliating black folks. Can you really beat this guy? And, Griff, isn't he the thug multiplier in reverse?"

"What are you talking about?"

"I mean, just 'cause he's black, all his Uncle Tom sins come down on black folks tenfold, right? He's much worse than any white guy we've taken a few bucks off of. I think a guy like that is an appropriate joint." She tried to keep a straight face for him.

"Appropriate, huh?"

"You know, equitable. Don't you think?"

"May I make a suggestion?"

"What's that?"

"I think we leave Mr. Thomas alone. That's a dangerous motherfucker, and I have a lot of experience with dangerous motherfuckers. They tend to go down on their own anyway." He searched her eyes.

Sidarra giggled into his turtleneck. During the song change, she could hear commotion coming from the pool lounge or beyond. Then it stopped, and it felt like Griff wanted to pull away.

"Wait, Griff," she said, holding him firmly. "Okay. I guess that sounds right. But I have to know something." She searched his hazel eyes again. "If there were something going on behind my back among you all, you gotta tell me now."

Griff silently held her gaze for a few seconds. Twice he looked ready to say something unexpected. Twice he restrained himself. "Of course I would. But it's a surprise, and it's just about time for you to see it for yourself. Now," he smiled broadly, "let's go see what I got you for your birthday." She started to beam with anticipation as he led her out of the dressing area. "Fellas," he said to Koob and Raul, who stepped in from just outside the maroon curtains, "now that Mr. Justice Thomas is safe again, let's show the lady what she got." Griff began to lead Sidarra toward the curtains out to the main bar. "Handkerchief, please," he said to Raul. As he reached over to hand him a black scarf, Raul gave Griff a long sideways look of pent-up menace. It was as if they had been enemies forever. Griff ignored the look and began to blindfold Sidarra. "Is everything set?" he asked Yakoob. Yakoob nodded. Sidarra could feel her heart flutter a little in her chest. "Okay, let me adjust your crown," Griff added. "All right. Gentlemen, the curtains."

And out they walked. "Surprise!!!" came the roar of about a dozen people seated under floodlights near a stage Q had set up for the night.

Griff eased the blindfold off of Sidarra's face and she scanned the scene with her mouth open wide. In the middle of the small crowd was a three-story white cake. On each table was a bottle of more Cristal on ice. Q stood proudly behind the bar along with Jeanette. On the small rented stage was a full band setup, including a drum set, piano, acoustic bass, guitar, and some horns, all flanked by a tremendous bank of speakers. In the center under a spotlight was a lone microphone on a stand.

Sidarra took in the crowd as Griff led her closer to them. There was Darrius and Justin, Yakoob's wife Marilyn, Aunt Chickie, and a tall, heavyset man Sidarra nearly couldn't make out in the low lights. She was shocked to see her aunt there, but as she approached her, the strange man stepped into her path.

"Happy birthday, Sidarra," he said, and grabbed her in a bear hug.

She couldn't believe it. "Alex?" It was her brother Alex from New Mexico and his wife Claire behind him. "Alex, how did you know? How did you get here?"

"Well, I know because you might remember I was there for the first one. How we got here is your friend Griff flew us out for the occasion. How are you, baby? You look smokin'."

Sidarra shook with happiness. She practically climbed onto her brother, hugging him so hard. "You folks don't understand," she kept saying to everyone in the room. "This is my big brother. This was my guy. I haven't seen him in . . ." And then she just went back to kissing his cheeks and holding him tight.

Alex held her in his strong arms and pulled back a little to search her face and her eyes. "There's my baby girl," he whispered. "I missed you."

Music began to play. Sidarra finally let go of her long-lost brother to ask Aunt Chickie where Raquel was if she wasn't with her.

"Michael filled in," she said. "Raquel's safe at home with him. Have a good time. Don't worry about it."

After she kissed everyone in the crowd and swallowed a few toasts, Sidarra wasn't sure how to approach the five men in dapper suits smiling a little awkwardly near the stage. "Um, Griff, do I know these cats, or are they just folks Q couldn't get out before this all started?" she whispered.

"No, sugar. You never met these guys in person, but you know something about them, I'm pretty sure. In fact," he called out, "maybe it's time they step up to the stage." The men stood up as one and bowed to Sidarra. Griff introduced each of them by name, and each kissed her hand. Then Griff climbed up the step to the stage, pulled the mike out of the stand, and said, "Sidarra, unfortunately Anita Baker was not available to sing 'Happy Birthday' with us tonight. So we got the next best thing to help us out. Ladies and gentlemen, Queen Sidarra, all the way from the Motor City, please welcome Anita Baker's band!"

Sidarra stood in a mouth-open stupor near tears while the band took their instruments onstage. Griff had to hold her to keep her knees from buckling. The horn player named Georgie seemed to be the crew's front man, and he stepped to the edge of the stage when they were all strapped in. "One, two—one, two, three, four," he counted, and the house began to sing "Happy Birthday" with a gusto (and a backup) nobody had heard in a long time. Sidarra jiggled and jumped like a prom queen, squeezing Griff's hand for support and smiling uncontrollably. Song after song, the band played, the champagne poured, the aroma of fresh pot smoke drifted in from the rear, and soon inhibitions went down like party cake. Then, with a very purposeful look and a demand for quiet, Aunt Chickie approached Sidarra.

"My darling niece," she began, "there is a reason Mr. Griff got this particular band for you tonight, you might have guessed. There's a reason your brother and his wife came all this way to see you. In case you were wondering, this is not the time to be sweet and silly and shy, okay? This is what you call a once-in-a-lifetime thing. The man here bought you a nightclub, a crowd, and the band you been singing with for more nights than I can probably remember. Here's the list, baby," she said, handing Sidarra the paper with a prearranged list of Anita Baker songs and breaking role just long enough to smile. "Do what I *know* you can do." Aunt Chickie kissed her and left her alone under the spotlight.

And Sidarra sang.

She got down like she was meant to get down. She sang from Anita's first album and she sang from her last. Sidarra sang from the bottom she had known and she sang for the top she would see. She sang past the boys who had forever looked just beyond her shy smiles. She sang sweet goodbye to Michael, and she sang for her brother as only he knew she would sing one day. She sang notes she had never quite reached before. Sidarra sang like she came from a world in which the lyrics to these songs still made good sense, like love calls from rotary phones with sympathetic operator assistance, a world in which people saved up important words for letters and paid important bills with money orders. She sang for her daughter who was not there to hear her mother take back her voice, and she sang for her parents who would never hear it again. She sang in thanks and she sang in sorrow. And she sang as if she would never get this chance again.

In the background near the bar, she could see Griff exchange long looks with Raul, then a few words from a short distance. The exchange lasted too long. She watched the man approach the boy until the boy stepped up to become a dog against him, and she kept singing while Q stepped in to end it all. Soon Raul was gone.

When the party ended late that morning and Sidarra was forty and almost a day, she realized that being a queen had never felt so good. Only Raul would never get to see that. For that night was the last time Sidarra would ever lay eyes upon him.

day they met before the brief court appearance. It was their first private conversation. "How you feeling? You scared?"

Whatever cool Tyrell used to have had been pretty well whupped out of him by Raul the night of Sidarra's Labor Day party. He was thin from drugs, his face permanently crooked, eyes bloodshot, and his leg was swelling up again. His sullen demeanor roamed between indifference and resignation. "Why should I be scared?" he whispered. " 'Cause I'm going up?"

"Nah, son," Griff answered. "That would be good news. You should be scared about trying to rob a well-connected chemist who's gonna want to make you dead wherever you go."

"Yeah? I didn't know, man," he said, looking adrift in the cramped wooden chair of the interview pen.

"You didn't know the cats you were helping?" Griff asked in mock disbelief.

"Not really. I know 'em like you know somebody in a crack house or a pool hall." There was nothing to see on the pale green walls, and Tyrell's fidgeting eyes could barely focus anyway. "I'm just hurt, man. See my leg? It don't work. I just needed drugs, that's all I wanted. Manny the only one got that crazy WeeWah dope. This shit right here don't never stop hurtin'."

Griff remained firm, but his eyes softened a little with compassion. "Then I'm afraid you're gonna have to be the nicest guy in the infirmary, Tyrell. And I don't know if you pray, but, my man, if you do, you need to pray they don't find out more about what your dead friends were really into."

"Don't even ask me, yo. I don't even know."

Griff didn't ask him what the hell WeeWah was either, because he really didn't need to know yet.

HE WORE HIS SUNDAY-BEST charcoal suit. She wore a long gold satin robe.

"How 'bout that Mike Tyson?" Sidarra asked Michael as she sat across the breakfast table from him. They had not been together the night before; they had not been together at night for a long time. But Michael had cornered her into what he called a very important brunch at her home, one he tried for weeks to have with her. Sidarra was still riding her birthday high, joking more than usual, unable to hide the acute attractiveness of a woman in love. Michael didn't know why. What explanations he had were his own concoction. The busier she became with the new life she was making, the deeper he thought their love could be. Today, while Sidarra was giddy, he was nervous. When Michael felt nervous, he wasn't funny or very interesting; his thick skin hung heavy from his face, and he just looked old. He watched her pore over the sports section as if nothing were up.

"Iron Mike back in the news?" he asked.

"Does he ever leave it?"

"I wish he'd leave me some of his money."

She glanced above the page at Michael for a second. "Me too," she said. And he'd make a worthy joint, she thought.

Lots of things about Sidarra moved Michael. He sat there reenchanted with her clear, soulful voice, how her hair pulled back that way opened her cheekbones to morning light and the full lemons of her lips. She was a mother like his had been, a friend to her daughter with a whip in her pocket. She was a civil servant, but unlike him, she must have had a plan. Michael had gotten over what that said about him. Sidarra was young; she still had the best to make of herself. Yet now the fact that she actually read the sports section, well, that's a wife. No sooner did he see his chance than Sidarra grabbed the first section of the paper from him.

"You through with that?"

"Sure, darling. Sure I am." He watched her smile and relieve him of the newspaper, not sure how he was gonna change the moment. "Nothing but awful in the world today," he added.

But the moment sure changed on its own as soon as Sidarra's eyes reached the lower right-hand corner of the front page. "You gotta be kidding me!" she exclaimed, putting a hand over her mouth. "Did you read this, Michael?"

"About that schools chancellor, Jack Eagleton?"

Oh no, Michael thought. Whatever it is was only gonna make this harder. Any other day he would want to make up for lost weekends discussing the news of the world with Sidarra, but not this one. "I glanced at it briefly," he said. "Guy's still dead, ain't he?"

"This says they think he was *murdered,* Michael." Sidarra read on with interest. Michael's heavy eyelids followed her eyeballs as they moved back and forth across the page like an old typewriter. "They did an autopsy, which raised a few questions at the time but nothing 'forensically indicative,' the medical examiner said."

"Meaning what? Natural causes?"

"That's what they thought at that time," she answered, still reading the page. "But somebody ordered an investigation, and it's been open for months. Going on almost a year now."

Michael was trying hard to care. "So what'd they find out?"

"Wait a minute," she said, squinting over the words and reaching to turn to the page where the story continued. She read on. "Nothing. They found nothing certain. But now they think they discovered a trace substance in his blood, a drug it says he was not known to take."

"But that's how it always is, isn't it? You got this fine, upstanding ofay. Rich as Rockefeller, been to all the best schools, ran a bunch of colleges, pillar of the community, skybox, first-table, black-tie guy. What happens? He's a pedophile. He's a pill-popper. Spied for the Commies. Always somethin' like that. Those guys are never what they make 'em out to be, you know, Sid?"

Sidarra had gone away in her thoughts. For a fleeting moment she was stuck in the flashback she had imagined of Eagleton's wife coming home to her husband dead on the floor. For months—

who knows how long—the woman must have lived in the shadow of his death, in his clothes-hanging idle, his saliva still staining certain glasses, his voice lingering in the air. But now somebody else was there with her. Now that Mrs. Eagleton knew he hadn't died naturally, he may not have died alone. It was all too much for Sidarra to think about right away.

"Sidarra, honey, there's something I've been thinking about. I want to tell you, but from the look on your face right now, I'm not sure this is the best time."

"What, Michael?" she snapped out of her daydream. "There's never a good time."

"Well," he started, then thought better. "I gotta say. I don't remember you having this kind of reaction when the guy died the first time."

"He was murdered!" she yelled. Her voice echoed up the high walls and surprised them both. Michael blinked hard. "I mean, he was murdered, sweetie. That's different than dropping dead. And, you know, there'll be gossip in my office now that they're investigating this. This is all anybody's gonna talk about." Her eyes dropped as she considered her next thought. "They'll probably want to talk to folks at the Board. I don't know. But that's all, Michael. I didn't mean to shout at you. That's all it is. Just shock. Now, talk to me about whatever it is you wanted to say."

There is a reason Michael had never done this before in fifty-three years of living, and this was probably it. He cleared his throat and looked at her. When the intensity of his gaze failed to match the intensity of hers, he looked away and cleared his throat again. Then he coughed.

"Want some water?" she asked.

"No, I'm all right. Well, maybe so." She handed him the glass beside his plate. He drank hard from it, slurping and spilling a little as though it were stronger than water. He looked over at her again and smiled. Then he took a deep breath and fished inside the pocket of his blazer. Whatever he took out he covered more quickly than Sidarra could see. He clasped it in his trembling hands and reached across the table to hers. "Your Aunt Chickie thought me babysitting was birthday present enough, but I knew better. Here you go, Sidarra. I hope you like it."

It was a small black box about the size of his palm. An odd feeling breezed through her, and her eyes opened wide. However, the sight of the thing did the trick he had intended, distracting her from seeing him drop down on one knee beside her. She opened it. Michael scooted closer to her lap.

"Michael!" she gasped.

"Look, I know it's nothing compared to what you can do for yourself these days. But I promise there's more where that came from. In my heart, I mean."

"Oh, Michael." She stared for a while at the delicate gold ring afloat in a blue velvet pond. The stone was no more than half a carat, but it had its brilliant little eye on her. No diamond had ever looked at her that way.

"Listen, Sid." His eyes nearly shut with sincerity. His lips still trembled slightly. "I know I haven't been the best guy to you all the time. I've been stubborn sometimes, and I know you think I was trying to hold you back. But I wasn't. I was learning. I was trying to learn from you, but I couldn't always keep up with you, to tell you the truth. Now, I realize that's not the best recipe. But folks do stranger things in this world. I know. I've been in it a bit longer than you. And I already know I'm not the prettiest man and that sometimes you might want that. I could be a lot smarter. But the thing I got on a lot of fellas is how you'll never wonder if I'm there when you turn around. I got your back, woman. I wanna be there all the time. You mean the world to me, Sidarra. I would do anything if you say you'll be my wife, darling. Please?"

"Oh, Michael," she repeated. Sidarra really didn't know what to say. There are songs for moods like this, but few words she could muster. She passed her eyes lovingly over his face and down his bent frame. Michael looked so gentle and gallant and pure just then. She smiled and leaned down to kiss him softly on the edge of his lips. He closed his eyes. She lifted herself away a little, and her gaze returned to the ring shining up into the late morning light. "I wish I knew what to say. I know I want to say thank you. I know I want to disagree with a lot of the things you just told me, but now I can't remember them all. You're a lovely man. You've been a prince to Raquel. She loves you. I love you." He waited and waded through her words, hoping to reach the other side with her. "I don't know what to say."

"Say you will, Sidarra. It's easier than you think. People grow old saying other things, baby."

"I can't."

He paused. "Then don't. Don't say nothing now. Think about it. Don't tell me today. I've made you wait almost four years. I can wait. We're not going anyplace, right?" She nodded. He paused again. "Would you at least do me the favor of trying it on?"

"Why, Michael?"

"Why?" He scratched his head. "Well, because for one thing it might not fit and I've been dying to know."

She looked at the tempting jewel glistening against the dark background. Sidarra wanted to free it from the box and see it cover her finger, but that might turn a long-held fantasy of hers into the start of a true story for him. "I'm not sure I can do that just yet, Michael. That doesn't feel like the right thing to do now."

He sat back over his heels on the kitchen floor, a little crestfallen but ready to be mature about it. Michael clasped his hands together and rested them on his lap. "You call it, Sid. I respect whatever you want to do."

| 25 |

THEY HAD TO GET AWAY TOGETHER. While Michael waited for Sidarra's answer, somebody else would have to look after Raquel. Sidarra had never been more than an hour away from her baby, let alone in another country. Aunt Chickie was fast becoming the master of the house and, offended by the notion that she couldn't care for a ten-year-old, agreed to watch Raquel while Sidarra took a weekend away with Griff. It was her first vacation in many years. Griff explained only that he was starting to get a bad feeling and thought they should escape for some fun. When she asked what he thought of the news about Eagleton's death, he was quiet. Without mentioning Manny or Tyrell by name, Griff vaguely mentioned his suspicions about a botched robbery and shoot-out at a drug lab in Spanish Harlem. It was just a bad feeling, he said, and Raul seemed to have something to do with it, since he grew up around the block. Sidarra wanted no part of bad feelings. She wanted only the feeling of being in love. To share it, they chose the one place Griff said he wanted to visit before he died: Belize.

The world visible below the clouds seemed to bend beneath her eye as the plane crossed borders she'd only heard existed. Short notice prevented them from getting a direct flight, so they had to connect through Chicago and travel straight down the continent. You could not see the border separating Mexico from Texas, but the pilot announced that it was there below. She held Griff's hand most of the way, though they sat in their dark shades and light colors and said very little. Behind their glasses, they looked worried and married; before them, cool. Sidarra stared downward at the earth. Her fingernails recorded everything new against Griff's palm, a huge glistening sea, a long deserted beach, sparsely covered mountains that dipped and tailed and peaked, then a vast flatness of scrappy greens and broken roads.

Griff leaned over and looked out for a minute with her. "It looks like the Southwest," he said.

"I've never been."

"I went there once, and I've crossed over it a few times on West Coast flights. Like it wants to be desert, but occasionally the plants win out over the dirt. It's almost ugly."

"I wonder," she said. "I have two brothers in the Southwest." Sidarra tried to imagine what her own flesh and blood was thinking, living every day in a landscape like that.

Belize was not ugly. Whatever gnarled tropical woods preceded it was but a greater power's preparation. The lazy sands were multicolored, and the beaches free and unpeopled to the water. Miles of long, bending palm trees contorted and competed to touch the aquamarine waves first. When Griff and Sidarra reached their villa, a small bungalow nestled not far from the shore, they undressed and made love. The small, mosquito-netted bed squeaked and squealed under the humid dance of their bodies. Afterward they drifted in the warm buoyancy of the water and let the sun impress them with a souvenir shine.

Sidarra had never been the curvaceous bronze figure strolling with the dark, handsome statue man on vacation commercials. She had not even prepared herself for that. The only thing they knew about the trip beforehand was that they had to go. They needed distance and clarity and, as Raquel would say, comfort. Undisturbed, they could think. They could be married or whoever they wanted to be. They could be wiser than fate as things changed back home, and they could talk about them.

But they didn't talk much. Not because Sidarra was afraid to know how Eagleton was killed, but because she was deliberately distracted. She and Griff went into town and watched people. They ate foods they should not have and lived to laugh about it. They raced each other in the sand. They held each other's body aloft in the water. They found simple things they'd never seen before in each other's faces and in the faces of the people walking proudly and slowly among them. The people walked so slow. The foliage raged supreme. The days lasted only as long as they were supposed to, and then the sun burned its way out again. That didn't seem to bother anybody. Sidarra had never known that. Why couldn't black folks all over do this? she briefly wondered. Then it was time to make love again.

Inside the cozy four-walled house there was a hammock. Off the room, blond levered doors opened to a small screened porch. Outside the bungalow, drums played a low drone from the beach. Bonfires sprayed with the rhythms. And on their last night together, as they curled naked in the swaying hammock, Griff finally started thinking like the lawyer he was. Against her back Sidarra could feel his heart speed up amid the drumming and mix badly. His head was active again. They were going home soon and Belize was starting to wear off of him. Sidarra pushed her bottom against his pelvis and reached an arm over her own head to stroke his scalp. She was not yet convinced by his sudden attack of caution. There were other ways to stay ahead of fear, she was learning.

"Shhh," she purred.

"It's gonna be all right, Sidarra. I promise you. Whatever happens. It's gonna be all right."

"Shhhhh," she purred again. "There are other places. Now I know. There are other ways. We have this." Griff only grunted. His back felt tight against her skin. "Isn't this what you said about Saturn returns? That they're necessary trouble?"

Griff turned around to stare into her eyes. She admired how the sun reflected off the sand beneath them and still found the side of his face. "Maybe I did, but I was misinformed, remember? Thanks anyway." And he kissed her lips gently.

In the taxi the next morning on the way to the airport, all the talking about Griff's bad feelings came down to a single ride. Griff spoke freely in the presence of a driver both of them knew could care less and would never see them again. Griff went over moves to make, tried out scenarios, and asked rhetorical questions about any identity thefts or investments that could be traced back to the Cicero Club. His mind fired rapidly, examining permutations of situations and what would happen if this, if that, and how to make things disappear. Breaking into a whisper, Griff finally mentioned Manny and the WeeWah connection. Yet because Tyrell was his client, Griff, even in Belize, wouldn't say his name.

Sidarra listened carefully. She sometimes chimed in with a steady remark or a correction of fact. But mostly she let him run the exercise both had been meaning to get to in their heads. By the time they got back on the plane home, they couldn't be too sure, but they were pretty sure they were outside of suspicion. A lot depended on Raul, of course. But a lot more depended on what Yakoob had done in the details. For that, they would have to wait till after his act early Tuesday night at the Full Count.

"Why were you and Raul arguing at my birthday party?" she finally asked Griff.

Griff squeezed her hand, but didn't remove his gaze from the airplane window. "He's a little maverick. He's starting to overstep the bounds, baby. Had to be checked." She waited for Griff to tell her the truth before she said anything else. Then he looked into her eyes and added, "I don't share too well."

She decided to let the issue go, but no matter what, as they sat quietly the rest of the plane ride, Griff's words continued making rounds in Sidarra's head. By the time the tires bounced onto the New York runway again, Sidarra was afraid she had figured out who killed the chancellor.

AS SOON AS YAKOOB PICKED UP THE MICROPHONE and began his act, it was clear to Griff and Sidarra that he had not been reading the papers.

I'm trying to figure out what's happening with white folks using the word "man" so much with me. I don't know about you. But me, whenever I walk into someplace and there's some white guy working there, I know I'm 'bout to get called "man." More than once. For all I know, it could be some private code for "nigger," but I suppose they're just trying to be friendly. They always say it with a smile. Guy behind the counter at the liquor store. "How you doin' tonight, man?" "Can I help you find what you're looking for, man?" "All right, have a good night. Man." It's too much. I can't trust that. Some of you remember they tried that shit in the seventies and it didn't work then.

You know what I think? I think white people—not white people, but white men above the age of about fourteen—white men have that word confused for some kind of password. I'm serious. I think they had one of those grand meetings and decided to go with it. You know, they had all the delegates at, like, the Republican National Convention take up the let's-call-black-guys-"man" plank. They discussed it, had a few "nigga experts" come up and make some speeches, you know, "Call 'em all 'man'!" they said. "We're gonna keep taking they shit, but from now on, we gonna call 'em 'man'!"

The smile suddenly left Koob's face as he looked hard into the stage lights.

And there was nobody there to say, "Hey, hold up. That shit is corny. Them niggas is bound to know what's up." Nobody to say that. So the word went out and they keep using it like they can't use it up. Like it makes some kinda difference. Like if you call me "man," I won't keep wanting to blow your fucking brains out. But guess what? I'd probably kill 'em anyway. My boss. The president. Schools chancellor. Bank officer—I don't give a fuck. 'Cause, man, you don't wanna mess with this nigga right here.

Yakoob flashed a peace sign at the crowd and started off the stage. *Shit . . . a black man ain't got a friend in the world.*

Not only was all that unfunny as far as Sidarra and Griff were concerned, it was reckless, especially to say such things in the Full Count. They got up and went straight to the lounge. As soon as Yakoob made it to the back room, Sidarra let him know.

"So you're a dangerous motherfucker now, huh? Givin' whiteboys a heads-up about you, huh? What kind of shit was that, Yakoob?"

He looked shocked to see his friends look at him that way. Griff gave him no help. "What do you mean? What's up? What'd I do?"

"Your bit, your set tonight, man, about all that 'man' shit," Griff explained. "That last part was foolish, Koob."

Koob, squinting over his usual neon-colored velour warm-up suit, shook it off. "C'mon, dude, don't play me. Y'all ain't got nothing to say about my act. Y'all ain't funny. Y'all don't know nothin' about funny. That's my art. I'm not hearing that."

"You damned sure better when you're running with me!" Sidarra told him.

Surprised and a little betrayed, Yakoob turned and faced her.

"How's my mouth your mouth all of a sudden, sistergirl? Why you got your fists up with me?"

"You should know better," she said more quietly, but disgusted nonetheless. He still looked perplexed.

"You haven't followed it, Koob?" Griff asked seriously. "You have no fucking idea?"

Sidarra abruptly put up her hand so no one would speak, walked round the table, sat her ass smack down on the Amistad, and looked straight into Yakoob's eyes. "Koob, I want you to tell me why Raul killed my boss."

Yakoob backed up and his eyes grew wide. Then he let his tight shoulders drop, walked in a half circle toward a stool, sat, removed his Kangol from his head, and started stroking his freshly minted cornrows. "Oh, okay, it's like that now." He reached into his pocket for a Kool, lit it, and took a long drag. He fought the urge to look at Griff. "Look, Sid, we gotta do what we do to—"

"I do not want to hear *that* shit, nigga."

"Hey, hey, I thought this was a 'nigger'-free zone in here?"

"Not when we got nigga infestation going on,"she snapped. "Now, if you'd been reading the paper the last week or so, you'd know that Jack Eagleton's death is now considered a homicide, that he was probably poisoned by somebody who got into his house, and that that somebody had to be connected to some dope they call WeeWah."

Yakoob just listened as smoke passed through his nostrils.

Griff spoke up in a low, calm voice. "And I happened to learn of at least one motherfucker who cooks WeeWah on the East Side and is now sitting in police custody at Bellevue Hospital, nursing a hole he got when three or four fools tried to take his shit." Griff still would not mention his client, Tyrell, by name. "A cop was shot and three young men died, Koob. This guy's gonna be tried. A guy named Manny."

"Manny?" Koob asked.

"Yeah."

Koob looked at the floor. "Damn, I know Manny. If that's the same Manny, Manny's all right."

"Not if Raul knows him, Koob," Sidarra said. "Does Raul know him?"

"I never thought about it." Koob scratched his scalp. "He might. Probably. Manny's from around my way, or he used to be. That's not my bag. I only used to know him. But, you know, Raul's kind of a resourceful motherfucker when he needs to be."

"He's still a knucklehead," said Sidarra.

Koob responded quickly. "So am I. So what? So they got Manny over whatever he's sellin' these days. He ain't sellin' that. He's selling morphine or meth or Ecstasy. If the chancellor dude died of that kind of shit, they'd *been* known about it, wouldn't they? I mean, nobody's gonna link some killer pothead to a spy-type murder just 'cause he knows a guy who got busted cookin' drugs. Where's the link? That shit makes no sense. We all right."

"That's not right, what you're saying," Sidarra said with a look of deep disappointment on her face. "C'mon, Koob." She grabbed the top of her thighs and leaned in toward him, exasperated. "What is that?" She slapped her legs in disbelief. "We never played for that kind of shit. Who told Raul to go and assassinate the goddamned schools chancellor, Koob?"

Koob sat up and crossed his arms. Then he slowly and deliberately turned toward Griff to see if he dared to add anything. He didn't and Yakoob turned back to Sidarra. "Baby, I think you know he do shit. Raul's like an entrepreneur now. You don't have to tell him shit exactly."

"That's good," Griff said to himself sarcastically.

"Hell yeah, it's good," said Yakoob.

"No, Koob. That's not good. What's good about taking the man's life?" Sidarra demanded.

Yakoob's surprised expression returned. "I can think of two

reasons offhand, baby. Getting paid and persuasion. We made a king-sized grip off all that shit. I know you're sleeping in some of yours; I'm ridin' in some of mine. And it was *y'all* that teamed up for persuasion. Remember dat? I didn't intolerate. You don't think I coulda? No, I listened. Y'all were righteous that night." He waved his hand. "Good fuckin' riddance to that bastard. More of them evil fucks need to go like that."

This was not supposed to be this. Sidarra planted her arms behind her on the table and let her head drop to keep from spinning too fast. She didn't understand and she couldn't make herself understood. The room started to crowd in on her, and she began to feel nauseous. Griff came over and reached out to steady her, but she couldn't even look up at him.

"You okay, sugar?"

"I need to, uh, I need to just get to the restroom for a minute. I don't feel so good."

Griff helped her off the table and guided her slowly toward the dressing area where the private bathroom was. Yakoob stood helplessly, not sure if his help was wanted or needed. When Sidarra got to the little door, she leaned in and quickly closed it behind her. Once alone, she sat on the toilet seat with her head in her hands and listened to the inaudible sounds of angry whispers coming from the pool room.

"This macho shit is a fuckin' mistake, Koob!" Griff shouted in a whisper.

"Don't you fuckin' step to me, man!" Koob yelled back in a whisper. "Now that the pussy's yours, you some kind of black motherfuckin' knight? You better recognize, my brother. You made this shit go as fast as I did. Don't *come* with this how-could-I-know shit now, Griff, don't do it!"

Griff knew enough to let Koob's rage settle. "All right. You finished? You cool? I hear you. But she's right now. The shit is hot. The shit is for real. Sid didn't know."

"I know she didn't know, motherfucker! Sometimes you act like can't another nigga think but you!"

Griff's right hand shot up and his fingers opened wide in front of his chest. "Whoa, whoa, black man. Try to put that shit on ice for me, a'ight? Just chill." Griff put his hand down and waited for Yakoob to stop twitching. "You right. You caught me watching my lady's back. But that's our girl in there too. She's got a right to be upset. You need to stay cool. You really do, blood." He walked around the pool table to the stand where his glass and a bottle of Hennessy rested. "I think you're right about the link. It's not there. But we're not waiting on that, dig? Shit's gotta get fixed."

"I'm hip."

"Okay then."

Sidarra walked back in the room. She looked better, resolute, and her color had returned. She asked nothing about all the whispering she'd heard.

"Sid," said Koob as he moved to embrace her, "I apologize, baby. I didn't mean to come off so hard. You know how they say don't hate the playa, hate the game? Well, I coulda played a different game. Okay? Don't be mad at me, sistergirl."

She let him hug her and she eventually held him back. When they separated, she looked up into Koob's eyes. "You still my nigga," she laughed. And they all laughed.

After that it was straight business. They filled their drinks together, sat down, and for the rest of the night figured out what they had to do.

BY THE NEXT MORNING, Yakoob officially got cold feet about doing Cavanaugh. With even fewer specifics than he had given Raul on the Eagleton job, Koob had again enlisted his muscle to make his point for him. But not only did Raul not read the papers, unfortunately he had also developed what he called a professional policy of not reporting back to Koob until he had completed his work. So Koob couldn't call him off; there was no sure way to reach him. And each day Koob would find a moment to peer inside the Fidelity Investments branch to see if Cavanaugh was still in one piece. But each time he went, Cavanaugh wasn't there.

| 26 |

BY THE EARLY SUMMER OF 1998, there were still two Central Parks. The first was the park of newly seeded lawns, keep-out fences, wildflowers, and mostly white families. That park had not come into being until maybe a decade before, and it was progressively taking over the huge urban sanctuary. The second Central Park, shrinking as it were, was the northern third, closest to the Harlem border, a little rockier and not as well kept. Here you still saw crowded family picnics of brown people and their soccer games, bands of boys, illegal barbecues, salsa and merengue in effect, dark lovers under trees, and unsafe cliffs you were wise to avoid. The families of freed slaves had seen their proud shacks demolished over a hundred years before to make room for the grounds on which their ancestors now breathed a little easier. The loop of road used by bicyclists, Rollerbladers, and joggers cut through both parks.

"Ready, Mom?" Raquel asked.

"Ready."

By now, Sidarra and Raquel had their own bikes for the times they wanted to ride together around the Central Park loop. Because it was such a long walk to the park entrance at 110th Street, they didn't do it often enough to justify the high price of their top-of-the-line mountain bikes. But that Sunday, the sun was too bright to ignore and they needed some uninterrupted time with each other. They wore matching warm-up suits, one lime green, the other pink. Sidarra had grown concerned that her daughter's progress at St. Augustine's was occurring at the expense of a connection to her own people, the kids on her block and the ones, until recently, in her old classroom. So she put Raquel in a subsidized day camp that met near Fort Tryon Park in upper Manhattan. Raquel spent her days as a kid again, jumping double Dutch, playing kickball, making arts-and-crafts picture frames out of dried noodles and cardboard and learning the words to songs played on radio stations she didn't listen to much anymore.

A long walk down Lenox Avenue used to be filled with Raquel's questions, mainly about her grandparents and what they used to do there, sometimes about what the people there were doing now. But today Raquel had other things on her mind, things far beyond the street. Like cumulus clouds overhead. Like weather patterns she had been studying before school let out.

"I think I want to be an astronomer, Mom," she declared at about 116th Street.

"That's a great idea, honey. A scientist. Astrology is some fascinating stuff."

Raquel looked up at her as if Sidarra had horns and a tail. "Astrology, Mom? Astrology might be neat to some people, but it's not science. As*tronomy* is the science of the universe. I like celestial bodies. Stuff you can't see in New York City, like stars. I love stars."

Forty years old and she still got those damn two words mixed up. Sidarra let the backslap go on account of her daughter being a Cancer. That's how they talk.

"Why stars, Rock?" Sidarra asked.

"Because," Raquel answered firmly, "whoever lives there probably thinks this is heaven."

They rode slowly through the park. They passed the point in the loop where Raquel had taken a fall for which she was hospitalized a few years back. Raquel's memory was sharper than Sidarra thought. She asked if they could pull over just past the spot. When they were safely beside the curb, Raquel got off her bike, held her mother's hand, and closed her eyes. Sidarra watched her lips moving slightly in a prayer she could not hear. Then Raquel crossed herself, smiled sweetly at her mother, and hopped back on the bike.

They rode on through the park's fresh meadows. They stopped to hear a live band or two and hit the swings at a playground near the children's zoo. Sidarra couldn't believe how much her daughter seemed to know at times. Raquel had a response to everything. She had opinions for days and always a keen eye for what the weather was doing. Days like this helped Sidarra to remember who she herself was and what she really wanted. Such a day helped her forget what the Cicero Club had done and what might happen to her. Nothing could happen to her, she decided.

For all her budding brainpower, Raquel had serious trouble working all the gears and speeds on her mountain bike. Sidarra herself almost fell over trying to change hers on a hill. Raquel said it was probably the fat tires that created resistance. That's why they struggled up the hills. Whatever it was, by the time they reached 106th Street on the East Side, they were walking again beside their bikes. Under a broad canopy of leaves, they stopped to have a hot dog and pretzel picnic.

"So you haven't told me much about camp, Raquel. How's it going?"

Raquel chewed her ketchup-covered frank and looked out at a field of families playing in the old Central Park. The shrieks and laughter sounded mostly Spanish, but they could also hear the distinct sound of dance hall music somewhere close behind them. Another mom and her daughter were sitting on the edge of a tall rock off to their right. Raquel's expression remained disinterested as she watched the pair swing their legs back and forth while they talked together. "It's okay. I'm the best girl in kickball."

"That's great, honey. Do you all play anything else?"

"Nah. They don't have anything up there. You know that. The boys play stickball, but I'm not playing that. I asked the counselor if we could get a lacrosse game together, but he just laughed at me. I wasn't trying to be funny."

Sidarra explained a little bit about the kind of camp it was and how it was important that Raquel remember that sometimes you try to make do with what's around you. They had fun anyway. Not all fun had to be St. Augustine's fun.

She was interrupted by a loud, sudden burst of laughter from the mother and her daughter on the rock above. She didn't know what they were laughing about. But Sidarra was reminded in that moment of all the times she had come with her own mother to this park before it divided, sat near rocks or under trees, and laughed over the lunch they packed in tinfoil from home.

"Oh, I play poor sometimes, Mom. Don't worry. But when this girl T'Quana heard me ask the counselor about playing lacrosse, she decided to jump bad with me."

"What'd you do?" Sidarra asked, bracing herself for the answer.

"Well, you know I'm not trying to hear that from *her.* I said, 'T, I'm not trying to hear that from *you.*' Mommy, T's mother is a crackhead. Either a crackhead or a ho. Anyway, T likes to fight. She fights like every day almost. So she comes at me with her fists up, rolling her neck and her eyes, tellin' me she's gonna bust me upside my face."

"Oh no, Raquel, how'd you handle it?"

"I'm not getting my nice stuff jacked up by a crack ho, nuh-uh. I called over the counselor. I told him, 'See this?' He stepped in and started to pull T'Quana away from me."

Sidarra's worried look subsided a little. "Well, that was pretty sensible, Raquel. Better than to fight."

Raquel seemed proud to add, "As he was dragging her away from me, I told her, 'You know I can have you! You know that. I can have you, T!' "

"What was that supposed to mean?"

"It means I own her. She ain't got nothin'," Raquel answered matter-of-factly.

Sidarra hauled up terrified and very nearly smacked Raquel across the ear. Instead, she smacked her own hip loudly. "Have you lost your goddamned mind, child?"

"Mom," she uttered softly, "that's using the Lord's name in vain. What's so wrong with what I said?"

"Get up! *Get up!* You don't talk to people like that. Just who the hell do you think you are, Raquel? I'm amazed at you and very disappointed." She helped Raquel to her feet by yanking her by the back of her shirt. They grabbed their bikes by the handlebars, and Sidarra led them on a march back uptown. She didn't know what she was doing exactly, or where they were going. She had to figure out what to say, and it felt instinctively like they needed to be closer to home if not actually there. What have I done? What have I done? Sidarra muttered inside her head.

Then it came to her. She stopped and turned to Raquel. "Look at me, Raquel. We're about to do something, and I don't want you to say a single solitary word, okay? Some people have so much money they have to buy themselves a lesson, and you're about to buy one." They marched ahead to the grass beneath the high rocks, stopped there, and Sidarra looked up. "Excuse me!" Sidarra called to the mother-daughter team swinging their legs above them. "Excuse me!"

Finally the daughter's face peeked out and looked down at Sidarra. She looked to her side and her mother's face soon peeked down and smiled. "Yes? Is something wrong?"

"We would come up, but it's a little steep with the bikes. Listen, I was just wondering if you all would be interested in these bicycles?"

The mother needed only a second to start shaking her head politely, but her daughter quickly encouraged her to hold up. Sidarra could see them consulting, but couldn't hear what they were saying.

"Look, maybe your daughter could just come take a quick look. It's not a scam. The bikes are ours and everything."

That was enough to warrant further investigation at least. Sidarra and a very sullen but silent Raquel waited while the mother and daughter gradually collected themselves and walked down a curling slope to them. The mom looked a little older than Sidarra, with a slight accent that could have been Caribbean. Her long-legged daughter had to be at least twelve.

"Why are you giving two nice mountain bikes away?" the girl asked with the beginnings of a Christmas smile on her cheeks.

"We sort of won them from a Wal-Mart in New Jersey where we live. We didn't really want them. It was a raffle. We don't really ride. You can tell they're still pretty new. They sat all winter. Today we thought we'd try them out in the park, but, honestly, we can't handle all the gears. So we've been looking for somebody who might make good use of them."

The mother and daughter checked each other's eyes to see if Sidarra's story checked out. The daughter didn't need much convincing. Her big eyes were busy running over the bikes' details. She looked back at her mom in what was supposed to be a private look of near-desperate acceptance. All she could say to her mom was, "Please?"

The mother had been looking at Sidarra's and Raquel's warm-up suits. Her only remaining look now was to check Sidarra's eyes for charity. She didn't want that. When she couldn't find it, she said okay. "Yes. We'd love to ride them."

"No, no, you may *have* them," Sidarra said.

"Okay, okay. Sure. What a nice surprise. Thank you, ma'am. Thank you both."

Sidarra nodded and beamed at them. She handed them each the bike, checking only to make sure Raquel stayed quiet. Then she took her daughter by the arm and they walked off again toward the park entrance at 110th Street.

"All I'm gonna add, Raquel, is that the nice thing about giving somebody something with wheels is that, all the days and years of your life when you're wondering about whatever happened to that great bike you talked your way out of, some other girl and her mother are covering ground, traveling to the places they like to go, seeing things, and just maybe feeling a lot more grateful than you do that their world got a little bit bigger."

"I just wish I knew their names," Raquel said. "It's easier to remember people when you know their names."

"Well, that's not a bad point," Sidarra replied, taking her hand as they crossed out of the park. "Maybe you can make some up." They walked in silence for a block or two until Sidarra could feel Raquel's grip on her arm return some affection again. She squeezed back and added, "I know how much you loved that bike, Rock. I hope you're not too mad, but that you got the message. You're my star, kid, and stars have to shine."

It wasn't exactly true. Raquel had steadily lost interest in bikes since her accident. She just liked to be out with her mom.

"You're mine too," she said.

"LADIES AND GENTLEMEN, on behalf of the mayor, who unfortunately could not attend today's historic meeting, I wish to introduce to you the new chancellor of the New York City public schools, Dr. Grace Blackwell."

Sidarra stood at the huge table in the City Hall conference hall and clapped furiously along with about thirty other people, some of them regulars at the monthly Thursday education meeting, many of them attending only for the ceremony. A two-term Republican mayor who had campaigned and served as stern father and vengeful master to the darker peoples of the metropolis had simply run out of takers for the job. Dr. Blackwell was a staunch Democrat with an unapologetic résumé. She had been the president of Spelman College, her alma mater, after receiving her doctorate from the Harvard Graduate School of Education. Then, after heading President Clinton's task force on educational reform in the former Bantustans of South Africa, she had accepted the post of schools supervisor over the troubled Gary, Indiana, school system. Beloved by most parents and many of the top administrators she had recruited, she made progress there until ongoing court battles over the use of school vouchers got in the way. When she refused to implement the voucher system on the ground that it discriminated against poor black children, she let her name be floated for job openings across the country. Now, at fifty-six, she, her husband, and their two teenage children would be moving into the chancellor's townhouse in Brooklyn Heights.

Sidarra held back her tears as she listened to the chancellor speak. Dr. Blackwell was a medium-sized woman of medium height, with shocks of gray hair and caramel skin. She wore a lightweight outfit of black and red robes that draped over her full bosom except when she occasionally tossed the front panel across her chest for emphasis. She spoke with unmistakable authority, a kind of no-nonsense lyricism punctuated by frequent smiles below her bright brown eyes. There would be reforms again, she told the group. Without going into detail at this event, she assured everyone in the room that she had her own methodology, an executive staff of experts she had worked with for years, and little of it resembled the "corporatized" approach of her capable predecessor, God rest his soul. The transition would necessarily take more time than usual, she explained, because of the ongoing investigation. Which, she added, would not penalize the children.

"Come with me, dear," she said to Sidarra through a warm smile when the meeting was over. "Please ride back with me."

How she knew who Sidarra was was a small mystery. No one had even informed Sidarra that the event would take place, and she only found out through watercooler rumor. Sidarra fairly bubbled with excitement at the introduction and the chance to sit in the town car with one of her heroes.

When they were crossing the Brooklyn Bridge and the first pleasantries had already passed, Sidarra spoke up honestly. "Look, Dr. Blackwell, I'm not saying this to jockey for anything. That I want you to know. I've read so much about you. I'm truly honored for the city that we have you. You've done wonderful work, a real model for me personally. I know you'll be making changes, and I may not fit into your plans. I just want you to know that I accept your judgment. I understand how these things work."

"Thank you, Sidarra. Thanks for your kindness. I could use that now. This won't be easy, you know." They sat with their legs crossed, smiled in each other's faces, and looked awkwardly out the window for a moment. "Of course, I could also use the names of a few decent restaurants nearby. Maybe you can help me out."

"That's the least I can do."

"Terrific."

SIDARRA MUST HAVE DONE QUITE A JOB on the restaurant list. Somehow it got her early entrée into the chancellor's office, a huge rectangular room with windows on three sides that Sidarra had never actually been inside before. During the first week of Dr. Blackwell's tenure, she was called there for at least two hours out of each day. Once she was surprised to see some of her own reports on Dr. Blackwell's gigantic oak desk. She said nothing about it, and nothing was said to her. She took notes at meetings alongside Dr. Blackwell's out-of-town staff and was often called upon to brief them on various aspects of Chancellor Eagleton's standardized curricula. When Sidarra was finally asked to deliver her own assessment of Eagleton's reforms, she let go without hesitation.

"You know that term they used to use about civilians killed by Central American governments?" she said to nods. "He simply 'disappeared' underachievers from the rolls."

There was a brief silence. Dr. Blackwell sighed into her desk and looked up. "That's what I thought," she said calmly.

Sidarra was even present the day Dr. Blackwell interviewed some of the former chancellor's top advisers. In walked Desiree Kronitz in a short, tight-fitting yellow suit that almost matched her hair. Desiree was all smiles. She spoke in rapid-fire breaths about what a huge fan she was of Dr. Blackwell's work, as she said Sidarra could attest, especially her principled stand on vouchers. Dr. Blackwell could not finish her questions without Desiree interrupting to give the long answer she thought the new chancellor wanted to hear. Sidarra could see Dr. Blackwell growing impatient, and finally gave over the questioning to her deputy, a short Asian man named Stanley. Stanley asked Desiree a few more questions, and Desiree immediately turned her full attention on him. Sidarra saw her pull some of the subtle flirtatious charms she used on Clayborne Reed when she first arrived. But they didn't last long. Stanley wrapped it up in a hurry.

"I've read her stuff," Dr. Blackwell said a little indifferently after Desiree had left. "What do you think, Stanley?"

"I think she's full of shit, Chancellor." He didn't even blink. "In Korean we would say that she lacks 'home-training.' "

"No doubt," the chancellor agreed. "We got that word too."

| 27 |

IN NEW YORK CITY, the newspapers had been silent about the ongoing investigation into Jack Eagleton's murder because it was stalled. That had given Griff time to retrace all the steps he personally knew about. What he found mostly encouraged him. The first dummy shell corporation they had formed offshore had long been dissolved, and foreign governments were slow to release the names of shareholders to any authority for fear of losing future business or getting indicted for money laundering. There were some smaller pots of money Yakoob had put together early on, especially on personal banking hits, and those accounts, now closed, could still have their names on them somehow. If the first shell stayed hidden, Griff was less worried about the second and third. He and Sidarra had created those together, and once they had learned the game a bit, two heads were better than one. The second shell had no name and no shareholders of record; in fact, it was completely illegal under securities laws. But Griff had seen Belinda move money into provisional holding companies that carried only an acronym for the first six months or until a dividend was distributed. Sidarra had suggested a way for the second to keep inventing itself so that the six months never ran out. As for the third and final shell, that one sat open waiting for Yakoob to deposit any newly liquidated gains, especially from the investments made with the Fidelity money. Beyond all that was the metaphysical problem that what lies in bytes of information never disappears entirely. The ultimate trick was to sever any link to Raul.

Whether by luck or skill, when schools chancellors are murdered, law enforcement has a funny way of getting its collective act together. Two things brought heat. Police forensic teams had pulled the chancellor's mansion apart. When that failed to yield anything that seemed like evidence, they pulled the grounds outside apart. It had been a long time since Raul had enjoyed the Manhattan skyline from the Brooklyn promenade. There'd been a lot of wind, rain, and snow, not to mention the irregular workings of city cleanup crews. But somebody was eating substantial numbers of chocolate bars in and around the gated door behind the building. Nestlé Crunch in particular. It was far from a trail, but there was one wrapper wedged in a flower bed and another that appeared to match a one-inch-square piece of foil found on the wall of the old servants' entrance where recyclables usually sat. The Brooklyn district attorney who had local jurisdiction of the case didn't find any of this particularly interesting. Then somebody decided to go back and pull the initial dustings of the parlor area where Eagleton died. There, inside a long green velvet drape, remained the smallest trace of a Nestlé Crunch bar, probably left by a fingernail. Which meant there was also a partial fingerprint. And since few people had walked over the scene in a house whose servants were no longer needed and whose bereaved host was moving out, there was still one good unidentified footprint on the rug. And another just inside a basement doorway. Dr. Blackwell and her family would have to wait to move in.

The second piece meant all the stops were pulled. The Manhattan Tombs is no place to wait for trial unless you're a water bug. Tyrell spent months awaiting his at Rikers Island, where nobody should go unless they're prepared to be stone cold and fearless. Somebody was. The police, with the cooperation of the DEA, placed informants in several cell blocks. Some were cops who had to hope for a quick lead and get out; some were men going nowhere fast. Tyrell happened to get a cop. He was a white guy, burly, with those upturned sideburns cut real short above the ear that only cops and men from a certain part of the city wore regularly. Tyrell paid him and the other half-mad men in the unit little mind until his leg swelled back up. Not moving around as much as usual, having no place to prop it up or ice to bring it down, just made it worse. No amount of nice could get him the infirmary attention he needed. The guards figured it was a healthy shock of detox. So Tyrell winced and occasionally wailed and got beat up for his noise more than once.

"Whaddya need?" Sideburns asked him one especially bad night.

Tyrell looked hard at him, shaken out of his stupor by the strange sympathetic presence standing over him. He was not about to get stomped. The guy seemed to be serious.

"What I need ain't in here, yo," he gasped.

"You don't always know that," said Sideburns.

No one else was around for some reason. Tyrell knew better than to trust that fact alone, but the pain was so bad. "WeeWah, motherfucker. You got some?"

Sideburns looked puzzled for a minute, which could have been part of his art. "The fuck is that?"

"C'mon, dog. I be a'ight."

"Nah, man, what is that shit? I might could get it for you."

Tyrell took the bait. "It's a painkiller. Street grade. Don't trip."

"What is that, like a morphine derivative?"

"Yeah, I think so," Tyrell gasped. As soon as it was out of his mouth he knew.

Tyrell never got his WeeWah. By the time he woke up the next day, Sideburns was gone, never to be seen around Rikers again.

THE INVESTIGATION NOW WAS UNSTUCK and heading straight to Manny's lab, thanks to Tyrell's slip about WeeWah to the informant. The press reported none of these new developments; however, that silence would not last long as the search widened. The Feds were deep into the matter now. Manny's lab evidence was distilled down to the smallest molecule. Suddenly everybody was ready for an education in WeeWah. A special crime lab at New York Hospital enlisted the help of two expert epidemiologists, one from California, the other from MIT. Within days the two had figured out how the stuff was synthesized, how much could put you into a nice painless sleep, and how much could put you to sleep forever.

Griff was always a day ahead of the latest tabloid report, but he was already a day late when he learned that investigators were working Manny over about his customers.

"I fucked up, I think," Tyrell told Griff when they met again in the pen at the Tombs.

"How so, son?" Griff was back to his old clothes again, a denim suit that flattered but dated him.

"I think I talked to a snitch, an informant at Rikers. A white guy."

There were white guys at Rikers, Griff knew. Not many, but a few. "What makes you think he was an informant?"

Tyrell sat up with a clarity in his eyes Griff didn't know was possible. "I told him about WeeWah. He asked me was that a 'morphine derivative.' You know any other motherfuckers out there who talk like that?" Griff surely did not and shook his head. "Plus, the motherfucker straight bounced off a dat. Gone."

Griff sat down and let out a long breath. He scratched the back of his neck for a second, then folded his legs and clasped his hands over his knee. "That's all I want to know, Tyrell. That might not be so bad." Tyrell looked only a little relieved. Griff kept thinking to himself. He reached into his briefcase and pulled out an envelope. Tyrell watched him with great interest. Griff put the envelope on the table between them under the light and very slowly, almost as if he wouldn't finish, started to pull out a small photograph. "You got three seconds to tell me if you've ever seen this man before." Griff allowed the image to peek out from the fold so Tyrell could see it. "One, two, three."

"Oh shiiit!" Tyrell yelled.

"Shhhh." Griff slipped the photo back into the envelope, folded it all up, and this time put it in his breast pocket.

"That's the nigga that fucked me up over by that teachuh house." Griff's eyebrows bent high. "That's how come I got this and this," Tyrell said, and pointed at his leg and his crooked face.

"Okay," Griff whispered. "Now, I want you to listen to me, son, and listen real good. His name is Raul. You keep that shit in your *fuckin'* head like it's a vault. You tell no one nothing until I say you do. If you open your goddamned mouth too soon, the attorney-client privilege will *not* save you from the people who want to make you gone. You dig?" Tyrell nodded like a little boy. "You already a snitch, young man. This time it might help you. Just watch your back in there, and keep your head up."

"Yes, sir."

AT ABOUT THE SAME TIME, Manny was on the well-guarded fourth floor of Bellevue Hospital with his lawyer, making almost the same deal with representatives from both the Manhattan and Brooklyn D.A.'s offices. They told him about the scientists they'd flown in and what they'd concluded. They told him that he was one of only three known sources of WeeWah in their entire search of New York City. And they told him that if WeeWah was in fact the substance in Eagleton's blood and that it was in fact what caused his death, he was looking at charges the likes of which he'd never imagined. The Feds wanted the case. Manny's lawyer thought they were bluffing. But Manny thought they knew more than they were telling him. He knew the difference between federal sentencing guidelines and what state judges give out.

"What do you want?" he asked the four men in the room with them.

"We want the guy."

YAKOOB KNEW BETTER THAN TO USE A CELL PHONE, but when he saw the *Daily News* the next morning he called Griff. Griff pretended it was a wrong number as he stood outside the Criminal Courts Building and called him back a few minutes later from a pay phone.

"Just be cool, blood," Griff said calmly. "Just bring your laptop and a blunt and pick me up in front of the pizza parlor on Chambers in a half hour." Griff got off, went to the clerk of the court to clear his day, and headed into the early July heat to meet a man who days before was too bad to care.

When Griff got in the Escalade, Koob was already soaked in sweat. "I can't go to jail, brother," he squealed. "You don't understand, man. I can't do time. I'd lose my woman."

Griff leaned back in the plush captain's seat and took in his friend's terrified look. "Drive, baby. Just drive."

Yakoob pulled the black SUV into traffic and headed toward

the West Side Highway. His hands shook on the steering wheel. Griff noticed half a blunt sitting idle in the ashtray and reached for it. He didn't normally smoke when he needed all his wits, but something about Yakoob suddenly losing it suggested it wouldn't be a bad idea this once.

"Somebody's been tracking our shit, Griff."

"What?" he gasped, and tossed the joint back in the tray.

"I can tell. They were pretty good, but there are ways to know, like fingerprints. Somebody's been trying to get at my trail."

"What are you saying? Man, pull this car over." Yakoob screeched a right turn off West Street onto a quiet cobblestone street in the West Village. "For how long?"

"I can't be sure. Not long. Mighta just started. Mighta been a few days."

Now Griff was pissed going on scared. "Motherfuck!" Before he could see his own life flash before his eyes, he refocused. "All right. What could they possibly put together? Go slowly. Take your time. Calm down."

"You don't think we should get Sid in on this, dog?"

Griff let out a long, smokeless breath. "Nah. Not yet. Let her sleep."

In the car, with the computer on but hardly in use, Yakoob and Griff methodically went down a long list of even more possibilities, including whether changes they had made since the last time they traced things could themselves be traced by police hackers.

"Okay," Griff said finally. "Now, we know what to tell Sidarra. Now, we know the exposure. Next, you gotta tell me exactly where a motherfucker finds Raul—all day, every day—I gotta know."

IT HAD RAINED ALL AFTERNOON despite the sun-filled July morning. Just as suddenly, about the time Sidarra had climbed the subway stairs and walked home, the sky bloomed lavender and a clear night commenced. She hurried home, practically running up the stoop.

"Raquel? Aunt Chickie?" she called out. From upstairs came no answer. She searched the parlor floor. Still no one. She knocked on the door to downstairs as she always did, as if her aunt ever required true privacy. No one answered. Sidarra rushed down the dark stairwell, almost stumbling on the way, and opened the unlocked door to the ground-floor apartment. "Raquel? Aunt Chickie?" Still no one answered. Just when her heart started to pound with fear, she peered beyond the little kitchen's windows and saw them with their backs to her on the small patio. They were hunched together over one of her aunt's flower beds, and she could hear Aunt Chickie's voice alone, singing.

"Summertime, and the livin' is easy . . . the cotton is high . . ." Then she broke into humming.

They were very busy, whatever they were doing out there. Sidarra just watched. This was another one of those scenes whose existence she had either forgotten or never knew about, like the people she saw in Belize lying down with the sun. They probably did this every Tuesday night when she was off being a pool queen. Aunt Chickie sang on, her voice so much raspier than Sidarra remembered as a child, still beautiful, possessed of practiced skill and nuance, but weak to the point of airlessness.

"I'm home," she said, pushing the door ajar.

"Hi, Mommy."

"Close the door, will you, Sidarra? You'll let the bugs in."

"Oh, c'mon, Aunt Chickie," she said. "There are no bugs in New York City."

Aunt Chickie looked at her as if she'd grown two horns and a tail. "Well, pretend that there are. We're out here picking enough of 'em out from under my tiger lilies that their cousins are bound to take up for 'em." Aunt Chickie turned back around to redirect

Raquel's fingers through the soil correctly. "There's wine inside if you'd like some, Sidarra."

"Thank you." Sidarra stepped back into the kitchen and searched the countertop. Sure enough, Aunt Chickie had some sweet blush wine out of a box. The glasses in her cupboards held the dirt flecks of bad eyesight and best efforts. Wine was just what Sidarra needed and she poured herself a glass. When she returned to the patio, the two were still at it. She sat down on a chair that was still moist from rain, put her feet up, and sipped. The evening air was still a little damp, less so than the grass and the leaves beyond them, but things had cooled and there was almost a breeze.

"Raquel, my love?"

"Yes, mom?"

"Would you mind going upstairs for a bit and changing into your bedclothes? I'd like to speak to your aunt a minute."

"She's your aunt too, you know."

"She knows that, fresh girl," said Aunt Chickie. "Now do as your mama says."

Off she went. One of the best things about their life with Aunt Chickie in the house was having a grown-up echo. Sidarra wondered for a moment if that was an advantage married parents had. "You want some wine, Aunt Chickie?"

"No, baby," she said, slowly squatting into a chair. "Whatcha thinkin' 'bout?"

"More than I can say, I'm afraid. But what I wanted to talk to you about is—" Sidarra suddenly realized she had forgotten the script she'd been writing in her head along the ride from Brooklyn. "Well, see, I want to do some estate planning, you know, for Raquel's sake. And I was wondering if I could have the deed redone and put you on as the owner of this place. It'd be easy. Then we'd get a lawyer to write your will so that you'd put the house in trust for Raquel. Sort of kill two birds with one stone."

"Who are the birds? You and me?" she asked skeptically.

"Figure of speech."

Aunt Chickie sat back and stared at her flowers for a moment. Then she turned to Sidarra, expecting the horns and tail to have disappeared by then. The look on her face said she still saw them. "I'ma tell you something, Sidarra. Maybe one or two things, come to think of it. I know you're busy doing what you do. I'm sure you have your reasons, and I probably wouldn't understand them if you explained them carefully to me. To tell you God's honest truth, I really don't care what you do with the deed as long as you don't create a family mess out of it. By the time you get it all done the way you plan, I will most likely be dead. See, I'm old. You prob'ly figured that out."

"Yes, ma'am, I was aware of that."

"Are you?" Aunt Chickie's eyelids seemed to hang halfway over her eyes, lending gravity to the slight look of disbelief she wanted Sidarra to notice. "Those flowers," she said, pointing, "they're perennials, you know. You heard my singing voice? That's what doctors call early-stage emphysema from all that smoking in France and whatnot. Diabetes is also a strange thing. It never likes you for long. Living in this city, breathing this air, walking up and down the steps in this house, I would have to say that there is an excellent chance I will not be around to see these little orange smiles bud again once they go down in a few weeks. Are you with me?"

"I'm with you, but I won't believe you," Sidarra said gently.

"Then do what you want. But don't say I didn't warn you."

| 28 |

EVEN THOUGH JEFF GEIGER HAD HEARD WATERCOOLER RUMORS about his name, it was damned exciting to see it appear on the victim list of a file being opened by his own office, the federal prosecutor for the Eastern District of New York in downtown Brooklyn. Geiger had leaped to the U.S. attorney's office after doing serious felony trials as an assistant in the Manhattan district attorney's office. His leap was not quite what he intended, though. He now prosecuted federal securities fraud offenses with a lot less rush and intrigue than the grand larceny cases he was starting to handle at the time he left the D.A.'s office. Not two years later, those two lives collided in a file.

At first the detectives thought there might be an African connection. No one was home at the time, but a search of the East Harlem apartment of a suspect named Yakoob who had known ties to another suspect wanted for murder turned up a yellow slice of legal-pad paper. Much of what was written there had been crossed out beyond recognition. A few notations appeared to be in code, but still decipherable were some personal names on a list that matched a state reporting bureau's list of people who had been victims of electronic funds misappropriation and credit card fraud. The dollar amounts were there too, small, but sure enough, there lay Geiger's long-lost $5,000 in black and white. Other units were piecing together whatever links might exist between the suspects and the crime or crimes involved. It could have been a terrorist murder-for-hire financing ring. Or gang activity. Or totally unrelated criminals whose paths crossed at convenient moments in time. Without knowing what to look for, the police hackers had done as much as they could. For his part, Geiger had to try to trace the small amounts of cash to larger stock purchases, transfers, and gains—securities violations.

The yellow slice of paper was not a lot to go on, and nothing else was found to incriminate "the African guy," as one detective called him. After interviewing him at the station house, they gave Yakoob what amounted to a summons to appear before a judge later. Without the main suspect, it wasn't clear whether Yakoob could even be linked to Geiger's $5,000 or anything else. But the file indicated that Yakoob would be put under surveillance, at least in the hours after work. And they knew where his wife worked.

Geiger studied the slender file for as many hours as he could spare from his docket of cases ready for trial. It was so random, nothing made sense. His unit chief wanted him to prepare a list of specific things police and FBI hackers could go back in for and to articulate legal grounds for a warrant to examine all of Yakoob's computer files and financial information. That had to be done within days. Whatever was going on in the case, Geiger was told, it was moving quickly. So Geiger set out on an aimless search for coincidences and petty identity theft. The murder suspect still had no name.

Soon enough, the main guy's predilections started to emerge.

The NYPD received a tip from a sickly inmate on Rikers Island about a guy who an illegal drug chemist named Manny called "the Candy Man." The chemist might have sold him a powerful sedative used in a high-level homicide. The kid in jail, who could at least call the suspect by his first name, Raul, had given the cops detailed information about Raul's mother's apartment, daytime habits, and a full physical description. Both men—Manny and Tyrell—had plea deals pending. That page of the file also said in bold letters that the suspect was probably aware that he was under suspicion and should be considered armed and extremely dangerous. Geiger did what he could about the money trail, but mostly he waited to hear if and when they brought in the Candy Man—Raul—for questioning.

NOT A FULL BLOCK AWAY FROM JEFF GEIGER'S OFFICE, in tall buildings that stood almost shoulder to shoulder, Sidarra was sitting at her desk cubicle at the Board of Miseducation about to receive her own promotion.

"You've got to be kidding," she told Dr. Blackwell.

"Don't be too happy just yet," said the chancellor. "We plan on doing it differently than you're used to."

"Our reorganization of the executive staff may look a lot like putting you right back where you were before the last reorganization had you reporting to what's her name," Stanley explained, "but we need your ideas."

"Actually, I'd like you to be one of my deputies, Sidarra," the chancellor added.

As soon as she had covered Dr. Blackwell with both arms, Sidarra realized that she probably had not really hugged another woman since she last held her mother. In fact, as the embrace nearly tripped them both over, she knew that was true.

However, Sidarra did not know that Yakoob had been in and

out of police custody the day before. She did not know what a wild chase was on for computer evidence of illegal stock trades involving her and the Cicero Club. And nobody knew exactly how close a small army of unmarked police cars was to closing in on Raul as he ate a late lunch at Conrad's Chicken & Waffle. The only thing Sidarra considered in that rare moment of rapture was that she had good news to tell her crew at the Full Count tonight, something she had worked long and hard for, and for the feeling, she would not creep through an alley tonight but would walk through the front door, proud of her own damned self for the first time in a long time.

EXACTLY WHAT RAUL WAS FINALLY GOING TO DO to Cavanaugh—short of murder—was going to hurt a lot. That much he knew. The man had been on vacation for at least three weeks, and the wait did not sit well with Raul. It took only a phone call to the receptionist to learn that this was the Monday Cavanaugh would return to his desk. All day Raul considered various options. It had to be good. It had to be memorable. It might be fatal, and for that reason it should come as Cavanaugh was leaving work around five. The hours grew long. Raul got hungry.

Conrad's Chicken & Waffle was located on West 145th Street. Raul loved their birds almost as much as he loved a chocolate bar. Waffles were a new thing he was trying out, and he bathed his in syrup. The breasts were so succulent he decided to have three. The waffles were so good, he asked the waitress for another round. Strawberry soda was the drink of the day. Together with the fist-sized corn biscuits, he had eaten so much and was bulging so bad that by two-thirty he had to move his Glock to the back of his waist. Home cooking has blinded many men. Being high on indica weed helps too. Raul sat in a lone booth near the back, fat on sweetness and protein, watching the door with a little less focus than usual. It was a small ecstasy he decided right then to start doing daily. He didn't even want to get up, but nature called.

"*Papi*, where's your bathroom?" he asked a middle-aged man with gray hair and a chef's white shirt.

"Just to the rear," the man replied in Spanish.

Raul lumbered to the back and practically fell into the little room.

As soon as the bathroom door closed shut, a SWAT-like commotion converged on the street outside. While Raul rested his Glock on the sink and lowered his baggy pants, six unmarked cars dove to a halt outside Conrad's. Pedestrians fell into form, checking the cops' eyes, seeing guns drawn, and scurrying to a safe place from which to watch. There was no bullhorn; folks knew what six cars meant. A paddy wagon screeched to a stop just down the street and men in black fatigues and helmets flew out of the doors and went racing front to back through adjacent stores with automatic rifles ready. While frenzied moms lifted paralyzed children out of the way, Raul enjoyed what a body does best. He sat with his arm on his knee and his hand on his chin and studied cracks in the linoleum floor. He finished just in time to hear what sounded like a chair fall over. Then his ears pricked up. He wasn't full anymore and grabbed his gun.

Raul let the door swing open on its own. The bustling restaurant suddenly had gone silent. The man with the white shirt was just trying to shuffle past him when Raul reached out and yanked him in by the collar. His eyes said everything.

"How many?" Raul asked in Spanish.

The man tried to unlock his jaw. "Don't," he stammered in Spanish. "Too many."

Before either man could say another word, a single gunshot rang past them and through the narrow hallway. Raul jerked away from the man, and the man darted through a door on the other side marked "Employees Only." Raul crouched. What the fuck? he thought. How you just be shooting in a fucking New York City restaurant like that?

"Raul!" came the loudspeaker at last. "Throw your weapon on the floor and show us your hands!"

Too mean to be scared, all Raul could think of was, New York's Fucking Finest. He waited for the first sound of them rushing him. He knew they would. His knees creaked in his crouch. He craned his short neck to peep down the hallway. At the end of it was a door, probably an exit. That's the way he would go, he decided, but he'd probably have to take a motherfucker out first to clear his way. And hope if he got hit they'd miss center mass. He started to count: one, two—then he heard the quick footsteps approaching and bolted out of the bathroom. The first shot missed him and he got off three or four devastating rounds of fiery light. Raul was almost to the back door when he felt the back of his thigh go numb. With one hand firing behind him, he pushed the exit open with the other. The door swung out to reveal a weed-ravaged garbage area and two rifles opening fire on him. The bullets shredded his chest and neck while others tore up his behind. His body could not fall at first, jerked back and forth by lead into a lifeless spasm. And though he was done, somebody's good measure blew his shoulder off. Raul's body finally dropped one way and his head another. In the quiet, his pooling blood seemed to smoke.

THEY EACH CAME TO THE FULL COUNT in different ways and in different looks than they had in a while, if ever. Sidarra parked her Mercedes right in front and bounced out of the driver's door in a short royal blue sundress, black heels, and her hair in a dark blue scarf. She walked straight through the bar scene to the back. Griff took three different cabs, a bus, and another cab, eventually walking carefully through the back door wearing thick black nerd glasses, ill-fitting pants, and a crooked-collared shirt with a pharmacist's pens lined up in the breast pocket. Yakoob parked his Escalade in the alley after circling the neighborhood five or six times and wore platform shoes, a nylon floral shirt, and polyester bell-bottoms. Before he walked through the back door, he put on a wig. The first thing they did was ask Koob why he looked like a clown. He told them he had a gig, the guy who went on after him was dressed in the wig, and the rest was pure pimp. No one said much more. Then Griff's music came on. The disk began, appropriately enough, with B.B. King's live version of "The Thrill Is Gone."

For the first little while, it just felt right to play pool, to talk pool, and to be billiard artists again as they had been that first night together. Nobody got high. Sidarra brought their drinks in along with bottles so she would not be seen at the bar again. Of course she and Griff wanted to know exactly what Yakoob had said to the police, but they let him unwind to himself.

"I'm okay," Koob told them before looking up. "Really," he added, finally looking into both their eyes. "They expected a dumb nigga, and that's what I gave 'em. They want Raul."

Griff and Sid remained quiet, editing questions in their heads until none were left. Koob had suffered enough interrogation for them all. Instead, they just enjoyed each other's company, complimenting each other's good shots and all-righting the missed ones.

"Fellas, I made deputy today," Sidarra finally said. They looked at her and smiled. It was clear they didn't understand. "Deputy to the new chancellor. She's a sister, you know. Maybe the mentor I never had. Dr. Grace Blackwell. She might be the first person in many years who actually read the things I used to write about the schools."

"Hey!" the men chimed. They raised their glasses. They hugged her each the same. They all wanted to say more, as if today were a different day and tomorrow completely unknown, but whatever it was, it wasn't that. So they just smiled about it and went on playing pool. Sidarra's news did not fit the mood and would have to wait.

A few minutes later, Q walked in through the maroon curtains. In the glint of low light, he looked like a man of steel. His presence was suddenly more welcome than ever before. They each could have used a superhero at the moment. Q greeted them all, kissed Sidarra on the cheek, and motioned to Griff with his index finger to come close. It looked at first like a phone call was waiting, but Q immediately leaned into Griff's ear and whispered a few words. Griff whispered back while Sid and Koob stopped playing. Q said something else, then turned to the other two and said, "I'm sorry, y'all." Then his big frame shook through the curtains and disappeared.

They waited for Griff to speak. He put his hands on his hips, searched the carpet, and took a few wandering steps toward the Amistad. Still they waited. "Raul's gone, folks. Had a shoot-out with the cops this afternoon, and he's dead."

Each of them stepped zombie-like toward the table, and one after the other rested their hands against the siderails. They studied the loose balls with blank faces. All hands were calm but Yakoob's, whose fingers began to squeeze the hard felt cushion and whose nails dug in with an anger he couldn't find words for. Griff stated the last of what he knew in a deadpan way, while Yakoob listened without letting go.

Sidarra wanted to say a prayer, but she was long lost for those words. Raquel would have known better, but Raquel had better never know. "I'm sorry for his mother," was all she could think to say. "He leaves for one journey, she starts on another."

"He loved you, girl, you know that, right?" Koob said, turning to her.

She nodded and whispered yes, then turned back to the balls

on the table. The huge stuffed purple teddy bear still sat in Raul's favorite corner, a dumb, inanimate smile forever on his mug, a bag or two of weed and a handful of candy bars in suspended spill from an opening in its side. For the moment, Griff said nothing and showed nothing.

Fighting a tear, Yakoob said, "He went out like his dad did. The guy just wanted to be a man."

"The guy was also 'bout to man us all the fuck upstate for life, Koob," Griff said without flinching. He gestured across the table. "C'mon. Lose the bear. For real, Koob. Don't save a thing."

Yakoob, in clown wig and pimp clothes, walked listlessly over to the stuffed animal. He lifted it into his arms with no sense of humor and dragged his feet toward the back door. Sidarra opened it for him and he disappeared into the alley. Alone between the buildings, Koob didn't know just what to do. He looked around for someplace to stash the bear. He looked at a small Dumpster, thought not, and squeezed the purple thing to him. He considered a group of trash cans at the far end of the alley, again squeezed the bear indecisively, and turned toward where his truck was parked. He carried the bear a few steps toward the Escalade, then stopped and turned. He turned again, then stopped and reached into the hole for the candy bars and the marijuana. He saved a bag of smoke as a souvenir and threw the rest into a nearby can. More decisively, he grabbed the bear, walked to his trunk, and opened the door. There were better places to toss such a noticeable thing, he figured. Resolved, Koob closed the door and started back along the side of the truck for the back door. Before he could get there, his head felt light. He reached out and put his hand on the brick to keep himself from falling. Suddenly he saw in his mind an image of his friend shot to pieces by police, and Koob's legs buckled at the knees. His back slid down the brick wall until he sat with his elbows on his knees. There by the back door Koob wept.

"Griff," Sidarra said sternly.

He had already taken a step toward her from behind. "Sidarra, this is a good thing in its way."

"That may be," she said, preventing an unexpected kiss. "But, c'mon, man, this has gone entirely too damned far."

Yakoob walked back inside at that moment. His expression had lightened a little, though his voice remained grave. "Are we cool now?" he said. "Do I need to hire a lawyer?" Before Griff could answer, Koob drained a very large shot of Tanqueray.

"Yeah, you need to hire a lawyer," Griff said. "We're not that cool."

"Fellas, wait up a minute," Sidarra tried to interrupt. "Please. Come sit down with me." They followed her over to one of the semicircular velvet couches, set down their glasses, and for perhaps the first time, sat down to talk there. "I love y'all. I *love* y'all. But somehow things got taken a little too literally, may I say that? Now, this has all gone too damned far, like—Griff had a term for it—some thug multiplier—"

"The thug is dead," Griff dryly declared.

"Oh c'mon. We enabled him. We couldn't stop wanting too much, am I right?"

They each loved her too in their own way, but they couldn't bring themselves to admit that just yet. To both of them, Sidarra, in her royal blue, sounded ready to resign herself to a fate just a little better than Raul's. Despite his tears, Yakoob was ready to beat it.

"Nah, baby," he said, swigging his drink dry. "You can't want too much when you start with nothin'. My lady Marilyn," he began, pulling a Kool out of his pimp pocket, "she's never been so happy or laughed so much. You don't know what that means to me. She's my heart, y'all. Do you know, you know how we met? We used to be working a night shift at a KFC in East New York. Ever been to East New York? Every other motherfucker in East

New York is dead, but they learn how to keep walking out there. We were there, her, me, and another guy, Ernesto, may he rest in peace. We used to be there till midnight from Tuesday to Saturday nights, scrubbing grease off grills, wearing them stupid hats, hoping the next thug on line was too drunk to shoot straight. That's how we fell in love. Hopin' we'd live to get the fuck outta there. You don't want to die with one of those hats on."

"What happened to Ernesto?" Griff asked.

"He split. Bounced. Said it was too dangerous. Became a manager of a White Castle on Atlantic Avenue. One night they held him up, took 'em all down to the basement, locked 'em in the freezer. That's where the brother died. Froze to death. Mexican guy. Left three little kids behind. I ain't goin' out like that." Koob squeezed off a long puff. "We smarter than you think, Sid. We gonna be all right. I'm telling you. They got who they wanted today, and I'm damned sorry they did. But we gonna be all right. Right?"

It sounded a little like he needed her to agree with him. Sidarra smiled knowingly and put her hand on Koob's soft cheek. "I hope you're right, baby. I know you're smart."

They sat there a moment in silence. Griff let out a long sigh and said, "We're probably looking at something, blood. I doubt we go down for the Eagleton joint, but they have a way of finding something. I know a lawyer you can talk to, a buddy of mine. He's good. He's in Brooklyn too. If it comes to that, he knows how to plead you down."

Yakoob looked stunned and laughed out loud. "I'm not goin' any damn place, Griff, so you need to man the fuck up. I'll be right here, next to you. Shiiiit." He looked at Sidarra and pointed at Griff. "Straight ahead, people. Just stay straight."

Sidarra giggled a little. She wanted to believe him. He was nearly convincing. Griff's heavy silence and distant gaze were the only things standing in her way. "You don't think we should—?" she began. "No, let me say it like this. Everything Raul ever saw was cash, right?"

"I think so," Griff said. "Yup."

"Okay," she continued. "Then, at this point, what else do we need to do, Koob? You know the files. You know the ins and outs I could never understand. If you were a man of excessive caution, if you had just one more thing you might do to cover your tracks, what would you do now?"

Yakoob was busy rolling a joint of Raul's weed. He had drained yet another full glass of gin. Even so, he pretended to scratch his chin in deep thought. "You know what I would do?" he asked. They looked at him with great suspense. "I would probably dance my motherfuckin' ass off!" He laughed loudly and bent down to feel it. "Man, I wish my woman was here. How 'bout some disco, Griff? This blues shit is giving me some."

Griff pulled his body off the narrow sofa, pulled some CDs from a shelf, and tossed one to Q through the curtain. The three waited like teenagers for something to happen. Yakoob lit the joint, took a long toke, and coughed out a huge puff of smoke. Then there was silence. Sidarra looked at the joint Yakoob was offering her and reluctantly decided to take it. Soon, fading in was the familiar sound of the Trammps from the *Saturday Night Fever* soundtrack singing "Disco Inferno."

Yakoob got up and grabbed Sidarra off her seat. He started bucking and jiving to the heavy beat and pretending to hustle. She smiled at him and reluctantly began to move her feet a little. He got a little freaky, spinning and whooping. Koob grabbed his cue stick and used it as a pretend microphone. He lip-synched the words until Sidarra and eventually Griff started to get into it with him. Once they joined him, Yakoob got wild, throwing the wig across the Amistad and juking like it was 1976. There was no denying the beat and nothing for any of them to do but get funky with it. Yakoob had already begun to break a sweat when the chorus came. He grabbed the stick to his mouth like a mike and screamed, *"I heard somebody say: Burn baby burn!"*

Again and again, they each twirled and kicked and shook it like they had back in high school. The longer it grooved, the more serious they danced, until the chorus came back each time, and together they looked at each other with big drunken eyes and sang: *"I heard somebody say!"*

29

RAQUEL WAS TRYING OUT A NEW ATTITUDE at day camp, Aunt Chickie was in her garden debugging the last tiger lilies of the season, and Sidarra had let her hair back down over her cheekbones. The Saks Fifth Avenue lobby was full of European tourists caring little and buying a lot.

"Good heavens, what the hell happened to you, girlfriend?" Darrius asked her as she leaned over his makeup counter with a friendly expression and tired eyes.

"I got promoted, but it's a long story I don't have time to tell," Sidarra answered. "When's your break time?"

"Whenever I say so."

"Then I'd like you to take a little walk with me, baby."

The cloudy Wednesday began to sprinkle a light rain as Sidarra and Darrius strolled out the side door toward Rockefeller Center. Darrius had one of those golf umbrellas that take up most of the sidewalk, and they walked under it together, parting incredulous crowds with impunity. The plaza across the street was regaled in its annual summer flower festival, and the wet fragrance slowed their steps.

"Let me get to it, Darrius. The following question has no bearing on my love for you, okay?"

"Shoot."

"Are you a trustworthy friend?"

"My dear, I am a proud Catholic. You see I work next to St. Patrick's Cathedral. I'm practically a vicar." He smiled sheepishly. "Practically."

"That's more than enough," she said. "Darrius, how would you like to live in Harlem?"

Darrius stopped and looked quizzically at her. "Sidarra, don't feel sorry for me just because I'm the token black faggot in Chelsea. Membership in that neighborhood has its privileges, you know." She laughed with him. "Justin, on the other hand, would love it. What are you talking about?"

"I'm talking about my place. Well, it's not mine. It's legally my aunt's. I'm thinking of going on a sabbatical for a while. It's not for sure yet, but if I do, I'd need somebody I can trust living there. Underneath the main apartment you saw is a rental unit. It would mean being a landlord too."

Darrius moved them along again. His brow furrowed a bit as he considered it. "I really don't know. There'd be some negotiation involved at home. How much do you want for it?"

"Nothing. I don't want anything. I would just want you to take care of it, cover your own utilities, be careful about who you rent to, get a fair price, and send most of the rent money to a friend of mine in the Bronx."

"Normally I wouldn't ask, but can I get some of the drugs you're taking?"

"I'm not on drugs. It's not really about me. It's about my daughter and my aunt. They may force me to do it, but I don't mind. I just need a little help. Can you swing it?"

Darrius pulled her arm closer as they strolled and pointed out a few particular flowers he'd never seen before. Their steps matched nicely. "Life is complicated, isn't it, darling? Never black and white." She clutched him in silence and breathed up the air. He was thinking. "Okay, Sidarra. I'm sure we can work something out. I'll help you. Don't count me among your troubles. You were so good at getting the sad off your face."

"Thank you, Darrius. I'll let you know soon if it's gonna happen. If it does, it will probably happen quickly."

IN FACT, IT WAS VERY FAST. When both the local police and the Feds team up over something, it goes down quickly. The death of the Candy Man only slowed it a little. Not when the FBI hackers came back to Jeff Geiger with more names, a possibly defunct shell corporation with what appeared to be large gains from an international betting consortium, and preliminary evidence of tax evasion. They had really wanted Manny. Geiger could have cared less since he didn't prosecute drug dealers anymore, but the Manhattan D.A. still wanted him locked up for a long time. Raul's death killed that. A day into his trial, Manny accepted a plea to illegal weapons possession, reckless endangerment, and drug distribution. His lawyer negotiated two years in state prison in return for the tips that helped nail Raul. With the news of an assassin's violent death in a Harlem shoot-out all over the tabloids for days, his attorney convinced the authorities that what was done was really now done, injured cop or no injured cop. Griff's line was similar for Tyrell. The D.A. almost liked Tyrell, who testified with rare conviction for a snitch. His every word made sense and his story never wavered. Manny might have done much harder time without Tyrell's story implicating Raul for him. So when Tyrell walked out of Rikers a free man, he had no one to thank but Griff. Even Griff's casual enemies in the Manhattan D.A.'s office thanked him for prepping his client so well. Until Jeff Geiger recognized Griff's name on a deleted shareholder file.

Realizing who Griff was set Geiger's mind on fire. You rarely forget a humbling and Geiger recalled the humbling he suffered over the stroller thief years ago. Hearing colleagues talk about Griff like an untouchable civil rights leader pissed him off. Geiger slept in his downtown Brooklyn office two nights straight trying to re-create a blueprint of credit card fraud, cash purchases of dummy stock, and an offshore shell corporation's bets on Internet mayhem scenarios. It was a tangled web they'd woven. The computer traces were not all going to hold up in court, he worried. Some might be excluded because the warrant had been issued after the fact. But there were surveillance photographs of Yakoob and Griff. Despite a masking technique, Yakoob had executed two traceable Solutions, Inc. trades on behalf of an oddly named holding company from his personal computer, and he, Griff, and another person were listed as the company's sole shareholders. Since the trades followed the IPO, the dollar amounts skyrocketed, and there were no corresponding capital gains tax filings by either man when the earnings were converted to cash. Where the cash was now was untraceable. It had simply vanished. That it existed once was a certainty, one that kept Geiger up at night—because it all seemed to start with his own $5,000.

Then another coincidence was uncovered. The police hackers performed a routine check of recent bank-related identity thefts based on amounts under $20,000. Because it wasn't a regular bank, Fidelity Investments didn't come up right away. But Fidelity's internal investigation turned up customer addresses—not even names—and one in particular that Geiger somehow found familiar. It was the same one police had gone to first in East Harlem, belonging to the guy they called "the African." The police techs were stuck trying to figure out where monies that left several Fidelity accounts wound up. Some seemed to have moved into and out of an account manager's account, but a lot had disappeared.

Yet seventy-two hours after he made the Fidelity connection, Geiger thought he had at least enough to arrest Griff and more than enough to get the Yakoob character. The only complete mystery remaining was the identity of the third shareholder of one of the shell corporations. He'd finally figured out the name that went with the initials "D.G." But who the hell *was* "Desiree Galore"?

"CAN YOU GET AWAY AGAIN?" Griff asked her over the phone.

Reluctant to talk, afraid to see him again, Sidarra let her heart speak for her. "Okay."

"Meet me at the Studio Museum by the last exhibit."

If Griff wanted to travel, Sidarra thought, then the pressure must have been all in her head. He was being cautiously romantic, not running away. Sidarra would have to check her Aunt Chickie's availability, but Aunt Chickie didn't mind babysitting another weekend as long as there was plenty of food in the house.

Sidarra packed underwear and a sundress in a small bag along with some toiletries and wore a bikini under her clothes. Raquel started to ask her the usual responsible questions about where she had to go in such a hurry.

"You too will be in love one day, darling," was all Sidarra told her.

"Whatever," she said.

And Sidarra was off, knowing she had probably forgotten something. She walked briskly to 125th Street, stopping in a couple of stores to make sure no one was following her. When she got to the museum, it was preparing to close. The uniformed guard inside started to give her the business until another woman in a suit relieved him and let Sidarra in without a word. Sidarra walked the blond shiny wood floors. Hard work and unspeakable passion filled the walls, the canvases crying quietly in their imagery, the halogens above them threatening to quit. The hard heels of one last couple could be heard randomly pacing one room, their voices speaking German, punctuated by "oohs." In the back corner, by a watercooler, was Griff with his back turned. He carried a leather bag shaped like an old-fashioned doctor's house-call kit.

"Hi," she said.

He wheeled around as if he were surprised and kissed her gently. "Hey." They looked at each other, their eyes searching for something new in the midst of something wonderfully familiar. "Let's go to Belize," he said.

She had a feeling that was his plan, but had to register a mild protest. "C'mon, baby. Isn't it past—"

Griff whipped out a thick envelope with airline tickets in them. "It's crazy, I know, but it's not stupid. You've probably survived the investigation at the Board of Ed or they wouldn't have promoted you. The only crime you're guilty of is having bad friends. If the police came to question you, for now they'd leave your family alone if you weren't home. I wouldn't ask you to do stupid. But crazy is kind of routine for lovers."

"You're my lover?" she asked.

"Not really," he said. "I'm just the man who loves you."

He led them through a side door to a patio. The patio sat between the backs of several buildings like a courtyard. Through a gate, they met a narrow alley which they took to the sidewalk on 124th Street. Griff had a town car waiting for them there.

The James Bond logistics brought Griff's mention of questioning cops to mind again. As the car started across 125th Street, Sidarra remembered the important something she'd left behind. "Wait!" she said. "I have to go back. I have to get something at my house."

"They could be watching your house," he whispered.

She looked scared at him. "Then I really have to get back there for something."

The driver followed her instructions while Griff crept low in the seat. When they reached the brownstone, Sidarra jumped out and Griff remained half hidden in the rear. She ran up the stairs, pulled out her key, and disappeared behind the door. While she was inside, a car pulled up behind the town car. It was an old car, a Chrysler, and a man sat behind the wheel. Griff waited and slumped lower, watching the Chrysler in the rearview mirror. Inside, Sidarra ran to her bedroom to retrieve Michael's engagement ring and hid it in her clothing. If cops came to search her house, she didn't trust them to leave a diamond behind. She made her way down the stairs of the empty upper apartment as fast as she could. Griff tried to decide what to do when she came back out. He saw her appear in the vestibule and open the front door to leave. Once she was visible at the top of the stoop, the driver's side door of the Chrysler opened. Griff looked hard at the man. There was no question. He was heading for Sidarra. Griff told the driver to wait and got out.

"Sidarra, honey," said the man.

Griff rushed up behind him as though he were about to snap the man's neck.

"Michael," she said in a frozen panic. "What are you doing here?"

Her fluttering eyes and the unnatural panic on her face made Michael turn around. Just as he did, Griff passed him and joined Sidarra on the bottom step. He looked up at the two of them as Griff brought his arm down around Sidarra's back.

"I was," Michael stammered, "I was wondering . . ." Michael interrupted himself to take a long look at Sidarra, then at Griff, who would not flinch or smile, and his shoulders dropped.

"Michael, please," Sidarra started.

He was past that. "Nah, Sid, I was just in the neighborhood and thought I'd check in on the Rock, that's all." He wouldn't look at Griff again. "She okay?"

"She's fine, Michael."

"Great," he said, resuming a stoic look of full dignity and turning away. "Then I'm off. Give her my love, Sidarra." He started back toward his car. "Take care of yourself."

"Let's go," Griff said as they watched Michael climb gingerly back into the Chrysler and pull away.

Sidarra followed Michael's trail with her eyes in the hope he would at least look back. He did not.

Griff's planning was typically deliberate, even at what must have been the last minute. He overpaid the driver out of the huge billfold of cash in large denominations he was carrying, and he made sure they did not sit together on the flight. Sidarra had a window at least. From there, she watched her country shrink and the countryside of another turn green and mountainous again. The scenery was a little different; the flight was direct this time. Still, it looked like the recurrence of a beautiful dream, one Sidarra started to worry she might never see again.

It had not been so long since their last clandestine visit there, but to Sidarra it still seemed strange that so little had changed about Belize. The weather had not moved. She even thought she recognized the cabdriver as the one they'd met before. And the palm trees still kept up their contorted hope of reaching the shore first. But she and Griff didn't stay in the same villa by the beach. This time Griff had arranged for them to stay in a brand-new high-rise condo British investors had completed months before. The suite was simple but well appointed, fully furnished with a galley kitchen, a bedroom, small living room, and den. Off the main room was a long balcony that overlooked the water and, by then, a long dark sky. The first thing Griff did after they undressed and bared themselves to the humidity was to order up a bottle of

Cuban rum. While Sidarra munched on a snack of good seafood, he promptly got drunk. She sat up on the bed looking out at the moonless night while he curled his worried body up against hers and went to sleep.

Griff slept hard for most of the next morning. She watched him twitch and jerk occasionally as if he were having nightmares, and she finally put on a robe and went outside on the balcony to watch the waves scatter against the shore. Clouds seemed painted on the horizon a thousand miles away like file tabs God had placed above the ocean to lift when He pleased and set the tides in motion. She had fallen back to sleep and only woke when a breeze rattled her teacup. Inside the suite, Griff was snoring gently. Sidarra decided to take a shower.

Perhaps the best thing about the suite was that shower. It was a circular glass enclosure in a triangular room furnished in bamboo and rattan fixtures. On the far side of the circle, the shower opened to a sunlit doorway, the doorway to a long tub, and the tub appeared to extend directly to the sea. Sidarra gently scrubbed her skin under the water and daydreamed to the vista. She had no idea how much time had passed when she felt a strong hand cup her hip. Griff had stood long enough absorbing the sight of her silhouette and now stepped into the water behind her. Realizing it was he, Sidarra closed her eyes and moaned happily. Their groggy hands awakened the skin all over their bodies, sudsing and cleansing until they were locked in full writhing embrace. They clawed and pulled and stretched against the sunlight.

Sidarra let his lips go for a minute to say, "I do love you, Griff." She roamed his eyes with her own. "I'm not sure I ever said that before. But I love you, statue man."

Griff's face took her in. A smile began to grow. "Don't you remember from high school, you're not supposed to say I love you during shower sex?"

Having attended a very different high school, Sidarra grinned, reached for the faucet handles, and turned off the water. "I love you," she repeated. "You're a good man."

He chuckled into her neck. "I was on my way there once, but thanks."

"The way is not closed, baby," she whispered. And they finished against the wet glass wall.

30

THEY HAD BREAKFAST brought up from a restaurant nearby and sat together on the balcony's two sun chairs in white terry cloth. They sat like married people, naked under robes that kept falling open, rubbing toes against each other in playful foot combat. But they ate like a first date, nibbling the edges of things and finishing nothing.

"I let some things slip past me, Griff. I know that," she said. He just listened. "It's hard to believe how needy I was, how scared I must have been. Maybe I should be more terrified now." The waves receded like old applause. "When Koob gave me that first credit card, I don't know, I felt liberated. I felt strong. I wanted to run through places and buy myself."

"Buy yourself what?"

"No, just buy myself. I was trying to buy the person I hoped to become."

Their feet tangled momentarily, then he stroked her calf with his big toe. You could hear children playing in a swimming pool twelve stories below.

"You're not gonna believe me, Sid, but I used to be a sucker for this country."

"Belize?"

"No, ours. That's part of why I went to law school. I really believed the hype. I was proud to say how much I loved America. I remember there were radical classmates of mine who used to assume I was a Republican. Me. I wanted to know all the first principles cold and be able to recite the Constitution as I defended it. Boy, what a wacko I was." He stared at the sea. "Or became."

Neither said a word. She scooted her lounge chair right up close to him so that there was no longer any distance between them and she could see the exact same view of the horizon he did. "Griff, what happened really? Why did people have to die so we could join the stock market?"

Griff turned his long neck up at the sky and almost laughed. Then he rested it back against the chair, grabbed her hand in both of his, and looked out. "I've been wondering a little of that myself, sugar. Basically," he said, turning on his side to face her, "we took advantage of opportunities that nobody expected would come to us. We got carried away with the Whiteboy talk. Once the Raul shit went down with that dealer he shot, he was eager to prove himself. When Koob was getting him ready to get into the chancellor's house, Raul would say shit about what he could do; he'd brag about what he could get away with. Koob always told him not to be so ambitious. One night Koob and I waited for you and talked about it. We talked about 'what if.' What if Raul goes into that house and gets trapped. We figured he's gonna shoot his way out. As long as no one could trace him to us, we might have a dead schools chancellor on our hands. Was there any profit in that? Hell yeah, it turned out, if you could stomach that online mayhem casino. Koob thought you might even be down with it, but I didn't. It didn't seem like something to bother you with at the time, because it didn't seem like something that was gonna happen. When it did, well, we took advantage of situations, Sidarra. I don't know what else to say."

She pulled back from him in her seat as if her stomach had turned. Disbelief grew on her forehead, and his words were starting to make her angry. A huge rush of anger swelled inside her like a rough tide. When Sidarra turned to him, she felt the urge to ball up her fist and punch him in the face. " 'We,' 'we,' 'we,' " she repeated, shaking her head.

"What do you mean '*we*,' Sidarra?"

She turned directly into his eyes with a sharp coldness. "Et tu, Griff?" she asked.

His face twisted up in confusion. "What?" he almost whimpered. Somewhere in the back of his mind he recalled the reference, something from college, but he wasn't sure. "What?" he repeated. Then it came back to him. Shakespeare. Julius Caesar.

"Et tu, *nigga*?" she repeated, cocked her elbow back, and slapped Griff hard across his cheek.

"Sidarra, I didn't betray you."

"No? Then who the fuck is 'we'? The Eagleton thing was bad enough, but *we* had to keep on going? Koob gets pissed off and wants to rob a fucking bank even after he knows a public official's been assassinated—"

"A corrupt corporate director, Sid," he interrupted. "A master pimp hoing black children for shareholder profit."

"He was a human being!" Sidarra screamed to the sky. She stood up and walked in a deliberate little circle before turning back to him. "Listen to how you talk about it even now, Griff. 'We.' Like I had any goddamned say at all. Like I'm just the girl in the movie. This ain't no movie, Griff! I ain't no girl! *This is real life,* man! This is *my* life!"

His eyes grew desperate. All his smarts dropped into the sea. "I know it is, baby. I got caught up."

She waited for him to come with something more, but she couldn't wait. It was all too clear now. "I'm afraid this is bullshit. You've been lying to me all this time, Griff, and now you're just rationalizing. What's wrong with you? How could you do this to me? I have a *child,* man! I'm all she's got." Suddenly tears pierced her rage. "You said you loved me!"

"I do."

"Then why would you take away from me the first chance I had to control my own life? I decided to invest in the stock market to save my life. I joined that club so that I would stop waking up wondering who was gonna fuck with me today. I had already rejected a man who wanted to run my show. Now you. So fucking typical, Griff. I really thought you were different. I thought you got it." Sidarra leaned on the banister and squinted at the sea. *" 'We'!"* she repeated. "What the fuck is wrong with men?"

At first it actually took Griff a moment to realize that Sidarra's horrified look of rage was meant for him. Had he lied? He guessed so. Did he love her? More than anyone or anything he could remember. Did he try to control her the way he couldn't control his own wife? Not on purpose, but the wrong he had put on her face panicked him. He searched it, hoping the anger would leave, but when it refused he was powerless to hold back his own tears.

"I never got to protect a woman," he said quietly. "I always wanted that, Sidarra. And then when I realized that I loved you, how deeply I respected you and wanted you to have, well, it seemed like . . . You're right." He shook his head and stared at his feet for a minute. Then he stood up. "I'm sorry," he nearly asked. "I'm so sorry, baby." He cried into her arms. "I really wanted to help." And locked in tears, they held and swayed.

After a while, their arms slowly fell off each other. Sidarra sniffled a bit and wiped her face with the wide sleeve of the terry cloth robe. She was okay. She even wiped his face dry. They settled back into their chairs.

"Why in the world didn't Yakoob just stop Raul?" she asked in a whisper. "Was he afraid of him?"

Griff pulled up a little surprised. "Yeah, he was." He paused. "Me too. That man was not just a little dangerous. He was completely dangerous. I mean, I failed, Sidarra, hard as it is to say it. The thing was complicated. They seemed to have some kind of undetectable history going on, like a big brother-little brother thing. By the time I really got it, it was too late."

Sidarra rubbed her eyes and shook her head. "Jesus, you guys really needed me. Thugs are my specialty." She closed her robe, folded her legs, and squinted at the blue wall of water before them for a while. "Are you going to prison, Griff?"

"Probably."

"Is the case strong?"

"Not nearly as strong as they'd like to think, I figure." He cleared his throat and got his strength back. "First of all, nobody really believes there's more than one black person on earth who could ever pull this off—and he's a Supreme Court justice. Second of all, they've got so many agencies involved—the Manhattan and Brooklyn D.A.s' offices, the U.S. Attorney, DEA, FBI, the IRS—that they're all probably tripping over themselves right now, I would guess, trying to get us on everything and giving each other as little as they can. At the end of the day, sugar, I think they'll have no chance of proving we knew anything certain about the chancellor's death. Whatever we gained is gonna look awfully lucky. There were three types of accounts, you know, and the cash ones are out of the question. The shell corporations are still an X factor, but I think we're probably okay on those. It's just the early ones, the ones we did on credit cards where we might have slipped up a little. I'm pretty sure Koob used some real names before that money got converted into stocks. They can't really follow them, I don't think. But they'll try. That's why people say you always want to follow the money. That's also why people say what they do about dead men talking."

"You could stand to be in prison?"

"Are you kidding?" He laughed a little falsely. "I've got more friends in there than I can count, Sid."

She turned toward Griff's face. "What about Yakoob? Is he gonna do time?"

"I have to think so, sweetheart. He's in as deep as me at least. They obviously started with his passwords and may not get too far, so they tend to want to stay with that first guy. If the Fidelity shit ever comes up, he could really go away. But he promised us both he'd never open an account in there, he'd just hack from outside. He should be clear of that one. Yakoob is a good brother. In a way, he's like *my* brother now. He just has to accept the system for what it is and not try to get too bold."

"Yakoob?" she giggled. "C'mon. What do you mean?"

"I mean, he told me he wants to go to trial. He still wants to plead innocent to everything and make 'em prove their shit. That's too risky. You gotta plea this shit out. You do that and all the colors of the masterpiece they want to paint for a jury sink down in a puddle. They already know my life is ruined. They know I'll be disbarred, won't practice another day of law in New York. They probably even know Belinda will never lay eyes on me again and will take everything I didn't hide. But Koob's got a woman. Nobody's gonna miss me but the brothers I meet inside. On the other hand, he's got somebody to get back to fast. So he's the last one who should be beating his chest." Griff turned close to Sidarra, grabbed her hand even tighter, and sat up a little. "The only question is whether I will have someone waiting for me, Sidarra."

"What are you talking about, baby? I, I assumed from all you've been saying that I'm going down too, for something anyway."

"No, darling," he said very clearly. "The 'we' ends there. If you just lay low and don't make it easy for them, I really don't think they're gonna get to you, Sid."

"Why not?"

Griff smiled into her eyes with an almost fatherly admiration. He seemed to be counting the things he could say to her, just as he had spent the last half hour expressing conclusions he had reached over many sleepless and calculating days. But this answer had nothing to do with the law.

"Because you're loved."

YAKOOB WOKE HAPPILY to the sculpture of Marilyn's sleeping body and sat up in the Sunday calm of a July morning, occasionally kissing points along her side. Periwinkle sheets twisted in long lines between her tawny thighs, up over one shoulder, and into a ball of clenched fingers against her peaceful face. He studied her eyelids for a long time, blew light breaths upon a single peeking nipple, and inhaled the warm weight of her scent. Then, for the first time in many months, Yakoob leaned into his wife's outstretched body and made love to her without the hope of pregnancy, but just to love her soundly.

Maybe an hour or so later it was Marilyn's turn to take in the unguarded perfection of her partner. His naked feet were never as bad as he made out, she smiled as her toes gently caressed his. He self-consciously snatched them back under the sheets and stirred with a chuckle. Her eyes looked distracted.

"What you thinking 'bout, baby?" he whispered hoarsely.

Marilyn leaned on her elbow and began to stroke Yakoob's chest hairs. "Is it really that good?" she asked.

"It's all good," he assured her, turning in the pillow to look into her eyes.

"No, sweetie. I mean, all the stuff we got now. Amazon.com

and McDonald's. Somebody told me you don't really see the money so fast with the stock market. I'm not doubting you. But how come we do, baby?"

The sun nearly fell across them like truth serum, and Yakoob felt the light of lies nearly blind him. He blinked hard and felt his pulse change. "Dividends, sugar," he said calmly. "Some people don't cash them when they come. We do."

She thought for a long moment, not completely satisfied with his response. "That makes me feel kind of stupid, Koob." He sat up beside her. "The idea that I don't know anything about the stock market, you know? And people just saying things about the stuff that's changed my *life* with you, baby, and I'm thinking I don't know *shit* about this. *I* want to be someone's mother? A *mother*—who doesn't know adult things?" Her brown eyes creased as they stared into his, and she drew up and kneeled on the mattress while squeezing the fingers on one hand with the other. "That's bullshit, isn't it? That shit's got to change for me. I have to know all about shit like that. You need to be a teacher, Yakoob. Okay?"

Suddenly disappointed in himself, he took a deep breath as he gazed back and forth between her eyes. "You're right, baby. I will. I'll try," he said with all the courage he could muster.

It was still early in the morning when they came, and well before there was any chance he might get away. They came with two vans, a few squad cars, a battering ram, and a warrant. Yakoob and Marilyn had both fallen back to sleep when the banging began at their front door. The neighbors woke too and watched as Yakoob was brought out into the sunlight in handcuffs, slippers, and only his velour warm-up pants to clothe him. Thing by thing, one by one, the marshals and agents carried his personal belongings into the street and onto the vans. The plasma TVs, sound systems, video games, racks of clothes, boxes of jewelry, a stash of herb, the basketball trophies, Bally shoes, three fur coats, a recliner stuffed with hundred-dollar bills, and, most importantly, the last of all his hard drives, monitors, backup systems and CD-ROMs were tagged with yellow "evidence" tape and removed. The black Escalade sat atop a flatbed truck waiting obliviously to be towed away. Yakoob lowered his head into his chest and dragged himself through the neighborhood perp walk while Marilyn, wearing only an old silk nightgown, screamed through her hysterical tears, *"Maricón, maricones, you fucking bastards!"* into the July air.

"I got you, baby!" she screamed after him with all her might. "Don't worry, baby, I'll get you out! *Maricones! Maricones motherfuckers!"*

| 31 |

SIDARRA'S MOTHER HAD A PHRASE she applied mostly to food storage: "Just to be on the safe side." Just to be on the safe side, Sidarra had emptied several different accounts she held with different banks into the money market fund with Raquel's name on it earlier in the week. She had closed most accounts that bore her own name and transferred a large amount of cash to a charter school fund she had set up in a small local bank based in California. Sidarra wanted to sell the Mercedes or give it away, but had decided at the last minute to simply pay it off. Now, as she and Griff prepared to leave the condo for a walk in the town before they would have to depart from Belize, she poured the contents of her travel bag onto the desk beside Griff's bulging billfold.

"What's all that?" he asked, pointing to the small pile of gum wrappers, tissues, receipts, lipstick, and plastic.

"Credit cards for the sea," she smiled. Arrayed before them she spread a half dozen plastic cards from department stores, American Express, Visa, and MasterCard, all in the name of her alias, Desiree Galore.

"Is that what you had to go back for when we were leaving?" Griff asked as he buckled his belt.

"Yes, these and a few personal items," she answered matter-of-factly. She opened the desk drawer, pulled out a pair of scissors, and methodically sliced each card into many pieces. He turned and walked into the bathroom for something. Sidarra pulled a small black box out from under the pile. She opened it, pulled Michael's radiant diamond from its blue velvet pond, wrapped it in a napkin, and stuck the ring in her jacket pocket. Then she collected the jagged pieces of credit cards, placed them in a paper bag she stuffed into her purse, tossed the rest of the stuff into the trash, and waited for Griff to take her for their stroll.

When Griff was finished with his own preparations, he came back to the desk area and picked up the billfold.

"Is that what I think it is?" she asked.

"Depends what you think, love. I've got something I need to do on our way out."

When they got downstairs to the marbled lobby, Griff stood with Sidarra under the overhead fans and asked to see the concierge. As they waited, Sidarra looked around and noticed that everyone working there was a deep, luscious brown. The pretty women at the front desk. The straitlaced doormen. The baggage assistants in their bright red uniforms. The janitors clearing cigarette butts from the ashtrays. Even the concierge of this British investment was brown.

"What can I do for you and your lovely wife, sir?" the man asked.

"Is unit number 12D where we stayed still available for sale?" Griff asked.

"Of course, sir. But we have much better for not much more money, American," the man replied.

"No. I think we like that one just fine. However, we're in a bit of a hurry to return to Chicago. We have a plane to catch." Griff reached into his slacks, retrieved the hefty grip so the man couldn't miss it, and patted the leather cover with one hand. "Can we do this quickly?"

"Of course," said the man. "We are quite happy to accommodate you. Let me bring you to the sales office and we can have you out of here in no time at all."

"I appreciate that."

Moments later they were seated in a small, plushly decorated room with a huge fish tank behind the sales manager's desk. She too was brown and a little too taken with Griff's hazel eyes for Sidarra's taste. A few lies, twenty-eight minutes, $65,000 in cash, plus a few years of prepaid condo fees later, Griff had an envelope with all the pertinent information and a quitclaim deed in his jacket pocket. On the way out of the lobby doors, he addressed it to a P.O. box, paid for the postage, and dropped it in a mail slot. In Sidarra's pocket was the sales office business card with a number she'd scribbled on the back while Griff was signing papers: Unit 12D.

"My instinct tells me I probably should turn around, go back up there, and move in when we're finished in town," he told her as they walked arm in arm to a taxi. "But at least I have someplace to come back to one day."

Sidarra wished she too had thought of such a move. That, in many ways, was the difference between her and Griff, the difference between Griff and Michael, and the person she had been looking for these forty years without knowing who. For a married man, Griff seemed to do so much so well alone, as if he were born to it. He made more peace than he knew. And now there was nothing worse than knowing the peace they had made together, a peace that didn't really rely on dollars and the Cicero Club, was in danger of locking shut.

They never walked so slowly. The slow town speeded by them as they walked its dusty streets with serene smiles. They dawdled over knickknacks, stopped to watch kids play music on the street, and fed each other snacks from sunlit stands selling God knows what. Their steps matched so perfectly, each leftward stride an elegant march into a hard-won future, each right foot forward a step closer to the gallows of the present.

"I promised myself I would not buy anything," Sidarra said as they passed a colorful hat stand, "but I think I might need to make just one exception."

She tried on a wide floppy straw hat with a Diana Ross brim and a red ribbon. It covered half her face, exposed a single sunglassed eye, and fit her head like a tropical gangster's. Long ago she had gotten her mother in trouble with Aunt Chickie over a hat like that. "Why not?" Griff said. "Keep your promise. I never bought you a birthday present."

She laughed like a silly schoolgirl again while Griff paid for the hat. Within minutes that street in Belize was a memory and they were in a cab on their way back to the airport.

Each mile under the old taxi's wheels spelled something foreboding. The time was running out. To distract her stomach from the death-defying drive over unbanked mountain curves, Sidarra decided to sing to Griff. She chose another Anita Baker number that had popped into her head, "Sometimes I Wonder Why." Griff's bones received every note. His spine tingled, and the driver slowed to a crawl as Sidarra lifted her voice and sang: *"This tightrope that I walk/A tightrope without a net below/And if I fall, child I just fall/Because I know/I know/I'll love you till I die . . ."*

Suddenly Sidarra stopped singing. "Driver?" she called out as the car ambled around a seaside cliff. "Please stop for a minute. I just want to get one more look at the water."

The man pulled the car over to the side of the road, Sidarra indicated to Griff to stay and jumped out of the door. She hurried across the dirt road in the breeze and stood at the edge of the cliff. The waters swirled in rock jetties way below. Griff watched Sidarra's profile against the sun. She pulled the small bag of credit card cuttings from her purse, opened it to insert a handful of pebbles she found at her feet, and flung the package over the side.

"Goodbye, kind lady," she whispered into an indifferent breeze.

When she saw it disappear under the white bubbles, she got back in the taxi.

She and Griff sailed through every checkpoint with the ease of man and wife. Smiles greeted them and their backs as they boarded. Griff had managed to seat them together for the first leg of the trip, a flight to Chicago before they had to change planes. As much as they had to say, they kept their shades on, clasped each other's hands as the borders flew by beneath them, and napped ear to ear. The landing in Chicago was bumpy and they woke to the loud bounce of rubber on tarmac.

Griff's face had already changed as they walked to the connecting gate at O'Hare. Sidarra decided not to tell him about that habit of his until they were back in New York. She would have the whole flight to think of things she thought they could change in their relationship. For all his legal calculations, Sidarra had a feeling he was not going anywhere without her.

They waited at the gate to board the final leg. Griff turned to her once the line of first-class passengers began moving forward. They stood together near the window, the nose of the plane just outside the pane. Griff lifted the wide straw brim of her new hat so he could see both her eyes. "I'm afraid we're not sitting together for this flight, Sid."

She shrugged. "I figured as much. That's okay. It's a short enough flight."

"I'm in the front. Unfortunately, you're back near the bathrooms."

"I'll survive," she said.

"I know you will. Listen, I, uh, want you to know how you've changed my life."

"C'mon, Griff. There's plenty of time for that." She squeezed him against her hips and touched his face. Griff let out a little surprised gasp, and his whole body tensed with unexpected delight.

"Sidarra?"

"Yes, baby?"

"I love you."

"I love you too."

"Please don't forget what I told you on the balcony."

"That I'm loved?"

"Yes."

"You think just because you say it it's true?"

He smiled. "Yup." He kissed her slowly and softly. "I'll meet you by the baggage claim."

They hugged. Her row was called, she blew him one last kiss and walked onto the plane alone.

You cannot hear sirens on the ground from a plane approaching a gate, but Sidarra still thought she did when they had landed in New York. She stood with the other passengers in the rear, waiting the interminable wait for the passengers up front to deplane. People all around her sighed hot, irritated breaths in her face, and she had to sit back down. Why Griff wanted to meet by the baggage claim when neither of them had any baggage was another question she would put to his know-it-all ass as soon as she relieved herself of the agitated arms and bodies around her. They waited and waited. the loudspeaker began to cackle overhead.

"I'm sorry, folks, but this is your captain speaking," it said. "The rest of you are being held up here at the gate while there's a police investigation going on. It should be just another few minutes or so. We appreciate your patience."

At that point Sidarra almost lost her mind. She immediately began to tremble with fear, and the first face she saw in her head was Raquel's. The panic was overwhelming. She looked around for a way to get out, but there were tightly packed bodies everywhere. She stood in a fret. The second face she saw in her mind was Griff's. Oh no! she almost said aloud, but something made her stop. She quieted herself. She tried to vanish from people's suspicious eyes. A few minutes later, and at last they were all moving again.

"Thank you. Hope to see you again soon," the captain and flight attendants told her as she deplaned, as if nothing were amiss.

Sidarra stepped cautiously up the ramp into the terminal. She lowered the wide straw brim over her shaded eyes, walked with a slight hunch, and gripped her bag for all it was worth. Once she was well inside the terminal, she sidestepped crowds of reuniting families and curious onlookers. There ahead in the long corridor was Griff, his back to her, his arms spread wide like a bird in flight, a circle of blue-uniformed police officers and airport security surrounding him. She got behind a black family and matched their strides. Sidarra kept her head down as she passed. She heard the steel cuffs snap shut and caught just a glimpse of Griff with his head thrown back and his eyes closed in a rare and powerful silence.

"You have the right to remain . . . Anything you say may be used against you . . ."

She quickened her pace once she got a few feet ahead of them. She wanted to run. The youngest kid in the black family launched into a tantrum. His parents tried to pull him away, but he wanted to see what was happening to the man with his arms out.

"Are they gonna shoot him?" the boy asked his father.

Sidarra hustled to a slow jog and disappeared down the corridor. When she got outside to the taxi stand, she cut the line. New

Yorkers cursed her as she handed the man directing cabs a twenty-dollar bill. She hopped in the taxi, slammed the door, and said, "Go! Upper Manhattan. Please go! I gotta go *now*!"

Inside the cab, safe for a minute on the Van Wyck Expressway, she fumbled for her cell phone. Her fingers were trembling so badly she dropped the phone. It wasn't on. She turned it on. It took forever to light up. When it did, the clock read 4:47. She dialed her home number. It rang and rang. Finally Aunt Chickie answered.

"It's me. Has anyone been to the house today?" she asked.

"No. What's the matter, Sidarra? Are you all right?"

"Is Raquel with you?"

"Yeah, she's right here. I'll put her on."

"Mommy?"

"Yes, sweetheart. It's Mommy. I'm back. I'm safe. I want you to go to your room. Don't ask me any questions now. It's very important. I want you to pretend we're in a movie."

"What kind of movie?"

Sidarra was stumped. "Um, a James Bond movie, okay? Now, first I want you to think about everything you got in there that you really, really want to have with you for a while. Get a suitcase and put it all in it. We're gonna take a really cool trip. When you're finished, I want you to sit on the suitcase and think, What have I forgot? Then I want you to go pack that too. But only enough to fit into one big suitcase. You can go into my closet and get one of mine. The Louis Vuitton bags. The biggest one you can find, okay?"

"Cool!"

"Good. Then, when you're finished, I want you to go to the kitchen and get the kennel box, the one we took the cat in when she had to go to the vet. Get it and get her. Put Pussy Galore in the cat box and wait for me. We're gonna take a trip. It's gonna be more fun than you've ever had, okay?"

"Okay!"

"Now, put your aunt back on the phone. And, Raquel, hurry!"

"What are you telling this girl, Sidarra? She's bouncing like a jitterbug."

"Aunt Chickie, I can't get into it over the phone. There's been a problem. Don't say anything out loud to scare Raquel. There's a guy. He might be stalking the house. We have to get out."

"Oh, Sidarra."

"Look, damnit! I'm not playing and I don't need any 'Oh, Sidarra's.' This shit is serious!"

There was a pause. "I'm sure you'll explain that one to me when I see you."

"I'm sorry. I will. But right now I need you to pack your most favorite things. What you can't fit into a couple of suitcases, try to pack into something else, and I'll arrange to have them picked up later. I know this sounds crazy. I know it's not fair. But just trust me right now. This guy is dangerous. We'll sort it all out soon. I'm on my way."

There was another long pause. "Okay. I'll do the best I can."

"Thank you, Aunt Chickie. Thank you. I gotta go now. Whatever you do, do not answer the door, and keep the lights off in the front of the house until I get there."

Aunt Chickie sighed. Sidarra could imagine the look she was giving the phone. "So much drama all the time, geez. You know, Sidarra, when we get a moment, I'd like to talk to you about the men in your life. Meantime, is there anything we should get for you?"

Sidarra thought for a second. "No. No, I'm okay. Just take care of yourselves and I'll be right there. Goodbye. Now, hang up and don't answer the phone again till you see me."

Sidarra hung up only to see the cabdriver's eyes bulging at her in the rearview mirror. "Just drive, please," she said as politely as she could. "I, uh, have an abusive ex-boyfriend. There's an order of protection out for him."

The man nodded. "I hope they get the guy," he said in a thick Middle Eastern accent. "They should cut off his balls!"

"Thank you, sir. Please, just drive as fast as you can. I'll be all right."

The driver muttered curses the whole rest of the way across the Triborough Bridge and onto the 138th Street bridge over the Harlem River. He raced like a professional, and they were in front of the garage where Sidarra had parked her Mercedes in about eleven minutes.

"No charge, lady. But please, get yourself a gun, okay? The Glock is good. I have one."

"That's very kind of you, sir. You're probably right."

"Pow pow!" he said. "Beautiful lady like you should not be running."

Sidarra ran up to the third floor of the parking garage and got into her car. She circled her block three times and finally double-parked in front of her brownstone. She raced up the stairs, realized she'd left the car running, ran back for the keys, and bolted into the house. "I'm home!" she screamed. Raquel came to the top of the stairs to greet her. Sidarra flew up and nearly tackled her, smothered her in wet kisses, and grabbed her up in one arm like Hercules. Raquel tried to protest and get down. She wanted to explain all that she had done already, including packing the cat and some of Sidarra's most precious things, but Sidarra wouldn't put her down. Instead, Sidarra listened and asked questions as she roamed frantically from room to room with the not-so-little girl hanging from her clenched bicep. Sidarra was ten minutes into packing up her own stuff and ready to move to the third floor when Aunt Chickie finally made it up the stairs.

"Sit down, Sidarra," she ordered.

"I can't, Aunt Chickie."

"Oh yes you can."

Sidarra finally stopped. She stood with Raquel still a few inches sideways off the floor and looked at her aunt, who absolutely was not playing. It struck her then. She could not breathe. She hadn't breathed since she got out of the cab. Raquel drifted slowly down to her feet. Aunt Chickie walked carefully to the banister and leaned back, staring suspiciously at her niece. "We can't stop till we go," Sidarra explained.

"I don't go like that. I'm a little too old for escapes. You wanna tell me what's going on?"

Sidarra looked around helplessly. She clenched her fingers and wiped sweat off her brow. "Okay. But quickly. Raquel, please go upstairs and put Grandma and Grandpa's shrine in a careful pile. That's coming too. Don't touch the photographs. I'll get the photographs." Only too glad to be part of the mad dash, Raquel raced upstairs with energy nobody else in the house could match. When they had both watched her skinny legs make it to the top of the stairs, Sidarra returned her aunt's powerful gaze. "I know this contradicts some of the good things you might have thought about me, Aunt Chickie. I know I seem wild. I want to explain it all to you. But right now, I want us all to be safe, and I think I know how to do it. So, please?"

Aunt Chickie washed her face with her hand. She began at the cheek and slowly moved it down her supple jowl and around her chin to her neck, where it rested in the gentle skin for a minute. "Baby, this is not how we do it. Let me try to help you."

Sidarra stared at her, first angrily for slowing things down, then desperately, and finally Sidarra's bottom lip began to quiver. Her eyes welled up with tears that soon streamed down her face. "I fucked up," she cried. "I fucked up, Aunt Chickie. It's a dangerous situation for all of us, okay? And I'm sorry," she sobbed. "I'm sorry to do this to you."

Aunt Chickie raced over to her as quickly as her body could manage and wrapped her arms around Sidarra's neck. "I'm here. What is it, baby? I'm here."

"I'm in trouble. I took advantage. I could lose you all," she cried. "We have to go. I need you, Aunt Chickie. We have to get out. We have to get away. Far away."

"Yes, yes," Aunt Chickie cooed, stroking the back of Sidarra's head. "It's gonna be all right. Let Aunt Chickie know. Calm down. You're hysterical. Slow down. Tell me about it, and we'll get through it."

"No, sweetie, this isn't like that," Sidarra wept, and pulled back enough to look her aunt in the eye. "They could come at any minute. I did something wrong, Aunt Chickie. I could go to jail!"

That did it. Aunt Chickie's expression changed all of a sudden. Her own eyes glassed up, and she searched Sidarra's face for exaggeration, but found none. She wiped Sidarra's tears away, but more just fell in their place. "I need you to concentrate, Sidarra. The baby's upstairs. You two are all I got. Now, tell me this: Do we really have to go? Right this minute? Do we?" she demanded.

Sidarra tried to hold her gaze. Her legs felt limp and she wanted to drop into her aunt's arms. Her lips quivered and tears streaked all over her face. "Yes. Please believe me. They already have the others. We have to go, Aunt Chickie. Please. I can't lose my child!"

Aunt Chickie shook Sidarra about the shoulders with a force she had not possessed in many years. "Okay, Sidarra! Okay. Then we'll go. C'mon now. I'll finish getting my things. You get yours. This is the time. We'll go."

"Thank you. Thank you," she cried.

"No. Thank me later. If you say we must go, then let's go. C'mon. *Go!*"

Sidarra sprang back into action. She turned and hurdled up the stairs to find Raquel. She helped her finish gathering the shrine and collected all the pictures. She found a box in a closet and threw all the things in it, trying to remember to get all the photos, hats, shoes, scarves, and CDs they might need. She found another box and threw a hundred small items in it that Darrius might not be able to find for her. Then she checked to make sure Raquel could handle the weight and told her to carry the things down to the vestibule so they could put them in the trunk of the car.

Finally she had to make the rounds of her own clothes and other items on the second floor. Raquel had done a hell of a job putting things into a few suitcases. Sidarra tried to make a mental picture of the trunk space, and so far everything seemed to fit. Raquel swore that she had everything she might need. Sidarra ordered her back up to see if there were other things in the house she might need for a really, really long vacation. Then Sidarra went to her bedroom and started putting her very best clothes, shoes, and some jewelry in a silver box she'd saved from Bergdorf Goodman's. It even had a small latch, and when it was full, she closed it. Next, she went to a drawer and pulled out her special jewelry. There was the gem-studded tiara Yakoob had so foolishly bought her for her fortieth birthday. She wrapped that in a scarf and tried to fit it in her coat pocket. It barely fit. She wormed her hand down to the bottom of the pocket, tossed away some napkins she'd hidden there along with a few idle pieces of crumpled paper, and found Michael's ring. She pulled that out and tried it on her finger. It fit perfectly. She stuffed the tiara in the empty pocket. Then she went to her bathroom closet, pulled back a makeup mirror, and retrieved $85,000 in cash from a box. She stuffed the money into several boxes. Nothing else remained. She looked around, trying to calm herself so she could think twice about things she might regret leaving behind. She pulled a mascara pen off the dressing table and put an *X* on the silver Bergdorf bag. Everything else was either in her pockets or stowed in the suitcases Raquel had mostly packed. She pushed them all down the stairs, ran after them, grabbed her family, and set the alarm. Sidarra paused for a moment and noticed that the huge mirror in the front hall had been neglected, it was covered in dust, and she almost thought to clean it. Then she saw her reflection, a resolute expression of pure craziness taunting her, and moved quickly out of the frame. She turned off the lights, locked the door, and headed down the stoop to help load the Mercedes.

"Where are we going, Bond? James Bond," Raquel asked as her mother tried to stuff the trunk with their life.

"Oh, I thought we'd visit your uncle for a while," Sidarra said.

"Goody! Can I sit in the front?" Raquel asked.

"Most definitely. I need a good copilot."

With the doors shut and no cars behind them, Sidarra, Raquel, Aunt Chickie, and Pussy Galore took off into the long July sunset. Sidarra drove around and around before settling onto the West Side Highway heading south.

While Raquel sang songs quietly to herself, Sidarra and Aunt Chickie remained mostly silent in their own heads. Sidarra finally pulled the car off at Chambers Street and headed east toward the Brooklyn Bridge. The early Sunday evening traffic was moving well enough, but not too fast, just as she wanted. Crossing the bridge, she was just another car. On the other side, she drove down Adams as usual and pulled up by the side entrance to her office at the Board of Miseducation.

"This is where your mommy used to work," she told Raquel. "I'll be right back," she told Aunt Chickie, and left the engine running. Sidarra then used her key to get in the side entrance, waved to the guard, and went upstairs. When she got to her floor, she went through her drawers and pulled out any personal information. So many idle years left few things of value. She grabbed up pictures, a few pens, and some stationery just in case. Then she logged on to her computer and sent a quick memo to everyone in her unit saying there had been a death in her family and that she would be taking an indefinite leave of absence. She listed a few important document numbers of things she had been working on since becoming a deputy and logged off. The next part was the hardest, and she took a long breath. She needed to create the impression of confusion in the administrative record. She needed to look like a victim and disappear from the file. Her name and employee record had to go. This moment and almost two decades would vanish with a few simple keystrokes: Control-86 Transfer Command.

Next, Sidarra tiptoed down the hall to the back stairs and went up to the chancellor's floor, her new floor, if only she had waited for her new executive office to be cleaned out. She was surprised to find Dr. Blackwell's office door unlocked. Sidarra feared turning on the light and instead walked carefully in the dark to the big leather chair behind the grand old desk. There she pulled from her pocket the gem-studded tiara Yakoob had given her and placed it carefully in the middle drawer of the desk. Then she made her way back downstairs, past the guard, who was covered in the sports pages, and left the building for the last time. Eight minutes later, she was on the Verrazano Bridge, speeding toward New Jersey.

Finding the Short Hills Mall after dark was tricky, but she did. It was the only place in New Jersey she knew, and New Jersey was roughly south and west, which is the direction the navigational system on her Mercedes told her to go. At the mall, she, Raquel, and Aunt Chickie had a bite to eat, bought a few items to make the ride more comfortable for them, and headed to a mailbox store that was about ready to close. Sidarra left the other two outside and went in to mail a few items. She sent the silver Bergdorf box full of clothes, jewelry, and just under $25,000 cash to Marilyn at the pharmacy where she worked at the corner of Duane and Reade streets. Then she scribbled a short note to Darrius and included the key and a little thank-you cash in the envelope, and sent that off too. Driving most of the night, they pulled into an Ohio motel by 3:00 A.M. The important thing, she realized as her head adjusted to the strange-smelling pillow, was that they were gone. Long gone in the slow lane to New Mexico.

| 32 |

ORIGINALLY, THE CASE OF THE UNITED STATES versus Griffin Haley Coleman and Yakoobiah B. Jones was tried as one. The two men sat in court with their lawyers at the defendants' table for several hearings at which they wore the same crisp dark suits and faced ahead like silent soldiers captured behind enemy lines. They sat beside each other and listened to the lawyers exchange technical arguments with the judge as the prosecution began disclosing evidence of the crimes with which they were charged. They were alleged to have violated both state and federal laws, but the charges were combined for a single trial in federal court. After some internal office wrangling, Jeffrey Geiger was named the lead prosecutor.

At times the case seemed stronger than Griff had thought. The police hackers had indeed reproduced the computer traces of credit card fraud by recovering files long deleted from Yakoob's hard drive. They identified a grand total of $172,000 which had been misappropriated from a victim list of twenty-one individuals. Geiger was one of them, but the judge allowed him to proceed with the prosecution despite the possible conflict of interest. The handwriting on the yellow piece of legal paper was identified as Griff's. Their bank accounts started to increase, then fluctuate wildly shortly after the first names were found on the system. Since the illicit monies had been used in stock purchases across state lines, the two men had engaged in interstate commerce, which could land them in federal, not state, prison. Anything purchased with the kitty was considered ill-gotten gain.

The rest of the case would have to proceed from that basis. And the prosecution would, of course, have to prove that the incredible accumulation of stock market wealth connected to the death of Chancellor Eagleton, a Solutions, Inc. director and shareholder, was more than coincidence—say, a lucky online bet. Griff and Koob would not only have to have known Raul Rodriguez, they would have to be shown to conspire with him for homicidal ends. That would amount to both securities fraud and murder. The only problem, Geiger discovered after the second court hearing before the judge, was that the key was in showing that Griff and Yakoob had benefited from the Solutions, Inc. IPO as illegal insiders. If they weren't invited to buy stock in their own identities, the government would have to show that they had somehow disguised themselves as angels during the angel round of financing. But, as Griff's attorney pointed out in pretrial conferences inside the judge's chambers, that would entitle the defense to examine the records of *all* the shareholders who were allowed to participate in the IPO. With a little resourcefulness, he had already learned that Jack Eagleton was not so upstanding after all. The chancellor had made timely announcements on education policy intended to artificially drive up the value of the company just before it went public. At the last minute he had also personally authorized the issuance of a thousand shares of Solutions, Inc. to his wife and children in the name of a nonexistent trust fund. That was insider trading. A trial on that charge would reveal publicly that the good chancellor was dirty. So the government decided to leave that count out.

Griff was right about one thing—that it was a good time to make a deal. All that was left of the charges against him were the credit card thefts, conspiracy to commit fraud, receipt of stolen goods, and, for failing to pay a cent in capital gains taxes on dividends, tax evasion for almost a million dollars' worth of traceable wealth. It was not nice to make online bets on the deaths of public figures, but it was not illegal to do so. Much to Jeffrey Geiger's supreme personal disgust, the United States Attorney's office agreed to a plea arrangement by which Griffin Haley Coleman would pay about $75,000 in restitution to his victims with interest, settle his debt plus penalties to the Internal Revenue Service, and serve a required minimum of seventeen months in a medium-security federal penitentiary designed for white-collar convicts. His license to practice law was also revoked. He would never vote again. The Full Count would be sold at auction—in all likelihood, back to Q. Griff's wife Belinda, who did not fly back from Japan to attend any of the proceedings, filed for immediate divorce and put their brownstone up for sale.

Encouraged by the busted securities fraud case, Yakoob stayed on to fight at trial. While Marilyn watched every day from the seat behind her husband, the prosecution showed a jury reams of technical computer evidence. They called Yakoob a "terrorist mastermind" and, over the objections of his defense lawyer, hammered repeated references to Yakoob's association with a neighborhood friend, Raul Rodriguez, a.k.a. the notorious "Candy Man," who had viciously assassinated the city's beloved schools chancellor in his home. When it was all over, Raul had been linked to at least two murders, the unprovoked near-bludgeoning-to-death of a

Harlem man named Tyrell Johnson, and assorted acts of wanton thuggery. It didn't matter that Raul was dead or that he was not on trial. Nor did the jury think Yakoob was the least bit funny. He faced all the same charges as Griff and was convicted of them all.

Yet the real problem with deciding not to take a plea as Griff had was that Yakoob's continuing trial gave the prosecution the time it needed to connect him to Fidelity. It wasn't just that by then the police hackers had become intimately familiar with Koob's hacking fingerprint—his methods and patterns of field deduction and decoding. It was that his computer showed him to be inside the bank itself. It was almost so obvious that for weeks they missed it. His own bank had been hit by rare identity thefts that, when properly traced, had to come from either a customer or an employee. The thief had to have a password, because the firewall had not yet been breached. Griff was fortunate that these facts came out *after* his plea was accepted for related crimes; he could not be retried. Yakoob was lucky that Cavanaugh was alive. Still, the judge sentenced Koob to a mandatory minimum of six years in prison.

Immediately after the sentence was announced, both Marilyn and Yakoob dropped lifelessly to the floor. Koob bumped his head on the defendant's table going down. He was still unconscious when Marilyn came to, crying to say goodbye and holding her stomach. While she waited for an ambulance with her mother, she watched them wheel her husband away on a gurney. An hour later, an emergency room doctor would tell her the good news. That cramp in her stomach was the developing embryo the fall did not injure at all. Koob too would survive.

Before the judge adjourned the trial, he had explained that the court would retain jurisdiction over the matter in the event the prosecution's unsuccessful efforts to locate the missing Desiree Galore changed. Unfortunately, she did not seem to exist. Unlike

Griff, this coconspirator used no password, left no computer trail, and received whatever gains she got through a fictitious identity. For all the government knew, she too was dead.

PERHAPS IT WAS SIDARRA'S SLOW, careful driving and too much air blowing through the car's open windows, but Raquel came down with one of those terrible summer colds that prevented her from seeing the beauty of the country they crossed. On the fever's first evening, Sidarra made a comfortable bed of blankets in the backseat for her to curl up on beside the cat. Aunt Chickie sat up front with Sidarra where they could finally talk. But they didn't really. It had been a pretty miserable first three days, and instead they began to argue. They argued and argued. The subject never got much bigger than its common beginnings—that Sidarra was hopelessly lost and refused to accept the fact and get help—but the pitch peaked quickly and stayed there. Sidarra's voice ranged high with short, sharp shrieks of defensiveness, while Chickie's loud accusations filled the small space with low, raspy sweeps of disgust and incredulity. It really came down to: How could you be so stupid? And Sidarra claiming that she was doing everything in her power not to be stupid. Back and forth, over and around each other it went, while Raquel and the old cat slept. It was never clear if they were arguing the same point. But it was true they were lost. After a while, Sidarra admitted that and pulled over onto the shoulder to look at a map.

"You just need to know how disappointed I am in you, Sidarra," Chickie said calmly to the landscape in front of the windshield as Sidarra puzzled over interstates.

"I know you are. You have a right to be," Sidarra whispered.

"Yes, but you must still hear it."

She heard it. With the car stopped, she even confessed a lot of what the Cicero Club did to get investment money. She didn't tell about the blood, though; Sidarra herself had trouble imagining what happened to Blane and the chancellor. She and Aunt Chickie continued on in silence for a while save for a few sniffles that signaled the spread of Raquel's cold.

"You think Alex will understand?" Sidarra asked.

"Your brother?" Aunt Chickie smirked. "Sure. He's not your problem. You can tell him a lot. He'll want to help you. Heck, he'll be glad to *get* some help, as many kids as he and that woman have running around that big place. No, I wouldn't worry about Alex. I'd worry about your brother Charles."

Sidarra grew somber. "You know we don't talk. Not in many years."

"That may be so, but him and Alex talk all the time. Alex moved out there to be near Charles. You need to remember that Charles has some strong feelings about this kind of stuff. You're not the first criminal in the family, you know."

Sidarra's eyes blinked hard and she turned to her aunt. "What's Kenny's record got to do with Charles?" she asked, recalling her youngest brother's bouts with the law.

"I'm not talking about Kenny, Sidarra." Aunt Chickie took a deep breath and tried to blow down the road ahead. "I'm talking about your father."

"Daddy?" Sidarra said in shock.

"Yes, precious. Your father. Your father spent most of the first two years of your brother Kenny's life in jail for running numbers. I guess you were too young to remember that. Maybe you blotted it out. So did Kenny. But Charles didn't."

"My God," Sidarra said softly. "Charles never forgave him?"

"Charles does not forgive."

Sidarra scanned the horizon, then looked over at her aunt, whose face looked tired yet peaceful bathed in the deep auburn light of late sunset, and smiled. She took a long breath, checked the rearview mirror for cars, and pulled out again onto the highway. The words stayed in the air. The long road had grown lonely of other travelers.

"Sidarra, are you done wasting yourself for men?" Aunt Chickie asked, surprising her.

"I didn't do this for a man, Aunt Chickie. I was broke. That cat managed money better than I did. Hell, I was past broke, I was broken. I'd run out of expectations. If it weren't for Raquel, I was ready to die. You might have noticed, but I was angry too. After Mommy and Daddy died. Very angry. So I was trying to live again, I think. I had forgotten how."

"You remember now?" Chickie grunted.

Sidarra shook her head. "I'm not sure. You think you know the secrets after a while—about your own feelings, about how to get the images out of your head, how you're gonna go on without your people. The pain subsides just enough for you to put your work clothes on again every day, and off you go, you know? On to the next best thing to save yourself from drowning in it all. Pretty soon you think you're really doing something. You've really turned a corner. Because you now have an understanding that you paid for with all that pain, and at least it's paid and you're out the other side. You know?" She looked over and Aunt Chickie had drifted off to sleep, her mouth open. Sidarra could speak freely, and aloud she continued. "But you're not. You're not on the other side of grief. Time has just passed. You thought your depression would kill you, but it didn't. So you had days and days to fill; you had a job and a daughter and needs to fulfill. No matter how selfish it seemed, you just couldn't stop thinking about your own life. You got distracted from your parents and stopped seeing them in their final moment of violence, stopped thinking about what they were supposed to be doing this day and that, stopped hoping they'd magically call and continue the conversation you never finished. You never decided to do your own thing again, you just did it. And lo and behold, your thing became some other thing that would *never* have been possible before, or desirable, when they were here. You never would have even looked at it. You would have seen it for the trouble that it is. But now you just did it, naturally, it seemed, because for all its stupid mischief it contained *love,* the one thing you knew you had to have. Again.

"I guess it takes longer to figure out than I thought."

THE TWO-LANE HIGHWAY CURVED gently through the earth. Aunt Chickie was fast asleep beside her while Pussy Galore's marigold eyes peered out at the sky from deep in the corner of her box. Still a little congested, Raquel snored gently in the backseat. So this is flight, Sidarra thought. Dusk fell in slow motion. The engine was a mere purr; the tires followed the asphalt edges effortlessly. An aimless observation struck her: the car really was pretty nice after all. This was what Alex was talking about when he first recommended it. Sidarra leaned way back in the seat with her knee pressed lightly against the steering wheel. One long-nailed finger, like a pool cue sketching angles, was all it took to continue along the line of progress westward. She was fleeing. The countryside in this light resembled the flat, rough terrain she and Griff had watched from planes overhead, the occasional ridge of beige hills like cattle backs, sun-singed bush, and gnarled trees. Down low, it made for peaceful escape. There was a good chance the police weren't even looking for her, but she was running anyway. Now, almost alone on this unknown highway, reality began to catch up. The loss of her beautiful home, maybe forever, and the room she had made. The loss of her job and what she was finally gonna be able to do. The loss of the only city she ever knew. The loss of Harlem in the morning. It would be forgiveness or insanity that would cure her. She had already tried insanity.

Forgiveness could begin with Griff, she realized. There would be no way to call or write to him in prison without the risk of being traced back and discovered. Maybe she should send her letters to the condo in Belize, Unit 12D. There would be no way to show him the charter school she was going to start in New Mexico. So she would have to take pictures at every stage of the project and send them down there, too. By now, the sun had nestled low enough below the horizon's hairless foothills that the last reds were burning into blue. It occurred to her: she could sing to Griff on tape. She could send him anonymous songs of love and faith. She could send those to the prison from anywhere. Griff would know who it was. A thoughtful man like him was going to have a hard time in prison. Somebody would need to sing to him.

Then, like a distraction, what her father would call the secret to this path she was on presented itself in one tiny mirror: the outlines of Raquel asleep, her small fists curled below her chin, her angelic eyelashes closed to dreams, that softest skin. This child would have to forgive Sidarra one day, too, for yanking her clear out of her life. The school she loved. The places in which she secured her own little comfort. Her friends. Michael. And when that happened, Sidarra might finally have grounds to forgive herself.

ON THE NIGHT when the Mercedes-Benz pulled into Alex's driveway just outside Santa Fe, New Mexico, she, Aunt Chickie, and the cat were all sick with Raquel's cold. By then Raquel was fine and fresh from a nap. It was almost ten at night, and everyone but her was so exhausted Alex nearly had to carry each of them into the house. Raquel was not tired at all. Her spirit caught hold of the newness of the surroundings and she could not help herself. The house was large but modest, at the end of a new subdivision by the edge of an endless field. It looked like the desert. The air was still warm, but a sweet-smelling breeze blew in from a distant mountain range. Inside the house you could smell the chicken dinner that still waited on low heat atop the kitchen stove. Raquel's cousins were all asleep by then except Erica, now twelve, whose parents let her stay up. Erica showed Raquel her music collection, walked her through the house, and immediately wanted to hear all about New York City, where she had never visited. Then she took Raquel down to the finished basement, where Alex and his wife Claire were already showing Sidarra and Aunt Chickie what would be their new windowless home. The sparse room was large, clean, and U-shaped, with enough cast-off furniture to swallow echoes. On one side was a long green pool table. Alex explained that he hadn't had time or enough guys willing to dismantle it yet. Nobody had played on it in years, and there'd be plenty more room once it was gone. At the opposite end were sliding glass doors that appeared to lead out to a patio.

"What's out there?" Raquel chirped, her eyes huge with anticipation.

"Oh," Erica answered excitedly, "that's the swimming pool! C'mon, I'll show you."

The four adults watched them practically dance across the basement to the doors. They slid them open together and leaped outside.

"Mommy!" Raquel screamed seconds later. "Quick! Come look!"

Sidarra smiled awkwardly at her big brother and made her way to the doorway. There they shined above them and engulfed the moon by the millions: "Stars!" Raquel shouted.

Stars.

© Thomas Dallal

David Dante Troutt's first published collection of short stories, *The Monkey Suit,* fictionalized ten actual legal controversies involving African Americans from slavery to the present. His nonfiction includes legal and political commentary and analysis for national periodicals and legal scholarship about poverty, race, urban development, and intellectual property. Troutt recently edited an anthology of essays, *After the Storm: Black Intellectuals Explore the Meaning of Hurricane Katrina*. He is a professor of law and Justice John J. Francis Scholar at Rutgers University Law School (Newark). Originally a native of Harlem, Troutt now lives with his wife and daughter in Brooklyn. *The Importance of Being Dangerous* is his first published novel.